CW01497173

The Companion's *Secret*

A Pride and Prejudice Variation

Linda C. Thompson

The Companion's Secret - A Pride and Prejudice Variation
First Edition -- REVISED

Copyright © 2015 Linda Thompson

This is a work of fiction. Names, characters, businesses, places, events and incidents are either the products of the author's imagination or used in a fictitious manner. Any resemblance to actual persons, living or dead, or actual events is purely coincidental.

For information, please contact:
Linda C. Thompson Books
1700 Lynhurst Lane
Denton, TX   76205

Cover Design and Graphic Flourishes: Karin Bench

ISBN-13: 978-1517518783
ISBN-10: 1517518784

DEDICATION

To my husband, Jim. There are no words to thank you for the love and support you have shown me as I began to write and publish. You have helped me live my dream!

In spite of the challenges we have faced, life with you has been filled with adventure, fun, and love. I look forward to eternity with you.

ACKNOWLEDGEMENTS

Thanks to my plot beta, Elizabeth Stolt, to my proofreaders, Julieanne Spoor and Betty Campbell Madden, and to my online author friends—you know who you are.

Special thanks to my niece, Karin Bench, for her beautiful cover design and for all the other invaluable assistance she has provided to me of late.

TABLE OF CONTENTS

AUTHOR'S NOTE

Miss Austen created one of her most ridiculous and memorable characters when she created Mr. William Collins. However, in this work, his first name has been changed to Walter. His role in this work is larger and more central to the plot, and I did not wish for confusion between William Collins and (Fitz)William Darcy.

The lone young woman wore her black mourning with quiet dignity that did nothing to hide her vulnerability. She was petite, her figure light and pleasing. Her delicate face was suffused with a rosy blush and her porcelain skin seemed to glow incandescently. In spite of the tell-tale redness left from her tears, her eyes glowed with life and sparkled with mischief. The rich brown color left him gasping for air like a drowning man. Her slight smile brightened the dreary room. Framing her face were luscious, soft curls that also graced her long, slender neck.

Her lovely appearance was accompanied by an almost tangible determination that could not mask her doubt and fear. She had shown kindness and compassion. Her soft, sweet voice spoke words of wit and intelligence.

He was lost to her in an instant.

PROLOGUE

June, 18___

THE WINDOWS OF THE MERYTON ASSEMBLY Hall shone with a soft golden light, but outside the music could not be heard above the heavy rain that pelted the town. It had been a very pleasant assembly. Even Mr. Bennet had enjoyed the event, having shared an interesting discussion with his friend, Sir William Lucas. As usual, Mrs. Bennet made sure they were among the very last to leave. She was certain if they were ever to leave early she would miss out on an important piece of gossip.

It was just after midnight when the music ended, allowing the remaining patrons to hear the sound of the driving rain pounding upon the roof of the assembly hall. The families moved quickly to the exit and boarded their carriages, hastily heading for the warmth and safety of home.

A simple misting rain had filled the air when the Bennets arrived at the assembly. Mr. Bennet was concerned that it had become such a downpour. It was disconcerting that no one had noticed the change in the weather prior to leaving the hall. The Bennet carriage was the last one in the queue, so Mr. Bennet hurriedly handed in his three youngest daughters and his wife. He cautioned the driver to be careful before Mr. Bennet himself entered the carriage and closed the door. The passengers were huddled together for both warmth and comfort. The ferocity of the storm had everyone's nerves on edge. Even before the lumbering carriage made the turn onto the road to Longbourn, the family members felt the wheels slip and slide on the muddy streets.

They were almost home; only one obstacle remained. They had to cross the narrow stone bridge that spanned the creek. The large creek meandered through Longbourn's acreage to the point where it joined the river. On both sides of the road were steep embankments leading down to the creek. The coachman slowed the carriage as it approached the bridge to ensure he was able to safely navigate the entrance onto the narrow structure. The darkness of the night sky and the heavy rain made the crossing more dangerous than usual.

The pair of horses had just stepped onto the bridge when multiple flashes of lightning appeared, striking a tree on the opposite bank. The horses began backing away from the bridge. A deafening crack of thunder quickly followed the lightning, further unsettling the animals, which now jerked forward. The coachman did his best to control the frightened horses, but the speed of their forward motion sent the carriage sliding sideways. The tongue connecting the horses to the carriage splintered as it hit the stone column of the bridge's parapet. The impact caused the passengers to scream in terror.

The carriage slid farther before flipping over as it moved down the embankment and came to a stop upside down in the rapidly moving water. Another crack of thunder caused the now-freed horses to rush forward. As the team reached the crest of the bridge, lightening again flashed. The horses reared, but as they came back towards the ground, they were not in the center of the narrow bridge. The foreleg of the horse nearest the parapet came crashing down against the stones. The impact snapped the bone in two, and the animal crumpled to the ground. Because the team was still tethered together, with the injury to the one, the pair was trapped upon the bridge. The animals would have a long wait as the raging storm drowned out the sounds of the accident and the screams of the injured horse.

1. TRAGEDY

ELIZABETH BENNET WOKE TO FIND DAZZLING sunshine streaming in around the drapes at her window. As the light did not bother her eyes, she knew she had recovered. Yesterday, she had been plagued with a debilitating headache. Her head throbbed, her eyes could not tolerate bright light, and she had suffered from nausea. Elizabeth had remained in her room with the curtains closed throughout the day. Her sister, Mary, had tucked her in bed with a dose of laudanum before going to the assembly with the rest of her family. Though it was not something he usually did, Mr. Bennet had accompanied his family to ensure his youngest daughters behaved with decorum. With Elizabeth not feeling well and Jane staying with the Gardiners in London, there was no other who would be in attendance to keep an eye on them.

Elizabeth looked at the clock and noticed the lateness of the hour. She was surprised to hear no sounds of the household coming to life. Hearing a rumble from her stomach, Elizabeth dressed quickly and made her way down to the kitchen. As she opened the door, Mrs. Phipps, the Longbourn cook, was busy pulling bread from the oven. Mrs. Hill, the family's housekeeper, was seated at the table, enjoying a cup of tea.

"Good morning, Miss Lizzy. How are you feeling today?" asked Mrs. Hill upon Elizabeth's entrance.

"I am feeling much better, Mrs. Hill. Thank you for your tender care yesterday." Turning to the cook, Elizabeth asked, smiling, "Mrs. Phipps, might I convince you to give me a slice of that warm bread with some butter and jam?"

"Of course, Miss Lizzy. You must be starved, as you ate almost nothing yesterday. Can I fix you anything else?"

"No, that is not necessary. I will wait to join the others when they break their fast. Perhaps just a cup of tea."

Mrs. Hill moved to get another cup and saucer for Elizabeth as Mrs. Phipps sliced her some bread. The cook placed the plate before Elizabeth, then went to fetch the butter and jam, bringing them to the table as well.

"The house seems unusually quiet for so late in the morning. My family must have come in very late last evening," Elizabeth remarked.

Just then the kitchen door abruptly opened and the groom, Sam, appeared in the doorway. Sam's family was one of the tenant families at Longbourn. He had gone home after dinner to check on his ailing mother. "I just returned from my parents' cottage, where the storm trapped me overnight. I went straight to the stable to apologize to Mr. Johns for not being here to help when they returned from the assembly last evening, but the coach and horses are not there," the young man said in a rush.

Elizabeth's face took on a look of concern at the groom's words. She jumped up from the table, intending to look for her family, but Mrs. Hill laid a hand on her arm to restrain her.

"You sit and finish your meal, Miss Lizzy. I will check on your family. Perhaps the storm prevented their return and they stayed at the Philips' last night. Sam, perhaps you should walk towards town and see if you come across them returning," directed Mrs. Hill.

"Wait, Sam. I will change and go with you. I did not get to take my walk yesterday, so I would enjoy the exercise in spite of the mud. I will see if my family is above stairs while I change." Lizzy rushed out of the room, only to return minutes later. Dressed in a dark brown gown, her oldest cloak around her shoulders, her pattens strapped to her walking boots, and tying the ribbons of her bonnet as she came through the kitchen door, she informed the group, "No one is there, so let us be on our way to Meryton."

Mrs. Hill's intuition told her something was not right and she wanted to protect Elizabeth from whatever that something was. "Miss Lizzy, you were so unwell yesterday; do you really think going for a walk this morning is for the best?"

"Do not worry, Mrs. Hill. The fresh air will do me good." Elizabeth gave Mrs. Hill a smile and a hug, then moved to the kitchen door.

"Well, then, you have a good time. Sam, you be sure to look after Miss Elizabeth and keep her safe," Mrs. Hill admonished. The housekeeper locked eyes with the young groom, hoping he would understand her meaning.

Elizabeth followed Sam out the door and around the house. The two of them moved down the driveway towards the road. The way was difficult, as the rain had turned the roads into a muddy morass. Elizabeth had to walk slowly and carefully because she could not see what lay beneath the puddles.

7

There could easily be a hidden hole waiting to cause injury.

After three-quarters of an hour, Elizabeth and Sam were in sight of the bridge. Elizabeth saw her father's carriage horses; they were still in their harnesses, but the carriage was nowhere in sight. With a scream, Elizabeth tried to run forward, but Sam wrapped his arms around her to prevent her from doing so.

"Stay here, Miss Elizabeth, and I will see what has happened. I will let go, but only if you promise you will stay here." At Elizabeth's nod, Sam removed his arms from around her waist and moved forward as quickly as conditions would allow.

It was obvious the horses were skittish, as the one standing on the bridge attempted to rear when the groom approached. Sam called the animals by name and spoke soothingly as he moved closer. Finally, he was near enough to grab the bridle. He reached out with his other hand to pat the horse's neck, all the while continuing to speak quietly to them. With his hand still holding the bridle of the standing horse, he leaned down to check the other animal. As it was down on the ground, he was sure it was injured. Sam ran his hands over the horse's front legs and the animal snorted in pain. He was dismayed to discover that its leg was broken and that he would have to return with a gun to put the animal out of its misery.

Sadly, Sam rested his hand against the bridge wall. It was then that he saw the carriage. Sam knew he had to get Miss Elizabeth away from the bridge so that she would not see what had happened. Removing the harness from the uninjured horse, he walked it towards Elizabeth.

"Miss Elizabeth, could you ride to Sir William's for help? Ask him to bring a wagon, pistol, and some ropes. While you are gone, I will continue to walk farther down the road and see if I find the carriage. It appears the trace bar snapped and the horses ran off."

"Why do you need a pistol?"

"The downed horse is injured, but I cannot tell how badly. After we take care of your family, we may need the wagon to transport the injured horse or the pistol to put him out of his misery."

Sam moved the horse to the grassy edge at the side of the road and helped Elizabeth to mount. She kept the horse to the grass and was able to make slightly better time than they had made on their trip down the road. As soon as Elizabeth was out of sight, Sam hurried to the other end of the bridge and scrambled down the slope.

Halfway down the slope he passed the body of Mr. Johns. From the odd positioning of the body, Sam assumed the coachman was dead, so he hurried on towards the overturned vehicle. When he reached the carriage, he yanked the door open. The sight that met his eyes made bile rise in his throat. As near as Sam could determine, one of the carriage windows had broken as the carriage rolled down the hill. When it landed upside down in the creek, water had filled the carriage and the injured passengers, now lying on the carriage roof, had drowned. Five bodies floated in the water that filled the interior.

Sam hurried to close the door, but it did not want to latch. It took all of his weight pushing against it to finally move the door back into place, keeping the ghastly sight from view. Pausing to catch his breath before he climbed back up the embankment, he rested his eyes on the carriage's

9

tongue. He looked at it, trying to determine what was odd. Then it dawned on him. The spot of the shaft where the carriage had split from the horses was visible. Sam would have expected the wood to be splintered all the way through. However, half of the wood was smooth, as though it had been sawed through part way. Upon this discovery, he again felt the bile rise in his throat.

Sam straightened and climbed back up the hillside to await help. He was standing on the bridge when Miss Elizabeth arrived, followed by Sir William and his oldest son, Robert, driving the wagon. There were a couple of farm hands in the back of the wagon. Miss Elizabeth stopped the horse in the grass again and slid down the side of the animal's body. Sam moved over to Elizabeth to prevent her from moving onto the bridge, where she might see the carriage.

Nodding to Sir William and his son, Sam said, "Miss Elizabeth, I found the carriage. You should hurry home and get hot water prepared for baths. Your family will be very cold." Sam did not wait for Elizabeth to answer before he reached out and lifted her back onto the horse. He turned the animal around and gave it a smack to get it moving.

When Elizabeth was no longer in sight, Sam turned to the gentlemen. He took his hat from his head before speaking. "Sir William, Mr. Lucas, please follow me and bring the pistol." As Sam led the men towards the horses, he said, "It was necessary to send Miss Elizabeth away, for I would not wish her to see what I found." He recounted the events since first finding the horses. Robert pulled out the pistol and shot the injured animal, releasing it from its pain.

The gentlemen followed Sam to the top of the embankment, where they could all see the overturned carriage. They were speechless at the sight and the thought of the loss it contained.

After a few moments of silence, Robert spoke. "Father, you take one of the horses and ride into Meryton. We are going to need additional help. Be sure to contact the undertaker and as many volunteers as you can. I believe Charlotte was going to walk to Longbourn to see if she could assist Mrs. Hill in making preparations. That is good because Miss Eliza will need a friend with her when she learns what happened to her family. It is unfortunate that Mr. and Mrs. Philips are visiting the Gardiners at the present. I am sure his help would be most useful at this difficult time. While you are gone, Sam and I will try to retrieve the bodies from the carriage."

Sam climbed into the wagon and moved it across the bridge, then backed it toward the side of the road near the carriage wreckage. He set the brake before jumping down and moving to unhitch one of the horses. He walked it to where Sir William and Robert stood. While Sam held the horse, Robert gave his father a leg up. Sir William moved off in the direction of Meryton as quickly as the road conditions would allow.

After much discussion, Sam and Robert decided the best way to retrieve the bodies would be for Sam to take a rope down the slope and loop it around the carriage wheel. Once it was secured, Robert would tie the other end around the nearest tree. Then, using the rope as an anchor, the two men would carry the bodies up to the roadside.

The two men worked diligently while they waited for help to arrive. They managed to retrieve the four women, as they were small enough for the men to carry one at a time. They were discussing the best way to bring up Mr. Bennet when Sir William and the others arrived. Using the supplies the others had brought, they were able to fashion a stretcher. Sam and Robert went down and worked together to lift Mr. Bennet's body onto the makeshift bed. They followed as it ascended the embankment, pulled by one of the horses that had arrived. By the time they reached the top, some of the other men had loaded the ladies' bodies onto the Lucas' wagon. Mr. Bennet was loaded into a different wagon and both vehicles moved off in the direction of Longbourn. Those remaining worked to remove the carriage from the water.

While the men worked at the accident site, Charlotte Lucas arrived at Longbourn. "Charlotte, what are you doing here?" asked Elizabeth when her friend appeared in the doorway of the sitting room.

"When Mother told me why you had ridden over, I thought I might be of some help here," she answered as she advanced into the room and hugged her friend.

"How thoughtful of you! I have already spoken to Mrs. Hill and water is being heated for both baths and tea. I expect them to be arriving soon. Please come and join me as we wait."

The ladies were enjoying a cup of tea when they heard the sounds of vehicles coming up the drive. They moved to the window and saw two wagons approaching, but Elizabeth was surprised when they both continued around to the stables.

"I do not see my family in either wagon. I wonder where they could be," Elizabeth said, confusion evident on her face.

Soon Sir William and Robert joined the two ladies. It was obvious from the looks the men wore that they came bearing bad news. Pulling up a chair directly across from where Elizabeth sat on the sofa,

Sir William reached out and took one of Elizabeth's hands in both of his. Charlotte reached over and held Elizabeth's remaining hand. She had no idea what her father was going to say, but she knew the news would not be pleasant.

"Miss Elizabeth, I am not sure how to tell you this. We located your family and the carriage." Her face took on an expectant look. "Unfortunately, it had slipped down the embankment and landed upside down in the creek."

Not taking Sir William's meaning immediately, Elizabeth said, "Oh, my poor family! They must have been so cold sitting in the water during the night! Why have you not returned them to the house yet?"

"They have returned, Miss Elizabeth, and you need not worry about their being cold. They are beyond feeling any discomforts in this world."

Finally understanding what had occurred, Elizabeth Bennet fainted for the first time in her life. When her eyes were once again open, she saw Mrs. Hill standing beside the couch, tears streaming down her face. Charlotte was seated beside her, her two hands firmly clasping one of Elizabeth's. At the remembrance of what had brought her to this place, Elizabeth began to sob uncontrollably.

In walked Mr. Jones, Meryton's apothecary. Mrs. Hill had sent for him as soon as Elizabeth returned. She felt certain there would be some injuries that would need tending as a result of the carriage accident. Charlotte and Mrs. Hill helped Elizabeth to her room, followed by the apothecary. He gave Elizabeth a draught to calm her and make her sleep.

While Elizabeth rested, several of the ladies of the neighborhood arrived to help prepare the bodies for burial. In all the confusion, no one thought to send a letter to the Gardiners or the Philips informing them of the tragedy.

Upon waking, Charlotte told Elizabeth of what had transpired and the plans that had been made. Learning the bodies had been prepared and the coffins placed in the sitting room, Elizabeth went to her father's library. Though she had loved all of her sisters, she had been close to only her older sister, Jane. Jane was her dearest friend in the world and they shared all of each other's confidences. Mrs. Bennet had never been too happy with Elizabeth. She was supposed to be a boy—the heir to break the entailment on Longbourn—and her mother had never forgiven Elizabeth for being a girl. Her father, however, had doted on Elizabeth. He recognized her intelligence at an early age and raised her as if she had been his son and heir. She was well read, knew about estate management as well as household management, and shared her father's dry wit.

Elizabeth assumed Sir William had sent a message to her family in London and knew she could do nothing but await their arrival. She needed her dear Jane but desperately hoped the sad news would not further complicate her Aunt Gardiner's pregnancy. Would Jane even be able to return home? Aunt Gardiner was dependent upon Jane's help at the present time.

These worries could not keep her attention for long, as her thoughts returned to the bodies of her family lying just a few rooms away. Elizabeth was curled up in her father's desk chair, lost in memories, when she heard a knock at the door. When she called, "Come," Mrs. Hill opened the door to inform her that two visitors were in the small parlor. Before Elizabeth could inquire as to their identities, Mr.

Harold Collins swept into her father's library, followed by his son, Walter.

Harold Collins was a distant cousin of her father's. He was also her father's heir. He usually invited himself for a visit each fall after the harvest, so his unexpected arrival was quite odd. No one in the family liked Mr. Collins. He treated Mrs. Bennet poorly because she was not a member of the gentry, though Mr. Collins could only barely claim to be a member of the gentry himself. He treated Mr. Philips, who was a solicitor in Meryton, disdainfully and he ignored the Gardiners all together, as they were of the merchant class. When he visited, he made pointed references to changes he would make when the estate was his. He was brusque and arrogant, and his visits were a miserable experience for all those at Longbourn, family and servants alike.

"My dear Cousin Elizabeth," he cried as he advanced upon her with arms extended as though to embrace her. "You poor, poor, dear. How fortunate my unexpected arrival is, as I shall be able to take over immediately and help you during this dreadful time."

"Mr. Collins!" Elizabeth replied, startled. "What are you doing here? Normally you do not visit until the fall." She stood quickly upon his approach and placed herself behind her father's chair, using it to keep the unwelcomed gentleman at a distance.

"That is true, but I was passing through the area after business to the north of here and decided to stop for a visit. What a fortunate coincidence I have arrived, as you will certainly need family support while you face this sad event and the changes it must surely bring. Have you written to your mother's relatives?" he asked, distaste clear on his face.

"I believe Sir William Lucas handled that. I think I heard him speaking of my Uncle Philips."

Mr. Collins was well aware of the opinion of his relatives and was not surprised at her cold response to him. "I shall send him a note immediately to find out for certain. If he has not done so, I will send them an express this very evening. Now, perhaps you should go to the sitting room, Cousin Elizabeth, as I will need the use of this room. I will need to see where matters stand immediately so the estate does not fall into further disrepair. Your father was neglectful of many things, which I must now put to right."

Elizabeth's indignation quickly rose in defense of her beloved father. "How dare you speak so of my father, Mr. Collins? Have you no compassion or decency? I lost my family this day, and you have the temerity to speak ill of my father when he is not yet in his grave!" With that, Elizabeth ran from the room, slamming the door as she departed.

Elizabeth ran right into the arms of Mrs. Hill, who had been hovering nearby in case Elizabeth needed her. Mrs. Hill put her arm around Elizabeth's shoulder and led her into the small parlor at the back of the house. Mrs. Bennet had always used this room for her meetings with the housekeeper. Mrs. Hill ushered Elizabeth to a chair and prepared a cup of tea for her. She had requested the tea tray when the visitors arrived and was glad she had, for Elizabeth's sake.

After her outburst, Elizabeth felt drained. She did not think she had the patience or the fortitude to face Mr. Collins again that day. Consequently, she begged Mrs. Hill to tell him she had retired, as she was not feeling well. The housekeeper promised to do as bid and to bring a dinner tray to Elizabeth shortly. Elizabeth arranged a time for the maid to wake her and help her prepare to receive the visitors who would come to pay their respects.

Elizabeth returned her dinner tray to the kitchen barely touched. With the assistance of Sally, the maid she had shared with her mother and sisters, Elizabeth settled in her bed very early. She lay staring at the ceiling, trying to comprehend how her world had changed so drastically in less than the span of a day. Finally, tears overtook her and Elizabeth cried until sleep claimed her.

Immediately after Elizabeth ran from the room, Mr. Collins sat behind the desk. He reached for paper and dashed off a note to Sir William Lucas to verify whether the Gardiners and the Philips had been notified of the accident. He dispatched the message with Sam and asked that he wait for a reply. After he had sent the note, Harold Collins sat back in the chair, relishing the feeling of power that came with being a landed gentleman and thinking of the life he led before.

Harold Collins' father, Jacob, had been the minister of a small parish. Being a second son, Jacob was careful when selecting a wife. He chose the only daughter, Lavinia, of the largest landowner in the area. She brought with her a respectable dowry of seven thousand pounds. She was a quiet girl and somewhat plain, but she had a very sweet nature. After a year and a half of marriage, she presented Jacob with a son and heir. Lavinia was a loving mother and doted on Harold. Two years later she died in childbirth along with the daughter she was carrying, leaving Jacob alone to raise Harold. Rather than remarry, Jacob had his spinster aunt keep house for him and help with both Harold and the care of his parishioners. Jacob was strict, very religious, and kept a tight rein on the activities of his family to prevent them from becoming mired in the evils of the world. As Jacob was also rather parsimonious, the fortune of his bride had grown since the time of their marriage.

Fortunately for Harold, his father died when Harold was only 25. Freed from his father's restrictions and in control of the family's finances, Harold sent his aunt back to her family home and rushed off to London to enjoy all the things of which his father disapproved. He began gambling, but was very bad at it and lost a substantial sum of money. He quickly went through almost half his inheritance.

Harold was a handsome man with strong features, much as his father had been. With his good looks and the appearance of a prosperous gentleman—though he had never owned any property—Harold set out to find a wife to shore up his financial situation. Like his father, Harold managed to marry well. The young lady was almost on the shelf and not particularly attractive, but she would inherit a small estate from her mother upon her marriage. She also brought with her a dowry of ten thousand pounds.

Harold and his bride, Harriet, moved into her estate immediately upon their marriage. Harold had always thought well of himself. However, his arrogance and condescension quickly gave his new neighbors a dislike of him. His wife was a shy girl whom he frequently mistreated. Shortly after discovering Harriet was increasing, he rushed off to town to enjoy the company of ladies of questionable repute.

Harold's lack of experience in running an estate, as well as his negligence as he indulged his desires, soon affected the estate's profitability. Within ten months of marriage, his wife gave him his heir and promptly died. Disgusted with his employer's behavior and the poor way in which he had treated his young wife, the estate's steward quit. Harold quickly hired a new man but did not take the time to thoroughly check his references. Then he sent for the aunt he had callously abandoned just over a year prior. Harold installed her at his estate to care for his son, Walter, while he returned to his activities in town. More concerned with his pleasures than his responsibilities, Harold Collins spent little time with his son. Walter was a great disappointment to him, as the young man favored his mother in both looks and intelligence.

By the time Walter was ten, the steward had bankrupted the estate. Harold was furious. He installed his aunt and son in a small house in the best section of London he could afford. First, he attempted to replace his lost funds at cards but succeeded only in losing more. He felt work was beneath him, but he was clever and managed to pull off a few successful swindles to improve his fortunes. It was at this time that he learned he was the heir to his cousin Bennet's estate.

He immediately took himself and Walter off to meet this branch of their family. He had made a point of returning every year to check on his inheritance.

Mr. Collins' son, Walter, observed his father from his chair before the desk, watching the changing expressions that crossed his face. Finally, he spoke. "I do not believe Cousin Elizabeth was very happy to see us. I also think you upset her by criticizing her father. I do not believe she will wish to marry me if you behave in such a manner, Father."

Mr. Collins was about to deliver a set down when he realized his worthless son might have a point. "You may be correct, Walter. We will have to appease her sensibilities for a few days."

"The timing of our visit seems providential," remarked Walter, "almost as if you knew something bad was going to happen." He studied his father as he awaited a reply.

"Yes, our arriving now was indeed fortunate, but how could I have known there would be trouble?" replied his father without meeting Walter's eye.

They heard a knock on the door. Mr. Collins called, "Come" and the door opened to admit Sam. He held out the letter to his master and left the room. Mr. Collins opened the letter and read through it, a satisfied expression appearing on his face. Looking at his son, he said, "Find something to occupy yourself. I have work to do."

Walter Collins stood, but he stopped at the door and looked back at his father, who was already bent over a piece of paper, busily writing. He shook his head as he exited the room.

2. FAREWELLS

ELIZABETH AWOKE THE NEXT MORNING, HEARING a persistent knocking at the door. She trudged over to admit Sally, who was carrying two pails of water and was followed by Mr. Hill with the hip bath and Mrs. Hill with more water. After placing the tub before the fire, Mr. Hill and Mrs. Hill departed when Sally handed him her empty buckets. He returned several more times with additional buckets of water. Sally added some of the lavender fragrance Elizabeth preferred and helped her into the tub.

Mrs. Hill came back carrying a black gown as Elizabeth sat in the chair near the fire, drying her hair. Surprised, Elizabeth asked, "Where did that come from, Mrs. Hill? I had not even given a thought to needing such a thing."

"Mrs. Stone, the seamstress, sent it as a gift, Miss Lizzy. She did not want you to have to worry about such things at this difficult time. I will lay it here and fetch you a breakfast tray. Could I tempt you to take more than tea and toast?" the housekeeper asked with concern.

"No thank you, Mrs. Hill. I am not sure I would be able to get even that down this morning."

"Now, Miss Lizzy, you will eat everything I bring you if I have to feed you myself. You will need your strength today. I will not let you go wasting away. I am sure Mr. Gardiner will take you away to

21

London with him when he comes. You will need your strength to travel as well," said Mrs. Hill firmly.

The devoted housekeeper returned shortly afterward, carrying a breakfast tray. She remained until Elizabeth had eaten every bite and drunk two cups of tea. Sally then helped Elizabeth into her dress and styled her hair in a neat bun. Finally prepared, at least physically, Elizabeth descended the stairs to the sitting room where she would receive those who came to pay their respects. She hoped she would have the emotional strength she needed to face this difficult day.

Elizabeth knew saying goodbye to her family would be very difficult. Deciding to leave it until after the neighbors had all come and gone, she took a chair just inside the sitting room to greet the visitors as they arrived. It was not long before Mr. Collins and his son also appeared. They stood to the left of her chair so the visitors would have to greet them first. Whenever anyone attempted to speak directly to Elizabeth, Mr. Collins interrupted the conversation and turned it to another topic, not allowing her to receive any personal comfort. After an hour of such treatment, Elizabeth removed to a chair on the opposite side of the room. If Mr. Collins wished to be the first to greet everyone, it was fine with Elizabeth. However, she would be sure to speak with them before they departed and to thank them for their visit.

During a lapse in visitors, Mr. Collins spoke abruptly to her. "Cousin Elizabeth, I require you to return to my side to receive the visitors."

"I cannot do so, Mr. Collins. If you wish to receive the visitors, I must of necessity stay here to farewell them and thank them for coming." Elizabeth spoke firmly and did not even bother to look at the hated gentleman who was ruining this solemn day.

Turning to his son, Collins whispered, "Go stand beside her. Change the conversation if it appears anyone is offering her assistance. It is imperative we keep her secluded and here with us." So saying, he gave his son a slight shove.

Though Elizabeth could not hear their conversation, her suspicions were raised by his strange behavior and unexpected arrival. Walter Collins was very different from his father. Elizabeth had never been able to determine if he was shy or just stupid. He had very little conversation but to reiterate his father's words. She had never seen him as other than his father's shadow. She knew he was in his final year at university, but she had no idea how he had progressed so far, as she could never seem to make any sense of his rambling soliloquies. Each time Elizabeth tried to speak to one of her neighbors as they departed, Walter began to cough and clear his throat loudly to drown out any chance at conversation.

Finally, the Lucas family arrived. After greeting the family, Mr. Collins detained Sir William as his family moved on to view the Bennet family. "Sir William, I thank you for your prompt reply to my note last evening. I immediately wrote an express to Cousin Elizabeth's other relatives upon receiving it."

"Oh, capital," said Sir William before moving to join his family, but he glanced back to see a satisfied smile appear on Mr. Collins' face. When the gentleman realized he was being observed, he looked down quickly and rearranged his expression to one more appropriate for the occasion.

Robert Lucas had finished paying his respects and exited the front door of Longbourn to await the rest of his family. He was looking down the drive when Sam came around the side of the house, asking for a word with him. When he nodded in agreement, Sam led Robert back the way he had come so they could speak privately.

"Mr. Lucas, sir, I do not wish to speak out of turn, but I am concerned. I noticed something odd at the accident scene yesterday, but it slipped my mind in the busyness of caring for the dead. I am not sure the accident was really that. I noticed how the tongue on the carriage appeared to be cut part way through. The other part was splintered as one would expect in a carriage accident."

"That is odd, Sam, but why are you concerned?"

"It is that there Mr. Collins. He comes every year to visit Longbourn but only after the harvest. No one in the family is fond of him; if I may be blunt, sir, they despise him. And, well, it just seemed odd to me, his showing up now. Almost like he knew something had happened."

"Sam, I certainly understand the family's feelings about the man. He is rather repellent," said Robert with a grimace. "However, perhaps you are correct. The best thing you could do would be to keep your mouth closed and your eyes and ears open. If he did have some part in what happened, perhaps you will overhear something that gives him away. You must always keep a close watch over Miss Eliza. If she needs assistance or protection, send a note to Lucas Lodge immediately."

"Yes, sir, Mr. Lucas. I was sure you would know what was best."

"Thank you for telling me, Sam. If you learn anything else you believe I need to know, please notify me."

Sam nodded and made his way back to the stables.

Elizabeth was completely drained by the time the last visitor left. There had been a steady stream of people throughout the day. Each of the twenty-four families that made up the cream of Meryton's society had come to pay their respects. They had also received calls from some of the merchants in the village, and all of Longbourn's tenants had come to pay their respects. Elizabeth's heart was touched by the community's outpouring of respect and care for her family.

Pointedly staring at the Collins men, Elizabeth asked for some privacy to say goodbye to her family. As he moved towards the door, Mr. Collins turned, giving her an oily smile, and said, "I hope you will join us soon, my dear cousin. Your presence is like a ray of sunshine at this sad time." Had she not been so tired, Elizabeth would have rolled her eyes at the ridiculous statement.

When the gentlemen had exited and the door was closed behind them, Elizabeth moved to Lydia's casket. Placing her hand on the top, she whispered softly, "Goodbye dear Lydia. I hope you shall find the joy you always sought."

She moved to Kitty's coffin, then Mary's, and spoke soft words of farewell to each of her sisters. Moving to stand beside her mother, Elizabeth folded her arms across her chest. "Mama, I am sorry I could not be what you wished me to be. I hope you find peace to soothe your nerves."

Finally, Elizabeth stepped up to her father's coffin. "Oh, Papa, how could you leave me?" she cried as she slumped to the floor. Her head resting against the coffin's side, Elizabeth sobbed, heartbroken. She could find no words to express her sense of grief at losing her dear father. He had loved, guided, and taught her throughout her life. His library had been a refuge from her mother's harsh criticism, and he had always managed to say something to make her feel better.

Almost an hour after she had been left alone, Mrs. Hill quietly opened the doors to the parlor. Seeing Elizabeth sobbing upon the floor, she called for Sally. Between the two women, they managed to get Elizabeth upstairs and settled into bed. Her sobs had dwindled to hiccups, and she was completely spent. Giving Elizabeth a small glass of wine with laudanum mixed in it, they left the distraught young woman to sleep.

3. ADJUSTMENTS

THE GRAY AND OVERCAST SKIES MATCHED Elizabeth's mood when she awoke the next morning. It was Sunday, and the funeral would be that day after church. Even though women were not permitted to attend funerals, Elizabeth did not think she could stand to be anywhere near the church today regardless. She did not wish to see the empty graves and the coffins waiting to be placed in them.

She grabbed the bell pull to alert Sally that she was awake. When the maid arrived in the room, Elizabeth asked her to bring tea and toast and to have Mrs. Hill inform the gentlemen she was indisposed that morning and would not be joining them for church.

A short time later, a knock sounded at her door. At Elizabeth's call to enter, Sally came in carrying the breakfast tray, followed by a worried Mrs. Hill. "Miss Lizzy, Sally said you were not feeling well. Do I need to summon Mr. Jones?"

"No, Mrs. Hill, I just do not think I could bear to be near the church this morning. I wish to wait here for Uncle Gardiner, and hopefully Jane, to arrive."

The housekeeper moved over to the bed and began to fluff and rearrange Elizabeth's pillows so she could sit up in bed to eat her breakfast. Once she was sure Elizabeth was comfortable, Mrs. Hill stood by the bed, encouraging her to eat. The tray was half empty when Mrs. Hill hurried back downstairs to ensure things were prepared in the dining room for the men to break their fast. She was about to return to the kitchen when Mr. Collins and his son entered the room.

Mr. Collins did not believe common courtesies were necessary for servants; therefore, he did not greet Mrs. Hill. When he noticed her hesitating in the doorway, he abruptly remarked, "Did you want something, Mrs. Hill?"

"I just wanted to inform you that Miss Elizabeth will not be attending church this morning." She was surprised to note the look of anger on his face. It was quickly replaced by a pleased look, which confused her further. She hesitated to say more, as the moods of this man were so mercurial, but she needed additional information. "Mr. Collins, what time do you expect to return from the funeral? We will need to prepare to greet and feed the mourners after the service."

"Due to Cousin Elizabeth's indisposition, I will inform the gentleman that we will not be receiving this morning. You need not worry about feeding a gathering." Mrs. Hill was shocked at this blatant disregard for propriety, and the look must have shown on her face, for her employer curtly remarked, "You are dismissed."

Mrs. Hill returned to the kitchen to explain the situation to Mrs. Phipps. The two women were scandalized at the disrespect the new master was showing for his relatives, but there was little they could do about it. They decided it would be best to keep the information from Elizabeth so as not to cause her further distress.

As the gentlemen finished their meal and prepared to depart for the church, Mr. Collins summoned the housekeeper. Mrs. Hill stood at the door of the dining room, waiting to be acknowledged.

"When we return, I should like to meet with you to review the household expenses and see what economies we can make."

"Yes, sir."

With that, Mr. Collins and Walter departed for the church. Though it was close enough to walk, Mr. Collins believed it to be beneath his consequence to arrive at the church on foot. As the largest landholder in the area, he was determined the neighbors should think him all the crack. He did not speak to anyone as he entered the church, but nodded condescendingly. With a smug expression on his face, he walked to the front and took his place in the Longbourn pew.

Many in the congregation looked askance at his behavior. The Bennet family had been well-liked, and it did not sit well with his neighbors, to whom Mr. Collins showed no dolor. There was concern among many that Miss Elizabeth was not in attendance. Many of the ladies of the community determined to call upon her in the coming week.

When the gentlemen returned from the funeral, Mr. Collins wore an almost gleeful expression. A look from his son caused him to adjust his countenance to one more appropriate for the occasion. Elizabeth had heard the door and knew she must go down to greet the mourners from the funeral. However, to her surprise, no one was there but Mr. Collins and Walter.

"Where are the others? I am sure Mrs. Hill has refreshments ready for the gentlemen from the funeral," Elizabeth remarked as she looked around in confusion.

"I explained you were indisposed, and we would not be receiving this afternoon," replied Mr. Collins in an off-hand manner.

Tears welled in Elizabeth's eyes as she cried, "How could you be so cruel and disrespectful to my family?"

Knowing his father would likely respond angrily to his cousin's words, Walter Collins spoke before his father could. "Please calm yourself, Cousin Elizabeth. I am sure Father did not mean to be disrespectful. He was most likely thinking of your well-being and did not realize it would be unseemly to not allow the others to return."

By this time, Mr. Collins had reined in his anger and was able to reply politely. "Dear cousin, I know how difficult this has been for you. You were already feeling unwell this morning. I did not wish you to tax yourself with entertaining others. I did not realize how it might seem. I was concerned only with your welfare."

Tears still in her eyes, Elizabeth rushed up the stairs and back to her room. She threw herself on her bed in distress and cried, "Oh, Uncle Edward, please hurry and arrive," before she dissolved into tears.

After the scene with Elizabeth, Walter went for a ride around the estate while Mr. Collins settled in the chair behind the desk in the study and rang for the housekeeper. Mrs. Hill appeared quickly, carrying the household ledgers. She gave the books to the master and he began to page through them. He was heard to "humph" frequently and he made notes on a piece of paper alongside the ledger. As he had not offered the housekeeper a seat, Mrs. Hill was forced to stand before the desk and wait for him to address her.

Finally, Mr. Collins closed the book and looked up at the housekeeper. "Mr. Bennet was very lax in matters of business, and he allowed much waste to occur at Longbourn. But things will change beginning immediately. From this point forward the servants are to have only gruel or porridge in the mornings. You may have a slice of bread with a slice of meat and cheese for your mid-day meal. Also, you will be buying much cheaper cuts of meat for your evening meal. I will not pay for you to eat as well as your masters. You must also purchase the cheapest tea for the servants. It is a waste for you to drink anything better. And, unless we are entertaining, one course is sufficient for the family meals, as well. For the next week or two you will present me with the weekly menus, showing both my meal and that of the servants until I am sure you understand my wishes. I will expect to see the menus for the week by the end of the day," he said.

"Another thing I believe should be done is to dismiss one of the girls in the laundry. Since there is only one lady in the house, the ladies' maid can assist in the laundry. Perhaps we should also let go of one of the scullery maids, as meals will be smaller and we will not often be entertaining due to the mourning period. Do you understand the things I have explained to you, Mrs. Hill? I will expect to note a decrease in the expenses immediately. If you are incapable of running the household as I request, I will find a replacement. You are dismissed."

"Yes, sir," said Mrs. Hill as she turned to leave the study. She had managed to contain her anger, but only until she made her way to the kitchen. "Oh, that man," Mrs. Hill cried as the kitchen door closed behind her.

"What did he say?" asked Mrs. Phipps in concern.

Mrs. Hill related the master's dictates to the waiting staff, whose expressions were equally displeased. "I will stay until Miss Lizzy is safely away to London with the Gardiner family. Then perhaps it is time to take my sister up on her offer to help at the inn she and her husband own," remarked the housekeeper with some heat. "Would you wish to join us if she needs a cook?"

Mrs. Phipps looked thoughtful as she considered the matter.

Mr. Collins remained in the study for most of the afternoon. At teatime, a request was made for Elizabeth to join them if she felt up to it. Much to his annoyance, she replied that she did not feel up to returning downstairs. Walter had returned from his ride and joined his father in the study. Mrs. Hill deposited the tea tray with a decided clank before departing.

"I wonder how many days I will have to cater to the tender feelings of our cousin," sneered Mr. Collins. "I want this matter resolved quickly!"

"I will pay kind attention to Miss Elizabeth at every opportunity and give her a reason to leave her room, Father, while you continue to learn of the estate," said his son in a placating manner.

"The steward is paid to do the work; I wish only to receive the monies to enjoy," replied his father dismissively.

"But Father, do you not remember what happened the last time? Perhaps you should learn, at least a little bit, to prevent such from happening again," Walter suggested hesitantly.

Giving his son's words some thought, he finally replied. "Perhaps you are not as stupid as you appear. It is a good idea for you to pay attention to Elizabeth, and perhaps I should oversee things a little bit to avoid a repeat of what occurred with that scoundrel, Griggs."

It was not until the evening meal that Elizabeth again appeared downstairs. She did not wish to be in Mr. Collins' company. However, as her Uncle Gardiner had not yet arrived, she needed to ensure Mr. Collins had indeed written to them. If they did not arrive tomorrow, Elizabeth would write to them herself the following day.

The gentlemen were seated at the table. After the blessing had been offered, she asked her question. "Mr. Collins, you did write to my relatives in London, did you not?"

"I did, indeed, Cousin Elizabeth. I wrote to them on the day of my arrival." The expression on his face caused Elizabeth confusion.

"Oh, I thought they would have arrived by now," she replied sadly.

"Perhaps they were detained, or perhaps your uncle is away on business. Do not give it a second thought, dear cousin. Walter and I are delighted to have you here with us." He accompanied his words with a smile that made Elizabeth very uncomfortable.

Immediately after dinner, Elizabeth retired to her room.

It was over brandy after dinner that the subject was raised again. "I wonder what could have delayed Miss Elizabeth's family?" Walter asked dubiously, observing his father closely.

"I am sure they will come as soon as they receive the notification," was all Walter said in reply.

"What are your plans for tomorrow?"

"I have arranged for the steward to meet with me and ride the estate. Then we will return and go over the books and the expectations for the harvest. I hope to see great changes to many of the problems of Longbourn by that time." The smile Mr. Collins wore was decidedly eager.

The next morning, Elizabeth took up a position in the window seat in Jane's room that looked out over the front of the house and the driveway. She prayed her family would come that day, as she could not wait to be away from Mr. Collins and the sad memories that now filled Longbourn. She was so upset when no one had arrived by nightfall that she refused to eat. Mrs. Hill took the untouched tray and returned to Elizabeth's room with it.

"Miss Lizzy, if you do not eat properly, you will be too sick to travel when your family gets here. Now, you sit yourself down and eat your dinner." Mrs. Hill stood over Elizabeth until she had consumed almost everything on the tray. Then, returning to her usual motherly tones, the housekeeper said, "That is better. Now, let me help you get ready for bed."

"Could you or Sally come back to do that in a half hour or so? I want to write to Uncle Gardiner before I return. Then you can put it with the other post for me when you go down."

"All right, one of us will be back in a bit to help ready you for bed."

Elizabeth sat at the small desk in her room and pulled out the necessary supplies to write her uncle. She had just sanded and sealed it when Sally entered. Elizabeth allowed the maid to help ready her for bed. As she settled under the bedcovers, she pointed to the desk and asked, "Sally will you please take the letter from the desk and put it with the outgoing post?"

"Certainly, Miss Lizzy. Good night and rest well." Sally picked up the letter and left the room.

Elizabeth reached for the book on her bedside table before remembering she had finished it the night before. She would have to find time to retrieve all of her books from her father's library and bring them to her room. Mr. Collins had made it clear she was not welcome in *his* study, so she would try to remove them the next time he went out.

As she returned downstairs, Sally placed the letter in the tray on the hall table. Unfortunately for Elizabeth, Mr. Collins noticed the letter. Seeing to whom it was addressed, he took it from the tray and into his study where he tossed it into the fire. When all traces of the letter had turned to ash, he summoned his housekeeper.

"Mrs. Hill, beginning immediately, I would like all incoming and outgoing mail to be placed on my desk. I will sort it and distribute the mail to the members of the household or arrange for it to be sent. Is this understood?"

"Yes, sir."

Things continued in this pattern for most of the following week. Elizabeth spent most of the day in her room watching for her family who never came.

Mr. Collins was growing very impatient with Elizabeth's behavior. He had definite plans for her, but he would be unable to accomplish them with her always in her room. Things would have to change soon.

4. SECRETS

ON SATURDAY MORNING, ELIZABETH WOKE VERY early. Without calling for Sally to attend her, she dressed and prepared for her usual morning walk. She had spent too much time cooped up inside the last week and needed the peace she found in nature. Once she was ready, she headed down to the kitchen.

"Good morning, Mrs. Hill, Mrs. Phipps."

"Good morning, Miss Lizzy, how are you feeling today?" Mrs. Hill's voice held solicitous concern.

"I am in great need of a long walk after the past several days. Could I convince you, Mrs. Phipps, to part with a couple of your delicious buns for me to take along?"

"Certainly, Miss Lizzy. Just let me wrap them up for you."

Elizabeth took the food from the cook with a word of thanks. "I will be walking to Oakham Mount this morning. I will try not to be gone long."

With a wave to the ladies, Elizabeth left through the kitchen door. She exited the garden by the back gate and headed along the path leading to Oakham Mount. Usually when her mind was filled with thoughts, she walked quickly. However, the sadness filling her heart and mind slowed her steps. She arrived at her destination just as the sun crested the horizon. Elizabeth took a seat on a flat rock atop the mount and pulled up her knees, wrapping her

37

arms around them as the pinks and oranges of the sunrise filled the morning sky.

"Oh, Papa! How can everything look the same and yet be so different? What shall I do without you?" cried Elizabeth as she burst into tears. She put her head on her knees as sobs overtook her.

It was some time before her tears subsided. Her father was gone. All of her family, except for Jane, was gone. What were they to do? Why had none of her other family members returned? Had something happened to her aunt to prevent their return? She hoped with all her heart they would come that day. She wished to leave Longbourn and the presence of the odious Collinses.

Finally, she noticed how high the sun had risen in the sky. She knew she must return to Longbourn, no matter her wish to be away. She tried to walk with more purpose on the return, but had no desire to face Mr. Collins.

She entered through the kitchen. As she passed the library door on the way to the stairs, she heard Mr. Collins call out to her. "Cousin Elizabeth, where have you been?" His voice was harsh, his question rude.

"As you know from previous visits, I always walk in the early morning, sir. That is where I have been."

Walter Collins cleared his throat softly, which caused his father to pause before replying angrily. "I know it is your habit to walk great distances in the morning, but we were worried, dear cousin. You may be quite familiar with the area, but neither Walter nor I can claim the same. If you were to become injured, we would have no idea where to begin looking for you. Until we are more comfortable with our surroundings, would you please humor me?

Either have Walter accompany you on your walks or limit them to the gardens." Though he managed to keep his voice even, Mr. Collins' anger was visible in his eyes and the way he appeared to clench his jaw.

Walter stood and bowed. "I should be delighted to accompany you, Cousin Elizabeth." He gave her an easy smile and bowed again.

Elizabeth was not pleased with his request or the thought of being forced into Walter's company, but Mr. Collins had presented his case so reasonably, she could not politely deny him. With as much grace as Elizabeth could muster, she agreed before proceeding to her room.

Though she was becoming tired of her room, Elizabeth planned to spend the day there, as loneliness was preferable to the company of the Collinses. However, just before the time for breakfast to be served, a knock sounded at the door. She opened it to find Mrs. Hill, but the housekeeper did not have her breakfast tray as Elizabeth had expected.

"Mr. Collins requires you to join him in the breakfast room, Miss Lizzy."

Elizabeth looked at the housekeeper expectantly, but Mrs. Hill gave a small shrug, indicating she was unaware of his reasons. Lizzy smoothed her dress, checked her hair in the mirror, and headed downstairs. The two gentlemen were waiting for her.

"Ah, Cousin Elizabeth. I believe it is time for you to leave your rooms and join us for meals."

"I thank you for the invitation, sir, but I prefer to remain in my room." Elizabeth turned about, intending to the mount the stairs, but Mr. Collins' voice halted her.

"I must insist you begin taking all your meals with us." His tone was brusque, so he attempted to moderate it. "It is not healthy for you to remain in your room wallowing in your grief. It would be much better for you to find something useful to do. It will give you something else to think about than your loss." Elizabeth complied with the request, though she was resentful of his words. He may have compelled her presence, but he could not make her speak to him.

Over breakfast, Mr. Collins put the first steps of his plan in place. He had coached Walter in his behavior and could only hope the boy would be successful. If Walter met with resistance, he hoped his son had the backbone to do what was necessary.

"Cousin Elizabeth, I do not know if you are aware of this, but Walter has long had a fondness for you. He has been too shy to speak of it." Mr. Collins gave a speaking look to his son.

Walter Collins understood what his father wished and though his mouth was full of food, he delivered his much-practiced speech. "Indeed, my dear cousin. What my father says is true. I wish you to know you are not without family. I would be most happy to be your closest family now."

Fearing what the man would say next, Elizabeth abruptly excused herself, claiming a headache coming on. She rushed to her room and locked the door behind her. Both Mr. Collins and his son came to see her during the day, attempting to gain entrance to her room. In each case, she replied she should be better the following day if she were to rest quietly and undisturbed.

Elizabeth knew she could not miss church two Sundays in a row. Consequently, she was dressed and in her place at the table shortly after the men seated themselves. After the meal, they exited the house. Elizabeth was startled to see the curricle and a horse awaiting them.

"This is not necessary. It is a very short walk to church," said Elizabeth. "In fact, I enjoy the walk."

"Cousin Elizabeth, as the largest landholder in the area in the absence of any residents at Netherfield Park, it is up to me to set the standards of behavior. It would be beneath my dignity to walk to church." Mr. Collins' tone was haughty.

Elizabeth bit her tongue to keep from uttering a sharp retort. Instead, she moved down the drive at a brisk walk. Mr. Collins mounted his horse and moved it down the drive to block Elizabeth's path.

"Cousin Elizabeth, as I am now the master of Longbourn, things will be done as I see fit. While you are still with us, you will be obliged to follow my instructions. Now, please get in the curricle with Walter and we shall make our way to the church." He gave her a look that brooked no argument.

Walter Collins had stepped down from the curricle to assist Elizabeth, but she ignored his offered hand and climbed into the seat, crossing her arms over her chest. Walter cast a worried look at his father and shook his head as he hurried around to the other side and returned to his seat. He moved the vehicle forward, following his father.

"I am sorry if my father seems overbearing. He is trying to find his place in this neighborhood," Walter offered apologetically.

"He will not be successful with this superior attitude he is displaying," came her terse reply. "The people here are warm and welcoming, but they do not much care for those who think themselves above their company—especially when they have no reason to feel that way." Elizabeth clamped her lips closed after delivering this opinion and they rode the rest of the way in silence.

When they arrived at the church, Elizabeth did not wait to be assisted from the curricle. She jumped down lightly and hurried into the building. She was greeted by several of the neighborhood ladies and was busy answering their questions when she felt Mr. Collins grab her by the elbow, guiding her away from the group and to the family pew. Allowing Walter to enter first, he then pushed in Elizabeth, placing her between the two men. Elizabeth sat straight and tall, never allowing her gaze to waver from the view of the altar. She had no need for a hymnal or prayer book, as she knew the service and many of the hymns by heart.

When the service concluded, Mr. Collins again rushed her away, not even taking the time to greet Mr. Carter, the vicar. Many of the neighbors discussed Mr. Collins' strange behavior.

When they returned home, Elizabeth moved to the rear parlor and remained there for the day. Her cousin had told her she was no longer to spend time in her room during the day, but Elizabeth was determined to not be in his presence either. Elizabeth had only her stitching to occupy her time, so she determined to sneak into the study after dinner, remove her books from the shelves, and take them to her room.

Though she followed Mr. Collins' directions and remained below stairs, she avoided his company and that of his son. She also refused to speak unless directly addressed. She hoped to make things so uncomfortable that Mr. Collins would change his mind and allow her to remain in her room. She retired for the evening as early as possible. Elizabeth remained dressed and took a seat near the window as she waited for the household to settle in for the night. As usual, her thoughts drifted to the Gardiners and Jane; she wondered why they did not come for her.

It was well past midnight, and the house had been quiet for some time when Elizabeth finally emerged from her room. She would get her personal books from her father's library and bring them to her room. However, she refused to ask Mr. Collins for the right to do so. She had made it halfway down the stairs, avoiding those that squeaked, when she saw light coming from the library. Apparently she had not waited long enough. She was about to return to her bedchamber when she heard Mr. Collins speak her name.

"I do not think we will be able to move as quickly with Elizabeth as I had hoped. I notified her mother's family that she had died in the carriage accident with the rest of them, so I doubt we shall be bothered by them."

"Father, how could you! They will find out eventually, you know."

"Of course I know, but we need to keep her here until you have married her. By then it will be too late for anyone to do anything about it. Also, I am sure her older sister will choose to remain with her London relations rather than return here with us in residence. It seems, too, that Elizabeth truly mourns for her family."

"That is the case in most families, Father," said Walter, adding under his breath, "with the exception of you."

"We do not have time for sentimental drivel and cannot wait for the end of her mourning. She will almost be of age by then, and as soon as the Philips return to Meryton, Elizabeth will learn of her inheritance. Once she is aware of it, we will never be able to convince her to become your wife."

"How did you find out about Elizabeth's inheritance?"

"Mr. Philips came by with his new will during one of our visits. I listened outside the study door as they spoke of it." Harold Collins' sarcastic laugh caused a shiver to run up Elizabeth's spine. "Yes, indeed, that was a lucky day. On her twenty-first birthday, Elizabeth stands to inherit a very large sum from a long-dead great-aunt on the Bennet side. Elizabeth must be named for her or some such nonsense. It is doubtful she even knew the lady. My cousin, Bennet, refused to make his estate as profitable as it could be because he did not wish for me to profit from his hard work. So we get this dump and nothing with which to improve it. I also have some debts in London I must pay off quickly. We need to get our hands on that money!"

"Is marriage the only way to obtain it?"

"Yes, if Elizabeth does not inherit, the money will be given to charity."

"Father, must I marry her? I find Elizabeth very disconcerting and do not believe I would enjoy being married to her, nor she to me."

"I just told you marriage is the only way. Give no thought to her wants. She is a woman; it is her lot in life to be married and submissive to her husband."

Elizabeth felt her hackles rising at Mr. Collins' words. 'We will just see about that!' she thought.

"Now, tomorrow you must be more obvious in your solicitousness to your cousin. You must do everything in your power to woo her and convince her of your love for her," Mr. Collins ordered. "If you cannot make her fall in love with you, are you prepared to do whatever it takes to gain Elizabeth as your wife?"

Walter gave his father a disapproving look.

"If you have made no progress within a few days, be prepared to compromise her. If you do not have the stomach for it, I just might have to take her in hand. Once she is ruined, no other man would ever want her, so she would have no choice but to agree to be your wife. It matters not who ruins her, does it?" The lascivious look on his face and Mr. Collins' obscene chuckle made his son more than a little uncomfortable.

"Remember, you need to marry her, but that does not necessarily mean it must be a long marriage," Mr. Collins continued. "Perhaps she will meet with an accident as the rest of her family did."

Walter shuddered at his father's words. Was he actually evil or merely self-absorbed? If he had killed Elizabeth's family, how had he managed to separate her from them? Walter was not sure he wished to know the answers to these questions.

Elizabeth was frozen in place by the shocking conversation she had just overheard. Only footsteps from within the room, announcing its occupants were preparing to exit, brought her to recognition of her current precarious position. She quickly turned and raced up the stairs and into her room, closing the door silently. She locked the door and leaned against it, trying to catch her breath. She remained in this position long after the footsteps in the hallway had ceased.

Elizabeth began to pace, scattered thoughts racing madly through her mind. She was shocked to learn her remaining family thought her dead. Even more surprising was the news she was an heiress—or would be when she reached her next birthday. She could not begin to imagine being married to the younger Mr. Collins. He was pleasant enough, but not nearly as intelligent as she would wish her husband to be. And the veiled threats made by the elder Collins were terrifying. What did he imply about her family's accident? Was it an accident or did he have something to do with it? Elizabeth paced unceasingly, but still she could not determine what to do. Finally, exhausted, she fell into bed.

Elizabeth barely woke in time to dress and join the gentlemen for breakfast, but her brief sleep had brought her the answers she sought. She would need to learn the gentlemen's schedule each day and make her plans from there. It was obvious to Elizabeth that she would need to leave the only home she had ever known, and do so very soon. Although she was uncertain where she would go, she felt sure she was capable of taking care of herself.

She slipped quietly into her place at the table. She kept her head down and spoke not a word.

"You are late, Cousin Elizabeth," noted Mr. Collins. "Please do not let it happen again. Regular meal times will be observed in this house going forward."

Elizabeth nodded. "I am sorry, Mr. Collins."

Though she did not speak much, Elizabeth listened to all that was said. Mr. Collins indicated he would be going out with Mr. Chapman. They were to inspect the fields farthest from the house. Elizabeth assumed they would be meeting with the tenants in that area as well, which should give her plenty of time to move her books.

When the meal ended, Elizabeth hurried to her room and summoned Mrs. Hill. She knew the faithful housekeeper would provide her with whatever assistance she could while keeping her secrets. When Mrs. Hill arrived, Elizabeth related what she had overheard in the library and explained her plan. When she was through, Mrs. Hill quickly packed some essentials for her into two small valises. She knew Elizabeth would need to be gone for at least nine months, when she would turn one and twenty. When she finished packing as much into the bags as she could, Mrs. Hill carried them down to the kitchen and hid them carefully.

Meanwhile, Elizabeth rushed to her father's library. She approached the bookshelves and reached to the top shelf to pull down a book. However, when she opened the front cover, it proved to be a small box. Mr. Bennet kept some funds within that he used to purchase new books. She quickly put the money in the pocket of her gown and returned the book to the shelf. She moved to another section of the shelves and pulled another book from the shelf. It was a book of poems by Donne and was the last gift her father had given her.

She was standing there holding it to her chest, tears quietly tracing down her checks, when the door opened. Elizabeth jumped at the unexpected sound and turned to find Mr. Collins standing in the doorway.

He looked at Elizabeth suspiciously. "What are you doing in my study, Cousin Elizabeth?" he asked harshly.

Elizabeth dashed the tears from her cheeks and squared her shoulders before she turned to answer. "I wished to retrieve my book. It was a gift from my father. All of the books he gifted to me are here in the library. I should like to take them to my room. Then I will not have to disturb you when I wish to read one of them."

"How many books do you claim are yours?" Mr. Collins asked gruffly.

"There are twenty-four. I have received one for my birthday and one for Christmas each year since I was eight. All of them are inscribed to me." Elizabeth's voice was haughty and her glare imperious.

Realizing it would not do to antagonize Elizabeth if they hoped to convince her to accept them as her family, Mr. Collins moderated his voice. "Please feel free to remove them from my study, Cousin Elizabeth, so you may have easy access to them."

Mr. Collins moved into the room and took a seat at one of the chairs in front of the desk. He watched Elizabeth as she removed the books from the shelves. It took her three trips to carry them from the study to her room. As she exited for the last time, she spoke to him. "I shall be upstairs packing the belongings of my mother and younger sisters. I will prepare them for delivery to Mr. Carter. He will give them to the poor of the parish."

"As you wish." Then Mr. Collins added, "Please be mindful not to remove anything that is a part of the estate. In fact, perhaps you should bring me your mother's and sisters' jewelry chests so I may put them in the safe. They should certainly not go to the poor."

"My younger sisters had only one necklace each, and they were buried in them. As to my mother's jewelry, I do not believe any of it was inherited with the estate. She had a set of pearls my father gave her as a wedding gift, but they are to go to my eldest sister, Jane, upon Mama's death. I shall pack the pearls to take to Jane when I go up to town with my uncle. I am surprised he has not yet come or at least sent me a note." Elizabeth watched Mr. Collins carefully as she spoke, and was surprised to see he showed no signs of discomfort at her questioning. The man was obviously an accomplished liar.

"As I said, perhaps he is away on business," Mr. Collins said. "You have already indicated neither your aunt nor your sister can travel. I will pass along any letter for you the moment it arrives, dear cousin."

Elizabeth returned above stairs and entered her youngest sister's room. She pulled Lydia's trunk from the closet and began placing her belongings in it. Anything Elizabeth wished to save was set aside. She would pack one trunk of special items and request it be sent to the Lucas' for safekeeping.

Elizabeth was delighted to find her sister had yet to spend any of her most recent allowance. She placed the money pouch in the pocket of her dress. She knew she would need funds for her escape and hoped she would find enough to support herself until she could find a position. She hoped to find additional funds in each of her sister's rooms.

Elizabeth remained above stairs most of the day, but at teatime Walter Collins came with a message that his father wished her to join them. Elizabeth indicated she would join them momentarily and continued to fold the dress in her hands, placing it in the nearly filled trunk.

Some ten minutes had passed before Elizabeth appeared in the parlor. "Cousin Elizabeth, I believe you were asked to join us some time ago. I would again ask you to respect my wishes regarding promptness in my home."

"I am sorry, Cousin Harold, I was trying to be useful as you instructed earlier and complete my task with the packing. I have finished with Lydia's belongings and have half of Kitty's packed. Tomorrow I should be able to finish with Kitty's and Mary's belongings. The next day I will work on my mother's things. Do you wish to have me pack my father's belongings as well, or would you prefer Mr. Hill to do so?"

"I would prefer you ask Mr. Hill to pack your father's things. It would not be appropriate for you to be in my bedchambers."

"Very well, I shall ask him as soon as the tea has ended. Everything should be packed and ready to be transported to the vicarage by Friday morning. If it would be acceptable to you, I would like to accompany them, as I feel the need of counsel from Mr. Carter."

Mr. Collins was not pleased with her request, but he knew he could not deny her the comfort of the vicar. Reluctantly he replied, "Of course, you may go. I will have Walter accompany you so you need not be alone in your sadness."

Knowing she would be unable to carry out her plans if Walter Collins accompanied her, she quickly searched her mind for a response that would appease him. "Perhaps I could ride in with Mr. Hill when he delivers the trunks and then Cousin Walter could come to retrieve me. There is so much turmoil in my heart at so great a loss; I expect to spend quite some time with Mr. Carter. Then I would like to sit at the graveside for a while, saying goodbye to my family. He could come to retrieve me at half past three so we shall return in time for tea, if that would be acceptable," Elizabeth stated reservedly.

Pleased she had suggested a way to spend time with his son, Mr. Collins agreed to Elizabeth's suggestion. With that, she excused herself and returned to packing.

Dinner was a tedious affair, and Elizabeth's nerves made it difficult for her to eat. "Cousin Elizabeth, you must eat something; it would not do for you to fall ill," Mr. Collins remarked.

"No, fair cousin, I would be devastated if you were to become ill," echoed Walter Collins dutifully.

"Perhaps I am just tired from all the activity of today. If you will excuse me, I should like to retire." Without waiting for an answer, Elizabeth rose from the table and went to her room. She rang for Mrs. Hill and requested that Mr. Hill pack all of her father's belongings in the morning. She also asked Mrs. Hill to have her husband set aside a few specific items she wanted to save. Mrs. Hill promised to have him do so. She also said she would have him bring to Elizabeth any money or valuables he found among Mr. Bennet's belongings.

When the gentlemen could no longer hear Elizabeth's footsteps, Mr. Collins turned to his son. "Now, Walter, you must make good use of your time alone with Elizabeth on Friday. She will not be able to leave the curricle, so you must propose to her before you return to the house. If she refuses you, very publicly kiss her, but make sure you are witnessed doing so."

"I know what you wish me to do, Father," said Walter in a surly tone. "Are you sure there is no other way to get the money? Though she is subdued now because of her sadness, that attitude will not last forever. I am not sure what would be worse, being chased by an angry bear or being married to an angry Elizabeth."

"There is no other way. I told you if she does not inherit the money, it will go to some charity of which the old lady was fond," growled Mr. Collins. "Now, I do not want to hear any more about this. You know what I expect; do not let me down." The look Mr. Collins turned on his son caused Walter to shift away.

"Of course, Father."

Since returning to her room, Elizabeth had busily written notes in preparation for her departure. An hour later, as a knock sounded at her chamber door, she covered the papers and moved to answer it.

Mrs. Hill waited on the other side of the door with a tray in hand. "I brought some tea to help you sleep, Miss Elizabeth."

"Thank you, Mrs. Hill, please come in," replied Elizabeth in a tired voice.

When the door was firmly closed and locked behind her, the two moved to sit on the edge of the bed.

"I have gained Mr. Collins' permission to go with Mr. Hill on Friday when the trunks are taken to the vicarage. I told him I needed Mr. Carter's counsel and time to say good-bye to my parents. Cousin Walter is to come for me at half past three to bring me home in time for tea. If you can think of a way to delay his departure, it will give me even more time to make my way from the neighborhood."

"I will confer with the others to see if we can find a way to stall him. Also, any messages you wish to have delivered you should give to me. Mr. Collins has been examining all the incoming and outgoing mail since the day after his arrival. He has also turned away both Lady Lucas and Charlotte, as well as Mrs. Long. He has been telling everyone you were indisposed due to your grief. I am sure it was part of his plan to isolate you and keep you from finding help or relief from others. He wanted you to be dependent on them, I am guessing. You best drink this tea and get to bed, Miss Lizzy. There is still plenty for you to do tomorrow. I think it is smart you are pretending to be agreeable. Mr. Collins is too full of himself to think you could outsmart him," said Mrs. Hill with a smile.

The next two days passed in much the same fashion. Elizabeth worked hard at searching for funds and saving special items as she finished packing the remainder of her sisters' and mother's personal possessions. Each day, when she spent time with the Collinses, she tried to be agreeable and reserved. She tolerated all of Walter's bumbling attempts at courting her, though she was particularly unhappy with the somewhat damp kisses he placed on the back of her hand. Those she tried to avoid whenever possible.

Everything was ready for her escape on the morrow. Mrs. Hill was attempting to gain the last needful thing. The only item that weighed heavily on Elizabeth's mind was what would happen to the servants she left behind. In many ways, they were part of her family, and she was concerned about their well-being.

She was in her room preparing for bed when a knock came at the door. She answered it, admitting the housekeeper, then locked the door behind her.

"Were you able to get what I needed from Sam?" asked Elizabeth.

"Yes, I packed it in the smaller valise. You can take it out and put your dress in it when you change.

"What about the horse?"

"Sam will saddle the horse and sneak away with it. He will meet you at the shed in back of the graveyard," replied Mrs. Hill.

"Good," Elizabeth replied with a nod of her head. She looked at the letters in her hand. "I packed all of my books in the small trunk that used to be Mama's. The large portmanteau contains the special items I wished to save from each of my family members. Could you please be sure both are discreetly delivered to Charlotte along with this letter?" Elizabeth placed a sealed letter in Mrs. Hill's hands.

"What about the letter to Miss Jane and the Gardiners?"

"I decided not to write one," Elizabeth whispered. "I know it is cruel to let them continue to think me dead, but perhaps it is safer for them. Mr. Collins may have caused the accident to my family. If he thought Jane and the Gardiners knew where I was, he might try to hurt them to get my cooperation. But since Mr. Collins told them I am dead, he cannot go to them and ask about me. Hopefully, that will keep them safe."

"Then you must let me know if you are safe and where you are."

"I will not be able to do so. There would be too great a risk that Mr. Collins would find out, and you would lose your position."

"I do not believe we will be remaining very long after your departure. My Jacob and I were talking about it, and neither of us wishes to work for Mr. Collins. My sister and her husband have an inn near Cambridge. Her husband has recently taken ill and can no longer work, and she needs to take care of him most of the time. They offered to give us the inn if they could remain there for room and board. Jacob and I decided to accept her offer. You could write to me there. Sally and Mrs. Phipps are coming with us, and Sam is looking for something else as well. We will be well. Do not worry. Your only concern should be keeping yourself safe. And if you cannot find any other options, come to us at the inn. We will hide you or help you."

Agreeing to the request, Elizabeth wrote down the name and directions to the inn.

"Is there anything else we can do for you, Miss Elizabeth?"

Thinking for several moments, she said, "Could you pack some food for me? I need to get as far away as I can, quickly. If I had food for my journey, it would save me both money and time. Perhaps you could pack it in saddlebags?" Elizabeth wondered.

Mrs. Hill agreed to do so first thing in the morning. The two women went over everything once more, including the timetable for the morning. Elizabeth then drank the tea Mrs. Hill had brought for her. After a tearful farewell, Mrs. Hill tucked Elizabeth into her bed and returned to the kitchen.

Fortunately, sleep came easily to Elizabeth, as the stress and activity of the past few days had left her exhausted. Her last thought as she closed her eyes was that this would be the last night she would ever spend in her childhood home.

5. DISASTER AVOIDED

AT FIVE AND TEN YEARS OF age, Georgiana Darcy was a beautiful young woman, possessing golden blonde curls and sapphire blue eyes. Wickham had been dancing attendance on her for two weeks now. Though she was lovely and in possession of an extremely large dowry, he was incredibly bored. The girl was so naive that, though he had convinced her of his undying love, she did not understand his hints to further their relationship. He would be required to be direct but would need to give careful thought to how he would press her into allowing him the liberties he wished and consenting to an elopement.

If it were not for the presence of Harriet Younge, Georgiana's attractive companion, he would be required to seek his pleasure elsewhere. He and Harriet had conspired to get her the position as Miss Darcy's companion. When Harriet was installed in Darcy House, they met on her day off, frequently spending the day in pursuits usually reserved for a married couple. Eventually, after earning Darcy's approbation, Mrs. Younge suggested Miss Darcy might enjoy a month or two at the seaside. After carefully considering all aspects of the request, Darcy had agreed and rented a house for his sister and her companion.

Darcy traveled to the resort town of Ramsgate with the ladies and stayed for a week before returning to London to handle matters of business that needed his attention. Darcy planned to return for the last two weeks of their stay. From there, they would travel to Pemberley in anticipation of visitors.

Though Georgiana would not have her regular lessons while at Ramsgate, her brother had hired art and music masters. The lessons with the masters would allow Georgiana to improve in her two favorite areas of study. The house Darcy had rented was located in an area of larger homes directly on the beach. Georgiana particularly enjoyed sitting on the porch at the back of the house, where she could watch the sea, the birds, and the sunrise. She was frequently found there with her sketchpad or watercolors.

Slightly more than a week after her brother's departure, Georgiana received quite a surprise. She and her companion had been strolling along the beach when she saw a gentleman walking towards them. There was something familiar about him, but he was as yet too distant for her to make out his features. When he drew nearer, Georgiana noticed a smile light his face. He removed his hat and bowed to her.

"Pardon me," said the gentleman, "but you would not be Miss Georgiana Darcy, would you?"

Georgiana blushed at the gentleman's forwardness, but gave a slight nod.

"You do not remember me?"

This time, Georgiana gave a slight shake of her head.

The gentleman bowed again, saying, "It is a pleasure to see you once more, Miss Darcy. I am George Wickham. It has been far too long since I was last in your delightful presence."

Georgiana blushed at his compliment and looked down. If she had not done so, she might have observed the exchange between her companion and the gentleman.

"May I accompany you ladies on your walk?" Wickham asked with a charming smile.

Georgiana looked to Mrs. Younge for guidance and, upon receiving her nod, agreed. Wickham offered his arm to Georgiana, who again sought permission from her companion. At Mrs. Younge's indication of agreement, Miss Darcy very hesitantly placed her hand on his arm. Her touch was as light as the fluttering wings of a butterfly.

For a week, Mr. Wickham met the ladies and escorted them on their morning walk. He filled his conversation with references to his friendship with her brother and memories of her parents and youth. Georgiana loved to hear about her family.

The second week of their encounters, Mrs. Younge encouraged Georgiana to invite Mr. Wickham to tea in the afternoon. Now he was in her presence twice each day. Georgiana had wished to write her brother of meeting his old friend, but Mrs. Younge told her it would be a much nicer surprise for her brother to meet Mr. Wickham by surprise when he joined them. During the third week of their acquaintance, Mr. Wickham accompanied them to an afternoon concert and a museum exhibit.

The ladies had been in Ramsgate just longer than a month when Mrs. Younge encouraged Miss Darcy to invite Mr. Wickham to dine with them. Georgiana would not have thought this appropriate, as there was no other gentleman in the house. However, as she believed herself to be in love with her brother's childhood friend, she pushed aside the uncomfortable feelings and issued the invitation.

As they sat in the parlor after dinner, Mrs. Younge made an excuse to leave the room, stating she needed to find a different thread for her needlework. As soon as she left, Mr. Wickham made his way to kneel before Georgiana. He took both of her hands in his as he gazed deeply into her eyes.

"My dear Miss Darcy, Georgiana, it can be no surprise to you that I have fallen in love with you during these past weeks. Memories of you are some of the most cherished of my youth. Now, seeing you before me as a grown woman, your beauty takes my breath away. Will you please accept my hand in marriage? Will you go away with me to Scotland to be married? We can return from there to Pemberley to surprise your brother," finished Wickham in a rush.

Georgiana's eyes grew round and large at his words, like a doe in the sights of a hunter. Her cheeks colored and her heart raced as she heard the words of love spoken by the man kneeling before her.

"Oh, Mr. Wickham . . . George," she said, her eyes shimmering with tears of joy. "I most happily accept your proposal."

Wickham started to stand to sweep her into an embrace, but her hand stayed him. "However, I do not believe I can elope. William is all the family I have left; I could not leave him to worry."

"But think, dear Georgiana, of his joy when you return married to his dear friend."

Georgiana looked down in confusion. Finally, she said, "Will you allow me a day or two to consider the matter, please?"

Wickham did an admirable job of masking his annoyance as he replied, "Of course, my dear, but I shall be in agony awaiting your decision." So saying, Wickham pulled Georgiana to her feet and wrapped his arms around her. Noting the nervousness in her eyes, he placed a chaste kiss upon her lips. As he attempted to deepen the kiss, he felt her stiffen in his arms. Reluctantly, he released her and stepped back to gaze at her as they heard the doorknob rattle upon Mrs. Younge's return to the room.

Georgiana's emotions were in such excited turmoil that she asked to be excused to retire for the night. Wickham and Mrs. Younge offered their wishes for a pleasant evening, and Mrs. Younge watched as her charge climbed the stairs. When she heard the door to Georgiana's room close behind her, Mrs. Younge returned to the drawing room and closed the doors.

"What did she say? When do we leave?" she eagerly questioned Wickham.

"Georgiana has agreed to the engagement but not the elopement. When is Darcy expected?"

"In ten days' time. He is to return to spend the last two weeks with us."

"Well, then, we will both have to work on her to get her agreement to the elopement. I wish to be gone well before Darcy arrives!"

"Did you seal the deal with a kiss?" Mrs. Younge's tone held the barest hint of jealousy.

"It could hardly be deemed as such," replied Wickham as he pulled Mrs. Younge into his embrace. "It cannot begin to compare with your charms, Harriet." He lowered his head and kissed her passionately. When he broke the kiss, he reminded her they must be patient, and they must both work to induce Georgiana to agree to elope. With a wave of his hat and a last kiss, Wickham departed.

The next morning, Mrs. Younge watched Georgiana carefully. The young lady had a moon-eyed look about her, but Mrs. Younge noted her forehead often crinkled in confusion or concern.

"Miss Darcy, are you well? You appear to be concerned about something. Might I be of help?"

At first Georgiana was hesitant, but then she remembered her companion was there to guide her. Certainly Mrs. Younge would know what she should do. "Mr. Wickham has proposed to me." Georgiana's eyes sparkled as she shared her news.

"I am delighted for you, my dear. Mr. Wickham appears to be all a gentleman should be." Georgiana failed to note the woman's expression or the sly tone of her voice. "What is it that concerns you, Miss Darcy?"

"He wishes to elope."

"Oh! How exciting!" replied her companion before Georgiana could say more. "It is a lovely, romantic idea."

"But I thought," Georgiana began hesitantly, "elopements were considered scandalous."

"I believe they were at one time, but I heard recently they were becoming all the rage," Mrs. Younge remarked encouragingly.

"How could I ever marry without my brother to give me away? He is the last member of my family. Would he not be sad and lonely if I were to elope?"

"Mr. Wickham is a dear old friend of his, and if you are happy, I am sure Mr. Darcy will be happy for you."

"I believe I shall take my sketch pad to the porch and do some sketching while I think."

"Certainly, Miss Darcy. I shall be here if you need me," said Mrs. Younge with a smile.

During the following week, both Mr. Wickham and Mrs. Younge continued to encourage her agreement whenever they were in her company. Finally, Georgiana made her decision.

Darcy had concluded his business in London early and traveled to Ramsgate to surprise his sister, Georgiana. The surprise had been on Darcy, however, when he walked into the parlor of the house he had rented for his sister's seaside vacation. Seated on the sofa beside his sister was none other than that scoundrel, George Wickham. Darcy heard Wickham's eloquent expression of affection as he told Georgiana that all of the arrangements had been made for the trip to Gretna Green on the morrow. Georgiana's eyes had been shyly downcast throughout Wickham's speech, but as she looked up to answer him, she saw her brother standing in the doorway. With a look both confused and delighted, Georgiana rushed across the room and into her brother's embrace. Over the top of her head, Darcy saw Wickham's face flush with anger. He also noted that the face of Georgiana's companion, Mrs. Younge, went deathly pale.

"William, what are you doing here? Oh, this is the most wonderful surprise. Now you can accompany us and give me away!"

With his sister tucked safely to his side, Darcy spoke. "What is this I hear about Gretna Green, Wickham?"

Before Wickham could come up with a suitable lie, Georgiana answered, "George has asked me to marry him. He wished to hurry to Gretna Green and then surprise you when we returned to Pemberley. Is it not wonderful that your childhood friend will be my husband?"

"I am afraid you have been misled, Georgie. It has been several years now since my friendship with Wickham ended."

Georgiana looked confused and tears welled in her eyes. She could not imagine being married to someone of whom her brother disapproved.

Turning to Wickham, Darcy continued. "I will say I never expected this of you, Wickham. Just when I thought you could not sink any lower, you do something more loathsome than ever before. Are you so heartless that you would ruin Georgiana's life to have your revenge on me?"

"You have it all wrong, Darcy," said Wickham with a smirk. "Your sister has practically thrown herself at me since we met a few weeks ago."

Darcy heard Georgiana gasp.

"I am quite certain Georgiana did nothing of the kind. I know you used her tender heart, your oily smile, questionable charm, and oft-used words of love to convince her that you loved her. Lest you forget, I have seen this behavior too often to doubt what occurred."

"Yes," Wickham sneered, "and I would have been successful again had it not been for your early arrival. This time I would finally have gotten all I deserved and my revenge on you!"

"However, this time you would have been the one disappointed. You see, there is a clause in father's will that says Georgiana's dowry is forfeited if she elopes."

"Your father would never treat Georgiana in such a negligent way."

"Oh, he was not being negligent. He just wished to protect her from fortune hunters like you."

At her brother's remark, Georgiana gasped before turning her face into Darcy's chest and sobbing as if her heart would break.

Darcy turned his glare upon Mrs. Younge. "The mere fact you allowed this to happen proves you were either part of the scheme or are completely unsuitable to be the companion of an impressionable young woman. No matter which it may be, you are dismissed immediately, Mrs. Younge. Provide me with your address and your belongings and wages will be sent to you."

As the frightened woman moved to comply, Wickham stopped her. He took her arm and moved towards the hall, where they waited for the servants to bring their outerwear. Mrs. Younge handed a card from her bag to the butler as she rushed out the door. Wickham remained in the doorway only long enough to cause more turmoil. "I guess I should be grateful for your arrival, Darcy. I may not get my money, but you stopped me from being stuck with this naïve little fool for the rest of my life." As he heard Georgiana break into renewed sobs, Wickham gave a heartless laugh and departed.

It was quite some time before Georgiana was cried out and able to speak rationally with her brother. She told him of her first meeting with Wickham. She had not recognized him, but he had introduced himself to her. Remembering him fondly from her childhood, she had been pleased with his attentions. Upon returning home after that first meeting, she had questioned Mrs. Younge regarding whether or not her behavior at accepting the introduction had been appropriate. Mrs. Young had reassured her it was, as Wickham was an old family friend. After that first meeting, Georgiana seemed to see Wickham everywhere she went. At Mrs. Younge's prompting, she had invited him to the house for tea.

"Georgie, what was his behavior like when he was here at the house? Did he behave as a gentleman should?" Darcy questioned.

"Yes, he never crossed the lines of propriety." As she finished speaking, her face became suffused with color and she would not meet her brother's eyes.

"Georgie?" The question in his tone was unmistakable.

"Well, he did begin to kiss my hand whenever he saw me or took his leave," she replied quietly. She was afraid to mention he had kissed her as well.

Darcy's anger, already to the boiling point, increased with her reply. *That miserable cad was preying on my innocent young sister! If I ever see him again, he will pay for this treachery*, Darcy thought. To Georgiana he said, "When did he ask you to marry him?"

"It was a little more than a week ago. I was so excited. I knew he was your friend and believed you would be happy for me. I wanted to write to you immediately, but George told me it would be much better to elope and surprise you. We had just finished making our plans when you arrived. We were to leave in the morning."

"Sweetheart, did Mrs. Younge agree that eloping was a good idea?"

"Yes. At first I could not imagine running off without telling you, but Mrs. Younge kept speaking of young love and how romantic an elopement was. She said elopements were becoming fashionable and you would be pleased for me." Georgiana again looked down, unable to meet her brother's eyes. Hesitantly, she spoke again. "Mrs. Younge's advice was incorrect, was it not?"

"It was."

In an even softer voice, she continued. "He did not really love me, did he?"

Darcy could hear the sadness in her voice and hesitated to make her feel worse, but he knew it was his silence regarding George Wickham and men like him that had placed his sister in this difficult situation.

"I do not know if he loved you or not, but because of his behavior, I would suspect he did not. No man who truly loves a woman would treat her with anything but the utmost respect. He would not try to convince such a young lady to run away from her family, but would approach her relatives and ask for her hand properly." Darcy saw tears again cascade down her cheeks.

Reaching out, he took her hand in his. "Dear Georgiana, you are not to blame for this situation. The fault rests squarely with me. I knew the kind of man he was even before Father died. I saw his behavior while we were at Cambridge. It was certainly not that of a gentleman." Darcy explained his history with Wickham, right up to the last time Darcy had refused to appoint him to the living that Wickham had willingly signed away for the sum of three thousand pounds.

Georgiana listened in silence, her face growing more and more shocked. Finally, she looked at Darcy and said, "William, could we please return to Pemberley tomorrow? I wish to go home."

"Certainly, Georgiana, we can leave at first light, but I must stop in town for a day or two before we continue to Pemberley. Will that suit you?"

Georgiana nodded tiredly and informed her brother she was going to retire due to an aching head.

Darcy pulled her into his arms and hugged her tightly. He kissed the top of her head and expressed his hope that she would have a pleasant rest. As she moved to the door, he reminded her to have her maid begin the packing for their departure.

Darcy called for Georgiana's maid to attend to her and sent his sister to rest. The rest of the household staff was sent into a flurry of packing, as Darcy planned to remove Georgiana from Ramsgate in the morning. Before having something to eat and retiring himself, Darcy sent an express regarding the events in the seaside town to his cousin, Colonel Richard Fitzwilliam, who was Georgiana's other guardian.

They traveled to London the next day and found the Colonel waiting for them at Darcy House. Richard greeted Georgiana cheerfully and reassured her of his love. She had only managed to apologize for her behavior before she burst into tears and rushed to her room.

Curse George Wickham! thought Darcy for the thousandth time in the last three days. Since Darcy's unexpected arrival in Ramsgate, Georgiana had wanted nothing more than to return to Pemberley. During their two days of travel, all Georgiana had done was cry and apologize. They had been delayed one day in London as Darcy attended to a matter of business that had arisen during his absence. That day they had gotten a later start leaving London than Darcy would have liked, and now they would have to stop early because of a problem with one of the horses. He hoped the issue could be handled promptly, as he wished to make an early start the next day. They would have two and a half long days of travel before they reached home.

Darcy was pulled from his thoughts as the carriage turned into the cobbled courtyard of the Knight's Rest in Stevenage.

6. ESCAPE

AT SIX-THIRTY IN THE MORNING, a quiet knock sounded at Elizabeth's door. Without waiting for the young lady's call, Sally entered with a pitcher of warm water and fresh towels for Elizabeth to use for her toilet. Once Elizabeth had refreshed herself and was buttoned into her black gown, Sally dressed her hair in a simple bun high on the back of her head. When it was time for Elizabeth to go down to break her fast, she stopped in the doorway and took one last look around. She had been forced to be selective in what she took with her. In that last look, she saw many of the childhood treasures she had collected over the years.

Elizabeth was in her place at the table when Harold and Walter Collins arrived. Mr. Collins smiled as he seated himself, taking his place at the table. He mistakenly assumed his strictures were the reason for her promptness. Elizabeth remained mostly silent throughout the meal, speaking only when addressed. Her silence also pleased Mr. Collins. He did not like women with spirit, like Elizabeth was. What he liked was breaking their spirit. In his conceit, he thought he had already achieved success.

When the meal was over, Elizabeth prepared to depart. She took her seat on the wagon with Mr. Hill, and they moved off down the drive. Elizabeth turned and called over her shoulder, as though she had just remembered something. "Once I am finished visiting with Mr. Carter, I must go to Mrs.

Stone, the dressmaker, and thank her for the black dress she sent to me. Perhaps Walter should meet me there." Mr. Hill slapped the reins over the horses and they increased their pace down the driveway, not giving Mr. Collins a chance to reply.

When the wagon arrived at the chapel in Meryton, Mr. Hill helped Elizabeth down and she moved inside to find Mr. Carter.

"Good morning, Miss Elizabeth," the cleric said kindly. "How are you doing, my dear girl?"

"Good morning, Mr. Carter. I am as well as can be expected. I packed up my family's clothes and brought them for you to distribute to the poor of the parish," responded Elizabeth quietly. "While you retrieve them, I wish to visit my family's graves and perhaps make my way inside later to speak with you, if that is acceptable."

"Certainly, my dear, I will be waiting here whenever you need me."

Elizabeth moved towards the front of the church and exited a side door to the graveyard. Mr. Carter watched her go before leaving to help Mr. Hill with the trunks.

Elizabeth was pleased the Bennets' graves could not be seen from the church. After moving out of sight of the chapel windows, she hurried to the storage shed at the rear of the churchyard. There she found Sam with the remaining carriage horse. The animal wore a small saddle. One of her valises was affixed to it as were a pair of full saddle bags. Sam held her other bag, which he quickly handed to Elizabeth. With the satchel in hand, she disappeared into the shed while Sam stood guard in front of the door. When it opened, Elizabeth stepped out dressed as a young lad in the set of clothes Mrs. Hill had obtained for her. She had a cap pulled down to cover her hair and wore a too-big pair of riding boots. Sam took the bag from her and attached it to her saddle. Then he gave Elizabeth a leg up on the horse.

Elizabeth looked down with a worried expression in her eyes. "How can I ever thank you for all your help? I hope you do not get into trouble for this. What will you tell Mr. Collins when he discovers the horse is missing?"

"You do not need to worry about that, Miss Lizzy. You just take care to get far away from them Collinses and stay safe. I have already talked with my folks, and I believe Sir William will take me on in his stables. If he cannot, I will find something else. Sally will travel with Mr. and Mrs. Hill and help out at the inn. They are taking Mrs. Phipps to her sister in Letchford on their way. When they wake up in the morning, they will not find any of us there, so do not worry." Sam gave the horse a gentle slap and watched as Elizabeth trotted away.

Elizabeth knew she would have at least a six-hour head start, and she expected Mr. Collins would believe she had gone to her relatives in London. Knowing as she did that Mr. Collins had told them she died, he would not be able to contact them directly regarding Elizabeth's whereabouts. She expected they would search the road to London, but did not know if they would check in other directions. Therefore, Elizabeth had carefully made her plans.

Fortunately, Elizabeth's walks had familiarized her with the surrounding countryside, and she had often studied the atlas and maps of England in her father's library. Elizabeth hoped to travel one day but had never dreamed she would be doing so dressed as a boy, alone, and on horseback.

Elizabeth kept to the woods alongside the road and headed in a westerly direction towards Aylesbury as quickly as she could. It was approaching mid-day when she arrived. Pulling her hat down over her face, Elizabeth stepped into the taproom of the inn and ordered a mug of cider. While she drank, she pondered her next step. Clearing her throat, she hailed the proprietor in the deepest voice she could manage and asked for directions to Oxford, as well as a recommendation for a place to stay.

When she finished her drink, Elizabeth exited the inn, calling out thanks for the directions to Oxford. She mounted the horse and headed west out of town in the direction she had been given. She traveled several miles before turning off and heading back the way she had come, circling around to the north of Aylesbury and heading for Luton.

When she arrived in Luton, she put on the same performance, this time asking for directions to Bedford. From Luton, Elizabeth continued to Stevenage. She knew the post from London to York would stop there. In each place the coach stopped, she planned to ask if the innkeeper was aware of anyone looking for a governess or companion. With any luck, she would find a position and a place to hide until her birthday in early April.

It was early afternoon when Elizabeth arrived in Stevenage. She picked one of the smaller inns and asked what time the coach to York came through. She was disappointed to learn she had missed it by half an hour. Now she would have to remain overnight and catch the stage in the morning. Armed with the information she needed, Elizabeth walked with her horse towards the center of town. She tied the horse to a post on the edge of the village green and sat under a tree to have a snack from the food Mrs. Phipps had packed for her.

She looked around, taking in all the activity. Stevenage was larger than Meryton and people bustled about everywhere. Still, the village retained a pleasant, peaceful air. There were several shops she would not mind entering, but she knew she would look out of place there dressed as a boy—except, perhaps, in the book shop. She also could not go shopping once she had changed, as then people would expect her to have a companion with her. Instead, Elizabeth remained on the green, watching the people and enjoying the sunshine.

As it drew near to teatime, she untethered her horse and led him towards her destination. Elizabeth selected the largest inn in the village and left her horse in the stable. With her saddlebags over her shoulder and struggling to carry her valise and satchel, she made her way through the garden and in the side door of the inn. Discreetly locating the necessary room, Elizabeth slipped inside and locked the door behind her.

She quickly divested herself of her boy's clothing and washed as thoroughly as possible with the water available. She donned her black dress and packed away the boy's clothing. She brushed out her hair and fixed it up in a bun before putting on the only hat she had been able to fit into her luggage. Now looking like a proper young lady, she took her bags and slipped out the garden door, being careful not to attract attention. Staying in the shadows of the garden, she waited for the next coach to arrive. As passengers disembarked, Elizabeth slipped in front of those exiting the carriage and entered the inn. As she stepped up to the desk and began to speak with the innkeeper regarding a room, the other passengers headed for the common room.

A young woman in black was standing at the desk, speaking with the innkeeper as Darcy entered. Recognizing Mr. Darcy, the proprietor turned away from the lady to give his full attention to Darcy. Neither of the gentlemen noticed the look of irritation on the young woman's face. It was quickly followed by a look of resignation. As the innkeeper turned to get the key, the handsome gentleman exited the inn, returning quickly with a lovely young woman on his arm. Tears were evident on her face, as was a look of intense sadness. The look was certainly something to which Elizabeth could relate.

Darcy stopped to retrieve the key and request bathwater to be sent to their suite immediately, with tea to follow in half an hour. As he made these arrangements with the innkeeper, the young lady tried to dry her eyes with her already sodden handkerchief. Noticing, Elizabeth pulled a dry handkerchief from her reticule and offered it to the young lady.

She had just taken it from Elizabeth when a loud laugh burst from the open door of the common room. The young woman before her started at the sound and glanced quickly around her. When the tearful girl saw a table of well-dressed young men— laughing and looking her way—all the color drained from the young woman's face and she dropped in a faint. Elizabeth reached out her arms in an attempt to catch the young woman as she called out for assistance. By the time Darcy turned to look in the direction of the call, he saw Georgiana limp in the arms of the young woman he had seen upon entering the inn.

He reached out and gathered Georgiana into his arms. Then Darcy quickly moved to follow the proprietor as he ascended the stairs, keys in hand. On the floor by her feet, Elizabeth noted the young woman's reticule and the two handkerchiefs. She picked up the items and moved to follow the men up the stairs. As she reached the top, the innkeeper exited a room halfway down the right side of the hall.

"Only guests are allowed upstairs," said the man belligerently.

"Had we not been interrupted earlier, perhaps I would be a guest by now," Elizabeth responded testily. "As for my reason to be above stairs, the young lady dropped these items when she fainted. I wished only to return them."

"Mr. Darcy would not wish to be bothered by the likes of you. I will return the items." The innkeeper grabbed the items from Elizabeth and turned again to the room he had just exited.

With one last irritated look in the innkeeper's direction, Elizabeth descended the stairs and again stood in the entrance, waiting to speak with the proprietor. Elizabeth was shocked to realize the innkeeper's opinion of her. In spite of the embarrassment she felt, she kept her head high as she awaited his return.

When the innkeeper was once again behind the desk and saw her waiting, he decided to deal with her quickly. "What is it you want?" he asked gruffly.

"I should like a room for the night, please."

"You be travelin' alone?" the man asked suspiciously.

"As you can plainly see, I am alone, but the circumstances are not of my making," replied Elizabeth with quiet dignity.

"Then what would be the reason?"

With as much dignity and calmness as she could muster, Elizabeth answered the man's question. "I have recently lost my family. The heir to my father's estate had a falling out with my father many years ago and refused to allow me to remain in my home, even until I could find a position. I had hoped to travel to London to look for work unless you know of a family in the area that might be in need of a governess or companion." Frustrated at having to humble herself in such a humiliating manner, she lifted her chin and haughtily added, "I am the daughter of a gentleman and very well educated."

The innkeeper was quiet for several minutes, staring at Elizabeth thoughtfully. It was apparent from her dress and speech that she was gently born. She appeared to be quite young, and the innkeeper could see the evidence of recent tears in her tired eyes. Finally, he spoke. "All my single rooms are taken for the night, but if you would be willing to wait in the common room, I could have a spare servant's room prepared for you. Would that be acceptable?"

Filled with relief and overwhelmed by the man's kindness, Elizabeth's eyes sparkled with unshed tears. "That would be acceptable. I appreciate your kindness."

The innkeeper personally escorted Elizabeth into the common room and placed her at a small table near the fire, saying, "I will have the girl bring you a meal and some tea while you wait." So saying, he moved off in the direction of the kitchen.

Elizabeth folded her hands in her lap as she waited for her meal. She had always imagined traveling and staying at an inn would be an exciting experience. In reality, she felt alone and somewhat frightened. *What will happen if I cannot find a position? Will I be able to find a position before my funds are depleted? Would it be safe to go to the Gardiners' if I can find no employment?* She was jolted from her thoughts when her meal appeared on the table in front of her. A buxom young woman with bright red hair and freckles sprinkled across her face gave her an annoyed look before moving over to flirt with the table of young gents.

Upon his return to the taproom after settling Georgiana in her room, Darcy found a corner table and ordered a glass of brandy. He had been able to get Georgiana to drink one cup of tea before she insisted she wished only to retire for the night. Leaving a footman stationed in the hallway outside her door, he had finally descended the stairs in search of food.

The buxom redhead quickly appeared. "What can I be doin' fer ye today, sir?" she asked Darcy with a wide smile.

Not bothering to look up, he asked for a simple bowl of stew. The young woman leaned down, offering Darcy a clear look at her exposed bosom. "Are you sure that is all ye be wantin'?" she asked.

Looking up for the first time since he sat down, Darcy was shocked to find the woman so close. Leaning well away from her, he said, "That will be all." The cold look he turned upon her convinced her to waste no more time with this gentleman. However, as she walked away, she could not stop herself from casting one last, lingering look at his very handsome person.

His meal being placed on the table before him returned Darcy from his morose thoughts. As he took the first bite of the stew, he looked around and noticed the young woman dressed in black sitting at a table near the fireplace. Had her attire not given away her mourning, her red eyes and the look of sadness that occasionally crossed her face would have. Darcy looked about, wondering where her traveling companion was. She appeared quite petite, but her posture and attitude gave him the impression she was trying to appear even smaller, as though she wished to make herself invisible.

As he took another bite of stew, he continued to watch as one of the rowdy young gentlemen from a nearby table approached her. It was obvious the man was slightly in his cups, and Darcy felt concern for the young woman who had shown such kindness to his sister. As his table was not a great distance from hers, he could hear the words spoken by the man.

"Such a lovely young lady and all alone," the gentleman said with a leer. "I am betting you would like some company, now, am I right?"

The young woman continued to eat, never once raising her eyes to look at the man before her. He seated himself next to her at the table but quickly jumped back up, wiping at his lap. In a graceful move that was almost unnoticeable, she had caused her cup of tea to spill into his lap.

Now that there was a greater distance between the two of them, she looked up at the man. Her expression appeared both grave and innocent, but Darcy thought he detected a twinkle in her eye.

"Oh, my! Sir, I am terribly sorry! My sadness seems to have made me clumsy. Please say you will forgive me, sir!" Darcy noted her eyes now appeared to have tears shimmering in them.

The man stopped brushing at his lap and noticed the tears in her eyes. His wet lap seemed to have sobered him somewhat, and a semblance of proper behavior returned. He bowed slightly, saying. "Think nothing of it, madam. I am sorry for your loss and for disturbing you."

He bowed again and returned to his comrades, where he was forced to endure some teasing. Darcy continued to watch her and noticed that when the man walked away, the young woman appeared to tremble and shrink back into herself. Then she quickly gave her shoulders a little shake and returned her attention to her meal.

Touched by the woman's sadness, impressed by the way she had handled such a difficult situation, and grateful for her earlier kindness to Georgiana, Darcy called to the landlord. "Could you please tell me what you know of the young woman who was of assistance to my sister earlier?"

The innkeeper repeated what he had learned of her earlier.

"So, she is the orphaned daughter of a gentleman and has found herself forced to seek work," said Darcy thoughtfully. He thanked the man for the information and dismissed him. He sat pondering a surprising idea. He had recently made such a blunder with selecting a companion for his sister. Could he dare consider an unknown young woman without references? Lost in thought, weighing the idea in his mind, he was startled to hear a sweet voice address him.

"Pardon me, sir. I know I should not approach you, but I will not be able to rest without assuring myself the young lady with you has recovered. She is better, I hope? I found some of her belongings on the floor and gave them to the innkeeper. I do hope you received them."

Darcy spoke. "Yes, I did receive them and thank you for your thoughtfulness. My sister has recently endured a trying situation. It has left her feeling a bit unwell, but I hope she will recover fully."

"I am glad to hear that, sir, and will say a prayer for her. Good night." Without another word, the lady in black turned to depart, quickly mounted the stairs, and disappeared from sight.

Darcy continued to ponder the situation. Not much time passed before he called again to the landlord, requesting writing supplies. He quickly wrote his note and asked the landlord to have it delivered immediately. He gave the landlord an additional instruction before retiring to the suite he shared with his sister.

7. EMPLOYMENT

E<small>LIZABETH</small> WAS SURPRISED TO SEE THE innkeeper at her door shortly after she had retired to her room. She was even more startled when he presented her with a note. Mr. Heath told her he was to wait for her answer. Elizabeth opened the note and looked at the message. The writing was bold and neat, yet precise, obviously written by a man. She quickly perused the information contained in it as shock registered on her face.

Eventually, she turned to the landlord and said, "I should like to meet with Mr. Darcy."

"What is your name, miss, so that I may make the introduction, if you please."

Elizabeth felt a moment of panic. She did not wish to conjure too many lies regarding her situation, but she knew she could not give the gentleman her real name, not if she wished to stay hidden from Mr. Collins. Thinking quickly, she replied, "Rose Lucas."

Fortunately, the landlord did not notice her hesitation in answering. After receiving the information he required, he led her down the hall to the stairs and down two flights, then down another hallway before stopping in front of a door and knocking.

Darcy heard the knock on the sitting room door. He moved to answer it and admitted the young lady in black. She was escorted by the landlord, who noted there was a maid in the room seated in the corner by the window.

81

"Mr. Darcy, may I present Miss Rose Lucas? Miss Lucas, this is Mr. Fitzwilliam Darcy of Pemberley in Derbyshire."

Darcy bowed and acknowledged the introduction while Elizabeth gave a polite curtsey. The landlord exited the room and remained stationed in the hallway as Mr. Darcy directed. He was to wait and escort the young lady back to her room when the meeting ended.

"Please be seated, Miss Lucas." Darcy indicated a chair across from his and took his seat again only after she had done so. "Miss Lucas, I realize this meeting is quite unorthodox, but I found myself in a difficult situation and was informed by the landlord that you are recently orphaned and seeking a position."

Elizabeth seemed to bristle a bit at the thought that Darcy had been enquiring about her, but said only, "Yes, sir."

"The young woman you saw earlier today is my younger sister. She is more than ten years my junior. Very recently I had to discharge her companion and now must find a new one for her. I would usually not act in such a precipitous manner, but I noticed you earlier this evening in the common room. I had already been impressed with your kindness and care towards my sister. Then I observed you protect yourself from a rather forward young gentleman. You were quick-witted and kind in spite of his manner and turned around what could have been a very difficult situation. These actions impressed me even further."

"Thank you, Mr. Darcy."

"Could you please tell me how you came to be in your current situation?"

Tears appeared in Elizabeth's eyes, but she dashed them away. She straightened her shoulders and looked directly at Darcy before answering. "Approximately two weeks ago my father, mother, and three younger sisters were killed in a carriage accident. My parents were only children, and my father's estate was entailed away from the female line. On the day after the accident, the heir, a distant cousin of my father's, arrived. He did not wish to be saddled with me, offering me a place as a servant in his home. I turned down his offer, packed my belongings, and left as soon as I could. I have been traveling for a short time, and at each carriage stop I ask if they know of someone in need of a governess or companion. I have met with disappointment all along the way, until now."

"Your behavior tells me you were raised as a gentlewoman."

Elizabeth nodded.

"Could you tell me a little about your education?"

Worry appeared in Elizabeth's eyes, but she answered him calmly. "I did not receive a formal education, sir. However, my father was a learned man and when he recognized my thirst for learning, he taught me as much as he would have a son. I am familiar with mathematics, history, geography, and a little with the sciences. I have a working knowledge of estate and household management. I can read Greek and Latin, can speak French and Italian fluently, and can read and speak Spanish and German to some degree. My sewing skills are quite good, I play piano tolerably well, and I have been told my singing voice is excellent. I am also a voracious reader and try to keep current on the war and the issues affecting our country." Elizabeth sat quietly.

She felt compelled to be accurate in answering his questions but hoped it did not appear as though she were boasting.

Darcy looked at the young lady across from him. He was impressed with the litany of her qualifications. However, after the fiasco with Mrs. Younge, he felt the need to test her veracity.

"Who is your favorite author?" Darcy asked in French.

"I very much enjoy the works of Shakespeare and the poetry of Cowper," Elizabeth replied flawlessly in the same language.

Darcy nodded, impressed.

They continued to discuss world affairs and a variety of other topics. Darcy finally realized the hour was growing late. He was surprised at how quickly the time had passed, as he usually found conversing with strangers a difficult task. "From my observations and our conversation, I believe you would make an excellent companion for my sister. Would you like to join us for breakfast tomorrow morning and meet her before you make a decision? If after meeting her, you wish to accept the position, we can discuss the particulars, if that would suit you, Miss Lucas."

"Yes, Mr. Darcy, I should enjoy meeting your sister. Until tomorrow, sir."

Darcy escorted Elizabeth to the door. The landlord stood waiting, so Darcy said, "Please join us in the private dining room tomorrow morning at nine for breakfast, Miss Lucas. I am sure Mr. Heath can direct you. Good night."

"Good night, Mr. Darcy." She dropped him a curtsey and turned to follow the innkeeper. Darcy stood watching her until she passed out of sight. Then he reentered the sitting room and closed the door. He returned to his chair, where he remained deep in thought for quite some time. When he finally retired for the night, he found himself very much looking forward to breakfast.

As Elizabeth settled into bed for the night, she thought about her interview with Mr. Darcy. He seemed a kind and intelligent man and was obviously a devoted brother. He was also very handsome. His near-black hair was cut short, but there was a curl that frequently fell onto his brow. His eyes were the color of emeralds, and Elizabeth thought of them as the windows to his soul. His face and expressions as he spoke to her always maintained a politely distant and serious mien, but if one glanced at his eyes, his true feelings were there for everyone to see. For a brief moment, Elizabeth allowed herself to realize he seemed to be exactly the type of gentleman she had one day hoped to meet. In approximately nine short months, she would be of age and an heiress. At that time, she would make an acceptable wife for such a gentleman. *Would he be able to see past my time as his employee and forgive me the deception? It was not all lies. I only gave an incorrect last name; the rest is all true, with a slight omission.* Elizabeth's thoughts attempted to justify her actions until sleep overtook her.

A few minutes before nine in the morning, Mr. Heath knocked at Elizabeth's door. She had been ready for some time and was waiting for him. She followed him down the stairs to the private dining room Mr. Darcy had engaged. He knocked on the door and waited for Darcy's call, then opened it to announce Elizabeth.

Darcy had risen to his feet when the door opened. Now he advanced towards Elizabeth.

"Good morning, Miss Lucas," said Darcy with a slight bow. "How are you this morning?"

"I am very well, sir. I thank you," Elizabeth replied with a curtsey.

Indicating his sister with his arm, Darcy continued. "Please allow me to present to you my sister, Miss Georgiana Darcy. Georgie, this is Miss Rose Lucas. She is the young lady who assisted you yesterday, so I invited her to join us for breakfast."

The young ladies exchanged curtseys and greetings before Darcy led them both to the table. He pulled out a chair for his sister. Elizabeth moved to seat herself, but Darcy was quick to assist her.

Once they were seated, Elizabeth looked at Georgiana. "You appear to be feeling better this morning, Miss Darcy. I hope that is the case."

"Yes, thank you." Georgiana's answer was so softly spoken that Elizabeth almost missed it. She looked at Mr. Darcy in confusion only to see him looking at his sister with concern.

Elizabeth determined to try again. "Your brother tells me you are returning to your home in Derbyshire. I have never traveled to that part of the country. What is it like?"

At the thought of home, Georgiana's mood seemed to improve. "Our estate, Pemberley, is the most perfect place you could ever find. There are rolling hills and a view of the Peaks in the distance. There is a beautiful lake, a hedge maze, formal gardens, and many areas where the beauties of nature have been left in peace. There are also many trails for walking or riding." Then, in a much less exuberant tone, she added, "It is my favorite place in the world, and I do not wish to leave it again for a long, long time."

"It sounds quite wondrous. When you are not enjoying the glories the outdoors has to offer, how do you enjoy spending your time? I prefer to spend my time in the library with my father and a good book if I cannot be walking the paths around my home." Elizabeth's eyes filled with tears, but she blinked them away. "I mean my former home." Her sadness was evident to both her companions.

Seeing Miss Lucas' distress, Georgiana's soft heart was moved. "Oh, how thoughtless of me. My brother explained you had recently lost your family and home. I am very sorry."

"Think nothing of it, Miss Darcy. It is just that it is recent, and sometimes the feelings are a bit overwhelming."

"I, too, know what it is like to lose family members," Georgiana responded quietly. "I have no memory of my mother, as she died when I was very young, and my father passed away five years ago. Though the heartache has eased, I still miss him every day." Tears glimmered in Georgiana's eyes, and Elizabeth reached out and patted her hand comfortingly.

"I am sorry for you, for you both," Elizabeth added with a look at Darcy. Then, wiping her eyes, she squared her small shoulders and continued with a determined effort. "There must be happier topics we can discuss. What of music? Do you play an instrument, Miss Darcy?"

The two young ladies began to talk of music and composers. Darcy was impressed with the way Elizabeth skillfully guided Georgiana from one topic to another, never allowing her to revert back to the shyness she had showed upon first meeting. Darcy was quite pleased with his unusually spontaneous decision of the previous evening, for he felt certain Miss Lucas would be just what Georgiana needed to recover from her heartache and prepare for the future. He sincerely hoped she would accept his offer of employment. He also hoped Miss Lucas might feel less alone in the world, as she would now be part of the Pemberley family.

As the meal concluded, Georgiana rose to refresh herself before they departed. When the door closed quietly behind her, Darcy turned to look at Miss Lucas. "I am very pleased with my sister's reaction to you. She can be very shy, and her recent experience could have a detrimental effect on her. Watching you with her this morning, I feel certain you are just what she needs to recover and prepare for her future. Will you accept the position as my sister's companion?"

"I would be most pleased to do so, sir. She is a delightful young lady." They briefly discussed salary and a few other particulars.

As they were about to leave the dining parlor, Elizabeth paused and looked again at Mr. Darcy. She appeared very nervous, and it took her a moment to find the words for the confession she must make. "Mr. Darcy, I feel honor-bound to tell you, I did not take a proper leave of this distant relation who took over my home. I may have helped myself to one of the horses when I left."

Darcy looked at her for a long moment before saying anything, and Elizabeth could not read his expression. "Was the situation really so insupportable?"

"I am afraid it was. He quickly made my life and those of all the servants a misery. The servants were so kind as to assist me in my escape. And I would not be at all surprised if he now found himself with no one to wait on him."

Darcy was mesmerized by the small smile that lurked in the corners of her mouth and the devilish twinkle in her eye. "Then I am sure he deserved to find a horse missing. However, since horse theft is a serious offense, perhaps you would allow me to arrange for its return."

Elizabeth considered this for a moment before replying. "I believe it should be my responsibility, Mr. Darcy, if you could just suggest the best way for me to do so."

"As you wish, Miss Lucas. I am sure Mr. Heath could arrange it for you."

"Thank you, Mr. Darcy. I will speak to him now and be ready to depart within fifteen minutes if that is acceptable?"

"Certainly, Miss Lucas. Please return to where we met last evening. We shall await you there." Darcy opened the door for her and watched as she moved to speak with Mr. Heath. Darcy caught his eye and gave him a nod. He could only hope the gentleman would understand his meaning.

Darcy then turned and mounted the stairs. He entered the sitting room and saw Georgiana's reticule and the two handkerchiefs sitting where he had placed them the previous afternoon. He picked up one of the handkerchiefs and, noticing it bore Georgiana's initials, set it aside with her reticule. Then he picked up the other handkerchief. He held it briefly to his nose and inhaled the sweet scent of roses, which he had also detected when he was near Miss Lucas. He straightened out the handkerchief and with a look of great surprise saw the initials in the corner. The letters ERB were stitched inside a ring of roses.

Darcy sat with the handkerchief still clutched in his hand. Was he making a huge mistake in bringing this young woman into his sister's life and into his home? His instincts about people did not often lead him astray, and his instincts said he should trust her. He thought about all he had learned of Miss Lucas. There was no mistaking her sadness when she spoke of the loss of her family or of her need to escape her current circumstances. It was quite obvious she was facing a very difficult situation. He then thought about the conversations both he and his sister had shared with her. Her intelligence could not be doubted, her manners were impeccable, and he had witnessed her kindness first hand. No, Darcy was sure he had made the right decision about Miss Lucas. He would do his best to provide her with a safe, comfortable environment and hope she would one day trust him with the truth about herself.

He was startled from his musings when Georgiana entered the room. Darcy quickly placed the handkerchief in an inside coat pocket. Georgiana moved towards the table where her reticule lay and looked at the belongings.

"William, were there not two handkerchiefs here? I do not see Miss Lucas'. There is only mine and my reticule."

"I thought there were two, but perhaps it only appeared so. Do not worry, Georgie, if it cannot be found, we shall purchase her a few new ones," Darcy replied evasively. "Are you packed and ready to depart?"

"Yes, William."

"Please wait here for Miss Lucas. I will go down and settle up with Mr. Heath and arrange for our luggage to be loaded on the carriage."

Darcy found Mr. Heath in the common room and requested a moment of his time. As they moved to the small counter in the entry, Darcy asked, "Were you able to assist Miss Lucas with her request?"

"Yes, sir, Mr. Darcy, but it is a funny thing. I thought she had come in on the stage. I did not even know she had a horse. Then there is another odd thing, sir. She asked that it be returned to a small town in Hertfordshire called Meryton, and if anyone asked, my son is to say he found it in Guilford. I am not sure I wish to be mixed up in such a havey-cavey business," said Mr. Heath with concern.

Darcy kept his expression blank. "I have spoken to Miss Lucas a great deal, and I do not think she would be mixed up in anything untoward. I would be happy to add a bonus to what she is paying you if that will ease your mind."

"Well, if you say it will be okay, Mr. Darcy, I will do as the lady requested."

Darcy settled up with the innkeeper, adding a little extra for his troubles, and returned to his suite. By this time Miss Lucas had appeared. "Well, ladies, shall we depart?" The ladies both nodded in agreement. Darcy offered his arm to his sister and turned, intending to offer the other arm to Miss Lucas, only to notice she was carrying a small valise and satchel with saddlebags over her shoulder. She almost appeared to be staggering from the weight. "Miss Lucas, please allow Jeffers to carry those for you. Darcy's valet moved from where he stood with the maid Elizabeth had seen the previous day. He took the bags from her and stepped back. Darcy again offered his arm to Elizabeth, who hesitated only a moment before taking his arm. Darcy's valet and Georgiana's maid followed them from the room.

After exiting the inn, Darcy handed first Georgiana and then Elizabeth into the carriage. He then entered himself and they were quickly underway.

8. PEMBERLEY

THE TRIP TO THE DARCY ESTATE took two and a half long days. On the third afternoon, they crested a hill just as the sun was setting, and it bathed Pemberley in its warm golden rays. Elizabeth gasped in shock at her first sight of the grand building.

"I did say it was the most perfect of places," said Georgiana with a smile.

"You did indeed, Miss Darcy, and I believe you must be right. I have never seen a place for which nature has done more, or where natural beauty has been so little counteracted by an awkward taste," Elizabeth replied with feeling.

By the time the carriage came to a stop at the entry, Elizabeth felt quite overwhelmed. An army of servants exited the front door as the carriage stopped. A small, slightly round woman in a neat gray dress, apron, and cap waited on the porch with a bright smile on her face.

"Master William, Miss Georgiana, it is wonderful to have you both home," the woman cried as she wrapped Georgiana in an embrace.

As Georgiana stepped back, the woman glanced around. Not seeing Georgiana's companion, she asked, "Where is Mrs. Younge?" She was surprised that such a simple question caused tears to appear in Georgiana's eyes. Elizabeth moved quickly to the young girl's side and clasped her hand, giving it a reassuring squeeze.

Darcy spoke up. "I am afraid Mrs. Younge was not able to continue with us. Georgiana had learned all she could from her. However, we were very fortunate to find Miss Rose Lucas to replace her. In fact, Mrs. Reynolds, would you please see to having the suite that connects to Georgiana's prepared for Miss Lucas? I believe it will be very beneficial for them to be close to each other." Darcy's words were accompanied by a smile at the two young ladies.

Mrs. Reynolds was shocked at her master's words. *Why was he installing his sister's companion in the family wing? Had this young woman used her wiles to worm her way into the family?*

Darcy had guessed at Mrs. Reynolds' thoughts and gave her a speaking look. Fortunately, Elizabeth's attention was focused on Miss Darcy.

Turning to Elizabeth, Darcy said, "Miss Lucas, may I introduce you to the woman who keeps Pemberley running perfectly? This is our housekeeper, Mrs. Reynolds. Mrs. Reynolds, this is Georgie's new companion, Miss Rose Lucas."

Elizabeth gave a curtsey. "It is a great pleasure to meet you, Mrs. Reynolds," she said with her usual warmth. "I have heard a great many wonderful things about you as we traveled the past two days. It is quite obvious how dear you are to Mr. and Miss Darcy."

Mrs. Reynolds was pleased with her words and was able to discern no artifice of any kind in the young lady's behavior, so she responded in kind. "It is nice to meet you as well, Miss Lucas. Welcome to Pemberley. I hope you will feel comfortable here."

"Thank you very much, Mrs. Reynolds. I am sure I shall, for I cannot imagine a more perfect place than what I see around me." As Elizabeth spoke, the family progressed into the hall. Elizabeth took in her surroundings, her jaw dropping briefly before she made a concerted effort to recover. Never in her life had Elizabeth seen a grander home. It was a bit intimidating.

Darcy recognized her discomfort and offered a distraction. "Georgiana, why do you not show Miss Elizabeth to her bedroom? Be sure to show her which door connects to the sitting room you will share."

Linking her arm through Elizabeth's, Georgiana mounted the stairs, happily chatting as she went. Darcy and Mrs. Reynolds watched as the young ladies disappeared down the hallway. Darcy turned to the housekeeper. "Mrs. Reynolds, as soon as everything is settled, would you please join me in my study?"

"Certainly, Mr. Darcy. Would you like me to have baths sent up, sir?"

"Yes, please arrange for three baths, and assign someone to assist Miss Lucas, if you please."

Again, Mrs. Reynolds was surprised at her master's words, but she only replied, "Yes, sir." As she bustled up the stairs after Georgiana and her companion, Mrs. Reynolds called for water to be carried up and asked to have two upstairs maids and Lucy sent to Miss Darcy's sitting room.

Mrs. Reynolds knocked on the door to the sitting room connected to Georgiana's suite. She entered at Miss Darcy's call.

"Miss Georgiana, Miss Lucas, baths have been ordered and should arrive shortly. Miss Lucas, I am sorry your suite is not yet ready, but it should not take long. I will ensure the dressing room and bathing chamber are attended to first so you may bathe and rest before dinner. If you would not mind waiting here, I will have your maid, Lucy, notify you when you bath is ready."

Elizabeth looked startled at Mrs. Reynolds' words. "Mrs. Reynolds, as an employee, it is not necessary for a maid to attend me. I can manage for myself," she replied humbly.

"Mr. Darcy's orders, miss." However, Mrs. Reynolds was pleased with her words, as they showed she understood and accepted her place in the household.

There was a knock at the sitting room door. At Georgiana's call, the maids entered. Mrs. Reynolds directed the maids to begin cleaning the adjoining suite and preparing it for occupancy. Then the housekeeper turned to Elizabeth. "Miss Lucas, please allow me to present Lucy. She will attend to your needs while you are at Pemberley."

"It is very nice to meet you, Lucy," remarked Elizabeth. "I shall endeavor not to require too much of your time."

"It is my pleasure to assist you, miss," Lucy replied. In spite of her surprise that she was to serve another employee of the household, she liked the quiet way of the pleasant young lady before her.

"Now, Lucy, would you please go and assist the girls in preparing the dressing room and bathing chamber? As soon as that is accomplished, arrange for a bath for Miss Lucas so she may bathe while you unpack her belongings and the others finish cleaning the bed chamber."

"Mrs. Reynolds," called Georgiana as the housekeeper prepared to depart. "You can see to William's bath before mine. I will stay and talk to Miss Lucas while she is waiting. Please have my water ready with hers so we can spend more time together after we have refreshed ourselves."

Darcy had quickly bathed, changed, and headed to his study to catch up on any work that had accumulated in his absence. He had been present for only a very few minutes when a knock was heard.

"Come in, Mrs. Reynolds," he called, a smile evident in his voice.

The housekeeper entered and closed the door behind her. She stood before Darcy's desk, her hands on her hips. "Just what game are you playing, Master William? Why have you placed that young lady, Miss Georgiana's *companion,* in the family wing?" Darcy did not miss her emphasis on the word companion. "I would never have expected such behavior from you!" The woman retained her stance, folding her arms across her chest as she waited for the explanation.

It was an obvious sign of the affection the two shared that Mrs. Reynolds would dare to address her employer in such a fashion. Replying kindly, Darcy raised his hands in surrender, saying, "Please be seated, Mrs. Reynolds, and let me explain things to you."

Darcy first told Mrs. Reynolds of the events in Ramsgate with George Wickham and explained why Mrs. Younge was no longer with them. He then explained all he had observed of Elizabeth at the inn and the things he had learned about her from the landlord. By the time he was through explaining about the loss of her family and the circumstances that had forced her to flee her family home, the housekeeper had tears in her eyes and was heard to mutter, "The poor dear."

Darcy continued. "I believe from what I know of Miss Lucas, she will be an excellent influence on and an example for Georgiana. I understand what it is like to lose one's parents, and Miss Lucas was unfortunate enough to lose not only both her parents but also her three sisters at the same time. I believe she needs us as much as we, uh, I mean, Georgiana, needs her." Mrs. Reynolds eyed her employer carefully. She had not missed his slip of the tongue.

"What is to be the young lady's status in the household? Placing her in the family wing, when Mrs. Younge had no such privilege, may give rise to talk."

Darcy was shocked at the implication in Mrs. Reynolds words. Thinking for a moment, Darcy finally spoke. "I believe it would be best to claim she is a poor relation who has come to stay with us as Georgiana's companion. It would not seem unusual for her to be in the family wing under such circumstances." Mrs. Reynolds gave an approving nod. "As to her status, I would like Miss Lucas to dine with us and be treated as part of the family. As she is currently in mourning and due to Georgiana's recent experience, I believe we will spend a quiet time at Pemberley until after the Christmas holidays. Of course, the Bingleys are scheduled to visit in August, but I do not feel it necessary to entertain them in any special way."

Mrs. Reynolds gave an approving nod. "Very well, Master William, I will gradually let her story be known to ensure there is no gossip. Dinner will be served at seven, sir." Mrs. Reynolds turned to depart.

"By the way, Mrs. Reynolds, could you please find out about the state of Miss Lucas' wardrobe? Based on the circumstances under which she left her home, I am certain she is in need of many things. Please arrange for those you can, and I will encourage

Georgiana and Miss Lucas to make a trip to see Mrs. Webb for new garments."

"Very good, sir. I will see what I can learn."

Darcy sat back in his chair with his gazed fixed on the view from the study window. He looked forward to observing Miss Lucas' relationship with Georgiana over the days and weeks ahead. He had been pleased with her reaction upon first seeing Pemberley and was curious to know her thoughts on the house. He particularly looked forward to showing her the library. With her love of reading, he looked forward to seeing her reaction. Shaking himself from his thoughts of the lovely Miss Lucas, he again focused on the work before him.

Elizabeth and Georgiana remained in the sitting room, talking until each received a call from her maid. As Elizabeth entered the room assigned to her, she stopped abruptly and stared. The room was large and airy. The furnishings were of satinwood. The walls were painted a very pale yellow. The bed covering was a beautiful floral design of light blue and yellow edged in white cutwork lace. Two cozy chairs covered in yellow stood before the fireplace; there was a light blue striped Recamier chaise lounge near one window and a small desk near the other. Elizabeth had never seen such a lovely room and had certainly never expected to inhabit one, especially not as an employee of someone else.

Her bath was another new experience. Her family had possessed two hip baths that all had shared. This bathing chamber was attached to her dressing room and contained a full-sized tub for her personal use. There was also a private water closet.

The dressing room was another wonder. She could not imagine having enough clothes to fill it. In fact, she doubted if all the clothes owned by the five Bennet sisters together would fill the space. The dressing room contained a lovely dressing table and mirror. By the time Elizabeth finished her bath and donned clean undergarments, Lucy had unpacked all her clothes. A freshly pressed pale yellow muslin gown awaited her on the bed.

"Lucy, I am in mourning and would prefer to wear my black gown."

"I am sorry, Miss Lucas, but the gown appeared a bit the worse for wear. I sent it to be laundered. It should be available to you tomorrow, but this will have to do for now," said the maid politely.

When Lucy had her dressed and her hair neatly arranged, Elizabeth knocked on the door to the sitting room. She heard Georgiana's call to enter and quietly stepped inside.

"You need not knock to enter the sitting room, Miss Lucas. You are welcome to use it at any time, whether I am present or not."

"That is very kind of you, Miss Darcy."

"I want to you feel at home here at Pemberley. As I said, it is my favorite place to be."

"I can certainly understand why," said Elizabeth with a laugh. "The rooms I have seen were obviously decorated lovingly and provide a feeling of welcome and comfort. As if that were not delightful enough, the view from every window is one of nature at her most beautiful. I cannot imagine a more wonderful place!"

Georgiana laughed, but before she could reply, a knock came on the sitting room door. A moment later, Mrs. Reynolds entered, carrying a tray. "I thought you young ladies might enjoy some tea and something to eat."

"Oh, my favorite biscuits! Thank you, Mrs. Reynolds, and please thank Mrs. Mason, as well."

"Certainly, Miss Georgiana. Now, dinner will be at seven, and Mr. Darcy is looking forward to joining you ladies then. Oh, but he did say, he wished for a moment of your time, Miss Georgiana, after you are finished with your tea."

"There must be some mistake, Mrs. Reynolds," said Elizabeth respectfully. "I believe I should be dining with the staff."

"No, miss, there is no mistake. Mr. Darcy requests that you dine with his sister and him for all meals."

Elizabeth blushed, but said no more.

"Enjoy your tea, ladies." The housekeeper gave the young ladies a warm smile and departed.

Georgiana entered the study at her brother's call. "You wanted to see me, William?"

"Yes, Dear One, have a seat." Georgiana sat in one of the chairs facing the desk. "Have you enjoyed your afternoon with Miss Lucas?"

"Oh, yes, she is wonderful company. I am so very glad we found her!"

"I am glad as well. Sister dear, I wanted to make you aware of some information and ask for your assistance.

"Certainly, brother, I am happy to assist you in any way I can. You know that."

"Yes, I do, and in this case I need your help with Miss Lucas." Georgiana looked at her brother in confusion. "Georgie, I have asked Mrs. Reynolds to let it be known Miss Lucas is a very distant poor relation. She is quite young to be a companion, and I needed an explanation that would not cause questions or gossip. You and I both know the devastation that comes from losing one's parents, and Miss Lucas lost not only her parents but also her three sisters in the same accident. I want her to feel comfortable and be treated as part of the family while she is with us. Also, I am sure she will need several new gowns and perhaps a riding habit so the two of you can ride together. I thought we could spend a quiet time at Pemberley until the holidays. The only plans we currently have are to entertain the Bingleys when they visit at the beginning of September."

Georgiana wrinkled her nose in distaste.

"I know Miss Bingley can be difficult, dear, but you will have Miss Lucas for company and can easily claim the need to study if she becomes too much of a trial for you," said Darcy with a grin.

Georgiana's spirits brightened considerably.

"I believe it will be difficult for Miss Lucas to accept the gowns as charity. Consequently, I plan to tell her they are necessary to her position, and that is why I will cover the cost. Do you think she will accept that?"

"I am not sure, William, but I will do my best to encourage her to accept them."

"Did she go to rest in her room when you came to see me?"

"No, I believe she is walking in the gardens. She told me she loves nature and was used to walking a great deal at her father's estate."

Darcy looked out the window and noticed Miss Lucas wandering the paths of the formal gardens. "Shall we go and join her?" he asked with a smile.

Georgiana looked at the expression on her brother's face and stored it away to think about when she was alone. She quickly agreed a walk would be lovely after their many days of travel.

Elizabeth had wandered the gardens for some time. She could not believe her good fortune in landing a position so quickly, especially one that brought her to this piece of heaven on earth. She stopped, her attention caught by the beds of roses surrounding her. At the sight, a picture of her sister, Jane, flashed into her mind. Tears filled her eyes and spilled over onto her cheeks. They continued to fall for several minutes.

When she heard the crunch of gravel heralding someone's approach, she quickly wiped away the tears.

"Miss Lucas, do you mind if we join you?" a deep voice said closely behind her.

Giving her eyes one last swipe, she turned and attempted to fix a smile on her face. "I would be pleased for the company," Elizabeth replied, though she kept her eyes focused on the distance.

Georgiana and Darcy both noticed the evidence of recent tears. "Oh, Miss Lucas, please do not be sad," cried Georgiana. "What has brought on your tears?"

"It is nothing. Please forgive me."

"There is nothing to forgive, Miss Lucas," Darcy soothed. "If anyone can understand what it is like to lose your family, it would be us, as we have already been through the pain of such a loss. But, it can help to talk about them. It keeps them near in your heart when you share your memories of them."

Darcy spoke the words with such gentleness that Elizabeth's heart was touched. He offered an arm to his sister and then to Elizabeth. As they set off down the path, he said, "Why do you not tell us about your family? For instance, who were you thinking of when we came upon you?"

"I was thinking of my dearest sister, Jane. We loved to tend the flowers at Longbourn and make perfume and lotions from them. The rose scent I am wearing right now I took from Jane's room when I packed to leave. It was a luxury to bring such an item, but it allows me to feel close to her."

"And what of your parents?" Georgiana asked to keep her talking.

"My father was a wonderful man, and I always felt his love for me. We were very alike in some ways. We shared a thirst for learning, a passion for the written word, and a similar sense of humor. We spent many hours talking and debating the things we read. We also enjoyed playing chess together. My mother was a very loving woman, though she could sometimes be excitable. She often worried about us making a good match and worried what would happen when my father passed. Having lived through that experience, I can more easily understand her fears."

"Tell me more of your sisters. I always wanted a sister, and you had several."

"The middle one, Mary, was quiet. She liked to read and she played the piano. My youngest sister, Lydia, was very happy and outgoing. She liked everyone, and everyone liked her. The second youngest, Kitty, was very much like Lydia, though not quite so outgoing. She also had a gift for drawing. They were all very dear to me."

Elizabeth had been so wrapped up in her thoughts, she did not realize all she had said, and she was startled by Georgiana's question. "I thought you said three of your sisters died in the accident, but you just told us about four sisters."

Elizabeth's face paled, but her intelligence did not fail her. "Oh, yes. One of my sisters had been gone for some time before the accident." She was relieved her answer was not a lie, just a slight distortion of the truth.

"Oh, you poor dear, that makes your loss even greater!" Georgiana exclaimed in concern.

Darcy had noticed her face pale and the way she relaxed when Georgiana accepted her words. He did not say anything, just stored the information away for future consideration. This beautiful young woman had certainly been dealt her share of heartache, and Darcy's heart softened to her a little more.

Dinner that evening was a pleasant affair. The Pemberley cook was extremely good. Elizabeth tasted a range of dishes she had never before experienced and she delighted in the delicacies. After dinner, Georgiana played for her brother. When she was through, she begged Elizabeth to play for them. Elizabeth complied and played one of her favorite sonatas by Mozart from memory. Darcy was impressed with her performance. Shortly thereafter, the young ladies retired for the night.

After Lucy had prepared Elizabeth for bed, she seated herself at the small desk in her room and pulled out a sheet of paper. Elizabeth dipped her quill in the ink and began to write.

Dear Mrs. Hill,

I am relieved to tell you I have found a wonderful position. I traveled away from Longbourn as though headed to Oxford. I stopped in Aylesbury and made sure to be seen and heard asking for directions to Oxford. However, once I was well the other side of Aylesbury, I doubled back and headed in a north easterly direction towards Bedford. I had determined to take the coach north from there, all the way to Scotland, if necessary, until I could find a position. But as fortune would have it, I met a gentleman and his sister who were in need of a companion for the young lady. Unusual circumstances had forced him to release the last companion hurriedly. They were traveling to their home in Derbyshire and offered to take me with them if I would accept the position.

The estate is the most beautiful place I have ever seen, and I am being treated well by my employer, his sister, and the staff. The young lady I look after is a true delight. The extensive education I received from my father has been a blessing in this endeavor, for which I shall be eternally grateful to Papa.

I will try to send you a letter as often as I can, but I do not wish to tell you exactly where I am for fear Mr. Collins will somehow find out. I hope things were not difficult for you and I look forward to the day I will be able to see you again. Perhaps when I come of age, I shall make my way to my Uncle Gardiner's by way of Cambridge.

With gratitude and love for all you have always done for me.

Lizzy

Elizabeth sanded and sealed the note and left it lying on the desk. She would take it with her when she went to breakfast the next morning and would deposit it in the tray in the hall where she had been instructed that any outgoing mail was to be left.

Elizabeth was distressed to find she had slept unusually late the next morning. She reminded herself she was an employee not a guest. Without ringing for Lucy, she completed her ablutions, then quickly dressed and prepared to go downstairs. As she opened the door between the dressing room and the bedroom, she heard two voices. She assumed it was the maids making up the room and was about to enter when she heard her name spoken.

"There be somethin' odd about this 'ere Miss Lucas," said a high-pitched voice. "Why she be sleepin' in the family wing? Missus Younge never did that." Elizabeth's face blushed at their words.

"There is nothing odd about it at all," said the other maid in a pleasant, more polished voice. She is a distant Darcy relation who just lost all her family, poor dear. She is family and is to be Miss Darcy's friend and companion. Be sure Mrs. Reynolds does not hear you say such things. She would be most displeased."

"Poor dear, indeed," said the first maid, though she did not sound convinced.

Elizabeth rattled the doorknob a bit before entering the bedroom. The blush still on her cheeks, she said, "Good morning," as she passed through the room and exited to the hallway. In spite of the delay caused by the maid's conversation, Elizabeth arrived in the breakfast room within half an hour of rising.

"Good morning, Miss Lucas," said Darcy pleasantly. "I hope you slept well."

"Yes, I did, too well. I am sorry to be so late."

"Nonsense," replied Darcy, "It is not uncommon to require additional rest during a time of grieving. Think nothing of it."

"I do not have the luxury of grieving. I am now in your employ and must immediately take up my duties. Perhaps you could spare me a few moments this morning to tell me what you expect."

"Certainly. When you have finished your meal, please join me in my study. I shall leave you two ladies to enjoy the remainder of your breakfast." Darcy kissed Georgiana's head, nodded to Elizabeth, and departed to his study.

A short time later, Darcy heard a light knock on his door. "Come in, Miss Lucas."

Elizabeth entered, pausing briefly to observe the room. It was large and dominated by a massive desk. There were bookshelves on the wall behind the desk and the one opposite the windows. There were two leather chairs before the desk and two leather wing-backs before the fireplace. A leather sofa paralleled the windows. It would offer good light for reading to anyone sitting there. The wood in the room was dark English walnut, and a rug of burgundy and gold filled the center of the room. Gold velvet drapes framed the windows, which were open to catch the breeze on that bright summer's day.

Elizabeth advanced into the room and seated herself in one of the chairs before the desk. She folded her hands in her lap and looked steadily at Darcy. Taking a deep breath, she began to speak. "Mr. Darcy, before we discuss my duties with Miss Darcy, I must ask you a few questions, if I may."

"Certainly, Miss Lucas."

"Why was I placed in the family wing? I have heard it said Mrs. Younge did not sleep there."

Darcy was concerned she had overheard something that was making her uncomfortable. "The answer is simple, Miss Lucas. I placed you there because I believe having you close to my sister will give the two of you a better chance of becoming acquainted and developing a close relationship."

"But why would you wish me to have a close relationship with your sister, sir? I am an employee, not a guest in your home."

"I believe you will find I have a reputation for treating all those in my employ extremely well," said Darcy with a small smile. "Let me tell you a bit about Georgiana. She is shy and has lived much of her life at Pemberley. When she was at school, she found it difficult to make friends. She was hurt to discover many of those who claimed friendship with her merely wished to use her to get close to me." Darcy blushed as he said this and would not meet her eye. "May I confide something in you, Miss Lucas, regarding Georgiana?"

"Certainly, sir. Anything you say will be kept in the strictest confidence."

"Earlier this summer, I rented a home for my sister and her companion in Ramsgate. After getting her settled, I was forced to return to London to attend to business. I was able to complete it earlier than expected and departed for Ramsgate to surprise my sister." Darcy went on to explain what had occurred in Ramsgate and to give her the history of Wickham.

"You are not likely to encounter Mr. Wickham here at Pemberley. In fact, after telling him of the restrictions on Georgiana's dowry, I hope we never see him again. Unfortunately, he has the habit of turning up regularly like a bad penny. His appearance is similar to mine in that he is on the tall side and has dark hair, though his eyes are brown. Unlike me, he is charming and glib. He has a knack for convincing others of his goodness, then leaves a wealth of destruction in his wake."

"Poor, Miss Darcy. Now I understand the look I occasionally catch on her face."

"Exactly. I watched how you dealt with the young man who tried to accost you at the inn. I believe you can be an excellent example for Georgiana. I would like her to develop your self-confidence and poise. Then no one will ever be able to take advantage of her again. Even though, as you say, you are in my employ, I would much prefer you to develop a true friendship with my sister rather than merely act as her companion. That is what she needs most at this point in her life. She has had an extensive education, but she would benefit from practice in the languages and from learning to debate her opinions on her readings. All of these things will build her confidence. That is the thing I most hope she learns from you."

"I have another question, Mr. Darcy."

He nodded for her to continue.

"Could you please explain why the maids seem to think I am a long-lost cousin who has come here as Miss Darcy's friend and companion?"

"I did that to protect your reputation. I did not wish to give anyone reason to question your position in this household. Mrs. Reynolds pointed out to me that your residing in the family wing might give people the wrong impression, as they believed you to be Georgiana's companion."

"I will accept your explanations, but if I hear it discussed again, I will request that my room be moved to one more appropriate for my position."

"Very well, Miss Lucas. Now, there are a few things I need to discuss with you. Understanding your situation and seeing the small amount of luggage with which you arrived, I wish you to go to the dressmaker in Lambton and order additional clothes. They will be necessary in the course of your duties, for you will accompany Georgiana everywhere she goes. You will also be dining with us and will be present much of the time when we are entertaining next month."

Elizabeth looked like she was about to protest, but he forestalled her.

"Miss Lucas, your presence will be necessary to protect Georgiana. We are entertaining my dearest friend, Charles Bingley, and his family. Mr. Bingley is all that is affable, but his unmarried sister can be a difficult guest. She has set her sights on being the next Mrs. Darcy. Her brother has frequently told her I am not interested in her, and I engage with her only to the extent dictated by good manners. However, she remains fixed in her delusions. One of the things she does in an attempt to gain my notice and approval is to constantly praise Georgiana and claim a closeness with her that does not exist. She has a strong personality that is sometimes overwhelming to Georgiana. I believe you will be able to act as a buffer between my sister and Miss Bingley."

Elizabeth nodded. "In that case, sir, I will acquiesce to your request.

"As I said, they will be necessary to your duties, so I will cover the cost of the clothing."

"I have sufficient funds of my own to cover the cost of a few new dresses, particularly as I need only clothes for mourning."

"I am happy to provide for all your needs in this respect and wondered if I might make a request of you."

"And that is?"

"I understand you are in mourning and respect you wish to honor your family in such a way. What I wondered was if you would be willing to also have some things made in the colors of half-mourning for special occasions?"

"I would be amenable to doing so, Mr. Darcy."

"Good. I would like to suggest you and Georgiana make your trip to see Mrs. Webb today. I will order the carriage for you while you prepare. When you return, we can give you a tour of the house."

"I would enjoy that, Mr. Darcy. However, you must allow me to assume my responsibilities the next day, or I will not be able to accept any wages from you." With a curtsey, Elizabeth departed to fetch Georgiana.

Darcy quickly called for the carriage to be brought around. While he waited, he wrote a note to Mrs. Webb. As he said good-bye to his sister, he slipped the note into her hand. As Georgiana stepped into the carriage, she glanced at the name on the note before taking her seat. The carriage moved off and Georgiana spoke little, wondering how best to deliver the note to Mrs. Webb without Elizabeth being aware of it. Finally, an idea came to her. She would arrange for Elizabeth to be taken away to be measured. Then she would give the note to the seamstress so they could discuss what needed to be done regarding Elizabeth's wardrobe.

Elizabeth was engrossed in the view from the window as the carriage passed through the lovely Derbyshire countryside. Wildflowers were abundant, and the rolling hills were much different from those in Hertfordshire.

"Miss Darcy, what is the name of the village closest to Pemberley?"

"It is Lambton, and that is where we are headed."

Elizabeth was startled at the familiar name. Her Aunt Gardiner was from Lambton. Thinking of her aunt, Elizabeth could not help but wonder about the woman's health. *Was she well or had the news of the tragic accident caused her condition to worsen? Had she had the baby yet? If so, were she and the baby all right? Would she ever get to see her family again?*

The village of Lambton was much like any other, Elizabeth assumed, but she had to agree that it was a lovely place. There was a beautiful stone church and a lovely village green graced with large old trees. They passed the mercantile that had belonged to Aunt Helen's family before she married Mr. Gardiner. Finally, they pulled up in front of a lovely little shop. In the window were a beautiful bolt of pink silk and several lace samples. Elizabeth pointed out the fabric to Georgiana. "That pink silk in the window would be lovely on you, Miss Darcy. Perhaps you should have a dress made up from it."

"It is very lovely," she agreed. "Now let us introduce you to Mrs. Webb." Georgiana linked her arm with Elizabeth's as they entered the shop.

"Miss Darcy, what a pleasure to see you," called Mrs. Webb. "I did not realize you had returned from London."

"We arrived only yesterday. Mrs. Webb, allow me to introduce you to my cousin, Miss Lucas. She has come to Pemberley to stay with us and will be helping prepare me for my debut.

"It is a pleasure to meet you, Mrs. Webb."

"The pleasure is mine, Miss Lucas. I am happy to be of assistance to another member of the Darcy family."

"Mrs. Webb, perhaps you could have someone measure my cousin. She has recently lost all her family and is in great need of mourning clothes, among other things."

"Certainly, Miss Darcy." Mrs. Webb called to her assistant and sent Elizabeth to the back room to be measured.

As soon as Georgiana was sure Elizabeth was out of hearing, she retrieved the note for Mrs. Webb. The dressmaker cast a look at her companion. "Do you know what is in the note?"

"Not exactly, but my brother and I discussed this somewhat yesterday."

"What do you believe to be necessary for Miss Lucas?"

"I would say no fewer than half a dozen day dresses, four mourning and two in half mourning, three dresses for afternoon, two in mourning and one in half mourning, and at least three evening gowns, all in half mourning. She will also need a riding habit."

"Mr. Darcy has given strict instructions about the riding habit in his note," confirmed Mrs. Webb. "Is there anything else?"

"Yes, please make at least two nightdresses and a robe, as well as all the necessary undergarments. We will allow Miss Lucas to select two of the morning dresses and one of the evening dresses. She insists she has money to cover her purchases, so please price those she selects reasonably and put the balance for them on the bill with the other items to be made for her. That bill should, of course, go to my brother."

When the measurements were done, Elizabeth joined the other ladies, and they looked at patterns, fabrics, and trims. Elizabeth's taste was simple but elegant. Mrs. Webb was delighted with the young lady's figure and took pleasure in selecting patterns that would most flatter her. In spite of the loveliness of the suggestions, Elizabeth insisted her dresses be quite modest as she thought befit her position. Mrs. Webb had noticed those she particularly liked in spite of her request for more modest requirements and determined to use them on the other items she would make for the lovely young lady. Elizabeth was concerned about the cost, but was surprised and relieved to realize her funds were sufficient for the purpose. She would also still have a good deal left over.

After an enjoyable few hours, the ladies returned to Pemberley. They sat down to luncheon shortly after arriving. When lunch was over, Mr. Darcy and Georgiana took Elizabeth on a tour of the house. Mr. Darcy was very knowledgeable about the history of many of the artifacts within the house. Elizabeth particularly enjoyed viewing the portraits in the gallery and learning a little about the Darcy history. When she stood before the portrait of Mrs. Darcy, she was startled by the resemblance to

Georgiana. "Your mother was very beautiful. You look just like her, Miss Darcy."

Georgiana blushed with pleasure at the comparison as they moved on to the next portrait.

"How handsome you are, Mr. Darcy! When was this made?" Elizabeth blushed bright red when she realized what she had said, but Darcy smiled at her warmly.

"Why, thank you, Miss Lucas. It was made just before my father's death, so a little more than five years ago. There is one more room to show you; please follow me. They went through the gallery to a set of doors near the head of the main staircase. Darcy turned his back to the door so he could watch Miss Lucas' expression. "I have saved the best for last." Darcy flung open the doors and backed into the room.

Elizabeth's eyes grew wide as she advanced to the center of the room. She turned about slowly so as to take in the exceptional space. When she once again faced the brother and sister, she said, "Perhaps I, too, have died, for this surely must be Heaven."

Darcy and Georgiana both laughed at her remark. "I can gladly assure you, you are very much alive. I want you to feel free to use this room at any time." Darcy's voice and expression were warmly insistent. I shall leave the two of you here to enjoy yourselves while I return to work. I shall see you for tea."

As Darcy departed, Georgiana moved into the room and picked up the novel she had been reading. She settled in a chair by the window and began to read. Elizabeth quietly walked around the room, perusing the shelves. The library was two stories tall, with the upper level consisting of a balcony that circled the room. Shelves covered all the wall space on both levels except where the massive windows had been placed. The library was flooded with light, and the furnishings were in shades of forest green and gold. Elizabeth loved the smell of the room. It reminded her of her father's book room back home. Tears suddenly filled her eyes and ran down her cheeks. She thought of how much her father would have loved this room.

Elizabeth continued to wander and look at the books. They appeared to be arranged by topic, and then author. Elizabeth knew that even if she spent the majority of the rest of her life reading, she would never be able to finish all the books contained in this magnificent library. Eventually, she selected a book of Wordsworth's poetry and took a seat near Georgiana.

The ladies remained quietly reading for quite some time. They were very surprised when they heard Mrs. Reynolds enter with the tea. Darcy was close on her heels. Over tea, they discussed the books they had been reading and several others they had all previously enjoyed. The conversation was intelligent and lively. It was one of the most wonderful days Elizabeth could recall.

The evening was a repeat of the previous one, and so ended Elizabeth's first full day at Pemberley. When she said her prayers that evening, she made sure to thank God for the blessing of the Darcys in her life.

9. LOST OPPORTUNITIES

IT WAS AFTER THREE-THIRTY WHEN Walter Collins arrived in Meryton to retrieve his cousin. The last thing she had said was to meet her at the dressmaker's. Being unfamiliar with the village, he required several minutes of looking at first one shop, then another, before he found it. However, when he stepped inside, the dressmaker, Mrs. Stone, said she had not seen Miss Elizabeth in quite some time.

Assuming his cousin had spent the entire day with the vicar, Walter turned the curricle back towards the church. He entered but found no one about, so he went next door to the vicarage and knocked on the door. A small woman dressed in black answered, and he asked to see the vicar. She asked him to wait while she checked to see if Mr. Carter was available. She returned in a moment and led him to the vicar's study. The woman announced Mr. Collins and left to gather a second cup and saucer so he could share the Reverend's tea.

Walter had to wait until the woman left the room before he could ask about his cousin. "Sir, I understand my cousin, Miss Elizabeth Bennet, came with Mr. Hill this morning to deliver some items for the parish poor. She said she intended to speak to you about her feelings from losing her family. Have you spoken to her yet?"

"No, I have not. When Miss Elizabeth came in, she said she wished to sit with her family before speaking to me."

"But sir, that was almost six hours ago. Did you not become concerned?"

"No, I have known Miss Lizzy all her life. She has a love of the outdoors and probably had much to say to her family. She was far too distraught immediately following the accident to say a proper goodbye to them. She will come in when she is ready to speak with me," the old gentleman said with a smile.

"I believe I should go to retrieve her. My father was expecting her home in time for tea."

Mr. Carter attempted to discourage the gentleman, not wanting him to upset Elizabeth with an interruption, but with no success. He watched as Mr. Collins walked from the house back to the church, disappearing around the side to the graveyard.

Walter walked around the tree that blocked the view of the Bennets' graves, but Elizabeth was nowhere in sight. He searched all around and found not a trace of her. Perplexed, Walter returned to the vicarage and entered without knocking.

"I did not see her anywhere."

The vicar looked at him in dismay, concerned for Elizabeth. The two men went out together and conducted a thorough search of the cemetery. "Perhaps after saying her goodbyes, she was able to resolve her feelings and no longer needed to speak to me," the vicar said in a reassuring tone. "Perhaps she wandered about town doing some shopping."

Walter Collins thanked Mr. Carter and departed. He jumped in his curricle and drove to the first shop in town. Walter tied up the horse and stepped down. Walking in, he took a look around and then asked for the proprietor. When speaking with the owner, he asked if Elizabeth Bennet had been in that day. He received a negative reply and thanked the person, then exited and went into the next shop along the walkway. He traveled all the way up one side of the street and back down the other, finding no trace of her at all. Walter trudged back to the curricle and despondently turned it in the direction of Longbourn.

Once the vehicle was underway, Walter breathed a sigh of relief. Elizabeth was gone, and he would not be forced into a marriage neither of them wanted. He was more relieved that he would not be forced to behave in the manner his father demanded and that Elizabeth would not be subjected to his father's attentions, either. Unfortunately, reality returned rather abruptly when he realized he was left to explain to his father that she had disappeared.

"Have you finally arrived?" came Harold Collins' voice. "Come, come, I am ready for my tea." Walter stepped to the doorway to face his father. The elder Mr. Collins looked up, prepared to offer his congratulations on the engagement, but saw only his son standing there. Before Walter could say a word, Mr. Collins was shouting. "Where is she?"

"I do not know, Father. I went to the dress shop in accordance with her last words, but the lady said she had not seen Cousin Elizabeth in some time. Deciding she was still with the vicar, I returned to the church. He claimed he had seen her only briefly first thing in the morning before she left to sit at her parents' graveside. He could offer no explanation except that perhaps she had resolved her feelings by talking with her family and had then gone shopping while waiting for my arrival. I checked with every store owner in town, and no one has seen her all day. It is as if she has vanished," he concluded meekly.

"Damn the girl! I guess that is what I get for trying to do things slowly and kindly. I should have just compromised her myself the moment the funerals were completed."

"Perhaps she has gone to her family in London. We could search along the road to London. Even though she has a head start of several hours, she is on foot. I am sure we can catch her," Walter half-heartedly offered.

Before deciding on his next step, Harold Collins screamed for his housekeeper. Mrs. Hill arrived promptly.

"Where is Cousin Elizabeth?" he demanded.

"I have not seen her since she left this morning, sir." The housekeeper began wringing her hands as tears filled her eyes, "Oh, my poor Miss Lizzy, I hope nothing has happened to her. Oh, where could she be?" Before Mr. Collins could say anything else, Mrs. Hill covered her face with her apron and fled the room.

"Have the horses saddled. We need to go after her immediately. You are correct; she could not have gotten very far on foot. I wonder if she had any funds. Perhaps she took the post to London. Did you check in the tavern to see if she had been there?"

"Of course not, Father. What would a lady be doing in a tavern?" As his father reached for the paperweight on his desk, Walter fled for the stables. When he reached the front door, he heard a thump as something hit the wall, followed by the sounds of shattering glass.

Seeing Sam in the stable yard, Walter asked him to saddle two horses immediately. Sam did as he was asked and soon appeared leading the horses.

"Hurry faster next time, or you will be looking for new employment without a reference," shouted Harold Collins. The two men mounted their horses and took off at a canter down the drive.

Sam stood, watching them depart with a small smile on his face. He walked to the back of the house and entered through the kitchen door. Everyone was there waiting for him. "They have gone," he said, and all sighed with relief.

"They were shouting about following her on the London road, believing her to be on foot. If we wait only long enough to allow them to reach town before we depart, we should have a good head start of our own," said Mr. Hill with a laugh. Soon everyone joined in.

After twenty minutes, the scene in the kitchen was different. The servants had all retrieved their packed bags and exited the back door of the house. Sam was going to the Lucas' to explain what had occurred that day. He was sure Robert Lucas would either take him on at Lucas Lodge or help him find work. Sam was going to stay in the area to keep an eye on the Collinses. He would also keep in touch with Mrs. Hill at the inn in Cambridge. The maid, Sally, was an orphan and very close to Mr. and Mrs. Hill, so she was going with them to the inn. They were to take Mrs. Phipps as far as Letchworth, where her sister lived. She would travel to the inn later if there was a position for her. Sam helped load the luggage in the back the of the Hills' hired wagon and then helped Sally and Mrs. Phipps into the back. He waved his friends away and then set out for the Lucas'.

Upon arriving at the kitchen door of Lucas Lodge, Sam asked to speak to Mr. Robert Lucas. They invited him into the kitchen while a maid retrieved Mr. Lucas. The maid returned quickly and told Sam to follow her. He was escorted to the study of Sir William Lucas and found the gentleman, his son, and his eldest daughter all within.

Robert looked intently at Sam and asked, "What has happened?"

Looking uncomfortably at the others in the room, Sam hesitated to speak.

Realizing the groom's concerns, Robert said, "My sister, Charlotte, received a delivery and letter from Miss Elizabeth earlier today, and she is very concerned for her friend. As my father is the magistrate for this area, it is safe to speak in front of them.

Sam nodded, then began. "Miss Elizabeth has run away. She overheard Mr. Collins and his son speaking late one night. What she heard makes my blood run cold. She felt the only safe thing to do was to leave and leave quickly."

"But where has Eliza gone?" cried Charlotte in concern.

"Nobody knows, but she has promised to contact Mrs. Hill when she is safely settled."

"Why did she not go to the Gardiners?" questioned Robert.

"Because of what she heard."

Sir William spoke for the first time. "Perhaps you should begin again and tell us what Miss Eliza overheard."

Sam repeated what Elizabeth had heard—about being forced to marry her cousin, by compromise if necessary, about him informing the Gardiners she was dead and telling his son that, after he married her, she could have an accident like her family did.

"I still do not understand why Miss Eliza did not go to London to the Gardiners," said Sir William thoughtfully.

"Mr. Collins cannot go to them and ask if she is there because of what he wrote. Miss Lizzy felt that if her family's accident was not really an accident, the Gardiners would be safer if they did not know her whereabouts."

"Why are they so desperate to have Eliza marry Walter Collins?" Charlotte wondered aloud. "It is not as if she has a large dowry."

Sam shrugged, deciding to remain quiet about the possible inheritance, but then continued speaking. "All the servants left today. That is one of the reasons I am here. I was hoping you might need an extra stable hand. I wanted to stay near my family and also keep an eye on the Collinses. Maybe I can learn something that might help Miss Lizzy."

Robert looked at his father, who nodded. "I believe we have room for you, Sam, but where have all the others gone?"

"Mrs. Hill's sister and her husband have an inn and needed help. Her husband got hurt and cannot work anymore. They are going to help her run the place from now on. The Hills are going to drop off Mrs. Phipps on the way, as she is to stay with her sister. Sally is going with the Hills, as there is a place for her at the inn."

"Why did the servants feel it necessary to leave?" asked Robert.

"We did not know what Mr. Collins might do to discover Miss Elizabeth's whereabouts. However, he cannot discover anything if no one is there, can he?" Sam replied with a grin.

"In that case, you will need to stay close to the estate so Mr. Collins does not find out you are here," added Robert. "Here, let me take you to the stables. I will explain your position to the coachman, and he can help you get settled."

Sam started to follow Robert Lucas from the room, but stopped at the door. "Oh, Miss Lucas, Miss Lizzy asked me to be sure to thank you for holding those items. She hopes to be back for them after she reaches her majority. She said it would be safe then."

When Sam was gone and the door closed behind him, Charlotte looked to her father with a worried expression. "Do you believe Eliza will be well, Father?"

"You know how intelligent Miss Eliza is; I am sure she will be fine," returned Sir William encouragingly. "However, I believe we should include her in our daily prayers until we know for certain."

Darkness had fallen when Harold and Walter Collins returned to Longbourn the next evening. Elizabeth had not been seen at the coaching inn, so they had started down the road towards London. They went as far as the inn at the halfway point but had seen no sign of her. They decided to stop for the night and continue to London in the morning. They were on the road very early and arrived in the city within a couple of hours. They had still seen no sign of Elizabeth. They stopped at the coaching inn on the edge of the city and decided to wait a while. Perhaps they had somehow passed Elizabeth and she would come here before going on to the Gardiners'.

Once mid-day had come and gone, they remounted and headed for Cheapside. As they rode through the streets, Harold kept his hat over his eyes and constantly watched for someone who might recognize him. It was dangerous for him to be in London, as several people to whom he owed money were looking for him. They were not the kind of people whom one angered, at least not if one wished to live.

Harold and Walter took up a place in a nearby park where they could observe the Gardiners' front door. As luck would have it, Mr. Gardiner was exiting the house with his wife and Jane Bennet. Harold watched them enter the carriage at the curb and pull away.

When the carriage turned the corner, Harold Collins turned to his son. "Go to the door and ask for Miss Elizabeth, but do not give your name. Watch the answer carefully to see if the servant is lying."

Walter did as instructed and knocked at the door of the Gardiners' residence. When the door was opened, he said, "Good afternoon, I would like to see Miss Elizabeth Bennet. I just learned from a mutual friend that she is staying here."

The maid's eyes filled with tears, and she reached into her pocket for a handkerchief. She used it to dry her eyes before answering. "I am sorry to tell you Miss Elizabeth was killed in an accident with her family a few weeks ago." Before Walter could say more, the maid closed the door.

Walter relayed the information to his father, who exclaimed, "Blast and damn! If Elizabeth is not here, I have no idea where to look for her. Perhaps we will have to spread out from Longbourn in several directions to see if there are reports of her. I wonder who assisted her in escaping. If it was any of the servants, I will beat the information regarding her whereabouts out of them!" Harold Collins' face was purple with rage. Walter was concerned he would have a fit of apoplexy if he did not calm down.

In an attempt to appease his father, Walter said, "Let us get a quick drink and be on our way home. We can return to Longbourn and set out again tomorrow in a different direction."

It was almost dark when the gentlemen turned into the drive of Longbourn, but fortunately, the light of the almost full moon allowed them to see clearly. The house was in total darkness. When they stopped the horses, Mr. Collins shouted for a groom. Tired and angry, he threw his reins to his son and marched through the front door, shouting.

"Mrs. Hill, why is the house dark? Wake up, you lazy woman, and get me something to eat now!"

Not a sound was heard in reply. Using the light of the moon, Mr. Collins made his way to the mantle in the parlor. He fumbled a bit before finding the tinderbox, but eventually was able to light a candle. He looked around the room. Everything seemed to be as it should, but still no one had answered his call.

Candle in hand, he stomped through the house, looking for the servants. Finally, he entered the kitchen, but it was empty. Not even embers glowed in the fireplace. He threw open the doors of the servants' rooms, but still found no one. He went so far as to check in one of the closets, but there were no clothes or personal items to be seen anywhere.

Harold Collins stomped back through the house to where his son still waited with the horses' reins in hand. Protecting the candle flame with one hand, Mr. Collins marched to the stables, Walter following with the horses. The stable was empty as well except for the two horses used for working on the estate. He noticed the lone surviving carriage horse was gone. Had Elizabeth taken it, or had one of the servants stolen it? Lighting a candle he found sitting on a barrel, Mr. Collins ordered his son to care for the horses before returning to the house. Staring at his father in confusion, Walter put the horses into stalls before unsaddling, brushing, and feeding them.

Mr. Collins was livid. He had done everything he could to get his hands on his inheritance sooner rather than later. He had planned everything so well, but somehow it had all gone awry. Now he had a poorly producing estate with little in the way of cash reserves, his cousin's inheritance had slipped through his fingers with her disappearance, and the servants had all abandoned him. He poured himself a glass of Mr. Bennet's port and downed it in one gulp before pouring a second.

Carrying the candle from the barn, Walter entered the house and heard the mumbling and swearing coming from his father's study. Knowing he would be in a foul mood, Walter plucked up his courage to speak with his father.

"Father, face the fact that Elizabeth is gone. There is no point in searching further."

"I will not be denied my due! That stubborn, strong-willed wench will not get away with this. Now quit your complaining. We will be leaving to search further in the morning. You will do as you are told, or I will take out my displeasure on you in her absence."

Walter did not speak another word, but turned and exited the room, making his way to the kitchen. He found a wrapped loaf of bread in the larder, as well as a wedge of cheese. He cut himself a slice of both and set them on the table. Then he found a glass and pumped water into a pan in the sink. Filling his glass, he returned to the table to eat. As he did, he made some decisions and a few plans of his own. He would pack his belongings and offer to search in the direction of Oxford. However, he would not return from that search, but instead arrive early for his last term at school. He would send his father notes about following a lead, then eventually say it had come to nothing and discontinue corresponding with his father, at least until he was settled in a position somewhere. Walter had no intention of remaining to bear the brunt of his father's anger or to be at his beck and call.

When finished with his meal, Walter went straight up to bed, exhausted. Two days in the saddle was not something he was used to, and he ached all over. If his father was in any condition to do so, he knew they would both be on the road the next day.

In spite of a bad headache that made Mr. Collins' temper worse than usual, both men were searching again the next morning. Walter headed west and Mr. Collins headed east. The plan was for them to travel the entire day away from Longbourn. They would stop at each inn they came to and ask about a woman traveling alone. Walter thought he had something when he reached Aylesbury. No one remembered a young lady, but they did remember a *pretty lad* who had asked for directions to Oxford. Walter asked whether the lad had been riding or on foot. The description of the horse he received matched the missing carriage horse. Thrilled with the information, Walter mounted his horse and continued. Though he asked at every inn he came across, he received no additional information. When he arrived in Oxford, he visited every inn in the city, but still there was no luck. As it was approaching dusk, Walter found an inn with a room for the night. After enjoying a bowl of stew and a pint in the taproom, he took himself off to bed. He would send a message to Longbourn in the morning, as planned. Then he would apply for admission to his rooms at the university and await the start of the term.

Harold Collins had headed east in the search for Elizabeth. The first stop was Luton. He asked about a woman with a horse and was told the same information his son had heard in Aylesbury. He was not surprised to hear she had dressed as a lad; he knew she was too smart for her own good. But in Luton, Harold was told the lad had asked for directions to Bedford. He remounted his horse and headed in that direction. By the time he stopped at a well-kept inn in Stevenage, Harold's temper was very short. He had drunk far too much the evening before, and the heat was making him even more uncomfortable. Entering the Knight's Rest, he shouted for the proprietor. He demanded information about a lady or lad who would have come through in the last few days, describing Elizabeth as well as the horse. Mr. Heath recognized the description immediately and was glad the young lady had left the day before. Assuming this was the obnoxious heir, he told Mr. Collins he had seen no one matching that description.

Harold remounted and continued towards Bedford. After searching all the inns there with no success, he decided to keep traveling. He arrived in Northampton but had no more reports on Elizabeth. Cursing her under his breath, he arranged for a room and a meal before he, too, retired for the night.

On the return trip to Longbourn after his fruitless search for Elizabeth, Harold Collins busily sought other avenues which might lead him to his missing cousin. He decided to report the missing horse to the magistrate, Sir William Lucas, on the morrow. A search for the missing horse might lead him to Elizabeth. However, when he dismounted his horse at the Longbourn stables, he was surprised to see the missing carriage horse was in its stall. His anger flared at his being thwarted yet again.

Entering the house, he was surprised to find a note from his son that must have been shoved under the door. For a moment hope soared, but upon reading what Walter wrote, his hope died. Walter said he would continue his search to the west and notify his father if he found any clue as to Elizabeth's whereabouts.

Just as Walter had surmised, his father did not take their failure well. Mr. Collins picked up a few of the knick-knacks at hand and threw them across the room. Harold was furious with Elizabeth and vowed that if he ever found her, he would make her pay for the trouble she had caused him—first with her inheritance and then with her life. His face twisted into an evil grin as he thought about making her suffer.

He also had no idea how he would replace the missing servants. It would not do to broadcast the fact that the servants had abandoned him. Mr.

Harold Collins retired for the night in a very foul mood.

10. SETTLING IN

ELIZABETH ROSE EARLY THE NEXT MORNING, as was her habit. She dressed quickly and descended the stairs, hoping to take a walk. She found the front door unlocked and decided to walk to the lake in front of the house. She noticed benches stationed in several spots around the lake. She selected one that faced east so she could watch the sun rise. It had just begun to peek over the horizon when she heard a deep voice beside her.

"Do you mind if I join you?"

Seeing Mr. Darcy looking down at her, she said, "Please do."

"You are up very early this morning. After your reaction to being somewhat later in arising yesterday, I would guess you are up early most mornings." Elizabeth could hear the question in his voice.

"Indeed, my habit at home was to arise early and take a long walk through the fields of my father's estate and the surrounding environs. I always do my best thinking when I walk." Elizabeth laughed softly, and Darcy raised his brow in question. "My father always said he could tell my mood by how I walked. When I was happy, he said I practically skipped. When I was angry about something, it was apparently more like stomping. When I was deep in thought, he said I meandered slowly and brushed my fingers along everything they could reach."

"What was your walk like this morning?"

"I would say it was steady and content."

"What brought on those feelings, if I might be so bold as to inquire?"

"I would say it was appreciation of the blessing of meeting you and your sister in my hour of need. I always wanted to travel, but when I was forced to leave home I found myself somewhat fearful about my future. I managed to set out only by reminding myself it could not be worse than what I was leaving behind. Even in my most hopeful moments, I did not imagine I would find such a wonderful situation so quickly. I cannot thank you enough for the opportunity you have given me."

"You are a blessing to us as well, Miss Lucas; please do not forget that. I hope you will feel comfortable here at Pemberley, and I hope you know you can trust us should you ever need assistance."

"Thank you, Mr. Darcy. Your kindness at this time means a great deal to me."

After enjoying the sunrise together, the pair returned to the house to break their fast. They found Georgiana already in the breakfast room. Darcy and Elizabeth each prepared themselves a plate from the sideboard and joined her at the table.

"What do you ladies have planned for the day?"

"I thought Miss Darcy and I would spend some time in the library. I need to gain an understanding of where she currently is with her studies so I can best plan our time for lessons. Do you have a specific amount of time each day you wish her to study, Mr. Darcy?"

"No, not at all. I believe the two of you are best suited to determine such things. I will, however, look forward to hearing from Georgiana of your daily activities over dinner," Darcy responded.

As Darcy completed his meal, he stood to depart.

"Ladies, if you will excuse me. I have a great many estate matters to which I must attend. Should you have need of me, I will be in my study. Otherwise, I shall look forward to joining you for luncheon."

Once they had finished their breakfast, the ladies moved to a table in the library. Elizabeth asked Georgiana many questions about her studies, which topics she enjoyed the most, which languages she had studied, and many other things. She also asked Georgiana what she knew of household management and estate issues. Elizabeth asked Georgiana to explain the layout of the library so she would know where to look for the items she would use for teaching. Georgiana happily explained to Elizabeth the organization of the library and showed her how to use the catalog system that had been set up to allow one to find a specific book. When Elizabeth felt comfortable that she knew what she needed to begin planning lessons for Georgiana, she dismissed the girl to practice the pianoforte as she began writing out her plans.

She spent a great deal of time looking through the catalog for books her father had used to teach her, finding the Pemberley library contained many of them. She discovered several atlases, as well as a recently made globe. There were a few books she did not find, so she made her way to Darcy's study, knocking lightly.

At Darcy's call to enter, Elizabeth moved to stand before his desk.

"Please, Miss Lucas, be seated. How may I be of assistance?"

"Mr. Darcy, after my discussions with Miss Darcy, I was able to find most of the books I would need to continue her education in your wonderful library. The cataloging system is most ingenious and certainly made my task much easier. However, there were two additional books I could not locate. I wondered if I might order them?"

"What books were you not able to find?"

Elizabeth gave him the titles and authors.

"I see no difficulty with that. I will send a note to Mr. Edwards, who owns the bookstore in Lambton, having you added to the account. Then you may purchase what you feel necessary for your work."

"That is very kind of you, but it is not necessary, sir."

"I insist, Miss Lucas. It would be much easier for you to order what you need than to have to request my assistance each time. You are a valued member of my household. I trust your judgment in this matter."

Elizabeth was very surprised that Mr. Darcy would be so trusting of her. She was deeply honored and determined to do everything in her power to be worthy of his trust in her. "Thank you, Mr. Darcy. If you would be so kind as to request he order these two books when you send the note, I would greatly appreciate it.

"I will send the note this afternoon, and the next time we are in Lambton, I will introduce you to Mr. Edwards."

From Darcy's study, Elizabeth made her way to the music room to find Miss Darcy. She stopped in the doorway to study her charge. Georgiana's eyes were closed, her faced suffused with feeling as her skillful fingers coaxed the passionate melody from the instrument. When she had finished playing, Elizabeth applauded. Georgiana started at the sound, and a deep blush covered her face.

"Forgive me for startling you. I do not think I have ever heard that piece played so well. I am afraid your abilities on the pianoforte are well beyond mine. I believe I will need to speak with your brother about hiring you a master for your music lessons. As things stand now, there is much you could teach me on this subject." Elizabeth gave Georgiana a rueful smile that drew the young lady from her embarrassment.

"Perhaps we could practice duets together," suggested Georgiana. "I have never had anyone to share my music with except William. Not many people know, but he plays very well."

Elizabeth was surprised at this piece of information. "Does he play for you often?"

"Not so often as I would like. Perhaps we can coax him into playing one evening soon."

"I thought perhaps we could take a walk before luncheon, and then after dining we will return to the library to begin our studies. How does that sound?"

"I would enjoy a walk. I will show you the hedge maze, if you would like."

"That sounds delightful. I have heard of such but have never seen one before. Shall you teach me how to make my way to the center?"

"I will show you the way today, but perhaps it would be best for you to learn for yourself. Then one day when you are confident and know your way about, we can race to see who reaches the center first," suggested Georgiana.

The ladies retrieved their bonnets and gloves and made their way out of the house to the rear garden. The maze was situated at the side of the house and served to separate the gardens from the stables. The ladies wandered arm-in-arm. Georgiana led Elizabeth in one entrance to the center and back out again. Then they moved to a different entrance and did the same. They had traversed all four paths from the exterior to the center of the maze and back out, finishing just as the time for luncheon arrived.

Mr. Darcy left word with Mrs. Reynolds that he had to visit one of the tenants and would be unable to dine with them, but would return to join them for tea. After completing their meal, the ladies returned to the library. Elizabeth had asked Mr. Darcy for the most recent paper if he was finished with it. Elizabeth used an article from the paper to teach a lesson on geography to her young pupil. They had completed the lesson and were perusing the other items in the paper, laughing together, as Darcy entered the room. He stopped at the sound. He had always loved to hear his sister laugh. It was a sweet sound, like a tinkling bell. The sound of Miss Lucas' laugh was something surprising. It was low, rich, and warm and had an infectiousness that was utterly charming.

"I had no idea lessons could be so much fun. I certainly do not recall my tutors ever doing something to inspire so much laughter during lessons."

Fearing Mr. Darcy thought she was lacking in her duties, Elizabeth said, "I apologize, sir. We finished our lesson and were finding a bit of amusement from the ridiculous items in the gossip column."

"There is no need to apologize, Miss Lucas. I am sure lessons are much more enjoyable when humor is included, and it was a delight to hear your laughter ringing through the room." The smile he bestowed on Elizabeth and Georgiana brought a blush to Elizabeth's cheeks.

They had just settled themselves before the fireplace when Mrs. Reynolds entered with the tea tray. As she moved to pour the tea for the three people present, Darcy remarked, "Please do not bother, Mrs. Reynolds. I am sure Miss Lucas would not mind pouring, and it will be good for Georgiana to watch and practice so she may serve as my hostess during the Bingleys' visit."

Mrs. Reynolds set down the teapot and nodded at her master as she moved to exit the room, closing the door behind her. Elizabeth reached for the tea service and began to pour a cup of tea for Georgiana. "How do you take your tea, Miss Darcy?"

"Two sugars and a little milk, if you please, Miss Lucas."

Elizabeth prepared the cup and passed it to Georgiana before beginning to pour for Mr. Darcy. "How do you prefer your tea, Mr. Darcy?"

"Just a little sugar, please." Elizabeth handed him his cup, and he took a sip. "That is perfect, Miss Lucas. I find many people do not understand what a *little* sugar is."

Elizabeth was pleased with his compliment. "As it is the way I prefer my tea, it was an easy request to interpret," she replied with a smile.

Georgiana began to describe the history lesson she had with Miss Lucas. As she told Darcy of using the newspaper and the description of the battles to review the geography, Darcy was impressed. She was learning about geography, but he appreciated the subtle way she was learning about the world around her at the same time. Again, he was pleased with the decision he had made to hire Miss Lucas as Georgiana's companion.

Their days at Pemberley settled into a pleasant routine. Elizabeth walked early every morning. Mr. Darcy frequently joined her, taking her to some of the best vantage points of the estate. As they watched the sun rise from the ridge of the hill behind the house one morning, Elizabeth reminisced. "This view reminds me very much of Oakham Mount. It was one of my favorite walking destinations back home. I could watch the sun stretch forth its light to cover the nearby estates and village from that perspective."

Georgiana practiced her music every day. Elizabeth always stayed to listen to the younger woman's remarkable playing while working on needlework or sewing. Frequently, the two young ladies practiced duets to perform in the evening. One day Georgiana convinced Elizabeth to sing to her accompaniment. Darcy was in his study, but as the door was ajar, he, too, enjoyed listening to Georgiana practice.

Suddenly, the house was filled with the most exquisite sound Darcy had ever heard. He left his study and drifted towards the music room. Elizabeth was standing beside the pianoforte. Her eyes were closed, and she was singing *Barbara Allen*. The emotion in her voice was incredibly moving. Darcy had never heard the song performed so passionately.

As the last note died away, Georgiana spoke reverently. "I have never heard a more beautiful voice. Miss Lucas, that was wonderful."

"I would have to agree with my sister, Miss Lucas. I have been so fortunate as to hear many talented professional singers, but I can honestly say none more talented than you. I hope you will perform for us frequently."

Elizabeth blushed with the praise and quietly expressed her thanks.

Several mornings a week, she and Georgiana spent their time in the library. Elizabeth often had Georgiana read aloud to help her gain confidence. In the beginning, Georgiana's voice was barely above a whisper, but as time passed, she spoke more loudly and used more emotion when she read. Eventually, she used different voices for each of the characters.

Soon the confidence she developed by reading carried over into her discussions with Elizabeth and her brother when they spoke of books, philosophy, or even the state of the nation. Darcy could not help but notice the difference in his sister. He was delighted with her progress and very grateful to Miss Lucas for helping her to blossom.

Mr. Darcy was often busy with the estate, but made a point of spending time with the ladies at least once per week in addition to joining them at teatime and for meals. Once Elizabeth's riding habit arrived, he selected a mount for her from his extensive stables, and they began riding out over the estate. Darcy and Georgiana delighted in taking her to see the hidden beauties of Pemberley that could be reached only by horseback. Many times they would take a picnic with them.

Darcy recalled the day he first took Miss Lucas to the stables to meet her mount. They left through one of Pemberley's side doors and headed in the direction of the barns. Miss Lucas had stopped short, saying, "Oh, my!" when she got her first look at the stable complex.

"Is anything wrong?" Darcy had questioned worriedly.

"No, it is just that your stables appear to be as large as the family home on my father's estate," said Miss Lucas with a laugh. Darcy smiled at her reaction. She stared for a few more moments before they began walking again.

The stable complex at Pemberley was unlike anything she had seen before. Two long buildings faced each other across a cobbled courtyard. One of the buildings housed the family's coaches, wagons, and other vehicles used to maintain the estate. The other building housed the animals. There were at least twenty doors facing the courtyard. As the building had a center aisle, there were twenty on the other side of the building as well. Halfway down, the building appeared to be separated by rooms of some kind. Inside the first ten stalls on each side were the carriage and work horses. The rooms in the middle contained an office for the stable manager and the tack room. Continuing down the aisle past the office was the area where the horses for riding and the hunters were kept. At the back of the courtyard was a riding ring, and beyond that another, smaller barn that Darcy explained was for foaling mares and their new offspring.

As they continued walking, Darcy discovered a new facet to this rather remarkable young woman.

"Mr. Darcy, I must thank you again for the riding habit. The design is truly lovely," she remarked, smoothing the skirt.

Darcy turned to assess the young woman at his side. The skirt of her new habit was considerably fuller than a typical dress and was black in color. The jacket accompanying her habit was burgundy with black velvet collar, cuffs, and trim. Perched upon her dark curls was a short black top hat with a burgundy ribbon and a jaunty matching feather for decoration. She also wore a new pair of black riding boots and gloves.

"Very lovely indeed, Miss Lucas." The warmth of Darcy's reply and the way he looked at her caused the young lady to blush.

Shaking his head slightly to release himself from the spell the woman always seemed to cast over him, Darcy asked, "Miss Lucas, as I remember, you borrowed a horse to make your escape. I take it you enjoy riding?"

"I do indeed, Mr. Darcy, but it was not something I often had the chance to do. Our estate was somewhat small, so in addition to the workhorses, we maintained only a pair of carriage horses, my father's stallion, and one mare that my sisters and I shared. It was because I could not ride as often as I liked that I began walking so much. I just wished to be out of doors."

"Tell me about the horse you rode."

"I was supposed to ride the mare, Buttercup. She was a sweet old thing, but could not be urged any faster than a slow trot. One day I convinced my father to allow me to ride his stallion. It was glorious to be racing along, the wind in my face, or flying over a fence. It was quite exhilarating!"

Darcy gave a pleased chuckle in response. "I quite agree, Miss Lucas. It is the way I prefer to ride as well. Though the horse cannot maintain such a pace all the time, it is by far the most invigorating part of my daily ride."

By this time, they had arrived at the stables. "After listening to your remarks, I think I will assign you a different horse than I originally intended." They stopped at a stall and glanced in to see a small brown mare.

"This is Bramble," said Darcy. "Not knowing your skill level, I thought she would be a good choice for you, as she is sweet tempered and dependable. However," he moved down the row, stopping three stalls later, "I believe Gambit would be the perfect mount for you."

Elizabeth stepped up to the stall and came almost nose-to-nose with a beautiful dapple gray thoroughbred. "My, what a beautiful girl you are!" Elizabeth reached out and the horse nuzzled her hand. The animal moved forward, her head hanging over the stall door. Elizabeth reached up to stroke the horse's nose and patted her neck as she reached into the pocket of her habit with her other hand. Elizabeth brought out a bit of apple, which she held out to Gambit in her palm. The horse quickly ate it from her hand. All the while Elizabeth had maintained a steady stream of softly spoken words to the animal. As she turned to look at Darcy, the horse edged forward, again nudging her shoulder to regain Elizabeth's attention.

"Well, I believe you have made a devoted friend, Miss Lucas." Darcy laughed softly at the animal's actions.

Elizabeth reached out to stroke Gambit's neck as her gaze remained fixed on Mr. Darcy. "She is a beautiful horse. I am sure I will enjoy riding her immensely."

Darcy beckoned to a stable hand and requested that Gambit be saddled with a sidesaddle and then to saddle both his horse and Georgiana's. As soon as the horse was saddled, Darcy led Gambit to the exit and into the riding ring, stopping beside the mounting block. He held the horse steady as Elizabeth mounted. When he let loose of the reins, Elizabeth began walking the horse around the ring at the back of the courtyard. There she put Gambit through her paces, first walking her, then increasing to a trot, and then a gallop.

Darcy watched closely. It was obvious Elizabeth was a natural horsewoman. She had an excellent seat and a light touch. She never used her riding crop but was able to communicate her every wish to the horse.

They were shortly joined by Georgiana and took off on the first of many rides around the magnificent estate.

One afternoon, Elizabeth entered the library to find Darcy seated at a table. He was looking through a book and muttering to himself. "May I be of assistance, Mr. Darcy?"

Darcy looked up at her with a grimace. "Forgive me, Miss Lucas. I was trying to find a piece I recently read regarding a new idea on crop rotations. It was by Simon Harris, but he is not the one who wrote the book."

"Was it the article that talked about plants that add nutrients to the soil?"

Darcy looked at Elizabeth in surprise and nodded.

"Where would I find the books on agriculture?"

Darcy pointed her in the right direction. She moved quickly to the shelves and ran her finger along the spines as she looked at the titles. Finally, she stopped and, standing on her toes, reached to the shelf and took down a book, saying, "Ah, here it is!"

She thumbed through the pages as she carried it back to the table where Darcy sat. "I believe this is the article for which you were looking."

"It is, indeed. I am astonished, Miss Lucas. Yet another interesting facet of your character is revealed."

"Did I not tell you my father taught me as he would a son? I am familiar with most aspects of estate management, as well as assisting the tenants," Elizabeth replied.

Since the death of Lady Anne Darcy, there had not been anyone at Pemberley to undertake the visits to the tenants. His mother had found great pleasure in ensuring all those who supported Pemberley were doing well. Georgiana had always been too shy to visit the tenants on her own, and Fitzwilliam met with them only on matters of business. With Darcy's permission, Elizabeth encouraged Georgiana to begin regular tenant visits with her. Elizabeth's kind manners and natural friendliness made the tenants feel at ease, and the visits were quite pleasant. Georgiana and Elizabeth always returned with a list of needs they observed, even if the families had not asked for anything. Elizabeth had enjoyed caring for Longbourn's tenants, and Georgiana was gradually becoming more comfortable with Pemberley's tenants with each visit they made.

As a result of their visits, Elizabeth and Georgiana began making clothing for some of the estate's children. They also began work on plans for the harvest celebration to be held at the beginning of October.

11. SURPRISE VISITOR

IN THIS PLEASANT FASHION, JULY AND the beginning of August flew past. It was the beginning of the third week in August. The trio was about to set out on one of their mid-day adventures when a figure in the bright red coat of the British Army rode into the stable yard. Darcy jumped from his horse and rushed to greet the rider.

"Richard! Welcome! How good to see you! Why did you not tell us you were coming for a visit?"

"It is not a visit, but I did receive permission to pause for two nights so that I might check in on you. I am delivering some things from the War Department to the general of the battalion stationed in Newcastle."

By this time, Georgiana and Elizabeth had dismounted as well. Georgiana rushed to throw herself into her cousin's arms. Richard picked her up and swung her about before setting her on her feet and giving each of her cheeks a kiss.

"I am glad you have," Georgiana said. "Please tell me you can stay for a long visit. I have missed you so much!"

"I have missed you, too, Georgie. Though I cannot stay for long, we shall have to make the most of it. Where were you heading?"

"We were going to show Miss Lucas the waterfall and have a picnic lunch there."

Though Richard had noticed the attractive young woman standing quietly by, he asked, "Who is Miss Lucas?"

Richard was surprised when Darcy answered instead of his sister. "Miss Lucas is Georgiana's new companion." He took his cousin by the elbow and steered him in Elizabeth's direction. "Miss Lucas, allow me to present my cousin, Colonel Richard Fitzwilliam. Richard, this is Miss Rose Lucas. She was of assistance to Georgiana when we stopped at the inn in Bedford. As it so happened, Miss Lucas was looking for employment, and her skills and experience make her the perfect companion for Georgie."

Richard was shocked to hear how this young lady had come to be hired as his ward's companion. He looked the young woman over from head to toe and did not see anything that would give him cause to worry. However, the look on his face as he regarded Darcy appeared to question his cousin's sanity. Darcy was actually smiling at the young woman. Richard knew he would have to interrogate his cousin about this matter very soon.

"Do you feel up to coming with us, Richard?" begged Georgiana.

"Well, if Darcy would loan me a fresh mount, I would be happy to join you."

Darcy called out to the stable hand to have Paladin saddled for the Colonel. As they waited, Elizabeth led Gambit back to the nearest mounting block and returned herself to the saddle. The colonel reached down and lifted Georgiana back into the saddle. When his horse was brought forward, he and Darcy quickly mounted, and the group took off in the desired direction for the day's adventure.

Richard rode beside Darcy, and the ladies followed a little behind them. "Darcy, were you out of your head to hire a stranger to replace Mrs. Younge? We made a huge mistake with her, then you compounded it by making a bigger one."

"Calm down, Richard. I know my actions were unusual, but I am confident I made the perfect choice for Georgiana's companion. Give the young lady a chance before you pass judgment. I am certain you will be impressed with her."

"I can see she is a beauty, but I would never have expected you to be the type to chase your sister's companion!"

Through tightly gritted teeth, Darcy ground out, "How dare you, Richard. Miss Lucas is a properly brought up gentleman's daughter and a very fine young lady. I will not have you insult her in such a way."

Richard was shocked at Darcy's manner, but decided to quietly observe the young lady for the remainder of the day. "Fine, Darcy. I will do as you request, but I expect you to tell me all you know about this young lady and how she came to be Georgiana's companion."

Still somewhat angry at Richard's words, Darcy gave him a terse nod. Darcy slowed his horse and moved back to where Georgiana and Elizabeth rode. As the path was not wide enough for three horses, Georgiana moved up to speak with her cousin.

"How do you like your new companion?" he asked nonchalantly.

"Oh, she is the most wonderful person I know. She seems more like a friend than a companion. It has been wonderful having her here and having someone I can talk to," came Georgiana's enthusiastic reply.

151

"Liking her is all well and good," said Richard with a chuckle, "but are you learning anything from her?"

Georgiana launched into an account of her recent geography lessons. Then she told Richard about the visits to the tenants and the clothes they had been making for some of the children. Richard could see that Georgiana's confidence had increased and he was grudgingly impressed with the geography lesson technique.

After riding for three-quarters of an hour, they arrived at the base of a tall rock face. There the path forked, and the right branch led up to a plateau at the top of the rocks. The left fork led slightly downward along the cliff. They stopped and dismounted near a stand of trees, tying the horses loosely so they could graze. They continued around the rock and came out on a round, flat spot of ground shaded by the cliff. A little way off, water rushed down the rock face into a small pool at the base. From there a steadily moving stream meandered down the hillside.

"Oh, what a beautiful spot!" cried Elizabeth with delight. "Each new vista you show me as we travel about Pemberley is more beautiful than the last. I am constantly amazed, and it confirms my opinion that Pemberley is, in fact, a piece of Heaven on earth." Darcy beamed with pleasure and pride at her words.

Elizabeth and Georgiana took the blanket from Richard and spread it on the ground. Darcy handed Richard one set of the saddlebags that had been packed with their luncheon. There was cold chicken, a loaf of bread, a wedge of cheese, a bunch of grapes, and biscuits. There were also several bottles of cider. The group settled on the blanket and began to enjoy their lunch. Darcy steered the conversation to topics that would allow Richard to see Miss Lucas' intelligence and wit.

They had finished dining, and Richard, Darcy, and Elizabeth were discussing the war with Napoleon. Georgiana had brought her sketch pad with her and began to create a sketch of Miss Lucas. As she put down her pencil and cocked her head at the drawing, Darcy realized Georgiana was inspecting the finished work.

"May I see your sketch, Dear One?"

"I am not sure it is quite right, but you may see it if you like." Georgiana handed the sketchbook to her brother.

A small gasp escaped Darcy as he looked down at the picture his sister had drawn of her companion. Georgiana had managed to capture her lovely smile, the sparkle in Miss Lucas' eyes, and the many little curls that escaped her coiffure to frame her face and rest upon her neck. Darcy was entranced. "I must disagree, dear sister, you have done a remarkable job capturing Miss Lucas. I believe it is one of your best!" Both the artist and subject blushed at his words.

Darcy handed the picture to the colonel, who examined it for several moments before speaking. "Darcy is correct, Georgie. You did a wonderful job with this portrait. Your skills have improved greatly since the last sketch you showed me."

Finally, the picture was handed to Elizabeth. "Miss Darcy, you have a remarkable talent. Sketching people was never something I mastered, but this is extremely well done. I wish I had such a talent, for then I would be able to sketch my lost family members, and I would always have them with me." The sadness in her voice and her wistful expression touched Georgiana's tender heart.

"Perhaps you could describe them to me, and we could work together to create sketches you would be able to keep. I would be happy to try to help you."

"Thank you, Miss Darcy. That is a very generous offer. If we can find time to work on them without disrupting your studies too much, I will gladly accept." Tears pooled in Elizabeth's eyes as she spoke. Georgiana reached out and gave Elizabeth's hand a comforting squeeze.

Both gentlemen observed Georgiana's thoughtfulness with pride. Darcy, glancing up and noticing that the sky was beginning to cloud over, suggested a thunderstorm might soon be upon them. "I believe we should pack up and return quickly; otherwise we might find ourselves getting soaked."

The others looked at the clouds gathering overhead and quickly began to pack the remainder of their meal and fold the blankets. They hurried to their horses. The blankets were secured behind the ladies' saddles. Richard reached out and lifted Georgiana into hers.

Darcy looked at Miss Lucas hesitantly. "Miss Lucas, would you allow me to assist you into the saddle?" At her nod, he put his hands around her waist and lifted her onto Gambit. The gentlemen slung the saddlebags over their horses and mounted. Darcy led them farther down the hill and into an open meadow. Before anyone else, Elizabeth gave Gambit her head and raced across the field at a full gallop. The others quickly followed. Stargazer and Paladin raced after Gambit. Richard realized there was no way Winsome would be able to keep up with the larger horses, so he slowed slightly to ride next to Georgiana. He was impressed, however, that Miss Lucas and Gambit never gave up, and Stargazer was able to take the lead only shortly before they arrived at the stables.

When Georgiana and Richard arrived a few moments after the others, Richard was surprised to hear Darcy laughing and complimenting Miss Lucas on a well-run race. Just as Georgiana and Richard joined them, the heavens opened up and large raindrops began to pelt them. The group ran for the rear of the house, laughing all the way.

Baths were soon drawn for everyone, as Mrs. Reynolds hurried them off to their rooms, worrying they would catch a chill. When the ladies were bathed and changed, they returned to their studies in the library. Once he had refreshed himself, Richard made his way to his cousin's study. After receiving Darcy's call to enter, Richard poked his head around the door and asked, "Feel like a game of billiards?"

"Are you ready to be trounced?" Darcy returned with a laugh. Darcy stood to join him, and they moved towards the billiards room.

They spoke of inconsequential things during their first game, and Darcy handily defeated his cousin. Richard broke for the second game. As Darcy stepped up to take his shot, Richard said, "Whatever else Miss Lucas is, she is an excellent horsewoman."

"She is, indeed. It is one of her many wonderful attributes."

"Are you going to tell me why you hired a perfect stranger to be the companion to our dear Georgie?"

"I am happy to tell you. Would you like to wait until you are again defeated or would you like to forfeit and we can discuss this over a drink?" Darcy questioned with a grin.

"Looking at what you have managed to clear on your first turn, I believe I will forfeit with my dignity intact rather than give you something else to gloat about," said Richard in disgust, though he had a hard time preventing his grin from appearing.

The gentlemen laid aside their cues, and Darcy moved to pour them both a drink from the decanter on the sideboard. They settled in the chairs near the window, and both took a sip of their drinks. Darcy stared out at the pouring rain as he gathered his thoughts. Richard kept his eyes focused on his cousin as he waited for Darcy to speak.

"You know what took place in Ramsgate."

Richard nodded, a look of intense anger on his face.

"You also saw the state Georgie was in when we arrived in London."

Again, Richard nodded.

Darcy went on to speak of her continuous tears as they traveled the first day and of the trouble with the horse that caused them to stop. He shared with his cousin their arrival at the Knight's Rest Inn, Miss Lucas' assistance to Georgiana, his observance of Miss Lucas' handling of the unwanted attentions of the man in the dining room, and her inquiry into Georgiana's well-being and her offer of prayers for the girl's continued improvement. Then Darcy told him what the landlord had learned of Miss Lucas before deciding to rent her a room. At Darcy's last words, Richard picked up his first clues as to Darcy's reasoning—he empathized with her orphan status and could not resist rescuing someone in distress.

Continuing his tale, Darcy told Richard of his good impression of her manners, her ability to handle difficult situations, and her compassion for others. "She possessed all the qualities I hope for Georgiana to acquire. I felt impressed she would make an excellent example for Georgiana, as well as a good companion and possible friend." Darcy then told Richard of writing the note and the interview that was conducted. "We spoke at great length about her background and education. I even tested her on some of what she said. The next morning, she joined us for breakfast and did a remarkable job of drawing Georgie out of her shyness. After breakfast, Georgiana expressed her pleasure at Miss Lucas' company and claimed she would be delighted to have such a companion."

"How do you know she is not involved in a scam with Wickham like the last one was?" Richard asked dubiously.

"You have now spent time in her company. Have you noticed any artifice in her at any time?"

"Well, no, but—"

"When she accepted the position, she did confess to me that, with the servants' help, she had made her escape from the heir's home, appropriating one of his horses to do so. She asked if I could offer her some direction on how best to return it. I referred her to Mr. Heath, sure he would be able to assist her. I will also tell you that her name is probably not Rose Lucas, as the initials on the handkerchief she loaned Georgie were ERB."

Richard nearly shouted at Darcy. "You know she is not being truthful, and you still hired her! I am beginning to doubt your sanity, Cousin." Richard jumped up and began pacing.

"Lower your voice, Richard. I would not wish for Miss Lucas to hear you."

The colonel gave his cousin a look of irritation as he plopped back in his chair.

LINDA C. THOMPSON

"I do not think she is evil, but perhaps she is in trouble. Do you know many gently raised young women who would go hunting for a job if they did not have to? I believe she needs our help, not condemnation, and she is certainly attempting to be strong and self-sufficient. When we go up to London after the holidays, I plan to do some investigating. I know the general area of where the horse was to be left upon its return. Assuming it is near where she came from, I plan to make further inquiries about a dreadful accident in the area. Maybe I can learn what happened to her family and their estate. I also know she sent word to a Mrs. Hill the day after our arrival here. The letter was addressed to her at an inn in Cambridge. What was the name again?" Darcy thought for a moment. "Ah, yes, it was called the Book and Barrel Inn. I plan to try to find out more about this Mrs. Hill as well."

"And to where was this horse returned?" asked Richard skeptically.

"It was to a small town in Hertfordshire called Meryton. Also, you need not worry about her being a fortune hunter. Because of her circumstances, I offered to purchase additional gowns for her, stating they would be required, as she would go everywhere with Georgiana. She refused to allow me to buy anything for her, stating she had funds for a new dress or two. However, Georgiana and I chose to ignore her request. We did permit her to pay for three dresses, but then Georgiana selected and I paid for several additional gowns and her riding habit. She wished to remain in mourning to honor her family, but I convinced her to allow some of the gowns to be in half mourning as well."

Richard still looked dubious but agreed to allow Miss Lucas to continue in her capacity as

Georgiana's companion until definite proof existed that she was not fit for the position. However, he felt a warning to his cousin was necessary. "Darcy, you need to distance yourself from this young woman. It is plain to see you are infatuated with her. Even if she is a gentleman's daughter, her current circumstances make her entirely unsuitable to marry someone like you."

Darcy looked at Richard in shock. "I believe you need to have your eyes examined, Richard. I have done nothing that could make anyone think I have any such intentions! All I feel for the young lady is compassion. Georgiana and I can certainly understand the sense of loss she is experiencing. In fact, her situation is even more painful, as she lost all of her siblings and her parents. Her sadness is frequently apparent, though she does try very hard to hide it and remain positive and supportive around Georgie."

"Methinks thou doth protest too much," (1) Richard muttered under his breath.

Darcy glanced at the clock, saying, "I believe it is time to meet the ladies in the parlor for tea." He moved towards the door, the colonel following, and strode to the library. He was surprised to find it empty. Noticing a footman standing nearby, he asked, "Where are Miss Darcy and Miss Lucas?"

"I believe they moved to the yellow drawing room, sir. I heard Miss Lucas tell Miss Darcy it would not be proper to receive a guest for tea in such an informal setting."

"Thank you." Darcy glanced at Richard with an amused expression on his face as they moved to join the ladies.

The gentlemen entered the room to find Georgiana and Miss Lucas seated on the small sofa across from two large chairs. The tea tray was on the table before the sofa. Elizabeth's and Georgiana's heads were close together, and their voices spoke in whispers.

"Good afternoon, ladies. Are you both recovered from our outing?"

"Yes, thank you, sir," was Miss Lucas' demure reply.

"Certainly, Brother. It is not the first time we have been caught in a summer rain, and I am sure it will not be the last."

Richard and Darcy both gave a chuckle.

"May I pour you some tea?" There was a hint of nervousness in Georgiana's voice.

"Certainly," replied her guardian, an eyebrow cocked in surprise.

"I believe you prefer your tea plain, do you not, Richard?"

"You have an excellent memory, Georgie." He watched as she poured his tea, noting that her hand shook just slightly.

As she passed him his cup of tea, she turned to offer to pour one for her brother. She prepared his tea as requested and passed the cup to him. Next she did the same for Miss Lucas. Darcy and Richard both noted that by the time she prepared her own cup, her hand no longer trembled.

Darcy inquired about the afternoon's lessons, and Georgiana took up the debate with her brother regarding the book she had read. Both Darcy and Richard were pleased to see the confidence with which she discussed her point of view. They were delighted that she refused to give in and continued to defend her opinion. Miss Lucas spoke not at all, allowing Georgiana the moment to shine.

As Richard prepared to exit his room after changing for dinner, he stopped abruptly and pushed the door almost closed again. What had surprised him was seeing Georgiana knocking on the door that connected with her sitting room and to watch Miss Lucas exit. When they were out of sight, he rushed to his cousin's room to knock on the door.

Darcy opened the door, dressed and preparing to exit. Richard put his hand on Darcy's chest, pushed him backward into the room, and closed the door behind him.

Startled, Darcy barked, "Richard, what do you think—"

"Why the devil is Miss Lucas living in the family wing? If word of this gets out, everyone will believe the worst of her, and Georgiana's reputation will be ruined by association."

"Calm down, Richard, and, again, lower your voice. I placed Miss Lucas there because I truly believe having her close to Georgiana is of benefit to them both. When Mrs. Reynolds learned of it, she took me to task with almost the same accusation." Richard could not quite understand the small smile on his cousin's face. "After understanding her point, we decided to let it be known that Miss Lucas is a poor, distant relation who has lost all her family and come to be Georgiana's friend and companion. Satisfied?"

Richard nodded his head, but he still looked unsettled.

"Let us join the ladies so we are not late."

Darcy escorted the ladies to dinner, as had become his habit. However, when he seated Georgiana in her usual spot, Elizabeth pulled out the chair next to Georgiana and seated herself. Darcy was about to ask why she was not sitting in her usual seat, but a small shake of her head discouraged him. From the corner of his eye, Darcy noted his cousin about to take the place on Darcy's other side, which was usually occupied by Miss Lucas.

Dinner began somewhat quietly, and Elizabeth noted the colonel was frequently watching her. Finally, to ease the situation, she spoke. "Miss Darcy, have you told your cousin of the new piece of music you are learning?"

At her words, Georgiana eagerly launched into an explanation of the new music and her practicing. "I was going to play it for William for the first time this evening. I am glad you are here to hear it as well." Her words seemed to ease the tension, and the conversation flowed pleasantly through the remainder of the meal. Elizabeth rarely contributed unless the conversation seemed to lag. She preferred for the family to enjoy their time together.

Richard continued to study Elizabeth frequently throughout the evening, though he did not speak directly to her. Georgiana gave an excellent performance of the new piece she had been learning. "That was lovely, Georgie. I have not heard it before."

"It is a piece by Beethoven. It is the Opus 81a Piano Sonatas #26 in E Flat Major," (2) she informed Richard. "But, Richard, if you wish to hear something lovely, you must convince Miss Lucas to sing for you."

Though she was somewhat uncomfortable with the colonel's continued staring, Elizabeth allowed herself to be convinced to sing. "I shall agree, but only if you will play for me, Miss Darcy." Georgiana nodded in happy agreement.

Elizabeth moved to the piano and searched through the music for a piece she knew well. Finding one she had noticed a few days earlier, she placed the music on the piano for Georgiana. Then, taking her position beside the instrument, she sang "Lavender's Blue." (3)

The performance was very well received, with Georgiana and Darcy both complimenting her. Even Colonel Fitzwilliam was impressed enough to speak. "You do have a remarkable talent, Miss Lucas. Should you ever find yourself in the position of needing employment in the future, perhaps you should give the theater a try."

Both Darcy and Georgiana gasped in shock at Richard's rude remark. And though both Richard and Darcy could see anger in her eyes, her reply was quite calm. "Yes, I am afraid orphaned gentlewomen, like second sons, must earn their keep. However, I feel certain my education will always allow me to find employment without having to take such drastic measures. If you will please excuse me, I believe I shall retire for the evening." So saying, Elizabeth turned on her heels and departed the music room, closing the door behind her. Once out of sight, she fled to her room.

While Lucy assisted in preparing her for the night, Elizabeth managed to maintain her composure. Once she was tucked in her bed, she cried herself to sleep. She had gained a great deal of knowledge from books, but it had not prepared her for the meanness of spirit she would encounter in her new position in life.

After Miss Lucas' hurried departure, both Georgiana and Darcy turned on their cousin.

"Richard, how could you be so mean to Miss Lucas? She has lost her entire family and been forced to leave her home. In the time she has been here, she has been the best friend I have ever had. If she leaves because of your rude remarks, I shall never speak to you again." Tears welled in her eyes as Georgiana finished speaking, and she, too, fled from the music room. She knocked softly on the door to Elizabeth's room, but received no answer. Georgiana retired sadly for the night, including in her prayers a wish for Miss Lucas to remain with her.

Darcy was angry with Richard for his remark, and seeing the way it hurt Georgiana made him even angrier. "Richard, how dare you speak to a guest in my home in such a disrespectful manner?" The colonel started to speak, but Darcy held up a hand, forestalling him. "If you cannot apologize and behave in a more appropriate manner to Miss Lucas, you will not be welcome to remain another night." Not wishing to converse further with his cousin, Mr. Darcy also said goodnight and departed.

Though Richard was concerned his cousins were being taken advantage of, he cared for them and was sorry for upsetting them. He would have to apologize the next day and find some time to question Miss Lucas privately. He also determined he would stop by the Book and Barrel in Cambridge on his return to London. Perhaps he could learn some information from this Mrs. Hill.

Richard made his way to his room. When he was prepared for bed, he poured himself a brandy and sat in the chair before the fire. He was attempting to find the best way to apologize and still gain the information he felt he needed to protect his family—even if they did not feel they needed protection.

The next morning, Elizabeth was up early, as usual. She was seated on a bench by the lake, preparing to watch the sunrise. She had been highly insulted by the colonel's remarks and planned to excuse herself from the family for meals and tea. She did not wish to cause friction between the Darcys and their remaining family members. Elizabeth knew her feelings for Mr. Darcy were hopeless, and she tried to keep them under tight control. Perhaps something in her countenance caused the colonel to suspect her feelings and assume she was an adventuress.

A voice at her side startled her, particularly because it was not the voice she was accustomed to hearing most mornings.

"Good morning, Miss Lucas. May I join you?" came the voice of Colonel Richard Fitzwilliam.

Elizabeth eyed him warily and moved to the farthest end of the bench as she gave him a slight nod.

Richard gave a chuckle. "I imagine I deserve that reaction. I apologize for my behavior and words last evening. Would you permit me to explain why I reacted as I did?"

Though she would not look at him, Elizabeth again nodded.

"My cousin, Darcy, has been the target of scheming mothers and daughters since he first appeared in society. Since he became the master of Pemberley, the scheming has increased, and the ladies seem to be remarkably clever. It was very unlike my cousin to make the snap decision he made to hire you. I was concerned he had become entrapped by a conniving young woman."

"Do you have so little trust in your cousin's judgment?"

"Of course not!" replied the colonel, stung.

"Then there must have been something in my behavior to cause you to think so meanly of me."

"No, there was not, and I watched you closely."

"Yes, though I might have phrased it 'stared rudely.'"

Richard gave a chuckle as he witnessed the sharp wit Darcy had mentioned. "Will you accept my apology and allow us to start over?"

Elizabeth hesitated only a moment before agreeing.

"Thank goodness you forgave me. Otherwise, Darcy threatened to boot me out of the house."

"Oh, no. You must not leave on my account. If it is causing difficulties for the Darcys to have me here, I must leave immediately."

She rose to depart, but Richard reached out to stop her. "That will not be necessary," he said with another chuckle. "If they thought I forced you to leave, they would never allow me to set foot in Pemberley again. I received quite the tongue-lashing after your departure last evening, first from Georgiana and then from Darcy. Would you mind reviewing with me what led to your employment? I understand you recently lost your family."

Tears welled in Elizabeth's eyes at the mention of her family. She looked away from the colonel and dashed the tears from her face while she tried to regain her composure. She told him of the accident that claimed five of her family members. She told him of the arrival of the heir on the day after the accident and his unwillingness to have her in his home unless it was as a servant. She told of the help the servants had given her to get away to find a better life for herself. She told of seeing Miss Darcy in tears and offering her handkerchief, as well as catching her as she fainted. Elizabeth told him about the note the landlord had brought her from Mr. Darcy requesting the interview and of meeting with Miss Darcy the next morning before accepting the position.

Richard had watched her throughout the recitation. He noticed no hesitation that would indicate she was less than truthful. The grief she felt at the loss of her family was also obvious, as was her disdain for the heir. However, when she spoke of him Richard thought he detected a bit of fear in her eyes as well.

"Please tell me something about your education."

Elizabeth told him the same things she had told Mr. Darcy during the interview. She could not help but smile when Richard, too, spoke to her in French to test what she had said.

"I thank you for your honesty, Miss Lucas. Again, I apologize for last evening. Since we failed to notice the sunrise as we spoke, may I accompany you back to the house for breakfast?"

He rose and extended an arm to Elizabeth. She looked at him for several moments, trying to determine if this was another test of some kind. Using caution, she answered, "I would be glad to walk with you, sir, but it is not necessary to offer your arm."

"Oh, but it is. I am attempting to improve the impression I made on you last evening." Richard's face wore a charming smile, and his eyes had a slight look of pleading.

Elizabeth gave a soft laugh and accepted his arm. The two moved across the lawn toward the house. The colonel still held Elizabeth's arm as they entered the breakfast room. She saw that Georgiana and Mr. Darcy were both at the table. Elizabeth noticed that Darcy glared at her hand resting on the colonel's arm. Dropping it, she stepped away from the colonel. Turning to the sideboard, she prepared a plate and seated herself in the chair next to

Georgiana. She kept her gaze downcast as a flush of embarrassment suffused her cheeks.

The colonel, on the other hand, chuckled at the looks of surprise his cousins both wore. "Good morning, Darcy, Georgie. I saw Miss Elizabeth beside the lake as I was about to take an early morning ride. I used the opportunity to apologize for my behavior last evening, and she was gracious enough to grant me her forgiveness." Though Georgiana's face expressed her relief, Richard was not quite sure what had caused Darcy's glare of disapproval. Shrugging it off, he helped himself to a plate from the sideboard and joined the others at the table.

Plans for the day were discussed, then everyone separated to their activities. Richard joined Darcy in his study, where he read while his cousin worked, occasionally engaging in desultory conversation.

Richard's opinion of Elizabeth improved throughout the day, and so he teased her and attempted to flirt with her on occasion. She used her wit to return his teases, but never once did she respond to his flirtatiousness. By the time he departed the following day, he was quite in agreement with Darcy about her suitability as Georgiana's companion.

And, though he believed what she had told him, he still intended to speak with Mrs. Hill. Perhaps he could learn something that would help Miss Lucas.

12. GUESTS ARRIVE

BECAUSE OF HER MOURNING STATE, ELIZABETH asked to be excused from being in company as much as possible during the Bingleys' visit. Both Darcy and Georgiana tried to convince her they would like to have her with them, but she was adamant. Elizabeth felt it was safer for her to interact with as few people as possible while she hid from Mr. Collins and his son. She did make a concession and agree that she would join them for the events tied to the celebration of Georgiana's sixteenth birthday at the end of the second week of the visit.

On the Wednesday of the first week of September, the Bingley family arrived. Elizabeth was seated in the library with the doors open when she heard voices in the hallway. Discreetly she moved into the upstairs hall, where she had a view of the visitors below. According to Georgiana, the Bingleys were returning from a visit to their relatives in the north and were expected to stay for three weeks before going on to London. She could hear Mr. Darcy greeting his guests.

"Bingley, how good to see you. Welcome to Pemberley."

"Darcy, old friend! We are delighted to be here!" Mr. Charles Bingley was a handsome man with reddish blond hair and bright blue eyes. His nature was happy and outgoing. Bingley had attended Cambridge with Darcy, though he was a year behind him. In spite of their very different natures, they had become fast friends. Bingley brought levity to Darcy's serious nature. Darcy shared his knowledge of estate management and life in the first circles with Bingley as the gentleman tried to become the first in his family to be part of the landed gentry. The Bingley family fortune was extensive, but it derived from the efforts of several generations of his family in the milling and manufacture of cotton goods and other forms of trade.

Accompanying Mr. Bingley was his elder sister, Mrs. Louisa Hurst. She had dark auburn hair, and was short and slightly plump. She seemed a pleasant sort of woman but did not speak much when in company with her younger sister. Her husband, Mr. Gilbert Hurst, was the eldest son of a gentleman with an estate in Lincolnshire whose worth was just less than four thousand per annum. Mr. Hurst's manner was indolent, but Elizabeth noted a look of humor and intelligence in his eyes that reminded her of her father.

The last member of the party was Miss Caroline Bingley. She was Mr. Bingley's next older sister, and they could not have been more different. There was a close resemblance in their appearances, but Miss Bingley was several inches taller than her elder sister. She had Louisa's same dark auburn hair, which, unfortunately, clashed with the orange dress she wore. Where her brother's eyes were a bright blue, Miss Bingley's were a pale, almost colorless, blue. She carried herself well, but with such an affected air she appeared almost ludicrous.

"Mr. Darcy, how wonderful to be at Pemberley again!" enthused Caroline Bingley as she rushed to her host with her hand extended. Elizabeth was shocked at the lady's voice. It was somewhat shrill and artificial. Mr. Darcy stepped back from the approaching Miss Bingley, bowing slightly, but not taking her hand. However, Miss Bingley was not to be deterred. She wrapped her arm around Mr. Darcy's, asking, "Where is dear Miss Darcy?"

Darcy unwrapped her arm and stepped away before replying. "She is awaiting us in the drawing room. Refreshments will be served in half an hour to allow you time to refresh yourselves from your travel." He turned to the waiting Mrs. Reynolds. "Would you please show our guests to their rooms?"

"Certainly, sir. If you would please follow me," said the housekeeper as she turned to the stairs.

At Darcy's words, Elizabeth moved back into the library and closed one of the doors before Mrs. Reynolds and the visitors arrived in the upstairs hallway. Darcy had glanced up as he spoke and noticed a quick movement near the top of the stairs. With a small smile playing around the corners of his mouth, Darcy waited until the others were out of sight, then quickly mounted the stairs. He ducked his head around the door in the library and saw Elizabeth sitting in a chair near the window, a book in her lap.

"So, what is your impression of our guests?"

Elizabeth started at the sound of his voice, and color suffused her face. "I am sorry, sir, it was wrong of me to be so curious."

"It is quite all right. As I have said, you are more than welcome to join us, if you would like."

"No, sir, I would prefer to keep to myself when I am not working with Miss Georgiana. Would I be likely to encounter anyone in the early morning hours if I were to continue my walks?"

Darcy laughed. "I do not think you need worry about that. Neither Bingley nor his sisters are early risers, and Miss Bingley and Mrs. Hurst often take a tray in their rooms in the morning. However, you did not answer my question. What is your impression of our guests?"

"Mr. Bingley seems a pleasant, happy man, but Mr. and Mrs. Hurst did not speak enough to leave an impression."

"And what of Miss Bingley?"

Elizabeth wondered how to answer both truthfully and tactfully. "Miss Bingley seems to be a determined young woman who is excessively fond of Pemberley."

Again, Darcy laughed. "You are very observant, Miss Lucas. I do wish you would reconsider and join us. Georgiana is not particularly comfortable around Miss Bingley. Nor am I, for that matter," he said with another quiet chuckle.

"I do not wish for Miss Darcy to be distressed," said Elizabeth with a frown. "She could always claim the need to attend to her lessons. I would be happy to give her additional work if that is the wish of both of you."

"I will recommend that to her," said Darcy with a smile, "or perhaps we will just allow her to use that as an excuse should she need one. Please remember, should you change your mind, you are welcome to join us at any time."

"Thank you, Mr. Darcy, but I shall be perfectly content on my own. I will still be able to enjoy my time with Miss Darcy, but I shall miss our rides."

"As will I."

"But, you will still be riding, just with different companions."

"It will not be the same without you. Your appreciation of the beauty of the estate helps me see it with fresh eyes."

Elizabeth blushed further at Darcy's words. She found herself attracted to this thoughtful, kind man. She was very grateful they had met when they did, as being here at Pemberley, far from her home and the Collinses, was a source of great relief. If only thoughts of what might have happened had she met Darcy when she was a well-dowered young lady, instead of his sister's companion, would leave her alone.

"Well, enjoy your book, Miss Lucas. I shall join Georgiana as we await our guests for tea." As Darcy stepped into the hallway, he encountered one of the maids. He quietly instructed her to be sure a tea tray was sent to Miss Lucas in the library when they were brought to the drawing room for the new arrivals.

The others were all present when Miss Bingley waltzed into the drawing room. She moved in the direction of the sofa where Miss Darcy was seated. "My dear Miss Darcy, how delighted I am to be with you again! It has been far too long since last we were in company."

"It is nice to see you again, Miss Bingley." Her quiet voice and downcast eyes caused Darcy to looked at Georgiana in surprise. Her confidence had been steadily growing since Miss Lucas had joined them. Now, in Miss Bingley's presence, she seemed to have reverted back to her shyness. He made a note to ask her about it later.

"It is so pleasant to be in such superior society again, for there was none to be found in York. I find I no longer know what to say to my relatives when we visit. We are so comfortable in the ton, we no longer have any common areas of interest with those of the family in trade." She spoke the word *trade* as though it left an unpleasant taste on her tongue. "They know

173

nothing of fashion from London, and what passes for entertainment there is laughable. I declare, I am relieved to be away and again in the company of such wonderful friends as you, Mr. Darcy." The look she gave Darcy was somewhat proprietary, as well as prurient. Quickly realizing she had overlooked Georgiana, she hurried to add, "And, of course, Miss Darcy. She is such a dear, sweet friend, and I long for more time to spend with her."

At that moment, Mrs. Reynolds entered the room, followed by another maid bringing refreshments. The trays were set in front of Georgiana, who, acting as hostess, began to pour for everyone. Noting Georgiana's hands were shaking slightly, Caroline assumed it was because she was not comfortable with her duties and abilities as hostess. Trying to show Darcy how perfect she would be as mistress of Pemberley, Caroline kept pointing out Georgiana's mistakes and offering suggestions on the correct way to serve tea. Between each suggestion, she gave Darcy a superior smile, failing to note how unhappy he was with her criticism of his sister.

Trying to turn the attention away from Georgiana, Darcy said, "We are pleased you and your family could join us, Charles."

"Thank you, Darcy, I do—"

Caroline spoke over her brother, not allowing him to finish his sentence. "Oh, we are so pleased to be here. Pemberley is like a second home. And after the horrors of travel and the places we were forced to stay, arriving here is quite a relief. Mr. Darcy, you would not believe what passes for quality in an inn. Charles insisted we were staying in the best establishments, but the service was dreadful and the meals barely tolerable. I am sure I should not have survived had I not had the thought of recovering at Pemberley with our dear friends to sustain me."

Turning to his friend in concern, Darcy asked, "Were you not able to stay in the places I recommended to you, Bingley? I have used all of those inns before and have always found the service and food to be excellent." At Mr. Darcy's words, Caroline's face paled.

"Pay no mind to Caroline, Darcy. You know how fastidious she can be. We did stay in the inns you recommended, and I found them to be just as you described. I was very pleased with the service we received." Miss Bingley cast a scornful glance at her brother.

Trying to make up for her *faux pas*, Caroline began to babble about the wonders of Pemberley. However, for every compliment she offered, she mentioned how she would change something else. When, after half an hour, Miss Bingley paused for breath, Georgiana took the opportunity to speak.

"William, I beg of you to excuse me. I have an assignment I must finish before lessons tomorrow. I would like to do so now so that I may rest before dinner."

"Oh, but certainly your companion cannot expect you to attend to your studies while we are visiting. I long for the opportunity to spend time with you, dear Miss Darcy," pouted Miss Bingley.

Ignoring Miss Bingley's remarks, Darcy turned to reply to his sister. "Yes, Georgiana, you may be excused. It is important for you to attend to your lessons." The look of relief Georgiana gave her brother almost caused him to chuckle.

Georgiana had barely cleared the doorway when she heard her brother speak again. "I am sorry if it disappoints you, Miss Bingley, but my sister will

175

be much occupied with her studies, even during your visit. I deem her education to be of vital importance as she prepares to make her debut. She will, of course, join us for meals and any other entertainments we undertake. Now, I suggest we all retire to rest before dinner, which is at seven. Bingley, might I have a word with you before you retire?"

Miss Bingley was frustrated at being dismissed when Charles remained in company with the object of her desires.

Wishing to get far from Miss Bingley, Georgiana quickly mounted the stairs, intending to go to her sitting room, but she heard a soft laugh coming from the library. She peeked her head around the door and found Miss Lucas just where Darcy had—in the chair by the window.

"Miss Lucas, would you mind joining me in our sitting room?"

"Of course not, Miss Darcy." Elizabeth glanced at the clock and was surprised at the time. She rose and started walking towards the door. "Did tea end so early?" she asked.

Georgiana linked her arm with Elizabeth's and headed down the hall. When they arrived in the sitting room, Georgiana collapsed onto one of the sofas and heaved a large sigh.

"Was it as bad as all that?" Elizabeth asked with a soft laugh.

"It was even worse than usual. I cannot bear the way she fusses over me. It makes me very uncomfortable." Georgiana gave a small shudder.

"From my brief observation of her when she first arrived, I can understand your feelings.

However, as the hostess, you must speak to your guests and attempt to guide the conversation to more appropriate topics."

"However would I do that? She barely pauses for breath and does not even allow one to answer the questions she poses."

Elizabeth gave another laugh. "I wonder if she sings; she does seem to have remarkable breath control." This brought a laugh from Georgiana as well.

"I hope you will find lots of work for me to do over the course of the Bingleys' visit. Though I enjoy Mr. Bingley's company, I would much prefer to never be alone in Miss Bingley's company."

"I am sure we can find enough to keep us busy. Will we still be able to use the library, or do we need to work here in the sitting room?"

"Miss Bingley is not fond of books, so—" The look of shock on Elizabeth's face caused a bubble of laughter to escape Georgiana before she could finish. "I believe the library will afford us the privacy we seek. In spite of Miss Bingley's presence, I hope we shall be able to maintain our usual schedule for the most part. I would be very sad if we were forced to give up our rides and music practice."

"Your brother has given me permission to stay withdrawn from the visitors because I am in mourning. I will expect you to maintain your schedule of practices, but I will mostly likely not ride while the Bingleys are here."

"Oh, how disappointing. That means all of our rides will be close to home, with no opportunity for a good gallop. Miss Bingley is not a particularly good horsewoman, so it will severely limit the places we can go. Also, William has not shared many of the places we have visited since your arrival with many people outside of the family. He prefers that visitors keep to the more public portions of the estate." Georgiana could not miss the blush that graced her companion's face as she spoke of the sights William had shared with them.

"Yes, I will miss our rides, but it cannot be helped," said Elizabeth sadly.

"Well, I must rest so I can face Miss Bingley over dinner," said Georgiana with a grimace. "If only I were in need of losing some weight, Miss Bingley's presence would be useful because I usually lose my appetite when she is visiting." With an unrepentant giggle, Georgiana departed for her room.

When the Hursts and Miss Bingley departed from the drawing room, Darcy looked at his friend and asked, "Would you care to join me in my study, Bingley? I feel the need for something a little stronger than tea."

"Of course, Darcy, lead the way."

When they were each seated with a glass of port, Darcy gave his friend a grimace. "I see your sister has not changed." Darcy took a gulp of his drink before continuing. "You do understand my position in regards to your sister?"

"Yes, Darcy. I know you have no desire for a closer relationship with her, in spite of her wishes. I know you tolerate her only for my sake, and I do appreciate it. I have spoken to her about her behavior around you, but she seems incapable of understanding anything I tell her."

"I hope you will help to keep her from imposing on Georgiana. My dear little sister is uncomfortable with her constant attentions." Under his breath he added, "As am I."

After a bit more discussion, the gentlemen finished their drinks and departed for their chambers to prepare for dinner.

Elizabeth had taken a dinner tray in the sitting room and spent some time writing to Mrs. Hill as she waited for Georgiana's return. Away from Miss Bingley, Georgiana's confidence returned as she relayed Miss Bingley's ridiculous dinner conversation and the way she hung onto Darcy's arm. Georgiana had to look away to keep from giggling as she watched her brother try to disentangle himself from Miss Bingley's ever-grasping hands. Though the ladies laughed at her behavior, Elizabeth felt it incumbent upon her to remind Miss Darcy she should try to be kind to the lady if at all possible.

"Perhaps Miss Bingley behaves in such a manner due to a lack of self-confidence or concern over fitting in with the new society her brother is entering."

Georgiana stared at Elizabeth in shock. She could discern the trace of a smile at the corners of Elizabeth's mouth. When Georgiana's lips began to curl into a smile of her own, the young ladies burst into uncontrollable giggles that lasted for quite some time.

When they eventually regained control of their mirth, Georgiana looked at Elizabeth and said in all seriousness, "I do understand your message and know it is important to always treat others with kindness. It is just that Miss Bingley's overbearing ways make it difficult to remember in her case."

179

With that, the two young ladies wished each other good night and sweet dreams before retiring to their rooms.   Elizabeth had just closed her bedchamber door behind her when she heard the sound of muttering coming from her dressing room. She opened the door and looked in to find Lucy going about her duties, preparing Elizabeth's clothes and things for bed, all the while murmuring to herself. Elizabeth knocked on the open door and Lucy looked up, startled.

"Is everything alright, Lucy?"

"Yes, miss," the maid replied with her eyes downcast.

"Why is it I do not believe you?"   Elizabeth looked at Lucy with her brow arched in question.

"It is nothing for you to worry about, miss."

"Lucy, you are worried, and I would like to help if I can." Elizabeth accompanied her words with a friendly smile. Lucy looked up and saw Elizabeth's expression. She fidgeted a moment before deciding to reply.

"It is my younger sister, Hannah, Miss. She has been assigned to tend Miss Bingley during her stay. Apparently, Miss Bingley discharged her maid before coming here."

"And you are worried for your sister's sake?"

"Yes, miss. I do not think Miss Bingley has brought the same maid with her on any of her visits. She is particular in her wishes and not always . . ." Lucy's words trailed off because she knew there was not a polite way to finish her thought.

"Oh, I see. Well, Lucy, please try not to worry, and if you or your sister should need my assistance, please do not hesitate to ask."   Elizabeth gave the maid an encouraging look.

"Thank you very much, miss," said the maid with a look of relief.

Breakfast became the only meal Georgiana enjoyed over the next week and a half, for Mrs. Hurst and Miss Bingley took trays in their rooms. Georgiana spent as much time studying with Miss Lucas as was possible during the Bingleys' stay; she even began to close and lock the door to the music room during her piano practice. The locked door allowed Elizabeth to join her by way of the servant passages. When Georgiana worked on one of the pieces assigned by her music master, Elizabeth sat and listened as she worked on her embroidery or made blankets for the estate's newest additions. At other times, they would practice their duets together. Occasionally during these practices, Mr. Darcy also made use of the servant passages to join them. He tried to spend as much of his time in manly pursuits with Bingley and Mr. Hurst as possible, but as a good host he could not avoid the ladies altogether. However, Miss Bingley's fawning and clinging drove him to distraction and only the beautiful music and soothing presence of his sister and Miss Lucas could bolster him enough to again tolerate her presence for a time.

On one such day after tea, Miss Bingley mentioned the locked door of the music room.

"My sister prefers not to have distractions when she practices," was Darcy's firm reply.

Not being willing to let the matter drop, Miss Bingley continued. "But it is so disappointing to be denied the opportunity to enjoy her playing. She is so accomplished on the pianoforte. Sometimes I am certain there are two players performing."

"Yes, my companion plays with me on occasion."

"I was not aware Mrs. Younge played the pianoforte. I do not remember hearing her do so in the past."

Georgiana's face paled at the mention of her former companion and her near escape in Ramsgate. "Family matters forced Mrs. Younge to resign her position. Georgiana's new companion, Miss Lucas, is very talented on the pianoforte and has a beautiful singing voice," was Darcy's terse reply.

"When shall we meet this paragon?" questioned Miss Bingley with jealousy tingeing her voice. Caroline had watched the expression on Darcy's face as he spoke of Miss Lucas. She would need to see the woman for herself, and if she proved to be a distraction to Mr. Darcy, Caroline would have to find a way to discredit her and get her dismissed.

"Miss Lucas is in mourning, having recently lost her entire family in a tragic accident. She prefers to keep to herself while our guests visit, but she will be joining us for the activities on Georgiana's birthday. You will meet her in a few days."

On the morning before Georgiana's birthday celebration, Elizabeth was seated in the library, awaiting Georgiana's arrival. Suddenly she heard footsteps enter the room and the sound of the door closing. She could not see who had entered and thought it might be Georgiana until she heard a familiar shrill voice.

"Our visit is to end in a week, Louisa, and still Mr. Darcy has not proposed to me. Why does he delay? I have tried to show him at every turn that I would be the perfect mistress for Pemberley and an excellent example for that sister of his. I do not know what else to do to gain his attention. Do you think I should attempt a compromise?"

"Caroline, you cannot be serious!" replied her sister in shock.

"Perhaps he is shy and waiting for me to demonstrate my feelings before he will say anything," Caroline countered.

Elizabeth had to clap her hands over her mouth to keep her laughter from escaping.

"We still have a little over a week before we leave. Perhaps you could be a bit more demonstrative, but I would not attempt to compromise yourself except as a last resort."

"But what about the new companion? He speaks of her with great respect and always smiles when her name is mentioned," whined Caroline.

"Do not be ridiculous, sister. Mr. Darcy would no more be interested in a servant than you would," sniffed Mrs. Hurst in disdain.

"Well, when I am Mrs. Darcy, there will be no companion around to distract him. In fact, if I get my way, Miss Darcy will be shipped off to a boarding school until she makes her debut."

Her sister nodded in agreement before saying, "We should go down to join the gentlemen now. You can make no impression on Mr. Darcy if you are not in his presence."

Without another word, the ladies departed from the room. Elizabeth sat in stunned silence at the disgusting insinuations Miss Bingley had made regarding both Mr. Darcy and herself. She was indignant on Miss Darcy's behalf for the dreadful way the young woman would be treated should Miss Bingley succeed in her goals. In spite of the embarrassment it might cause her, Elizabeth knew she would have to relate to Mr. Darcy the conversation she had overheard. She hoped he would not think her presumptuous, and would understand her warning was made out of concern for his sister and him.

Then a pleasant thought struck her. Miss Bingley said Mr. Darcy spoke of her with respect and smiled when her name was mentioned. Elizabeth knew herself to be greatly attracted to Mr. Darcy and wished they could have met under different circumstances. She could easily be falling in love with this man. *Is it possible he is attracted to me as well?*

Elizabeth was lost in thought with a soft smile on her face when Georgiana finally entered the room. After having called her name twice with no response, Georgiana dropped a book onto the table where Elizabeth sat.

Elizabeth started at the loud thump, her hand flying to her heart. "Good morning, Miss Darcy. You appear to have caught me woolgathering. Please forgive me."

"What were you thinking about that brought such a lovely smile to your face?"

A soft pink blush suffused Elizabeth's face as she replied. "I was merely thinking of the blessing of a loving family. Now, shall we get started with this morning's lesson?"

"Before we start, may I make a request?"

"Certainly, what is it you wish?"

"Would you please call me Georgiana or Georgie as my family does?"

"I would not object to doing so, but I am not sure it would be proper."

"I am sure my brother would agree it is proper if I ask you to do so. Besides, you are the closest friend I have ever had. While I was at school, I found most of the girls only pretended to be my friend so they could gain an introduction to my brother. The minute they met him they would act so differently from anything I had observed in them previously. Then if William did not pay them any attention, they no longer spoke to me afterward."

The tears filling Georgiana's eyes nearly broke Elizabeth's heart. She reached out, wrapped her arms around the young girl, and held her until her tears stopped. She pushed Georgiana away from her embrace but maintained a hold of her arms. Giving Georgiana a bright smile, Elizabeth said, "If your brother finds it acceptable for me to call you Georgiana, I will do so, but only if you will call me Rose."

"Oh, thank you! I will ask him the very next time I see him," Georgiana replied excitedly.

As was his custom most nights, Darcy stopped at the door to his sister's sitting room to escort her to dinner. That evening she had him step in for a moment so she might speak to him. The door had barely closed behind them when Georgiana began to speak. "Fitzwilliam, I wish for Miss Lucas to call me Georgiana instead of Miss Darcy, but she did not feel it was appropriate. Would you please tell her you do not mind? She is my dearest friend, and I do not wish to be so formal with her."

Darcy looked to where Miss Lucas was seated before giving his attention again to his sister. "I do not have an objection to the two of you addressing each other less formally. I am very pleased you have developed such a close relationship. In fact, I am particularly pleased with the progress you have made since Miss Lucas joined us. I believe she has been good for both of us. Pemberley is a much happier place since Miss Lucas has joined us here." A lovely blush spread over Elizabeth's face at Mr. Darcy's words.

"Oh, thank you, William!" Georgiana squeezed the arm she held in appreciation as brother and sister smiled at the other occupant of the room.

13. MISS BINGLEY MEETS THE COMPANION

THE MORNING OF GEORGIANA'S SIXTEENTH BIRTHDAY dawned bright and clear. Elizabeth had promised she would spend the entire day in company and participate in the events that had been planned. She donned a light gray mourning dress trimmed in black, and Lucy arranged her hair in a complex twist of braids that would serve her well for the day's activities. Elizabeth stepped into the girls' shared sitting room to await Georgiana. She did not have long to wait before her friend came through the door, nearly bouncing with excitement.

"Good morning, Georgiana. Happy birthday!"

"Good morning Rose. You look very pretty this morning."

"As do you. Is that one of your new dresses from Mrs. Webb?"

"Yes, it is," replied Georgiana as she pirouetted to show off the gown. "It turned out very well, did it not?"

"It did, indeed, and the light blue color suits you very well. Shall we go down to break our fast? It will be pleasant to dine in the dining room again," said Elizabeth, a smile on her face. What she was thinking, however, was that it would be nice to dine with Mr. Darcy again.

Darcy was the only one present in the dining room when the girls entered. He rose from his place at the table and moved to greet his sister. "Happy birthday, Georgie! I cannot believe you are sixteen. Where has the time gone? Instead of a beloved little sister standing before me, I see a beautiful young lady."

Georgiana blushed at her brother's words as he leaned down to kiss her cheek and escorted her to her chair. After seating her on his left, he seated Miss Lucas in her usual place on his right. Elizabeth had remained standing, uncertain where she should sit, as the Darcys were entertaining guests. She was delighted when he seated her beside him.

"Do not worry, brother dear. I will always be your little sister, and you shall always be the most perfect of brothers."

Darcy felt a lump grow in his throat at his sister's words and was spared the need to reply by Bingley's entrance into the room.

Bingley paused in the doorway at the sight of the lovely young woman seated to Darcy's right. Recovering quickly, he said, "Good morning, Miss Darcy, and happy birthday. I hope you are well this morning."

"Thank you, Mr. Bingley, I am very well."

Darcy had risen at his friend's entry. "Bingley, allow me to introduce you to Miss Lucas. She is a distant relation and dear friend who also serves as Georgiana's companion."

"Good morning, Miss Lucas. It is a pleasure to meet you," offered Bingley with a bow.

Elizabeth rose and made her curtsey as she replied. "It is very nice to meet you as well, Mr. Bingley."

Bingley took the seat next to Georgiana. Before Darcy could beckon the footman to serve the special breakfast that had been prepared for

Georgiana's birthday, the Hursts entered the dining room, and introductions were again made. The Hursts placed themselves next to Miss Lucas and finally the meal was served.

With Mr. Bingley and Elizabeth both present, conversation at the breakfast table was cheerful and animated. It was into this lively atmosphere that Miss Bingley arrived to make her grand entrance. She was dressed in a chartreuse gown, cut too low for daytime wear, which made her skin look quite sallow.

Those already at the table were so engrossed in their conversation, no one noticed her entrance or greeted her. She began to move to her place at the table on Darcy's right when she noticed it was already occupied by a rather attractive young woman dressed in half mourning. Refusing to take a lower place at the table, she turned around and stomped from the room. She returned to her room and screeched for the maid to attend her. Hannah timidly entered from the dressing room.

"Fetch me a tray of tea and toast, and be quick about it. When you return, lay out my riding habit. I will change for our outing as soon as I am done eating." The maid scurried off to do as she was bid.

After the group had finished dining, they moved to the music room, where Darcy had a surprise for his sister. When they opened the door, Georgiana gave a small cry and rushed forward. A new pianoforte stood where the old one had been just the previous evening.

"Oh, William, it is beautiful," cried Georgiana as she threw herself into her brother's arms and hugged him tightly.

189

William laughed as he caught her. "You are very welcome, Georgie, but I insist you play something for me immediately, so we may hear how it sounds."

The doors to the music room were closed as Georgiana took her place before the instrument. She ran her fingers lightly up and down the keys, playing a scale or two to get a feel for the instrument. Then she began to play a piece by Bach, which she knew well.

When the applause for her playing died down, she said, "Lizzy, will you please sing *The Last Rose of Summer*? I would love to hear how you sound with the new piano."

Elizabeth looked embarrassed by the request, but when Georgiana pleaded, "Please, for my birthday," she knew she could not refuse.

As Elizabeth's mesmerizing voice was heard, both Darcy and Bingley failed to note his sister's arrival in the doorway. She had not missed the soft look on Darcy's face as he stared at the young woman singing. The last notes died away, and the applause for the performance was quite loud.

"You must be the Miss Lucas about whom we have heard so much. It was so kind of you to finally allow Miss Darcy some time away from her studies," said Miss Bingley with sarcasm evident in her tone. "You have kept our dear friend away from her guests, which was badly done of you. And though you may possess some talent, it is quite indecorous of you to attempt to steal the attention from the birthday girl." Her voice dripped with disdain.

One could hear the indrawn breaths from those present. Elizabeth gave Georgianna a bright smile to show she was unaffected by the remark. "As Georgiana's companion, it is my responsibility to see she gains the education she will need for her future. Her study schedule is determined by Mr. Darcy and me with full input from Georgiana. Perhaps something she is studying at the moment was more important to her right now than other considerations." Darcy had to clear his throat to cover the laugh that tried to escape at Miss Lucas' words, while Georgiana smiled and nodded. "And as for my song, it was a request from Georgiana as a birthday gift."

"You are on very familiar terms with your charge. Do you always push yourself forward in such a way?"

Before Elizabeth could reply to this latest assault, Georgiana spoke up. "Miss Lucas, Rose is the dearest friend I have ever had. It was I who requested we address each other less formally, and my brother wholeheartedly supported my decision."

Darcy had to bite back the retort he wished to make, but he was pleased to see Georgiana stand up for her friend.

"If you will excuse me, *Miss* Bingley," Elizabeth said, "I shall go to change for our outing. Would you like to join me, Georgiana?" The young girl stepped up to take Elizabeth's arm, and together they left the room. Both were smiling and holding their heads high.

"She is quite impertinent for a servant. I would not tolerate such behavior in my home."

"It is fortunate, then, that this is not your home," said Darcy pithily as he followed the ladies from the room.

"Yes, but . . . but," stuttered Miss Bingley to his retreating back.

As Charles moved to pass his sister, he took a firm grip on her upper arm. "You will behave today, Caroline. It is Miss Darcy's birthday, and I will not have you ruin it. She is very fond of her companion, so keep your opinions of the woman to yourself. Do I make myself understood?"

Caroline jerked her arm away from her brother, saying, "Do not be ridiculous, Charles. I am always a perfect lady. And what does it matter what I say to a servant?"

"She is not just any servant, Caroline. She is a distant relation who came to stay with Georgiana as her companion when she lost her family in the accident Darcy mentioned."

Caroline looked at him askance. "A relation, you say? I thought his only cousins were Miss de Bourgh, the colonel, and the viscount. Where has this other supposed cousin come from?"

"That is none of your concern, Caroline. Now remember what I said and behave." Charles moved past his sister and mounted the stairs.

Caroline was furious. Georgiana Darcy's companion was an attractive, talented relative, and she was residing at Pemberley. Caroline did not like it one bit. She looked about for something to throw but realized she would most likely be heard if she threw something here. Caroline stormed back to her suite and grasped the first thing she could find, a small glass dish on a table near the door. She hurled it in the direction of the dressing room door just as it opened. Fortunately, it missed Hannah, but hit the doorframe and smashed into a thousand pieces. Some of the glass bounced back at the maid, small pieces lodging in both her cheek and forearm.

Not caring that she had hurt the young girl, Caroline screamed, "Clean up this mess before I return, you stupid girl," before turning and exiting the room.

Elizabeth had hurried through her toilet to find a moment to speak with Mr. Darcy. She rushed from the room without her gloves and moved down the hall to knock on the door to his sitting room. Darcy opened the door, surprise on his face at seeing who it was.

"Mr. Darcy, I know this may not be the best place to speak with you, but it is quite urgent, and I was not sure when I might get another opportunity."

"Has something happened? Is Georgiana alright?"

"Yes, sir, she is fine, but what I have to say does concern her."

Darcy turned into the room to call for Palmer, his valet. When the man arrived, he said, "Please stand at the open door to ensure no one comes near. Miss Lucas, please be seated." Darcy led her to a sofa in his sitting room and seated her, taking a seat nearby so they could speak confidentially. "Please, Miss Lucas, feel free to speak. I wish to know what concerns you."

"It is actually concern for you and Georgiana that causes me to speak. And because I believe I know your feelings for Miss Bingley, I hope you will not find my behavior an impertinence," said Elizabeth by way of preamble. She went on to relate to Darcy all she had heard from Mr. Bingley's sisters the previous day in the library. By the time she finished speaking, Elizabeth was very uneasy. Darcy's face was a mixture of emotions, of which anger seemed to be the primary one. He spoke not a word as he attempted to master them.

Finally, his face appeared calmer and he spoke. "I thank you very much for the information, Miss Lucas, and I appreciate your taking the opportunity to relay it to me. I can assure you, Miss Lucas, you have no need to worry. I will take all necessary steps to ensure I am not alone with Miss Bingley, and I can promise you I would never agree to send my sister away for any reason." He stood and offered her an arm as they moved toward the sitting room door. "Now, shall we join the others for our ride?"

"I shall join you momentarily. I must retrieve my gloves first."

Hannah knew the master and his guests would soon be leaving, so she hurried to Miss Lucas' room so her sister could help her remove the glass shards and tend to the wounds. She arrived in the dressing room to find Lucy alone.

Lucy cried out, "Hannah, you are hurt! What happened?"

"Miss Bingley was upset about something and threw a glass object at the door just as I opened it. Fortunately, her aim is poor, and it hit the doorframe beside my face. However, some of the glass bounced back at me rather forcefully. Could you help me with my wounds before I clean up the rest of the glass?"

Unbeknownst to either girl, Elizabeth had opened the door to the dressing room to retrieve her forgotten gloves and heard all that was said. When she spoke, her voice startled the sisters and made them jump. "Here, Lucy, I have some tweezers in my dressing table. Allow me to get the glass out while you get water and something to apply to the cuts. You should probably have Mrs. Reynolds take a look. I believe Hannah may need stitches for at least one of these cuts. I can take care of them if Mrs. Reynolds has the supplies."

"I can deal with it, Miss Lucas. You may get blood on your habit if you help me."

"Do not worry about that. Caring for your sister is what matters. If we both do something, she will be cared for more quickly."

After a moment's hesitation, Lucy hurried to the kitchen to get fresh water and clean rags. Elizabeth had all the glass removed from the wounds by the time her maid returned with the housekeeper in tow.

"Thank you for your help, Miss Lucas," said Lucy, out of breath, "but you had best leave now. I believe the others are already gathered in the hall."

"Is there someone here who can stitch up a wound, Mrs. Reynolds? If there is not, I would be happy to do so. I was trained by the apothecary back home in the proper way to place stitches."

"Yes, Miss Lucas, I will tend to things from here. You go on, as the others are waiting."

Elizabeth glanced about for her gloves and began pulling them on as she spoke. "Very well, then. I hope you will be feeling better soon, Hannah." The door closed behind her, leaving the two young women looking after her in astonishment.

It was Hannah who broke the silence, saying, "She must be the kindest young lady I have ever met."

"That she is, sister, and I must say it is a pleasure to serve someone who treats me kindly and is not above being friendly to a servant."

"She is a very fine lady, indeed," added the housekeeper.

Elizabeth arrived at the top of the stairs just as Georgiana was about to go look for her. Darcy moved to make his way to Elizabeth, only to be stopped by the clinging arms of Miss Bingley. Georgiana moved towards her companion, asking "Is everything well, Lizzy?"

While keeping her eyes focused on Caroline Bingley, Elizabeth replied, "Of course, Georgiana. I was just helping tend to one of the maids who was cut by glass *someone* thoughtlessly broke."

"Will the maid be well?" asked Darcy in concern. "Do we need to send for the doctor to attend her?"

Elizabeth transferred her gaze to Darcy. "I do not believe that will be necessary, Mr. Darcy. I had one of the other maids fetch Mrs. Reynolds. She assures me she can handle the stitches that will be required to close one of the wounds." Darcy relaxed at her words. It was obvious to Elizabeth that he cared deeply for those under his protection.

Darcy had finally managed to detach Miss Bingley from his arm and move away. "Shall we make our way to the stables, then?" He offered an arm to Georgiana and another to Elizabeth as he exited the house in the direction of the stables.

The horses had been prepared for the riders. As Georgiana and Elizabeth arrived at the stables, they released Mr. Darcy's arms and moved to speak to their mounts. Elizabeth stood before Gambit and offered her a treat from her pocket. Gambit ate it from her palm and then nuzzled her shoulder. Darcy knew Miss Lucas had visited Gambit at the stables while the others were out riding, but he could tell how much the horse had missed their rides. Gambit was excited, and Darcy hoped she would not be too much of a handful for Miss Lucas to manage.

Miss Bingley immediately turned her sights on Darcy, again attaching herself to his arm. "Oh, Mr. Darcy, how exciting our outing will be. Tell me again where we are going."

"We will ride to the ruins of an old monastery, where we will enjoy a picnic lunch."

By this time, they had arrived near the horses. Caroline looked at Miss Lucas and the beautiful gray horse. The first thing she noticed was the similarity of their habits, though Miss Lucas' was decidedly plain. Caroline's habit also had a plain black skirt, but the jacket was her favorite shade of burnt orange with massive quantities of gold braid upon it. To accompany it she had chosen a tall top hat, which sported two burnt orange ostrich plumes. She also noted the affection between the horse and rider and decided to make trouble.

"I believe I should like to ride the beautiful gray today," she stated as she marched over to Gambit and tugged the reins from Elizabeth's hands. She attempted to pull Gambit towards the mounting block near the riding ring, but the horse preferred to stay with Elizabeth. Caroline gave Elizabeth a supercilious look and in a falsely sweet voice said, "You do not mind if I ride this horse, do you, Miss Lucas?"

Elizabeth patted Gambit's nose and whispered, "Be good," as she replied, "Not at all, Miss Bingley."

Again she tried to pull the horse to the mounting block. Gambit grudgingly followed.

Darcy attempted to step in, not wishing Elizabeth to be deprived of her mount. "I believe, Miss Bingley, you are better suited to ride Bramble. You have had no complaints with her so far."

"I assure you, Mr. Darcy, I can handle any horse a servant can manage."

Stifling his anger, Darcy tried again. "It is just that Gambit has not been ridden in a few days. She may be a bit frisky today."

"As I said, I am capable of controlling any mount that would be suitable for the likes of Miss Lucas."

Darcy was about to try again when Bingley forestalled him. "Here, Caroline. I will give you a leg up and lead you into the ring where you can get the feel of your mount before we begin our adventure." He moved over and assisted his sister into the saddle. Then he led her into the soft dirt of the riding ring and handed her the reins.

She nudged the horse with her heel, but Gambit did not move. Caroline took her crop and, with all her might, smacked the horse several times on the flank. Gambit neighed and reared up on her hind legs, unseating Caroline Bingley, who landed with a hard thump on her derriere.

Caroline cried out in pain and screamed at the horse, who merely trotted over to Elizabeth and nuzzled her shoulder. Elizabeth buried her face in the horse's neck so no one would see the smile on her face. Georgiana, Darcy, Bingley, and Mr. Hurst all had to hide smiles of their own.

Without making any attempt to conceal his smile further, Mr. Hurst grabbed his wife's hand and led her to the ring. He assisted Caroline to her feet and said, "Louisa and I will help you to the house, Caroline. The others can ride without us today."

"That horse is a menace," cried Miss Bingley as they moved past Elizabeth and Gambit. "She should be put down."

Gambit sidestepped her back feet towards Miss Bingley, causing her to give a shriek of fear. With a look over his shoulder, Hurst gave the others a wink and a smile. As they moved off towards the house, Miss Bingley saw Mr. Darcy lifting Miss Lucas onto the gray's saddle. She leaned over and patted the horse, whispering something to it that caused all the others to laugh. The laughter floated on the breeze to Caroline, increasing her anger.

When she was back in her room with her sister beside her, Caroline burst out, "It is all that Miss Lucas' fault. She must have told the horse to misbehave. Perhaps she hurt her somehow."

"It was not anything Miss Lucas did, Caroline. You tried to ride a horse you could not handle and then struck the poor animal. That is why she dumped you to the ground."

"How mean you are, Louisa! I am in pain, and she is out there spending time with my Mr. Darcy. I must do something to stop it!"

"The best thing you can do is lie still and rest. As it is, you may have a difficult time sitting down to join us for dinner." Fortunately, Miss Bingley's eyes were closed, for she would have been exceedingly wroth had she seen the smile that graced her sister's face.

14. A BIRTHDAY DINNER

WHEN THE RIDERS RETURNED FROM THEIR outing, Caroline could hear the sound of their happy laughter from the hallway. Noting Mr. Darcy's rich, deep laugh among the sounds made her even more angry. She had to find something about Miss Lucas she could use to embarrass her in front of Mr. Darcy. Thinking Georgiana too naive to perceive anything unusual in her questions, she wrote a note requesting that Miss Darcy come to visit her as soon as she was changed. When her maid arrived, Caroline noted the bandages covering her cuts. Feeling no remorse for the injuries she caused, she merely said, "Deliver this to Miss Darcy and be quick about it."

Hannah bobbed a quick curtsey and nearly ran from the room.

When Georgiana had finished freshening up from their ride, she entered their shared sitting room with a note in her hand. "Why the long face, Georgiana?" her companion asked.

She dropped down in a chair before she said, "Miss Bingley begs me to visit, as she must rest until dinner if she wishes to be well enough to join us."

"Perhaps you could take a book and offer to read to her so you will not have to converse," suggested Elizabeth.

"Would you perhaps ask Mrs. Reynolds to come for me in fifteen minutes, certainly no more than half an hour, with a household issue I must address? I am sure I can manage to endure her company when I know it will be over soon." The two young ladies looked at each other before their suppressed giggles could no longer be contained.

Darcy was passing by in the hallway when he heard the sound of their laughter. Wishing to share in their joy, he knocked on the door. Georgiana opened it with a smile still gracing her face.

"The sound of your delightful laughter made me wish to join you. Do you mind?"

"Of course we would not mind, Fitzwilliam, but Miss Bingley has asked that I come and sit with her a while." Georgiana looked as though she were heading for the guillotine, not to a guest room down the hall.

"I shall be sure you are rescued soon, Georgie. Have no fear."

At his words, the two young women looked at each other and began to giggle again. Darcy looked between the two in confusion. Finally, Georgiana wiped the tears from her eyes and said, "I shall leave Rose to explain things to you as I head into the lion's den."

Darcy stepped aside and allowed his sister to pass. Then he looked again at Elizabeth and said, "Would you care to join me in the library, Miss Lucas? I look forward to your explanation of the merriment."

"I should be delighted to do so, Mr. Darcy."

When they arrived in the library, they took seats near the large window. Elizabeth seated herself on the sofa in front the window, while Darcy took the seat across from her. As she began to explain the cause of their laughter, Darcy was mesmerized. The sunlight coming through the window shone brightly around Miss Lucas. It glimmered on her hair, showing the many colors that made up her magnificent curls. It also suffused her skin with a warm golden glow that reflected in the sparkle of her eyes. As she reached the end of her tale, Darcy could not help but laugh.

Hearing the sound of the laughter coming from the library, Bingley stuck his head in the door. "I wondered where everyone went. What had you laughing?"

His question set Darcy and Elizabeth to laughing again. When Darcy regained control of his mirth, he explained that his sister had been requested by Miss Bingley to visit with her.

"We have to rescue Miss Darcy. How long has she been there?" Bingley's remark caused another round of laughter. Through his laughter, Darcy finished his story. By the end, Bingley was laughing with them.

When the three had finally stopped laughing, Mr. Darcy challenged his friend to a game of billiards. With a bow to Elizabeth, the gentlemen left the room. Elizabeth rang for Mrs. Reynolds, then picked up her book to read while she waited.

At Georgiana's hesitant knock on the door, Hannah opened it quickly. Georgiana noticed the bandages and the girl's frightened look.

Caroline's voice cut across her thoughts. "Leave, girl," she barked at the maid, who quickly fled the room. "My dear Miss Darcy, how kind of you to visit me."

"I hope you are feeling better, Miss Bingley."

"I am as well as can be expected after such an awful experience. You must have your brother put down that animal before she hurts someone else."

Miss Bingley's tone caused Georgiana to rush to the animal's defense. "No one has ever had to use a crop on Gambit; perhaps it startled her. She is an excellent horse, and we have never had trouble with her before."

A look of irritation passed over Caroline's face, but she quickly recovered and offered her guest a seat. Georgiana took the seat indicated, but perched on the edge as if in preparation for a hasty departure.

"What have you been learning that has taken so much of your attention of late?"

Knowing Miss Bingley did not like Rose, Georgiana thought carefully before answering. "We have been reading a new novel, but I must translate it into French before reading each sentence. We have also been studying the battles taking place in the war against Napoleon and using them as a geography lesson. And, of course, I practice my music many hours a day."

"I have never heard such ridiculousness. Certainly your brother cannot approve of this. Did he thoroughly check Miss Lucas' credentials? She hardly seems old enough for such an important position. How do you know she is not some adventuress out to capture your brother?"

"Actually, my brother is very impressed with her teaching methods. She manages to make learning interesting and relevant to what is happening around us. My fluency in and understanding of French grammar is also much improved, as is my Italian, which Miss Lucas also speaks. Even practicing my music is more enjoyable, for I have the opportunity to play with her and to learn to accompany someone who is singing. As Miss Lucas is a distant cousin who is recently orphaned, there is no doubt she is not an adventuress. Both William and I have much experience in spotting those," said Georgiana dryly.

"If she was a poor relation, how did she become so well educated? I would hate to think someone was taking advantage of my two dearest friends. I am only concerned about you both," was Miss Bingley's blatantly untrue response.

A knock came at the door, and Georgiana jumped to answer it. Seeing Mrs. Reynolds, Georgiana smiled in relief, but only the housekeeper could see her expression.

"I am sorry to interrupt, but there is a matter that requires your attention, Miss Darcy."

Georgiana turned back to Miss Bingley. "Please excuse me, Miss Bingley, but I must attend to household matters. Will you be joining us for tea or just for dinner?"

"I believe I will rest until dinner," Caroline pouted.

"I will be sure someone brings you a tea tray." Georgiana stepped into the hallway and, after closing the door, wrapped Mrs. Reynolds in a big hug. "Thank you for rescuing me! Do you know where I might find Rose?"

"I believe she is reading in the library, waiting for you to join her." With another quick hug for the housekeeper, Georgiana rushed down the hall to the library.

"Thank goodness that is over," said Georgiana as she dropped onto the sofa beside Elizabeth.

Elizabeth laughed softly. "What did you talk about?"

"You, mostly."

Elizabeth became unsettled at Georgiana's response. "What could she possibly want to know about me?" came her hesitant question.

"She kept asking what your qualifications are and from where you came. She accused you of being an adventuress trying to take advantage of us."

At that, Elizabeth had the grace to blush slightly, but Georgiana failed to notice. Elizabeth often felt guilty for being at Pemberley without having told the Darcys the entire truth. However, she reminded herself that harm could come to them if Mr. Collins knew they had assisted her. She promised herself she would tell them the truth as soon as it was safe. She prayed she would retain their friendship and good opinion.

The group had just settled in the drawing room for tea when Caroline Bingley waddled in. Her backside was stiff and sore, and it gave her a distinctive gait. She paused in the doorway for effect before announcing she could not let a little injury keep her away from her dearest Georgiana on such a special day. As she looked about for a seat, she was disturbed to see Miss Lucas seated beside Miss Darcy, with no room for her. She was forced to sit on the opposite sofa with Louisa and her husband.

When the tea tray and refreshments were brought in, the maid, Sally, who was new to service, bumped the tray against the table, causing the dishes to rattle loudly. Caroline Bingley cast a fierce look at the nervous young woman, saying, "Be careful, you foolish girl, you might break something." Then she turned to Darcy and suggested he dismiss the girl from service.

Poor Sally was near to tears, so Elizabeth turned to the maid, gave her a large smile, and softly commented, "It is quite alright, Sally; there was no harm done."

Sally cast a relieved look at Elizabeth and said, "Thank you, miss."

Mrs. Reynolds, who had followed the maid to observe, cast a grateful look at Elizabeth for her kindness. She bustled forward and took the maid's arm to lead her from the room.

Miss Bingley turned to stare at Elizabeth, her eyes sparking in anger. "How dare you contradict me—especially in front of the servants!" she cried angrily. With a sneer, she continued. "Perhaps I should not be surprised. Servants always look out for each other."

She looked as if she would say more, but Darcy spoke up. "It appears, Miss Bingley, that you require more rest to recover from your accident. Please allow Mrs. Reynolds to show you to your room *immediately*. I will have tea sent up to you." Darcy stood, pulled up Miss Bingley by her elbow, and led her to the hall.

Rather than recognizing Mr. Darcy's anger, Miss Bingley took his attentions as a compliment towards herself and assurance he would soon ask for her hand . . . perhaps that very day.

Mrs. Reynolds had settled Sally and sent the maid back to the kitchen. She was still in the hallway when her master suddenly appeared with Miss Bingley. Noting the housekeeper, Darcy said, "Miss Bingley seems to be out of spirits. Would you please accompany her to her room and have some tea sent to her? She will be remaining in her room until dinner."

Darcy's voice was cold, and the housekeeper could tell he was angry, though the woman whose arm he held was completely oblivious to his true emotions. She preened, and a superior smile could be observed on her face. However, she was surprised when Darcy abruptly departed her presence without a word.

When Darcy returned, Bingley gave him a shrug and rolled his eyes. Georgiana began pouring out the tea for the remaining guests and a pleasant conversation ensued.

Elizabeth had just finished dressing for dinner and sat waiting in the sitting room for Georgiana to join her. That night, in honor of Georgiana's birthday, she was wearing a pale lavender evening gown. The gown was very simple, with a square neckline front and back that showed off Elizabeth's décolletage to best advantage. There was a pale gray, almost silvery, lace edging the neckline and the short, puffed sleeves. Some of the same lace was threaded through her curls. Elizabeth's only adornments were a pair of pearl drop earrings and a single pearl on a chain that rested just above her bosom. Due to the warmth of the evening, she needed no wrap.

Elizabeth had not been waiting long when Georgiana stepped through the door. She was wearing the new pink silk dress they had purchased on their trip to Lambton.

"You look lovely, Georgiana! Your new dress turned out very well, and it suits you perfectly. You are a young woman on the cusp of the most exhilarating time in your life. Are you excited?"

"About some things, yes. It will be fun to go out more in company, but I do not wish to debut for at least two more years. I know many young ladies come out when they are seventeen, but I would prefer to wait. I do not wish to be courted yet, and it will be expected if I am presented."

"I am sure your brother will consider your wishes in this matter. Is there any particular reason you do not wish to be courted?" Georgiana had never opened up to Elizabeth about what had occurred at Ramsgate, but she hoped they had become close enough that the young lady would now be comfortable doing so.

"Perhaps we could talk about it after the Bingleys have departed," said Georgiana diffidently.

"I would be happy to speak with you whenever you wish," replied Elizabeth with a squeeze of her charge's hand.

A knock was heard at the door, and Georgiana opened it to find her brother. "I am here to escort the two loveliest ladies of Pemberley to dinner." Georgiana gave a laugh, and Elizabeth smiled delightedly as a rosy blush covered her cheeks. He held out an arm to each and led them towards the stairs.

Darcy entered the drawing room with a young lady on each arm. Caroline Bingley looked up eagerly, having heard the sound of Mr. Darcy's footsteps. Her words of greeting died in her throat when she saw the three enter the room. Darcy had his sister on one arm and the companion on the other. A lovely blush suffused Miss Lucas' face, and Miss Darcy was happily smiling at both of them.

Caroline's jealousy was aroused. Her eyes narrowed when she saw Darcy escorting the woman she considered no more than a servant. She did not seriously believe Darcy would consider the servant for more than an illicit relationship. However, she wished to have his total focus until she had secured his proposal. Once she was Mrs. Darcy, she did not care if he kept a mistress. She would take no chances. *A compromise will occur tonight! Darcy and Pemberley will be mine!*

She schooled her features and spoke. "Good evening, Mr. Darcy, Miss Darcy. How lovely you look this evening, Miss Darcy. That dress is exquisite! You have such excellent taste. Perhaps when you are next in London, you will come shopping with me. I am sure I would enjoy having your opinions on my gowns." In actuality, Caroline thought the gown dreadfully plain. There were no flounces and very little lace to make it fashionable. *Why is she dressed no better than the companion?*

Darcy and the ladies had not had an opportunity to sit down before Jeffers appeared and announced that dinner was served. Because the ladies were still on his arm, Darcy looked at his guests and said, "Please follow us," as he moved towards the dining room.

Bingley took Caroline's arm and led her to the dining table. He moved into the dining room following Darcy. Leaving his sister's side, Bingley pulled out the chair for Miss Darcy to be seated. Seeing that his sister was being attended to, Darcy moved around the table and seated Elizabeth on his left.

Caroline's mouth fell open in shock. Before she could cause trouble, Charles took her around the table and seated her on the same side as Miss Lucas, then settled himself between the two women. Mr. Hurst sat next to Miss Darcy with his wife on his other side.

Darcy realized placing Miss Lucas to his left while guests were present might not be appropriate, but he did not believe he had the patience to deal with Miss Bingley's behavior through another meal. He knew Miss Lucas' presence would make Miss Bingley more difficult than usual. Consequently, Darcy addressed his guests and said, "I hope you all forgive the informality of tonight's seating arrangement. It was Georgiana's wish for her birthday that we sit as we usually do when no guests are present."

From the far end of the table came the shrill voice of Caroline Bingley. "I would be happy to instruct Miss Darcy on proper seating arrangements during my stay. I imagine Miss Lucas has not had occasion to visit or observe how things are done in Miss Darcy's social circle. One cannot teach what one does not know, after all."

Darcy's tone was cool when he replied, "That will not be necessary, Miss Bingley. Miss Lucas is a distant cousin, and she knows all that is necessary for a properly brought up young lady." Darcy signaled for the first course to be served. Bingley, Darcy, Georgiana, and Elizabeth began a lively discussion that lasted the entire meal.

Because of her location at the table, Miss Bingley was not able to easily hear or participate in the conversation taking place around Mr. Darcy. Mrs. Hurst could see her sister's anger growing. She hoped Caroline would control her tongue following the meal, but she doubted that would be the case.

When the meal ended, Elizabeth nodded to Georgiana, reminding her that she should lead the ladies to withdraw. Georgiana understood her responsibility and invited the ladies to join her in the music room. Elizabeth stood to rise and join Georgiana, but Miss Bingley rushed around the table to take Georgiana's arm and practically drag her from the room. Elizabeth allowed Mrs. Hurst to precede her and followed the other ladies to the music room.

As she passed the grand staircase, Elizabeth realized she needed to return to her room to retrieve Georgiana's gifts. As she entered her bedchamber and crossed to the table where the gift lay, she heard sobbing coming from her dressing room.

Opening the door, she saw Lucy and Hannah. Hannah was softly crying, her face twisted in pain. Lucy held one of her sister's arms. Several wet rags rested across Hannah's arms, and Lucy was looking at a bright red mark that appeared there.

"Hannah, what has happened? Are those burn marks?" asked Elizabeth with concern.

Hannah was crying too hard to answer, but her head gave a barely perceptible nod. Lucy turned to Elizabeth with a tear-streaked face. "Miss Bingley said Hannah was too slow fixing her hair and struck her arms with the hot iron. Then she made her finish her hair before letting her get care for them. Hannah was so frightened of Miss Bingley's anger; she even picked the room up before coming to me." Lucy's anger was palpable and justified, stirring Elizabeth to action.

"Lucy, take Hannah to the sofa in my room and sit with her," Elizabeth commanded. She opened her bedroom door and asked a passing maid to fetch Mrs. Reynolds and her medicine bag. She then turned to the nearby footman and asked that he fetch Mr. Darcy.

Elizabeth remained in the hallway, awaiting Mrs. Reynolds. The woman came down the hallway carrying her bag and breathlessly spoke. "Miss Lucas, are you hurt, or Miss Georgiana? They said I was needed with my medical bags."

"No, Mrs. Reynolds, Georgiana and I are fine, but you are most definitely needed." Elizabeth opened the door to her bedroom, then led Mrs. Reynolds inside and to the sofa where the two maids sat. At first Mrs. Reynolds was disturbed to see the girls sitting in Miss Lucas' room. Before she could scold them, Elizabeth said, "Hannah has received several burns to her arm from the curling tongs. Would you be so kind as to care for her and see her put to bed to rest? I shall be right outside."

The gentlemen were lounging in their chairs, a glass of brandy in hand, when Charles spoke. "If that is the kind of dinner conversation you are treated to each day, it is no wonder you did not wish a more formal arrangement. Miss Darcy is usually so quiet when we visit, I had no idea she had such a delightful sense of humor. And Miss Lucas, what a pleasant young lady! You were very fortunate to find her."

A small smile played over Darcy's face. "I was indeed, Bingley, I was indeed."

Bingley was surprised at the soft look on his friend's face. It was certainly not one he could remember seeing in the past.

A footman entered and whispered something in Darcy's ear. The smile evaporated quickly as Darcy said, "Excuse me for a moment, gentlemen." Darcy hurried after the footman, leaving the gentlemen looking at one another in confusion.

Within another moment, Mr. Darcy arrived. "Miss Lucas, what has happened? Where is Georgiana?" asked Darcy with mounting concern.

"I believe she is in the music room with your other quests. If you would please step into my bedchamber, Mrs. Reynolds is tending to an injured servant."

Darcy looked surprised at her words but quickly followed her. When they entered, Darcy saw the two maids with Mrs. Reynolds kneeling before one of them, examining the wounds on both the girl's arms.

"What has caused the injury, Mrs. Reynolds?" asked Darcy in his Master of Pemberley voice.

"The girl has received several burns, sir, but I cannot get her to tell me the cause," replied the housekeeper.

"She is afraid of losing her position. That is why she will not speak against one of your guests, Mr. Darcy." Elizabeth's voice was firm and strong, and she faced her employer in righteous indignation.

"What are you saying, Miss Lucas?"

"Do you remember that I helped a servant earlier?"

Darcy nodded.

"Earlier today, probably shortly after our conversation with Miss Bingley in the music room, I believe she returned to her room to vent her anger. She threw a glass object at the dressing room door as poor Hannah opened it to enter the room. Fortunately for Hannah, the object hit the doorframe, but the shattering glass embedded pieces in her cheek and arm. I sent Lucy for water and bandages while I removed the pieces of glass from her flesh before joining you. This evening, Miss Bingley complained that Hannah was too slow at arranging her hair. She grabbed the hot tongs and smacked Hannah's arms several times, burning them. You can even see that the skin is beginning to blister." Elizabeth's chest heaved in her disapprobation.

Elizabeth could tell Darcy was once again attempting to control his anger before speaking. "Mrs. Reynolds, please do your best to tend to Hannah and then put her to bed. If the physician is needed, do not hesitate to send for him," Darcy said.

"Yes, sir. Miss Lucas has already asked me to attend to just that." The housekeeper looked at her employer proudly, pleased with the young lady's concern for the servants.

"Come, Miss Lucas, join me for a long-overdue conversation."

Darcy asked the footman outside the study to fetch Mr. Bingley and to ask Mr. Bingley to bring Miss Bingley to his study. The footman moved off to do as directed. Darcy opened the door of the study and allowed Elizabeth to enter before him. He positioned a chair next to his desk and asked Elizabeth to be seated.

The footman gave Mr. Bingley the message, and he went to the music room. When he announced that Mr. Darcy wished to see them in his study, Caroline's face beamed and a large smile appeared. Georgiana, on the other hand, became frighteningly pale.

When Bingley and Caroline entered the library, Miss Bingley's smile faltered when she saw Miss Lucas seated beside Darcy's desk. When the newcomers had taken their seats, Darcy stared at them for a moment before speaking.

"Do you allow the abuse of servants in your home on a regular basis, Bingley?"

"I say, Darcy, what are you implying? I would not tolerate the ill use of my servants. What do you take me for?" cried Bingley angrily.

"I take you for a good man but have to wonder if you know what goes on in your home. Does Miss Bingley have trouble maintaining a lady's maid?"

"Well, yes, she does, but what are you going on about, Darcy?"

"Twice today the maid who has been attending your sister has been injured at her hands."

Bingley looked appalled. Caroline cried, "The girl is a liar, Mr. Darcy. I came upon her cleaning up some glass she had broken this morning, and she dropped the curling tongs when fixing my hair. It was fortunate I was not burned. You could not possibly take the word of a servant over mine!"

The callousness of the woman filled Darcy with disgust. "Things could not have happened as you say, Miss Bingley. The girl's injuries prove that. Your maid is the sister to Miss Lucas' maid and she overheard the sisters speaking as one tended to the other. You also broke a valuable piece of crystal in your anger. Such behavior may be acceptable in some places, but it is *not* here at Pemberley. Please return to your room and remain there. You will be leaving my home tomorrow and are no longer welcome here at Pemberley or my house in town."

Caroline stood, shaking with anger. She pointed her finger at Elizabeth and screamed out. "You lying harlot! You are lying to get me out of your way. She knows about your feelings for me and is trying to get rid of me. She is stupid enough to think you would condescend to marry a servant or is determined to trap you in a forced marriage."

216

Elizabeth's face flamed in outrage and embarrassment.

"I would be stupid only if I condescended to marry a manipulative and heartless tradesman's daughter like you. Miss Lucas' actions today show she is indeed fit to be the mistress of a fine estate and to care for the welfare of its people, as she was raised to be. You, on the other hand, are not fit to work as a scullery maid in my home. Now you can retire to your room for the night and remain there until you depart, or I will have you driven to Lambton with only the clothes on your back, and you may take the stage to London. I care not so long as I never set eyes on you again." Darcy turned to look at his friend, saying, "I am sorry to be harsh, Bingley, but I cannot tolerate her behavior any longer, and I will not have the people under my stewardship mistreated."

Caroline was furious that Mr. Darcy had taken the word of two servants—for that was how she saw Miss Lucas—over herself. Miss Bingley leaned over Darcy's desk, getting as close to his face as she could before angrily screeching, "You will regret this, Mr. Darcy! That hussy will be the ruin of you!"

Darcy marched to the door and opened it to nod at the two footmen stationed in the hallway. "Please escort Miss Bingley to her rooms and ensure she remains within. She will be departing at first light."

Darcy remained near the door, waiting for her to exit, but Caroline only stood and stared at Miss Lucas, who turned towards one of the windows. Fighting to contain her fury was a losing battle. She had been spoiled all of her life, by her parents, her elder sister, and her younger brother. She could not believe a maid and companion had cost her the thing she most desired—Mr. Darcy and Pemberley—and she would not stand for it.

Looking over the desk, Caroline reached for the letter opener she saw lying there. She picked it up and began to raise her arm to throw the small knife-like object at her nemesis. Fortunately, Mr. Bingley grabbed her wrist and squeezed until she dropped the item on the desk.

Her brother whispered in her ear, "Have you completely lost your mind? You cannot hurl a knife at someone; you could kill them! What were you thinking?" Moving his grip to her elbow, he excused himself to escort his sister to her room, saying he would join the others in the music room shortly. Bingley was practically forced to drag her from the room, and they were followed up the stairs by the footmen, who remained in the hall. Fortunately for Caroline, Mr. Darcy had not seen her attempted attack on Miss Lucas.

Darcy rang for Mrs. Reynolds, who appeared promptly.

"How is Hannah?"

"I have sent for the doctor. I do not like the way the skin is blistering. Burns can be painful and easily infected. I am not comfortable treating burns as severe as the ones Hannah received."

"Very well," said her master. "Would you please send two or three of the most experienced maids to Miss Bingley's room to pack her belongings? Based on her behavior when she left this room, her mood will be wretched. I do not wish to have only one person there to do the work, as she may harm someone else in her anger. However, I believe Miss Lucas and I must quickly join the others in the music room. I would not wish to have this upset Georgiana's birthday celebration."

"I will send my assistant, Miss Watson, to oversee the maids and keep an eye on Miss Bingley as her belongings are packed."

"Excellent. Now, if you would excuse us." Darcy held out his arm to escort Miss Lucas to the music room.

Georgiana entertained Mr. and Mrs. Hurst on the piano as they waited for the others to return. She looked up as she heard the door open and saw her brother enter with Miss Lucas on his arm. However, Mr. and Miss Bingley were nowhere in sight. The two newcomers gave her a warm smile, which allowed Georgiana to relax. She brought her song to a close and received delighted applause and compliments on her abilities.

"Thank you again, William, for my wonderful gift. The new pianoforte plays beautifully."

"You are most welcome, Georgie. I am sorry for the delay; there was a small household emergency of which Miss Lucas made me aware. I am afraid Miss Bingley has retired with a headache. Bingley escorted her to her room and he should join us shortly." Darcy rang for a servant and asked for the tea, coffee, and dessert to be brought to the music room.

The servant arrived with the tea tray, followed by Mrs. Reynolds carrying a beautiful birthday cake for Georgiana. Bingley trailed behind the refreshments. Elizabeth offered to serve the tea and coffee in honor of Georgiana's birthday, and Mrs. Reynolds cut and served the cake.

Once everyone had finished their food, Elizabeth handed Georgiana her gift. Opening it,

Georgiana found a beautiful dark blue leather-bound journal with her name embossed in gold letters. Elizabeth had also taken the time to embroider several handkerchiefs with her initials encased in a ring of flowers. "Oh, Rose, this is wonderful! Thank you so much," enthused Georgiana.

Mr. Bingley presented her with a pale blue silk shawl embroidered with small pink flowers, from Caroline and him. The Hursts had purchased a small bottle of perfume in a delicate floral fragrance. It was not long afterward that last wishes for a joyous birthday were offered to Georgiana and most of the guests retired for the night. Georgiana and Elizabeth linked arms and went to their sitting room.

When they were comfortably settled on the sofa, Georgiana spoke. "I have always wished for a journal, but did not know what I would write in it."

"I have kept one as long as I can remember," answered Elizabeth. "I was able to bring only my most recent volume with me when I left my home. I asked a friend to hold the others for safekeeping. I hope someday to retrieve them from her. I have always found it useful to have an outlet for my hopes, dreams, thoughts, anger, and frustrations that was safe and private. It is a place where I can say what I truly think and feel. Now that you are almost grown and will someday be coming out into society, I am sure you will have many experiences to write about," declared Elizabeth with a smile.

"I may have something to write about tonight if you will answer a question," Georgiana said timidly.

"What question is that?"

"Do you know why my brother invited Mr. and Miss Bingley to his study tonight?"

"I do."

"Please tell me he did not propose to Miss Bingley," said Georgie with a worried expression.

Elizabeth laughed. "He most definitely did not!"

"Will you tell me what happened?"

"I will, but only if you promise not to allow it to ruin your joy in this day."

"I promise."

"Twice today, Miss Bingley has caused injury to the girl who has been serving as her lady's maid during her stay." Elizabeth went on to tell Georgiana of the two incidents and the injuries Hannah had sustained.

"Oh, the poor girl," said Miss Darcy. "Is there anything I can do?"

"No, the doctor was sent for, but if you would not mind, I would like to ring for Mrs. Reynolds to find out what the doctor said about her injuries."

Georgiana jumped up and reached for the bell cord. It was not long before the housekeeper appeared.

"Thank you for coming, Mrs. Reynolds. I wondered if you could tell me what the doctor said regarding Hannah's wounds. Will she make a complete recovery?" Elizabeth's concern was obvious to the housekeeper.

"It is hoped so, Miss Lucas. The doctor is concerned she may take an infection, which could be quite serious. The burns must be treated, and the bandages changed twice daily. It could take as long as two weeks before it will be sufficiently healed to no longer need bandaging, but Dr. Powell said we would have to wait and see."

"Please let me know if there is anything I can do to assist in her care," came Elizabeth's sincere offer.

"If you do not mind my saying so, you have already done a great deal. It was very brave of you to stand up for Hannah against one of Mr. Darcy's guests. It is not the first time Miss Bingley has mistreated a servant during her stay, but this is by far the most harmful thing she has done. Lucy and Hannah asked me in particular to tell you how much they appreciate your kindness, as do all the servants. You have been kind and considerate of everyone with whom you have come in contact here at Pemberley. It shows what a fine young lady you are."

Elizabeth was embarrassed by the housekeeper's words and sought to change the direction of the conversation. "Thank you again for coming to answer my questions, Mrs. Reynolds. As I said, I would be happy to assist in her care if it is needed. Is there someone to sit with her tonight?"

"That will not be necessary. The doctor gave her some laudanum, and Lucy shares a room with her sister, so she will know if Hannah needs anything during the night."

"Good night, Mrs. Reynolds," said Georgiana as the housekeeper turned to depart. After the door had closed, Georgiana turned to Elizabeth with wide eyes. "What exactly did you say to my brother, and what did he say to Miss Bingley?"

Elizabeth relayed the entire story to Georgiana about how she had discovered the two injuries and sent for Mr. Darcy. She continued with how the maids had been afraid to say what had happened and that she was the one to tell Mr. Darcy what she had overheard about how Hannah came to be injured. Then she told Georgiana of the conversation in the study, ending with the fact that Miss Bingley had been asked to leave in the morning and denied admittance to any of the Darcy homes in the future.

"Thank goodness," said Georgiana in relief, causing Elizabeth to laugh. "I know it may not be polite, but Miss Bingley is a sore trial. She is so forceful and unkind. I am quite relieved I will not often be in her company again!" Georgiana leaned over and gave Elizabeth a hug. "Good night, Rose. Will you please join us for breakfast since Miss Bingley will be departing?"

"I will if she has left, but I would not wish to be the cause of any unpleasantness if she is in attendance. Good night, Georgiana. I hope you enjoyed your birthday."

In Darcy's study, the two gentlemen enjoyed a glass of brandy. Neither had spoken much since they moved from the music room, but Darcy had watched the myriad of emotions that crossed his friend's face. "All right, Bingley, what is troubling you?" he finally asked.

"I hardly know what to say, Darcy. I had no idea Caroline treated the servants so dreadfully. Why has my housekeeper never mentioned the issue to me before?"

"Well, in your household, Caroline runs the house and deals with the staff. Perhaps the housekeeper feared reprisal from Miss Bingley if she learned of complaints that had been made to you."

"I can see I will need to have a long conversation with my housekeeper upon my return to London. I believe my family should depart tomorrow with Caroline. I am not sure I wish her to be alone with the servants just now. She is incredibly angry, and I do not trust her to behave as she should while she is in such temper."

223

"I am sorry to see you go. I hope you realize you and the Hursts are welcome to visit again, but I do not believe I can allow Caroline back in my home. I am sorry it has come to that. I have endured her behavior for many years out of respect for you, but I cannot allow her to mistreat those in my employ in such a way."

"I perfectly understand and agree with your actions. Caroline has been told of your disinterest numerous times, and I warned her to behave when we first arrived. I am uncertain whether she can correct this behavior or if there is something wrong with her that makes her act in such a way." Bingley gave a frustrated sigh.

"Perhaps you, Louisa, and Hurst should sit down to discuss this situation when you return to London," suggested Darcy kindly. "I know you take your responsibility to Caroline very seriously, but Louisa, as your elder sister, may have some helpful insights to share. I will help in any way I can; you know that." Darcy reached out and firmly gripped his friend's shoulder.

"Well, if we are to be away early, I should retire."

"Why do you not stay for breakfast and then depart? I will ask that a tray be taken to your sister."

"Thank you, my friend. I will see you in the morning."

15. A CELEBRATION

THE WEEKS AFTER THE BINGLEYS' DEPARTURE passed quickly. Darcy was busy with his steward every day as they checked on the progress of the harvest and the resulting yields.

One morning over breakfast Darcy's face paled, and he smacked his forehead. "How can I have forgotten something so important?" he mumbled.

"What is it, brother? What important thing have you forgotten?" asked his sister with concern.

"It is almost time for the Harvest Celebration, and I have not even thought about what should be done." When Georgiana began to giggle at his concerns, he looked at her and spoke sternly. "It is not a laughing matter, Georgiana. The celebration is used to show the tenants we appreciate the efforts they put forth to make Pemberley the successful estate it is. We would not have nearly as much without their hard work."

"I understand, William. I was only laughing because Miss Lucas and I have already taken care of all the preparations and plans for the celebration."

Darcy looked first at his sister and then at Elizabeth. "How can I ever thank you?" Darcy asked with a warm smile at his sister's companion. "How did you even know this needed to be done?"

"Well, I was raised on an estate, Mr. Darcy, even if it was not so large as Pemberley. We always held a small Harvest Celebration, and you were so busy, I thought this would be a good teaching opportunity for Miss Darcy. We met with Mrs. Reynolds and discussed how things were done at past celebrations. Then I had Georgiana list what she would like to keep and what she would like to change, and from there we made our plans. Miss Darcy has made a small change or two, and I believe you will find we will have a better celebration for less than was spent last year."

"I am very impressed, ladies, and I greatly appreciate your thoughtfulness in attending to this important matter. When is the event to occur?"

"After speaking with Mr. Martin, the steward, we decided to hold the celebration on the first day of October. He felt the harvest would be completed by then," his sister informed him. "Rose and I wrote all the invitations already, and one week before the celebration we will deliver them to the tenants and the others invited."

"What changes did you make to the celebration?"

Elizabeth nodded to let Georgiana know she should answer her brother's questions.

"We have added an area for children's games and have hired musicians for dancing in the evening. Everyone is invited to arrive at one in the afternoon. Rose insisted all the food be served by four o'clock, and then our servants can all join in the celebration. They will be off duty from four o'clock until after the dancing is through by ten in the evening. We plan to hold the event on the lawn by the lake. The men, from the groundskeepers to the grooms, are helping build a dais for the musicians and a dance floor. They will also put up several tents on the lawn for the people to relax in the shade. I was also able to get Mr. Bingley to donate some bolts of cotton in yellows, oranges, and reds to cover the tables. I thought we could put out the boats for people to row on the lake, and I have balls, hoops, and lawn bowling planned for the children, as well as several races. For the adults, there will be lawn bowling, croquet, shuttlecocks, and some races as well. We purchased prizes for both the adults and children to give to the winners of certain races."

When Georgiana paused for breath, her brother spoke up. "It sounds like it will be a wonderful celebration. I am very impressed with your plans, Georgie. My thanks to you and Miss Lucas for ensuring such an important event was not overlooked. I have only one question. What will you do if it is raining?"

"Oh, we have that all worked out. We will open the formal dining room, the ballroom, and the game room."

Laughing, Darcy remarked, "I see you have indeed thought of everything. I am very proud of you, Georgiana." She blushed in delight at her brother's praise. Then he turned to Miss Lucas. "Not only have Georgiana and I been blessed to have you here with us, but now your kindness has spread to my tenants and staff. You are a remarkable young lady, Miss Lucas."

Elizabeth blushed at his praise, and though she could not quite determine what the warm look in his eyes was meant to convey, she felt herself grow even redder as a feeling of warmth spread through her body.

The tenants' wives were very surprised when Miss Darcy and Miss Lucas appeared to deliver personal invitations to the Harvest Celebration. The ladies stayed to visit briefly and answer any questions the women might have. When the wives met one another, they could not help but discuss the kindness Miss Lucas showed to them and the thoughtful things she was teaching her young pupil. Elizabeth made sure Georgiana received all the credit for planning the event. "The master could not find a better young lady to be Pemberley's mistress," was often repeated.

When Darcy was made aware by Mrs. Reynolds of some of the comments going around, his longtime housekeeper heard him say, "Indeed, I could not," as he smiled wistfully. It was obvious to Abigail Reynolds that Master William was losing his heart to Miss Lucas. She determined to keep a keen eye on the situation to ensure nothing untoward happened which might hurt either of them.

The morning of the Harvest Celebration dawned bright and clear. The groundskeepers and other men from the estate kept busy setting up all the different areas on the lawn. An area away from the lake had been roped off for the children's games. Colorful rags and scraps of fabric had been tied to the rope, giving the area a cheerful feel. The dance floor and dais were placed near the lake on a level patch of ground. The many tents were erected around the area for dancing. The center tent directly opposite the dance floor was for the food, and there were smaller tents at both sides of the food tent. There were also blankets spread out over a portion of the lawn for those who preferred to sit there as they dined or visited rather than in one of the tents.

He watched from the terrace as Elizabeth and Georgiana kept busy covering the tables and decorating them with pumpkins, gourds, fall flowers, and other beauties of nature. Candles in glass containers were mixed in with the decorations and would be lit at dusk. There were also torches that would be lit later, before full dark. Between the full moon and the many candles and torches, the night would be brilliantly illuminated. The laughter of the two young women drifted across to Darcy on the light breeze. It was a delightful sound that he enjoyed hearing.

Because of the effort his sister and Miss Lucas had put into the planning, Darcy wished to ensure everything went well. He had purchased several additional rowboats to be used on the lake, as well as some balls, tops, and hoops for the children's area.

Though he was not particularly comfortable with large crowds, this was one event Darcy truly enjoyed. These were his people, and he cared for their well-being. That night Darcy even looked forward to the dancing and hoped Miss Lucas would favor him with a dance or two

As the tenants and villagers, whose livelihood depended on Pemberley, began to arrive, Darcy and Georgiana waited to greet their guests near what had been designated as the entrance. They had asked Elizabeth to join them, but she declined, saying she preferred to be of assistance in directing everyone or answering questions. Darcy noted she was wearing a forest green dress that day. She had a yellow shawl around her shoulders, and yellow flowers in her hair. Darcy had never seen anyone so lovely.

Many of the guests brought pies or cakes to contribute to the feast. Elizabeth stood off to the side, directing the guests as to where they could place the food and encouraging the children to enter the children's area. She told them they could play with the toys as they waited and that there would be games and races to come, with prizes for the winners. At the mention of prizes, the children's eyes lit up, and they skipped or ran for the children's area.

There was much laughter throughout the afternoon. There were a few challenges between the men, with some wagering to accompany them. The sounds of the children at play and the cheering for the races filled the air. The lake was filled with couples and families enjoying the rowboats. Everywhere one looked were signs of happy people enjoying themselves.

Elizabeth and Georgiana had arranged for only water, lemonade, and cider to be served before the meal. After the food had been served, kegs of ale were added to the libations. There were plenty of sweets to go around, as so many had contributed to what the kitchens had prepared for the day. It was a pleasure for Mr. Darcy to see many of the household servants dining together in one of the tents. He could see Mrs. Reynolds, Mrs. Mason, the Pemberley cook, and Miss Watson with their heads together, laughing and talking. He was delighted to see the women who shouldered so much of the responsibility for the house and family taking the time to enjoy themselves.

Darcy, Georgiana, and Elizabeth were seated in one of the tents with Reverend Wilkinson, the vicar of Kympton, and his wife, as well as Dr. Powell.

"I say, Mr. Darcy, this is one of the finest celebrations I have been to in many a year. You have outdone yourself," remarked Dr. Powell amiably.

"I am glad you are enjoying yourself, Dr. Powell, but all the credit goes to Georgiana and Miss

Lucas. They are the ones who planned this year's event."

"Well then, ladies, my congratulations to you both for an outstanding job."

"Oh, yes," said Mrs. Wilkinson, "it is a lovely party."

"I am looking forward to the opportunity to dance with my wife this evening," added Reverend Wilkinson with a smile at his bride of thirty years.

"Speaking of dancing," said Darcy, "I will open the dancing with my sister, but I hope you will favor me with a set or two, Miss Lucas."

Flushing prettily, Elizabeth replied, "I should be happy to accept, Mr. Darcy." They smiled at each other briefly before Georgiana's giggle caused them to look away.

As the evening progressed, the adults became more animated as many of the younger children fell asleep. Quilts and blankets had been placed on the ground in the children's area off to the side, so they could sleep peacefully as their parents continued to enjoy the festivities.

As dusk fell, several of the groundskeepers lit the torches and the candles placed around the area. The full moon began to rise, reflecting brightly off the lake, and the soft sounds of the musicians warming up could be heard. As the musicians quieted in preparation for the first dance, Mr. Darcy stepped onto the dais and called for everyone's attention.

"Ladies and gentlemen, I would like to take this opportunity to thank all of you for the hard work and dedication you put into making Pemberley such a magnificent estate. Many of you have been tenants here for several generations. You have seen the estate in prosperous times, as well as more lean times, and you never fail to give your very best efforts. I hope you have enjoyed the afternoon and looked forward to the dancing. I must ask you to please give thanks to my sister, Miss Darcy, and her companion, Miss Lucas, for planning this outstanding day that we have enjoyed."

Georgiana and Elizabeth were still seated together in their tent as Darcy waved a hand in their direction. Cheers and applause were heard as everyone turned to look at the young women.

When Darcy again had everyone's attention, he concluded his remarks. "Again, our thanks to each and every one of you for your dedication to Pemberley. Please enjoy the remainder of your evening."

Darcy stepped down and made his way to his sister's side, offering his arm to lead her to the dance floor. Georgiana stood up with him for a country dance. When the set was over, he returned his sister to their table and offered his hand to Miss Lucas. As they took their places at the head of the set, Darcy softly said, "You look lovely this evening, Miss Lucas. The green and yellow are very becoming on you."

A soft blush covered her cheeks, but she smiled as she replied, "I thank you very much, Mr. Darcy, but you really should not say such things. If someone were to overhear, your reputation would be ruined."

Darcy threw back his head and laughed as he passed her in the dance. "I believe being seen in your company can only enhance my reputation, Miss Lucas. Everywhere I go, I hear people singing your praises. Whether I am with tenants or in Lambton, even the household staff cannot say enough good about you. I believe you won their undying loyalty when you informed me of Miss Bingley's poor treatment of her maid."

"You must be exaggerating, sir, for I have done nothing unusual. I have only behaved as is proper."

"No, Miss Lucas. I, unfortunately, know far more ladies who lean towards Miss Bingley in their behaviors than towards you. You are quite unique, for you are a truly kind lady."

"I wish that were the case," she mumbled.

"Pardon me? I could not hear what you said."

"I said, it is easy to be kind when you are treated with kindness."

"If that were true, Miss Bingley would not be the person she is. She was showered with kind attention from both of her parents, as well as her siblings, yet she is the antithesis of her brother, no matter how she is treated. You treat everyone with the same degree of kindness, be they titled or a scullery maid. You are the most genuine person I know."

Elizabeth was thrilled to hear his words, but she knew she could not allow herself to take them seriously. She was his employee and the daughter of a small country gentleman from a far different social circle. When the dance ended, she did not wait for him to escort her from the dance floor but excused herself to find Georgiana.

She joined Georgiana in dancing with the older children and watched as Mr. Darcy danced with Mrs. Wilkinson and tried to convince Mrs. Reynolds to dance with him. He asked Elizabeth for a second set, but she politely declined, saying she was tired and preferred to watch.

After Darcy had finished dancing for the evening, he wandered towards the house. Entering through the French doors in the drawing room, he ascended the stairs and made his way to a balcony at the front of the house. There he sat in the dark and watched everyone enjoying themselves. He was able to observe Miss Lucas without her being aware of it. He wondered if he should ask her more directly about her past or continue to hope she would begin to trust him with her secrets.

As the end of the evening approached, the musicians announced the last dance. Darcy slowly made his way back to where the party was wrapping up. As parents gathered their families and picked up their sleeping children, Darcy and Georgiana stood at the entrance to the area and wished everyone a good night as they departed.

Darcy addressed the staff members who were still on the lawn, offering thanks for their efforts in preparing for the event. He expressed his hopes that they had enjoyed the evening and wished them a good night. Then he turned, offering an arm to his sister and another to Miss Lucas. He escorted the young ladies to the door of their sitting room. He opened the door for them and kissed his sister before she entered the room. Then he reached for Miss Lucas' hand and brought it to his lips. He placed a chaste kiss on the back before wishing her a good night. He paused at the door of his room and looked back to see her standing where he had left her. Her cheeks were tinted a soft pink, and her look was one of wonder and confusion. The corners of his mouth turned up in a slight smile. He nodded to her and entered his room.

When he had lifted her hand, Elizabeth felt a tingling feeling begin. When his surprisingly soft lips pressed against the bare skin of her hand, the feeling spread throughout her body, and her heart began to race. A rosy flush appeared at the edge of her gown and rose to completely cover her face. She was mesmerized by the look in his eyes, which never left hers. The moment was over quickly, but Elizabeth felt as though time had stopped. The soft sound of his door closing released her from the confusion his actions had caused.

In a daze, she turned to enter the sitting room. She expected to find it empty and was startled at the sound of Georgiana's voice.

"Elizabeth, are you feeling well? Your face is quite flushed."

Rallying herself, she replied in as normal a voice as she could. "I am well, thank you, just tired. It has been a very long, but very successful day. You did a wonderful job with the Harvest Celebration, Georgiana. Now, if you will excuse me, I shall retire and see you in the morning."

"Good night, Rose. Sleep well."

Elizabeth entered her room and found Lucy waiting to help prepare her for bed. Once she was in her night clothes, she sat at the dressing table as Lucy brushed out her hair. The maid happily chatted about the wonderful day, though Elizabeth was not so attentive as usual. Finally, she thanked Lucy for her assistance and dismissed her for the night.

In spite of her fatigue, Elizabeth's thoughts were too unsettled for sleep. She wandered to the window seat in her room that looked out over the lawn and the lake in front of the house. There she curled up and put her flushed face against the coolness of the glass. Her thoughts were filled with Mr. Darcy as she reviewed their interactions of the day. He had praised her efforts in preparing the Harvest Celebration. He had asked her to dance, twice, and had generously complimented her during that time. She had noticed his disappointment when she had refused his hand a second time, but she did not wish to do anything to cause talk by dancing with her employer more than once. She had felt his eyes upon her frequently throughout the event, and when their eyes happened to meet, he smiled warmly at her.

She had been very surprised when he kissed her hand, and the look in his eyes had confused her greatly. It had definitely been a look of admiration. But she was his employee and far beneath him socially. He could certainly have no feelings for her. Then, with a feeling of dread, she wondered if the feelings might be less than gentlemanly. *No! Mr. Darcy was far too honorable to have inappropriate designs on her. But what could his looks and actions mean? If only I were someone he could truly admire and with whom he might wish to have a courtship or, perhaps, marry.* At the realization such hopes were to no avail, she rested her head on her knees as tears silently began to fall. She sobbed softly for some time before falling asleep, curled in the window seat. The coolness of the room woke her several hours later. She moved stiffly to her bed and crawled under the coverlet. She rolled to her side and curled up into a ball as a few tears again rolled down her cheeks.

When Elizabeth had not summoned her by the usual time the next morning, Lucy went to check on her mistress. She was surprised to see Miss Lucas still sleeping. She opened the curtains, flooding the room with light before stepping to the bed to wake the young lady. Lucy called her name twice to no avail. Finally, she reached out and placed a hand gently on Elizabeth's shoulder, giving her a soft shake. Elizabeth stirred and rolled on her back. When she opened her eyes, she cried out in pain and quickly closed them again.

"Miss Lucas, are you well?"

Elizabeth could hear the concern in Lucy's voice and responded without opening her eyes. "I am sorry to have startled you, Lucy, but it appears I have one of my headaches this morning. Would you please close the curtains, as the light makes it worse."

Elizabeth could hear the young lady rush to do as she was bid. "They are closed, miss. What can I get you for your relief? Should I request the doctor?"

With her hand shielding her eyes, Elizabeth carefully opened them. Realizing the room was, indeed darkened, she carefully removed her hand. The first thing she saw was Lucy's worried expression.

"Do not look so concerned. I am accustomed to these headaches, and they are fortunately rare. I beg you to tell Miss Darcy I am ill and will be unable to attend her today. Please let her know they rarely last more than four and twenty hours, and I shall be perfectly well by breakfast tomorrow."

"Yes, miss," replied Lucy as she exited to the shared sitting room. She moved across the room and knocked at Miss Darcy's door. When Georgiana called out to enter, Lucy opened the door and entered with a curtsey.

"Miss Darcy, Miss Lucas is quite ill this morning and will not be able to join you today —"

Before she could complete the message, Miss Darcy gave a cry of concern. "Oh, the poor dear," she said and moved quickly to her companion's room. "Rose, Lucy tells me you are ill. Shall I send for the doctor?"

"Please do not be concerned, Georgiana. I am merely suffering from a megrim I get on occasion. There is nothing that can be done for it but to allow it time to dissipate. I shall be fine by morning, I assure you."

"Are you sure I cannot get you something for your comfort?"

"Unfortunately not. I require time, quiet, darkness, and sleep. As I said, it shall be gone by morning. That is always the case. Please express my regrets to Mr. Darcy for failing to do my duties today."

"Do not be ridiculous. I know Brother would agree your health is the most important thing. I shall leave you now and let you rest, but I will check on you throughout the day." Georgiana stepped closer to the bed and straightened the bedcovers, settling them comfortably around Elizabeth. "Lucy, please stay with Miss Lucas and ensure she has whatever she needs."

"Certainly, Miss Darcy."

As Georgiana moved to the door, she said, "I shall have Mrs. Reynolds send up a breakfast tray to you."

"That is not necessary, for the headache often causes my stomach to feel unwell. Do not concern yourself. I shall be well."

"Of course I shall concern myself. You are my dearest friend. Now rest and I will check on you later."

Georgiana paused in the doorway to catch her breath after her hurried descent to the breakfast room. Darcy was seated at the table, coffee cup in hand and a small smile on his lips. He was drawn from his reverie when he heard the soft sounds of a chair as his sister joined him. His smile quickly faded when he saw she was not accompanied by the subject of his musings.

"Where is Miss Lucas, Georgie?"

"She is not feeling well. Lucy and I insisted she remain in bed and not get up until she was completely recovered."

"What is wrong with her? Do we need to send for the doctor?" Worry was evident in Darcy's voice.

"It is a megrim. Miss Lucas said she has had them before and the only cure is quiet, darkness, rest, and time. Her maid will stay with her throughout the day to ensure it is nothing more serious, and I will have another one sit with her overnight. She said it was not necessary to send for the doctor. However, if it seems she is growing worse or is not recovered by the morning, I will not hesitate to call for Dr. Powell."

"Please let me know of any change in her condition. We must insure she returns to good health." The fervency in Darcy's voice caused his sister to stare at him for several moments. Lost in his worry, Darcy did not even notice.

"Brother, do you like, Miss Lucas?"

Startled, Darcy quickly replied, "Of course, I do."

Georgiana continued to stare at him, a thoughtful look on her face as she ate the breakfast the footman had placed before her.

Fortunately for all concerned, Elizabeth was returned to her normal good health the next day, just as she had indicated. Darcy was greatly relieved to see her arrive in the breakfast room and was solicitous in his attentions to her.

After breakfast, the ladies spent the morning in the library attending to Georgiana's missed lessons. After luncheon, they decided to go for a walk in the garden before returning to the library. As they stepped off the terrace, Elizabeth suggested they race to the center of the maze.

"Are you sure you are well enough, Rose?"

"Of course. I have been learning my way about the maze whenever I have a spare moment. I might even beat you to the center," was her challenging reply.

"Shall there be a prize for the winner?"

"Certainly, the pride of accomplishment."

"Agreed."

The young ladies chose their entrances to the maze. Elizabeth counted down to three, and they raced through the green hedge toward the center. They had chosen opposite sides, and each stepped into the center at the same moment.

"Well done, Rose!" cried Georgiana. "You shall have to race against Fitzwilliam to see if you can beat him."

"With his great long stride, I cannot imagine outdistancing him, but it might be fun to try."

The young ladies seated themselves on the benches surrounding the fountain in the middle of the maze. At first neither spoke, just sat absorbing the serenity of the scenery. Finally, Georgiana said, "I should like to speak to you about an event that recently took place."

Noting the serious tone of her charge's voice, Elizabeth replied, "I am happy to hear anything you wish to say. If I can assist you in some way, please know I will."

Slowly, Georgiana explained to her the events that had transpired in Ramsgate. Elizabeth listened quietly, using only a murmured word or a nod of her head to acknowledge Georgiana's words.

Elizabeth's heart broke for the young girl. She had been ill-used by her companion and this falsely charming young man. Her own good sense had stood her in good stead and had been overcome only by the lies of her companions. Elizabeth also felt a great deal of anger for the two people who had so mistreated her dear Georgie.

When the young girl had emptied her mind of the troubling thoughts that had plagued her for the past few months, Elizabeth offered these words.

"Do you still have feelings for the young man?"

"No."

"Did you learn something from this experience?"

"Oh, yes!"

"What have you learned?"

"First, love is much more than pretty words and behavior. Second, love does not force its way on the object of its affection. Third, I can always depend on my brother."

"Is there anything else?" Elizabeth's raised brow made Georgiana wonder what she had missed.

Hesitantly, she said, "To trust my own judgment and instincts."

"Very good," said Elizabeth. "Yes, love is much more than pretty words and behavior. When you love someone, it means putting the needs of your beloved before your own. Love always gives and cares. It does not push and take. And I certainly believe you will always be able to depend on your brother. He is one of the most hard-working and responsible men I have ever met. Most importantly, I am glad you know you can trust your judgment. At each turn, you questioned your companion about proper behavior. There would have been no trouble at all had she not given you erroneous information. You will not make that same mistake in the future."

"Why do I feel so bad about my choices then?"

"Let me teach you another lesson. Think only of the past as its remembrance give you pleasure." (4)

The young ladies continued to talk for quite some time. As tea time drew near, Georgiana spoke of wishing to retire with her journal for some time, requesting that tea be sent to her room.

16. WICKHAM ARRIVES IN MERYTON

IT WAS A SUNNY MORNING IN early October. There was a slight nip in the air, and the leaves on the trees presented a riot of colors. George Wickham looked around the quaint village of Meryton. The streets were relatively quiet, as it was not yet ten in the morning. The shopkeepers could be seen sweeping the walks in front of their stores or washing the windows so their wares would be clearly visible. The sleepy hamlet of Meryton seemed like the perfect place to hide from Darcy and his cousin, Colonel Fitzwilliam. Wickham, still angry from failing to gain Georgiana Darcy's dowry of thirty thousand pounds, knew there would be other opportunities to cause Darcy harm or extort additional funds from him. He simply needed a quiet place to plot and scheme. Perhaps he would find a few pigeons to fleece in this backwater town, thereby helping replenish his empty pockets.

He had run into an old friend, James Denny, while hiding in London. Listening to his tales of life in the militia, with minimal work, free food and lodging, a steady income, and many parties and balls, it sounded like the perfect solution to Wickham's current troubles.

As he stood gazing about the main street of Meryton, Wickham heard his name called. Turning to the sound of the voice, he saw his friend crossing the street towards him. The gentlemen greeted each other with the ease of long acquaintance.

"Come with me, and I will introduce you to Colonel Forster," offered Denny.

"Lead on, my friend," replied Wickham. "I look forward to the pleasant life you have described to me, particularly all the socializing." Wickham leered at his friend as both men laughed.

Less than half an hour later, Wickham was being fitted for his uniform and shown to his temporary lodging. That very evening he attended his first social affair. Colonel Forster was hosting a dinner at the Assembly Hall for all the gentlemen of the area. It was to earn the goodwill of the community and give them an opportunity to meet Colonel Forster and his officers. For Wickham, it presented the perfect opportunity to take the measure of the gentlemen in the neighborhood.

Wickham went prepared to charm. He knew people were more forthcoming to charming manners and a handsome face. He took up a position in the corner of the room and looked around him, observing the gentlemen as they arrived. Once he had been introduced to everyone, he moved about the room, listening and learning all he could about his new neighbors.

Wickham's pleasant manners and seeming openness allowed for easy acceptance from those he met. It was easy for Wickham to see which gentlemen were lacking in sense and might be easily exploited. He learned that the largest estate in the area, Netherfield Park, was currently available to let. He also discovered that a tragic accident had recently taken the life of the largest permanent landholder in the area, along with his wife and several daughters. These daughters were reputed to have been some of the most beautiful in the neighborhood. Wickham overheard Sir William Lucas discussing his distaste for the heir who had taken over the estate upon the family's demise. Wickham determined to meet the man at his earliest opportunity. From what he heard, he could not decide if the man would be an easy mark, a fellow schemer, or a cunning adversary.

As the evening wore on, Wickham easily observed which members of the community did not hold their liquor well and he targeted them for a fleecing at cards. He felt there would be several opportunities in the neighborhood to refill his empty pockets.

The duties that filled Wickham's daytime hours were not particularly onerous. They marched and drilled both morning and afternoon. Occasionally there was practice with swords as well as rifles and bayonets. Wickham also had guard duty twice a month, but was given a day off following that particular duty. He found plenty of opportunities to wander the streets of Meryton, observing the ladies who were to be found there. He had met the resident spinster, Miss Charlotte Lucas, but found himself uncomfortable in her presence. Wherever he went, Wickham repeated his tale of woe at the hands of Darcy. He describing how he had been denied a living in the church left to him by old Mr. Darcy because the current Mr. Darcy was jealous of his father's attentions to Wickham. In the past, he had always gained sympathy from, and often the comforting attentions of, the young ladies when they learned of his misfortunes. It unsettled him that Miss Lucas did not seem to believe his story.

Wickham already had a tavern maid warming his bed some nights. However, he considered himself a gentleman and believed he could do much better than a barmaid. Wickham believed himself attractive and charming and was constantly on the lookout for an heiress to marry. Unfortunately for any young ladies, Wickham had no intentions of staying married any longer than it took to gain control of their fortune. He was also not above dabbling with the daughters of the local gentlemen should one strike his fancy and such an opportunity arise.

Wickham soon set his sights on one of the neighborhood young ladies. He targeted her specifically because her elder sister was so suspicious of him. It was at the monthly assembly that he approached her for the first time. Wishing for more information, he turned on his most charming smile and approached her, a shy-looking young lady of fifteen.

"Good evening, Miss Maria, is it not?"

Maria Lucas looked up to see a very handsome gentleman with dark curls and brown eyes staring down at her with a friendly smile. Though not so plain as her elder sister, Maria was not used to receiving much attention from gentlemen because of her young age.

"Good evening, Lieutenant Wickham," replied the young lady with a blush. Though she had been introduced to the gentleman at a dinner one evening, they had not spoken previously. Maria had heard many of the young ladies in the neighborhood speak of the newest member of the militia, often remarking on his handsomeness.

Wickham asked the young lady to dance, and she could only nod in reply due to her surprise. They took their place in the set, and Wickham made polite conversation with the young lady. It took a good deal of effort on his part to draw her from her shyness. After a few more compliments, when the dance ended

Wickham was able to lead the young lady to a quiet corner for conversation. With only a few leading questions, he learned more about the families in the neighborhood, as well as about the tragic accident that had claimed the majority of the Bennet family. It was easy to get Maria Lucas to share all the gossip she knew about the residents of Meryton, and it was not long before Wickham knew everything there was to know about his neighbors.

At a previous event, he had learned of an affair in which one of the local gentlemen was involved, and he was now blackmailing the gentleman. Wickham was wise enough not to ask for too much, for the neighborhood was not a particularly well-to-do one, but it was a start. Wickham had also managed to charm most of the local merchants into extending him credit. Due to the patronage of the late Mr. Darcy, Wickham had expensive tastes, and he ran up debt with the merchants wherever he went. Unfortunately for the merchants, he usually departed without paying these debts.

It was not long after the evening at the Lucas' that Wickham finally met Mr. Harold Collins. Without Walter's restraining presence, Mr. Collins had returned to his preferred habits. His inflated opinion of himself had isolated him from the rest of the neighborhood. He was in mourning, so he did not receive invitations to the events that were held in the neighborhood. As he had yet to replace all of the servants, he could not entertain in his home, even had he not been in mourning. If he tried to do so, he would have further offended his neighbors, and most would not have attended out of respect for the Bennets.

When Mr. Collins encountered his neighbors in town or at church, his superior attitude kept them at a distance. Many were upset with the disrespectful way in which he had treated the deaths of the Bennet family, and all were concerned over the disappearance of Miss Elizabeth, wondering if he had harmed her in some way.

When Walter had been at Longbourn, he had managed to distract his father from heading to the tavern at night. "It would not be seemly for the largest landholder in the area to spend his time at the local public house," he would say. With Walter gone, there was no one to prevent Collins from indulging his habit of gaming. He was hiding in Meryton because he owed money to several unpleasant characters in London. He was a dreadful card player, and his luck had not improved with the change in locale.

It was on one such night that Wickham first encountered Harold Collins in the tavern in Meryton. Walter had run out of ready cash and had to excuse himself from the card game underway at a corner table. Because of his neighbors' dislike for him, many would not accept his vowels.

Angry at the treatment he received, Harold muttered into a pint of ale about his misfortunes. He was disgusted at being reduced to drinking ale, but the coins in his pocket would not allow for the purchase of anything better.

Wickham had observed the game from across the room. Harold Collins' behavior had made him easy to read, and Wickham quickly determined the best way to approach him. Collins considered himself superior to those around him, and Wickham knew that commiserating with him, one gentleman to another, would flatter Harold's ego. Wickham would pay for a round of drinks and get the man talking.

Wickham felt certain he could learn something that might be financially rewarding to himself.

"My sympathies, sir," began Wickham as he slid into the booth across from Mr. Collins. "A gentleman like you should not be reduced to playing with such rustics. Vowels are accepted in all the best establishments. Their lack of understanding merely proves their lowly station in life."

Harold eyed the gentleman across from him suspiciously. "What do you want?" he growled.

"Merely to buy you a drink," said Wickham good naturedly. "I recently arrived in town from London. Your stature and demeanor show you to be a well-bred gentleman—the kind with whom I am accustomed to associating. I merely wished to make your acquaintance, but after observing your poor treatment by the others at the card table, I thought I would offer you a drink and some better company with which to commiserate."

Harold Collins was about to tell Wickham to be off when Wickham asked the barmaid for two brandies. At the thought of drinking something more in keeping with his status, Collins offered a grudging, "Thank you."

When the drinks had been delivered, Wickham said, "Allow me to introduce myself. My name is George Wickham. I recently arrived in Meryton as a lieutenant in the militia."

"Harold Collins, master of Longbourn," said his companion gruffly.

"Longbourn...is that the attractive estate on the east side of town?"

Pleased by Wickham's flattery of the estate, Harold answered more civilly. "Yes, I recently inherited the estate from my cousin." Collins smirked as he added, "He and his family were the victims of a tragic accident not too long ago."

"How sad for them, but how fortunate for you," said Wickham with a smirk of his own.

"Yes, it was sad." Wickham noted that Mr. Collins' expression showed the opposite of his expressed emotion.

The gentlemen continued to converse over their brandies, with Wickham's flattery stroking the ego of Harold Collins. By the time the gentlemen parted, they were quite in harmony with one another. Collins had even issued an invitation to Wickham to join him for dinner in two nights, and Wickham was only too happy to accept.

Wickham arrived on the designated date and time, and the gentlemen sat down to dinner shortly after his arrival. Mr. Collins had managed to find a new cook, but her skills were sadly lacking. However, Wickham knew better than to do anything but flatter Collins. After dinner, Wickham talked Collins into a game of cards. He was careful to lose most of the hands to ensure there would be future opportunities to play again. The gentlemen enjoyed several glasses of Mr. Bennet's favorite port over their game, and Mr. Collins became more pompous with each hand he won.

Wickham and Collins often met in the weeks to come to share many a meal and a few hands of cards. Whenever the gentlemen met, large quantities of alcohol were consumed. Gradually, Wickham won more often than he lost, but he was always gracious and accepted vowels from Mr. Collins. Wickham wondered whether he would ever collect what he was owed, but he found that the information Collins inadvertently shared when in his cups more than made up for the difficulties. Collins had let slip some information Wickham could use to profitably blackmail him. Information of this magnitude would soon be earning a significant amount for Wickham.

Within a few days of Wickham's arrival in Meryton, another gentleman appeared in the quiet village. He was a rather nondescript fellow who was easy to overlook. That very quality was what made him an excellent investigator.

Richard Fitzwilliam had stopped at the Book and Barrel in Cambridge on his return trip to London. He asked about Mrs. Hill and was told she managed the inn. Upon speaking to her, he found a competent, pleasant woman who was knowledgeable about her business. However, when he asked what she had done before and from where she had come, she was a bit less forthcoming. When he mentioned the name of Rose Lucas, the woman excused herself with the remark that she had work to do. Through his army experiences, Richard was quite certain the woman was not involved in anything havey-cavey. She was obviously anxious when Miss Lucas' name was mentioned, glancing around to be sure no one had overheard the remarks. Richard felt certain she was concerned for the young lady's safety. Consequently, Richard had hired the investigator.

Mr. Shaw's appearance allowed him to listen in on many conversations and to glean a great deal of information without anyone taking note of his presence. Even his discreet questions always got the information he was seeking without anyone taking note of the questioner.

One evening, as Wickham and Collins sat in the taproom of the inn over a hand of cards, the gentlemen were unaware they were being observed. An ordinary man in the clothes of a farmer sat at a corner table. He appeared absorbed in his drink and half asleep, but he was watching the gentlemen at the nearby table and listening intently to their conversation. He was easily able to discern that the younger gentleman was cheating at cards and was quite shocked at the drunken disclosures made by the older gentleman.

After the departure of Collins, Mr. Shaw observed Wickham smile evilly and heard his muttered "Stupid old fool!" before he, too, quit the taproom for his lodgings. When both men had departed, Shaw retired to his room and began a letter to his employer.

Meryton Inn
Meryton, Hertfordshire

Colonel Fitzwilliam,

I have looked into the matter as you requested. I am afraid the information I have discovered is quite disturbing. On the last day of June, there was indeed a dreadful accident that claimed several lives. One daughter, the eldest, was out of town at the time of the accident. The second daughter had not been with her family at the local assembly due to illness. All those in the carriage were killed. After about a week, the daughter who had been ill disappeared suddenly without a trace. All the servants in the house also left, without notice, at about the same time.

The heir to the estate is Mr. Harold Collins. The gentleman has not been well received by his neighbors due to his callousness at the loss of the family and the neighborhood's concerns over the missing girl.

I have much additional information to share but do not feel comfortable putting it into a letter. I will be returning to London on the morrow and will arrange to call on you at your cousin's home upon reaching town.

One additional piece of information you may find interesting is that Mr. George Wickham is currently a member of the militia unit stationed in Meryton. He has been seen in frequent company with Mr. Collins.

I should be in town by noon.

Shaw

The investigator sealed the letter and went down to ask the landlord about arranging for an express rider. Though it was too late for someone to start at that time, the innkeeper informed him he had a rider in the taproom waiting for a return trip to London. He directed Shaw to the man and within minutes Shaw had turned over the letter and the fee. The rider would leave at first light.

17. BINGLEY MEETS AN ANGEL

BINGLEY WAS RELIEVED WHEN THE CARRIAGE rolled to a stop in front of his London townhouse. The family had been subjected to Caroline's foul temper, threats, and tantrums the entire trip from Pemberley to London. When they stopped at the inn for the first night, Bingley refused to allow a servant to attend his sister. When he told his sister she would have to dress and care for herself, she stared incomprehensibly at her brother. Unfortunately, the staring lasted only moments before she began complaining of his mistreatment. Bingley, however, could not be moved, insisting he would not risk anyone else being injured at Caroline's hand.

Her complaining continued as they entered their rented London townhouse, but Bingley ignored her and moved towards his study. He locked the door behind him to prevent her from entering and continuing her harangue. Just as quickly, the Hursts disappeared up the stairs to their suite.

Caroline moved to the drawing room and reached for the first knick-knack she saw. She grabbed it and, with a surprising unladylike curse, hurled it at the mirror over the fireplace. Unfortunately for Caroline, she broke the mirror, and the crash brought several of the servants and her brother to the door of the drawing room. Seeing the broken objects, Bingley grabbed his sister by the arm and dragged her from the room, up the stairs, and into the sitting room attached to her bedchamber. He roughly pushed her into a chair and stood over her. Caroline was taken aback at the look of menace on the face of her normally cheerful brother.

At the surprised look on her face, Bingley decided to press his advantage. "I have had more than enough of your childish behavior to last me a lifetime! For goodness sake, Caroline, you are four and twenty, not four years of age! You are confined to your suite until you can improve your behavior to everyone around you—family and staff alike. Also, I will not employ a new maid for you until I am certain your behavior has improved enough that you will not cause her harm. Your temper tantrums are bad enough, but that you would cause physical harm to another human being is repulsive. I have never been more appalled or humiliated than I was to discover how truly reprehensible your behavior has been.

"The funds to pay for the items you broke at Pemberley and those you broke upon our return home will come from your allowance. I will also send Darcy the funds he paid the physician for the wounds the young woman received, and I will send her five pounds for her injuries and trouble. All of this will come out of your funds, as will the cost of any items broken in the future. If the remainder of your quarterly allowance will not cover the costs, you will receive no additional funds until the next quarter, and I will take what is owed from it before you receive it. I will no longer allow you to overspend your allowance or treat our belongings with such careless disregard.

"Just as at the inns, the staff will not be providing you any, and I do mean any, services. You will fetch your own tray and eat in your room, then return your dishes to the kitchen and clean them yourself. You will act as your own lady's maid. If you desire a bath, you will fetch your own water and clean everything up after the bath is over. No one shall enter your bed chamber or dressing room for any reason. Coal will be provided, and you will maintain your own fires. Perhaps when you see how difficult the work of the servants is, you will learn to treat them better. Until such time, you shall be doing everything for yourself.

"Needless to say, as you are confined to your room, you will receive no visitors or attend any social events until there is a marked improvement in your behavior, as well as continued evidence you have changed. If you cannot abide by the rules of this household, I will arrange for you to live in York with Aunt Agatha until you are old enough to set up an establishment of your own. When that time comes, you can decide whether you prefer to remain with our aunt or set up house alone. However, you will not be welcomed in my home, and if your funds are released to you, I will no longer serve as your escort to social events. I will not allow you to damage the family name. Do you understand what I have said?"

A mutinous expression was the only response he received. As he turned to leave, Caroline grabbed the figurine from the table beside her and lobbed it at her brother. It struck Charles in the back and fell to the floor, where it shattered.

"I see you are confused about my instructions. I believe I will speak with the housekeeper about all the items that have been broken during the past year and allow you to pay for their replacement as well. With your temper, there may not be anything left of your *next* quarterly allowance to give you. With no funds, even should you improve your behavior, you would still not be enjoying the life you are used to living."

Bingley went directly to his study and requested the first footman he passed to send the butler and housekeeper to him. He poured himself a drink and sipped it as he waited. It was not long before the servants knocked. Upon bidding them enter, Bingley asked them both to be seated.

"Mr. and Mrs. Graves, it has recently come to my attention that not only has my sister been verbally unpleasant with our servants, but some of them have been physically harmed. As a result, she is confined to her suite for the time being. I would like the doors to the bedroom and dressing room locked from the outside, and I will maintain the keys."

"Miss Bingley has copies of the keys to her room, sir," said the housekeeper quietly.

"I shall get them back from her, then, Mrs. Graves. Graves, please have the largest footman we have stationed outside of my sister's sitting room door. She is confined to her room and is to receive no servants or visitors in her suite. I have decided she must see to her own needs until she can learn to treat the servants appropriately. The footman is not to let her out of the room unless she is going to fetch a meal or her bathwater, do her laundry, or other chores that would normally be done by servants. Please instruct the servants not to speak to her or accept any orders from her. The only thing she will be allowed is the food the servants receive. I will not disturb Mrs. Green by allowing my sister in her kitchen except to pick up her tray and return it to the kitchen, where she must wash her dishes.

"Mrs. Graves, I need you to determine what items my sister has broken within the past year. I intend to use her funds to replace them. Also, if she has caused physical harm to any of the servants or dismissed any unfairly, I wish to send them a recompense, so please provide me with names and any pertinent information. Also, I expect you to report all future incidents to me so I may rectify them as quickly as possible. In the interim, Mrs. Hurst is to be considered the hostess in my home. Any problems that arise from her orders or behavior are to be reported to me immediately."

"Yes, Mr. Bingley. I believe I have records of all the information you requested in my office. I will make a copy for you as soon as possible, sir."

"Very good, Mrs. Graves. Now, do either of you have any questions?" When they both shook their heads, Bingley continued. "Please keep me apprised of any information you feel I need to know and refer my sister to me if she gives you any problems. That will be all for now."

The servants exited the study and once the door was closed behind them, looked at each other in surprise and amusement. "It is about time," muttered Mrs. Graves.

"Amen to that," said her husband.

Next Bingley sent for his sister and brother-in-law and explained the situation to them. Louisa Hurst looked aghast at the punishment her brother had planned for Caroline.

"Charles, you cannot be serious. You plan to have our sister do a servant's work."

"I do indeed, Louisa. Perhaps when she realizes how easy her life is because of the servants, she will learn to treat them better. What she did to the young girl at Pemberley is behavior beyond the pale. I will no longer allow her to treat us or others as miserably as she has in the past." Bingley studied his sister contemplatively. "Were you aware of the full extent of her poor behavior towards the servants?"

Louisa Hurst looked down at her hands and said not a word.

"Louisa!" cried her husband and brother in surprise.

Appalled, Charles Bingley asked, "How could you be silent and allow this behavior from our sister?"

Still Louisa Hurst remained silent.

"Louisa, I demand an answer," came her husband's firm voice.

She looked up at Hurst, who saw tears glittering in her eyes, "The first time I realized how bad things were, Caroline was about ten and six years of age. When I reprimanded her for her behavior, she struck me several times with her hairbrush. I was left battered and bruised."

"Why did you not tell our parents?" asked Charles, aghast.

"The way the whole family catered to Caroline's whims, I am not sure they would have believed me," came the soft reply.

"Did it happen more than the one time?" Gilbert Hurst gently asked his wife.

"No, for I never mentioned it again. I was afraid of what she might do the next time."

Gilbert Hurst did something he had not done in some time. He drew his wife into an embrace and held her close, whispering words of love and encouragement.

"Do you think there is something inherently wrong with Caroline, or is her behavior just the result of the way she was spoiled?" mused Bingley as he observed the tender scene before him. After allowing

Louisa to recover her composure, Bingley asked, "Would you be willing to act as my hostess for the time being? I have notified Mrs. Graves you will be doing so. After hearing about your experience, I doubt it is necessary to say this; however, there is one thing I will not tolerate. You are not to help our sister get around any of her punishments. If you do not think you can abide by this request, perhaps it would be best for you and Hurst to visit with his family during this time. I will not relent in this behavior. I am hopeful she will improve quickly, but you know how stubborn she can be. If I do not see signs of improvement, I shall set her up in her own household. Should that happen, I will no longer serve as her escort nor cover her when she overspends her allowance."

Hurst had been trying to suppress a chuckle since Charles explained the punishment to them, but he could no longer do so. "I say, Charles, this is the grandest idea you have ever had. I cannot wait to see Caroline emptying her chamber pot!" He guffawed loudly. "Louisa will not assist her sister; I shall make sure of it. Oh, I cannot wait to see how she handles this, and I shall be sure you do not weaken in your resolve."

Caroline's shrill voice could be heard throughout the house for the remainder of the day. At first she refused to give up the keys to her room, but Charles merely threatened to have the locks changed. Then she screamed at the footman who would not permit her to leave her room. She screamed at the kitchen staff when she saw the meal she was expected to eat, and then again when she was told she would have to wash the dishes. Instead of complying, she smashed the dishes and stormed from

261

the room. Mrs. Graves was forced to add the items to the list for the master.

Things did not improve the next morning, when Caroline discovered she would have to empty her chamber pot. When Charles informed her of this further indignity, she made as if to toss the contents at her brother. However, he reminded her she would then have to wash his clothing, carry his bath water, and scrub the carpet to remove the mess if she followed through with her intentions. She quickly reconsidered, but another breakable object was hurled at the door upon his exit. He merely opened the door, looked at the object, and said, "The cost of this shall be added to the list. It is already quite extensive; you may not have any allowance left to receive when the next quarter arrives at the end of the month."

Caroline's cries and grumbling continued for quite some time. It had become necessary to hire a second large footman, as Caroline managed to sneak from her room during the first night of her captivity while the exhausted footman slept in a chair in the hall. She found her way to her brother's study, intending to destroy everything in the room. However, the door had been locked, so she moved to the library. The footman had awoken and discovered her gone. He quickly woke Bingley and they easily followed the noise to the library, where Caroline was discovered tearing up books. Now her door was guarded around the clock.

At the end of a week of Caroline's rantings, the Hursts made arrangements to travel to his family's estate. They planned to stay for some time. Bingley began spending more time at his club or in other manly pursuits, and accepted invitations for every evening, avoiding his home and the noise as much as possible. The noise gradually lessened, and finally the day came when the noise stopped. Charles did not believe Caroline had yet learned her lesson, but the entire household was grateful for the quiet.

They had been back in town for two weeks when Bingley had a meeting with a Mr. Gardiner of Gardiner Imports and Exports. Bingley planned to invest with the gentleman and perhaps arrange for the export of some of the cotton and woolen textiles from his mills in the north. Mr. Gardiner had access to far more markets than those to which Bingley was currently shipping his products. Charles was pleased with the results of the meeting and made a mental reminder to send Darcy a note of thanks for suggesting he meet with Mr. Gardiner.

The gentlemen met several more times over the course of the next week. When they finally had everything resolved, Mr. Gardiner invited Bingley to dine at his home in celebration of the mutually beneficial deal they had reached.

When Bingley arrived at the Gardiner home, he was shown into the parlor where the family was waiting to greet him. Mr. Gardiner was there with two attractive women; the younger one was the most beautiful lady Bingley had ever beheld.

"Mr. Bingley, welcome to our home," said his host pleasantly. "We are so pleased you could join us this evening."

"Thank you for the invitation, Mr. Gardiner. I am pleased to be here." Though Bingley's words were directed to Mr. Gardiner, he could not take his eyes off the blond-haired beauty dressed in mourning and seated on the sofa beside the woman he assumed to be Mr. Gardiner's wife.

Mr. Gardiner suppressed a smile as he said, "Please allow me to introduce you to my wife, Mrs. Helen Gardiner, and my niece, Miss Jane Bennet."

Bingley acknowledged the introductions with a bow to each lady. Miss Bennet stood and offered the gentleman a curtsey, though she spoke not a word.

"We are delighted you could join us this evening, Mr. Bingley," said Mrs. Gardiner, after offering her curtsey. "My husband tells me the two of you have agreed to an arrangement that should be mutually beneficial."

"Thank you for having me, Mrs. Gardiner. I hope it has not inconvenienced you in any way."

"Not at all, Mr. Bingley. Will you please be seated?"

Bingley took the chair next to Mr. Gardiner's, across from the sofa where the ladies sat. Bingley's outgoing manners and affability helped make the conversation flow. Mr. and Mrs. Gardiner even noted a small smile which occasionally graced Jane's face.

They had been talking for some twenty minutes when the butler arrived and announced that dinner was served. Mr. Gardiner offered his arm to his wife to lead her to the dining room. Bingley hesitated only briefly before offering his arm to Jane Bennet, who also hesitated for only the briefest of moments before accepting. The young couple followed the Gardiners into the dining room.

Dinner was a pleasant experience, and the evening passed far too quickly in Bingley's estimation. He had not been able to draw much conversation from Miss Bennet, but was quite enthralled with her beauty. Before departing, he did manage to ask if he might call on her again.

As Jane began to demur, Bingley said, "I understand you are in mourning, Miss Bennet, but certainly you do not need to shun all company. I should be most pleased to have the opportunity to know you better. Certainly making a new friend is not against the rules of mourning."

At the hopeful look on Bingley's face, Jane found she could not deny his request. "I would be pleased to receive your call, Mr. Bingley." His presence and conversation had brought Jane the first pleasure she had felt since the death of her family. *Perhaps his friendship will help me bear this terrible pain,* she thought. Jane graciously accepted his request, and with Mr. Gardiner's permission, Bingley arranged to call two days hence.

Over the next few weeks, Mr. Bingley could be found visiting the Gardiner home once or twice a week, sometimes more often. He had been visiting for almost a month before Jane opened up to him about the loss of her family.

"Who is it you are mourning?" Bingley had asked hesitantly, hoping it was not a lost betrothed.

"There was a carriage accident that killed my parents and all of my sisters. At least, we were originally told all my sisters had perished." Bingley noted the tears that filled her eyes at her reply.

"I am sorry for your loss, Miss Bennet. Was it recent?"

"It has been more than three months, but . . ." Jane's voice trailed off as she was again overcome with sadness.

"If it is not too painful for you to speak about, I should be happy to listen to anything you wish to say," Bingley remarked gently.

Jane recounted what she knew about the accident from the letter Mr. Gardiner had received. "The heir showed up on the day after the accident occurred, even though he had never visited our family at that time of year. He did not even notify us of what had occurred until after the funeral," sniffed Jane. "My uncle wrote requesting that we be allowed to come and pack up the rest of my belongings and to gather some items of special meaning. However, he denied us entry, saying he would have the housekeeper send the belongings to us."

"What did you mean when you said you were originally told all your sisters had perished?" Bingley asked in confusion.

"One of my uncles is the solicitor in the town nearest my family's estate. He was away on holiday at the time of the accident. When he returned home, my uncle learned that my next younger sister, Elizabeth, had not been in the carriage at the time of the accident. However, within a week or so of the accident, she had disappeared." Jane had to pause to collect herself before she could continue speaking. "We have not heard from her in all these months and have no idea where she is. I contacted a friend in the neighborhood, who told me the servants helped her escape. She had said she must stay away until she reaches her majority and then it would be safe. None of it makes any sense to me, and I am so worried about Lizzy's safety. Where could she be, and how is she managing on her own? I am so afraid I will never see her again!" said Jane before bursting into tears.

Though Bingley would have liked to take Jane in his arms to comfort her, he had to settle for patting her hand and trying to speak words that would give his angel, as he thought of Jane, some comfort.

Bingley met with the Gardiners and Miss Bennet many times in the coming weeks. With each meeting, his attraction to Jane Bennet grew, and he became more convinced the young lady he had met at Pemberley was Jane's missing sister.

Charles Bingley had been calling on Miss Bennet for a month before he was certain he was in love with Jane and wished to marry her. Bingley was scheduled to dine with the Gardiners that evening, but he decided to pay a call on Mr. Gardiner at his office earlier in the day. It was a nervous Bingley who was shown into the office of Edward Gardiner.

"Good morning, Mr. Bingley. How are you this fine day?"

"I am well, Mr. Gardiner," answered the young man. Nervousness obvious in his manner and his voice caused Edward Gardiner to raise his eyebrow and work to suppress a smile.

"Please have a seat." Gardiner waved the young man to the chairs before his desk and continued speaking when the young man was seated. "I had not expected to see you until this evening. Is there something particular I can do for you today, Mr. Bingley?"

"Actually, sir, there is. I would like your permission to marry Miss Bennet. If you feel it is too soon or have concerns due to her mourning state, I would be willing to settle for a formal courtship." The words had tumbled out in one breath that the young man now seemed to be holding.

"I take it you have not yet spoken to my niece?"

"No, sir. Because of her mourning status, I believed it more appropriate for me to discuss the situation with you first."

"You do realize that should I agree, Jane could not be married until the first of the year at the earliest. You also understand that Jane might prefer to wait until the full year of mourning is over before marrying. Do you think you will be able to wait more than seven months before a wedding?"

"I would be happy to wait as long as she needs. I just want to know she is mine and to have the world know it as well."

Mr. Gardiner was quiet for some time, staring at the young man. He believed Bingley to be Jane's perfect match and was only too happy to give his permission. Jane felt adrift without her family and needed someone she could love and for whom she could care. Mr. Gardiner and his wife had already noticed the tender care Mr. Bingley had shown for Jane. They believe he would make her a loving husband and provide her with the anchor she needed to recover from her loss. Finally, Mr. Gardiner gave the young man his answer.

"I will arrange for you and Jane to have a few minutes alone after dinner this evening. However, I must have your promise on one item. If you propose, and Jane wishes only for a courtship at this time, you will not press her to change her mind. Can you promise me this?"

"Of course, Mr. Gardiner. I love Jane and wish only the best for her. I am more than willing to allow her to dictate the pace of our relationship."

"Very well then. We will see you for dinner this evening, Mr. Bingley.

"I am very much looking forward to it, sir." Bingley could not disguise the smile on his face as he shook hands with Mr. Gardiner and departed.

Bingley arrived early for his dinner with the Gardiners and Jane. Relieved at having received her uncle's permission to speak to her, he could not stand to be separated from Jane. He only hoped his request would receive a positive response.

They enjoyed a delicious meal together, and it was decided they would forego the usual separation of the sexes after dinner. As they prepared to leave the dining room, Mr. Gardiner said, "Jane, would you lead Mr. Bingley to the parlor? I must speak with your aunt for just a moment, but we shall be with you shortly."

"Of course, Uncle." Jane turned to move in the direction of the parlor, but Mrs. Gardiner saw the nod her husband gave to their guest, as well as the huge smile that graced Mr. Bingley's face.

When they arrived in the parlor, Mr. Bingley seated himself on the sofa next to Jane. He reached out and took her hand in his, staring into her eyes as he tried to organize his thoughts.

"Miss Bennet, this time we have shared leads me to realize you are the young lady with whom I wish to share my life. I know your life has had many changes over the past several months. I wish to spend my life with you. I wish to be your family. I know no one will ever take their place, but I wish to offer you a chance to create a new family with me. Would you do me the very great honor of accepting my hand in marriage?"

Floundering since the death of her family and the disappearance of her dearest sister, Jane had wished for nothing more than a family to again call her own. Her eyes filled with tears at Mr. Bingley's words, and she was not sure she would be able to force the words from her suddenly dry throat. Nonetheless, she looked at Mr. Bingley and, nodding her head, said, "I thank you for your proposal, and I would like nothing better than to accept. When my family died, I felt as if a part of myself had died, too. My heart began beating again only when I met you."

Bingley could not believe his good fortune. He took the hand he held and brought it to his lips, placing a lingering kiss upon it. He would have loved to sweep Jane up into his embrace, but he truly meant what he told Mr. Gardiner. He would go as slowly as Jane needed as they planned their future life together.

"Would you be willing to wait until a full year of mourning has passed before we marry?"

"I will wait as long as you need. I just wished to know you would be mine."

The Gardiners joined them and congratulations were offered. They spoke of plans for Jane to get out more during her half-mourning and set a date for the wedding at the end of the first week in July.

18. DISTURBING NEWS & PLEASANT DAYS

COLONEL FITZWILLIAM ARRIVED AT DARCY HOUSE at half past eleven. He was greeted by Dixon, the long-time butler at Darcy's London townhouse.

"Good morning, Colonel. What brings you here today?"

"I have a meeting about noon, Dixon, and thought to make use of Darcy's study to conduct it. The matters are of a confidential nature, and some of the information could be hurtful to my cousins. I wished to ensure complete privacy for the discussion ahead of me."

Dixon was concerned by the colonel's words. "Are Mr. and Miss Darcy quite well, Colonel?"

"As far as I know, both are in excellent health. Now, if you would be so good as to conduct Mr. Shaw to the study when he arrives, I would appreciate it, Dixon."

"Certainly, Colonel."

As Richard moved down the hall in the direction of the study, he was met by Mrs. Dixon, the housekeeper.

"Good day to you, Mrs. Dixon. I would ask after your health, but as you grow lovelier each time I see you, there is no need." Richard accompanied his words with a toothy smile.

"Go on with you now, Colonel," replied Mrs. Dixon with a pleased smile. "Can I get anything for you or will you be staying for luncheon, sir?"

"No thank you, Mrs. Dixon. My conversation is more suited to a glass of my cousin's brandy than tea, and then I must be off back to the War Offices. As I told your husband, I just needed a quiet place to conduct a meeting on a sensitive subject."

"Well, you just ring if you change your mind," said Mrs. Dixon as she moved off to join her husband.

Richard entered the study and poured himself a glass of brandy. He placed it on the table between the chairs before the fireplace as he took a seat. In moments, a servant appeared to light the fire, for the days were getting cooler. As he watched the blaze come to life, the colonel sipped his brandy and pondered what other news Shaw might have to share that he did not wish to put in a letter. He hoped his cousins had not been taken in by someone whose intention was to harm them. However, from the information Shaw had written, he did not think that would be the case.

His musings were interrupted by a knock on the open door. "Mr. Shaw to see you, Colonel," said Dixon as the gentleman entered the room. The butler withdrew, closing the door behind him.

The colonel extended his hand to the newcomer. "Shaw, good to see you. Can I get you a drink?"

"No thank you, sir."

"Have a seat. I am anxious to hear the rest of your information."

Shaw took the chair the colonel indicated, but did not immediately speak as he arranged his thoughts. He did not delay long, as he could see the colonel's obvious concern and impatience. "If the missing young lady is the same one who is serving as your cousin's companion, I do not think you need have cause for concern. Everyone who spoke about her praised her for her kindness and compassion. She was well-regarded by all of her neighbors, and concern for her whereabouts and well-being were frequently expressed.

"Colonel, I believe the young lady had no choice but to leave her home, and it appears she was intelligent enough to do so without giving away her plans or getting caught. I overheard a drunken Mr. Collins, the heir to the estate, say several things that made my blood run cold."

Continuing, Shaw said, "He may have had a hand in the accident that killed the Bennet family. Due to an entailment, he was Mr. Bennet's heir. He also mentioned he had tried to arrange a marriage between his son and Miss Elizabeth Bennet, the missing young lady, due to an inheritance she would come into when she came of age. If the young lady had been unwilling, he was not above forcing himself upon his cousin, leaving her no other choice."

"Bloody hell! What a cur the man is. Does the man have any idea where Miss Bennet is?"

"I do not believe so, sir. He would have dragged her back if he knew. Mostly he cursed her for getting away and swore revenge if he ever saw her."

"Thank heaven for that!" the colonel remarked with feeling. "Were you able to get a description of the missing young lady? What about the man Collins? Were you able to get his likeness? It may be useful if we need to keep her safe from him."

"She was described as having dark curly hair, brown eyes that often sparkled with amusement, and a lively wit. I was also told she was quite intelligent.

As for Collins, I was able to make this sketch for you." He handed a folded paper to the colonel, who opened it and stared intently at the face drawn there as if committing it to memory. Richard saw a once-handsome face beginning to show signs of a life of dissipation. Folding the paper again, he looked at the investigator and spoke.

"Well, that description certainly fits the young lady currently at Pemberley, but it could also fit many other young ladies of my acquaintance. I will have to speak with my cousin and the young lady to determine her identity. If she turns out to be Miss Bennet, we will do what we can to protect her. Did you learn anything else of importance?"

"Yes, besides the family in Meryton, she has an aunt and uncle in London, where her elder sister is also residing."

"If she has family, why would she not turn to them for assistance?"

"I have a theory about that," said Shaw thoughtfully. "If she overheard anything that made her suspect the cousin's involvement with the deaths of her parents and younger sisters, she may have been afraid to put her remaining family in similar danger."

Richard nodded in agreement.

"As I mentioned, the young lady is to receive a large inheritance of some kind. I believe she may try to contact them when she reaches her majority. I am sure she will not feel safe returning to her family until the inheritance is tied up in such a way that it cannot be gained through marriage to her. If he cannot get at the inheritance, he would have no reason to bother Miss Bennet."

"Yes, if she is as intelligent as was reported, she may plan something exactly like that."

"Do you know who her family is or where they live?"

"Yes, sir. I took a few minutes to gather some information about them before coming here. It is the Gardiner family. They live in Cheapside. Mr. Gardiner is in the import/export business. From what I learned, he is extremely successful. Several members of the ton have invested with him, including Mr. Darcy and your father, I believe."

"I believe I have heard my father mention him. He is quite impressed with the man, from what I gather. So Miss Bennet is an heiress but orphaned and with no connections of which to speak. Is Collins just greedy, or is there some reason he needs to obtain Miss Bennet's inheritance?"

"I believe Mr. Collins owes some gambling debts to a few rather unsavory characters here in town. I would add a note of caution, Colonel. I do not believe Mr. Collins is the type of man to accept being thwarted in his desires. I believe he would attempt to revenge himself against the young lady, even if the money was no longer involved."

"Is there anything else to add?"

"Unfortunately, Colonel, Mr. Wickham is also aware of most of these facts. If Collins should ever learn of the young lady's whereabouts, he might ask his friend Wickham for assistance. We know how he feels about the Darcys. If Wickham learned the young lady was there, he would be happy to assist in obtaining her and may try to get at Miss Darcy again as well. Even if Wickham did not make another attempt at Miss Darcy, he would not be above double-crossing Mr. Collins in hopes of gaining the young lady's inheritance for himself. Either option would be dreadful for Miss Bennet."

"Bloody hell," the colonel said again.

"I took the liberty of buying up the debts Mr. Wickham has incurred since his arrival in Meryton. I assumed Mr. Darcy would wish to continue this practice, as it gives him greater leverage against Mr. Wickham," Shaw concluded.

The gentlemen continued to discuss what Shaw had learned about Mr. Collins' history, the situation in Meryton, and the condition of the estate. Shaw also told the colonel about Walter Collins.

"Collins' father speaks in a very derogatory manner regarding his son, frequently commenting on his lack of intelligence. I would guess he was most likely bullied by his father, complying with requests to keep the peace. Walter Collins is currently at Oxford, where he will finish his studies to be a parson in December. He appears to be a somewhat timid young man of average intelligence, but is well-liked by his peers. Most feel he has a true calling for the church. He has already been contacting possible patrons. If I am not mistaken, one of the people he contacted is Lady Catherine de Bourgh."

"That is all we need," said the colonel with a grimace. "If Lady Catherine were to find out about Miss Lucas or Bennet, Collins could find out where she is. Fortunately, I am going to Pemberley for the holidays. I will discuss everything with Darcy immediately upon my arrival. We will just have to hope nothing unusual occurs before then."

Shortly thereafter, the colonel finished his drink and the gentlemen went their separate ways.

The fall months passed pleasantly for the residents of Pemberley. The Harvest Celebration had been a huge success. It was still a topic of conversation whenever the tenants gathered or met with someone from the main house.

If what Darcy remembered most about the event was dancing with Miss Lucas, he tried not to dwell on it. She was his employee, but no one knew that, he argued with himself. She was a remarkable woman and the daughter of a gentleman. Never in his wildest dreams did he imagine he would meet such a woman. She challenged him intellectually and brightened a room with her presence. She was a wonderful example to Georgiana, caring towards the staff, and kind to all she met. He tried, unsuccessfully, to put her out of his mind, but she was rarely far from his thoughts and had even begun to invade his dreams.

For Elizabeth, her dance with Darcy at the Harvest Celebration was unlike any she had ever experienced. Darcy was an excellent dancer, but the feelings he stirred within her at the sound of his voice or the touch of his hand were new and unsettling. He could make her shiver and feel extremely warm at the same time. She did not understand her feelings and was a little frightened by them. There was a part of her that wished to trust Darcy with the truth of her situation, but she was terrified he would turn away from her when he learned of her deception.

With the Harvest Celebration behind them, Elizabeth had Georgiana focused on plans for the upcoming holiday season. The Fitzwilliam family was planning to arrive two days before Christmas and would be staying until the 28th of the month. Then the Darcys would be traveling to Lockwood for the Fitzwilliams' annual New Year's Eve Ball. It was one of the highlights of the holidays, and families came from all over Derbyshire and the surrounding counties to attend.

The young ladies made plans for decorating the house and reviewed what had been given to the families in the holiday baskets the previous year. Then they visited each of the families and began planning the baskets for the current year. Elizabeth taught Georgiana how to make small cloth dolls for the girls, and they tried to decide on a small gift they could give to all the boys.

Darcy was busy with the calculations from the harvest. He had to decide how much to hold back for the next year's planting, what to store, and what to sell. Then he needed to negotiate the best prices for the sales. After consultation with his steward, determinations had been made about what fall crops to plant, how much to plant, and which tenants would do the planting. Darcy still had to determine which fields he should leave fallow, as well as begin planning for the spring planting.

When the weather permitted, he and Elizabeth still took a weekly excursion to the most beautiful spots on the estate. Elizabeth delighted in seeing the changes in the landscape as summer waned and fall came forth in all its autumnal glory.

As the weeks passed, Elizabeth was surprised at how much colder Derbyshire was than Hertfordshire. When she left Longbourn she had tried to pack for any circumstance, but she had not imagined she might end up so far to the north. Winter clothing took much more space, so she had packed only her warmest cloak. The thin shawl she had packed did not give much warmth, nor did it dispel the chill of the northern climate. Darcy realized Miss Lucas was not accustomed to the Derbyshire climate, nor did she have an appropriate wardrobe for the colder weather. Consequently, he again sent the ladies into Lambton so warmer clothing could be made for Elizabeth and Georgiana.

Because her time of half mourning was approaching, Elizabeth chose to purchase gowns in dark shades of forest green and gray. She also purchased a lovely wool shawl in a pretty plaid that would complement many colors. Georgiana ordered three additional day dresses for Elizabeth in dark blue, deep plum, and a chocolate brown that matched Elizabeth's eyes, as well as a long-sleeved evening gown in burgundy silk. The Darcys also purchased two pairs of boots and a cloak lined with fur. Georgiana added a fur muff and several pairs of new gloves for Elizabeth as well. They also purchased a warmer robe for her and winter nightgowns in soft flannel. Elizabeth had, again, insisted on less and paying for her purchases, but, as before, Darcy and Georgiana ordered what they felt she would need regardless of the additional cost.

Soon the weather turned too wet for Elizabeth to enjoy her morning walks. Instead, she could often be found walking the halls of the house at a brisk pace or climbing the stairs from the ground floor to the top and back down again several times. The staff grew accustomed to her unusual habit and smiled when they saw her. Elizabeth knew them all by name and never failed to speak politely with them or ask after their health or that of their families. She was admired and respected by all. The staff was particularly pleased that her addition to the household seemed to make both Master William and Miss Georgiana happier, and the house was often filled with the warmth of her laughter.

When Georgiana's studies were done for the day, the two ladies could often be found seated on a couch in the library as Georgiana tried to create realistic sketches of people she had never seen. Elizabeth had described her family's personalities to Georgiana in great depth, telling her about their behaviors, their likes and dislikes, their favorite activities, and their individual idiosyncrasies. She described her sisters' features as compared to her own in an attempt to help Georgiana visualize them. Miss Darcy was endlessly patient as they worked to get each detail correct. It took several weeks, but eventually Georgiana produced sketches of all the members of the Bennet family, and the realism of the drawings brought tears to Elizabeth's eyes.

One afternoon as the Darcys and Elizabeth sat in the library, Darcy began to laugh aloud as he read a letter from Bingley.

"What does Mr. Bingley write that causes your humor, Brother?"

Darcy read the letter out loud to his sister and her companion. Bingley wrote of the trials of the trip to London and of the punishment he had devised for his sister. He wrote about watching as she emptied her chamber pot the first time and of watching her attempt to scrub her clothes and of her burning a favorite dress as she tried to press it. By the time he had finished reading, all three were laughing so hard they had tears streaming from their eyes.

"I would give anything to have seen what he describes," said Georgiana as she wiped away the tears.

"I wonder if it will truly make a difference in her behavior," mused Elizabeth.

"It will be easy to tell. She may be complying for the time being, but Bingley wrote that he must see 'marked improvement and continued evidence' of such before he will relent. She may be able to hide her feelings while she is hidden away in her room. I am not sure she will be able to maintain it when she is allowed back in company with her family," Darcy replied. "However, I do not plan to give Miss Bingley further thought, for she is not permitted in my homes."

Darcy received a second letter that day from Colonel Fitzwilliam. However, this one brought a frown to his face. Not wishing the ladies to see his expression, he stood and paced to the window with his back to them as he read the letter through a second time. One section, in particular, caused him a great deal of concern.

"I do not know for sure that Miss Lucas is the missing Miss Bennet, but she does match the description, and she did have the horse returned to the town from which the young lady disappeared. If she is Miss Bennet, she is in a great deal of danger."

He went on to inform Darcy that he would arrive well in advance of the rest of the family so they could talk to Miss Lucas and see what assistance they could provide.

Mrs. Reynolds arrived with the tea tray and Georgiana asked her brother if he would like some tea. He did not acknowledge her, and she asked again. Finally, she called, "William," in a loud, emphatic voice.

Darcy started at the sound of his name, turning to look at the ladies.

"Are you alright, Brother? You were lost in thought. I had to ask several times if you wished for a cup of tea."

"I am sorry, Dear One. I was just reading the most recent letter from Richard. He says his leave will allow him to arrive well before the rest of the family for the Christmas visit. I was wondering what I would do to entertain him on those extra days," Darcy replied haltingly.

Georgiana seemed to accept his answer, but Darcy noticed that Miss Lucas continued to gaze at him in concern.

Darcy affixed a smile on his face and returned to his seat, again noticing Miss Lucas looking at him with a puzzled expression on her face. Not wishing her to ask questions, Darcy quickly changed the subject by asking his sister if there was anything particular she wanted for Christmas. The conversation continued pleasantly throughout tea. When Georgiana departed to rest and change for dinner, Elizabeth held back.

"Pardon me for asking, Mr. Darcy, but was there something in your cousin's letter that caused you concern, perhaps something about which you did not wish Miss Darcy to be aware?"

Darcy stared for a moment, surprised at her perceptiveness. Thinking quickly, he said, "The Colonel mentioned there have been reports of highwayman in the area. Please be sure you take at least two footmen whenever you and Georgiana are away from the house. In fact, I should feel more comfortable if they were to follow you about when you are doing errands in Lambton also."

"Certainly, sir. I shall protect Miss Darcy with my life if necessary."

"I would hope it never comes to that, Miss Lucas, for I — Georgiana and I would be lost without you. You have brought life back to Pemberley." The warm smile that accompanied his words caused Elizabeth to blush. As the bright pink color flooded her cheeks, the look in his eyes intensified. Elizabeth did not understand the feelings his look engendered in her, but she dearly wished he would always look at her in such a fashion.

They stood staring until a knock at the open door startled them.

"Excuse me, Mr. Darcy, but I wanted to collect the tea tray." Mrs. Reynolds looked between her employer and his "cousin." It was clear to her that Master William had feelings for the young lady, and that his feelings were likely returned, though she saw hesitancy in Miss Lucas' expression. This situation was something she would have to watch. She liked Miss Lucas and would not wish to see anything untoward happen to the young lady, but what was the master thinking to be flirting with an employee?

When Darcy looked away to reply to the housekeeper, Elizabeth almost ran from the room.

Darcy remained in the library after Mrs. Reynolds removed the tea tray. He realized, as he watched Miss Lucas flee the room, that he had frightened her, and that had certainly not been his intention. As the months had passed, Darcy had fallen more and more under the spell of Miss Lucas. Her beauty was beyond compare, and she was the most fascinating young woman he had ever met. He enjoyed every discussion they had and was impressed with her intellect. She was also one of the kindest, most compassionate women he had ever met. Georgiana had blossomed in her presence. In fact, all of Pemberley felt more alive with her there. She had certainly proven she was a competent and capable mistress for Pemberley. The perfect mistress of his home! Darcy sat with a thump as he realized he thought of her as the mistress of his home. In fact, he could not imagine another woman of his acquaintance who would make a better one. *I love her*, he thought.

Darcy realized he would have to find a way to discuss his feelings with her, but he hesitated to do so. She had run away earlier. Did that mean she did not feel the same towards him? Perhaps she did, but had assumed he would be offended. Perhaps he could speak with her after supper. With that in mind, he rushed to change so he would be present when the ladies arrived in the drawing room.

Darcy was standing with his back to the room, looking out the window, when he heard the door open. He turned with a smile on his face to see his sister entering. He was surprised when she immediately closed the door.

"Where is Miss Lucas, Georgie?"

"She has another one of her dreadful headaches, and Lucy and I insisted she remain in bed and not get up until she was completely recovered."

"She said they were infrequent. I believe we should summon the doctor to be sure it is nothing more serious," said Darcy firmly. He moved to the bell pull to ring for a servant.

Within seconds, Mrs. Reynolds appeared in the doorway of the sitting room. She was about to announce that dinner was ready, but Darcy spoke before she could. "Thank you for coming so promptly, Mrs. Reynolds. Please send for Dr. Powell. Miss Lucas is again suffering from another of her headaches, and I am concerned about her health."

"Certainly, sir. In the meantime, dinner is served."

The housekeeper turned to request a footman to fetch the doctor as Darcy escorted Georgie into dinner. They had almost finished dining when Darcy heard a noise at the door, indicating the doctor's arrival. He stepped to the doorway of the dining room. "Doctor Powell, thank you for coming. The first time Miss Lucas suffered from one of these severe headaches after arriving at Pemberley, she told us they were very rare. However, this is the second one she has had since the Harvest Festival. I wish to be sure there is not another cause for her headaches or something else that could be wrong."

Dr. Powell was surprised to learn he had been summoned because of a headache. "Certainly, Mr. Darcy. I shall give her a thorough examination to ensure she is in good health." Following the housekeeper to the family quarters, Dr. Powell was deep in thought. At the Harvest Festival, he thought he had detected a partiality on Darcy's part for Miss Lucas. Having known the young man all of his life, he was pleased to see Darcy had finally met a young woman for whom he could care. Suspecting his affections, the doctor could more easily understand the young man's actions. Having lost his parents at such a young age, he always became quite concerned when someone for whom he cared was ill.

After completing his examination, the doctor opened the chamber door to find Mr. Darcy pacing in the hallway. He was forced to suppress a laugh.

"How is Miss Lucas?"

"Perhaps we could discuss it in your study rather than the hallway," the doctor responded with a raised eyebrow.

Darcy quickly led the way to his study. The door had barely closed behind them when Darcy stopped, turned to the doctor, and again asked, "How is Miss Lucas? Is there anything she needs? Should I send for a specialist from London?"

This time, the doctor could not suppress his laughter, though he tried to cover it with a cough. He moved to the decanters on the table at the side of the room and poured a small glass of brandy. He handed the glass to Darcy and gestured to the chairs before the fireplace. Darcy took a large pull of his brandy as he moved towards the chairs indicated.

Once they were seated, the doctor finally spoke. "I have thoroughly examined Miss Lucas and discussed her past headaches with her. I can assure you, she will be perfectly well very soon. She suffers from a particularly debilitating type of headache, called a megrim. These are usually resistant to powders and are improved only with time. Fortunately, they rarely last more than four and twenty hours.

"I left a new kind of powder for her to try. This formula has worked well for another patient who suffers from megrims. Miss Lucas said she would happily try most anything to gain some relief. I suggested she remain in bed all day tomorrow, though I imagine she will have made a complete recovery before then. As I said, they rarely last more than four and twenty hours."

"Thank goodness," Darcy breathed. "Is there truly nothing that can be done for her to reduce her suffering?"

"Other than quiet and, possibly, a cool compress, I am afraid not."

"Is there something in particular that causes these megrims?" Darcy was determined to eliminate the cause to prevent Miss Lucas from suffering in the future.

"As you know, the brain is quite a mystery in many ways. There is an abundance of theories, but no one is certain of the cause. Most often, they seem to come on in times of deep stress, or at a shock or fright of some kind. They can also be caused by changes in a woman's body, undue anxiety, or extreme exertion. There could also be other causes about which we know nothing. I have read of a case in which the patient was fine at night and woke up in pain where no outside stimulus appeared to be involved."

"You are sure there is no other form of illness except the pain in her head."

"I assure you, Mr. Darcy, Miss Lucas is quite healthy except for her headache."

At the words "times of stress, fright, or anxiety," Darcy's guilt returned. *Because the doctor insisted she was otherwise healthy, I must be the cause of her illness! Could it be that the thought I might have feelings for her makes her feel unwell?* Darcy worried. He was devastated at the thought; not only had he frightened her with the intensity of his feelings, but he had brought about the pain she was suffering. How was he ever to speak with her further without causing this to happen again?

Dr. Powell had been watching the changing emotions rapidly cross Darcy's face. It was quite obvious he felt somehow responsible for the young lady's headache. It was the doctor's chuckle that pulled Darcy's thoughts back to his companion. Dr.

Powell was looking at him and shaking his head with a rueful smile on his face. "Despite her current circumstances in life, Miss Lucas is a remarkable young woman, Darcy. A man would be lucky to come across someone like her even once in a lifetime."

Surprised by the doctor's words, Darcy answered without thinking. "Yes she is, but if I caused her pain by intimating my feelings, how can I ever speak further without causing more anxiety or pain?"

Pleased that his surmise had been correct, Dr. Powell spoke reassuringly. "Perhaps Miss Lucas was shocked by your inference, but that does not necessarily mean the information was unpleasant or unwelcome." The doctor stood from his chair and put his hand on Darcy's shoulder. "Go slowly. You will be able to see how your feelings are received." He gave Darcy a strong clap on the shoulder he was holding before departing.

Darcy was still staring at the doorway through which the doctor had disappeared when he heard the front door close. He leaned back in his chair and took another large swig from his glass. Dr. Powell had guessed at Darcy's feelings, but he had not sounded disapproving of the idea. After all, Miss Lucas was the daughter of a gentleman. Her job as Georgiana's companion was her first position, and he had created an acceptable explanation for her presence in his home. *Would his family be as accepting?* Darcy remained in his study, staring at the fire until it burned low. He had been lost in his musings, but he believed he would need to enlist his sister's help in determining the best way to approach Miss Lucas.

19. DISCONCERTING EVENTS

DARCY FOUND SLEEP DIFFICULT, SO HE was up even earlier than usual the next morning. The remainder of the day passed slowly, as he worried for Miss Lucas and about the future he hoped to have with her. Though a stack of correspondence on his desk needed replies, Darcy could not focus for more than a few moments at a time.

Darcy moved to the window, staring out but seeing nothing. Perhaps if he shared his feelings with Georgiana, she would be able to determine the best way to approach Miss Lucas. Having made a decision as to the best course of action, he returned to his desk and concentrated on answering all of his correspondence so that he could focus on winning Miss Lucas' heart.

He had almost reached the last letter in when a knock came at the door. Georgiana entered at his call, followed by a maid with the tea tray. She beckoned the maid to set the tray on the table between the chairs by the fireplace and remained standing before her brother's desk until the maid had left.

"When you did not appear for luncheon, I decided to bring something to you. You have obviously been busy today," remarked his sister. "Let us move to the chairs before the fire, and I will pour us some tea while you eat."

Darcy stood to join her and remarked, "Actually, I am glad you are here, Georgie. There is something I wished to discuss with you." As he seated himself next to his sister, Darcy hesitated. He would normally not share his innermost feelings with another, even his sister. However, *his* Rose was worth the discomfort he might feel during this conversation.

"Is something the matter, William?"

Darcy could hear the concern in her voice, as well as a tremor of trepidation. "No, Dear One, there is nothing the matter. I merely wish to ask your opinion on a matter." He could see Georgiana visibly relax. Not knowing where to start, he asked, "Have you checked on Miss Lucas recently? Does she appear to be improving?"

"Yes, I did see her shortly before joining you. I inquired if she would care to have tea sent up. She said she would enjoy that and asked for a few biscuits as well, so I am certain she is feeling much better."

A small smile lit Darcy's face at the news. She was no longer in pain, but would she stay that way if he were to speak to her of his feelings? No one was closer to Miss Lucas than Georgiana, so he was sure she could provide valuable insight into her companion. Perhaps she could even discover what Miss Lucas' feelings were for him.

"Dear One, have you and Miss Lucas discussed whether there were other gentlemen in her life besides her father? I mean, was there someone special she may have cared for before she was forced to leave her home?"

Whatever Georgiana had expected her brother to discuss, it had not been this. However, his question, coupled with Darcy's behavior in recent days, led his sister to the obvious conclusion.

Fitzwilliam cared for Miss Lucas as more than her companion. Georgiana was delighted and determined to do what she could to bring them together, as she would certainly enjoy having Rose for her sister.

"Though we have spoken of my experiences at Ramsgate, she has never mentioned any gentlemen." Georgiana had to look at her hands, which were folded in her lap, so Fitzwilliam would not see the smile that crept across her face as she heard him exhale in relief.

"You appear to enjoy having Miss Lucas as your companion; it is too bad she will leave us in just two short years."

That was not what Georgiana had expected to hear. Thinking quickly and hoping to provoke a reaction from her brother, she said, "Well, because we have been telling everyone she is a distant relation, perhaps some nice young man will wish to marry her when she appears with me at balls and the other events I will attend during my season."

"Do you think she would fit in with the ton?"

Georgiana could hear the nervousness in his voice and the look in his eyes led her to believe her answer would be very important. Consequently, she paused to order her thoughts. When she was ready to speak, she looked directly at her brother. "I believe Rose could fit in well anywhere. She is quite an intelligent woman, after all. Her manners and understanding are excellent, and she certainly demonstrated her strength of character when she stood up for Hannah against Miss Bingley. I believe she could handle the less polite members of the ton very well. She also has a gift for putting people at their ease. After all, look at us," she said with a soft laugh.

Georgiana's words brought a smile to Darcy's face as well.

"In fact, I would not be at all surprised if some perceptive gentleman should recognize her worth when she accompanies me to events during my season. We have allowed everyone to believe she is our cousin, so I would certainly encourage her to find love if the opportunity presented itself."

At the mention of some other gentleman recognizing her worth, Darcy's face paled and his determination increased. If he had his way, by the time she met the gentlemen of the ton, she would be his wife, or his betrothed at the very least.

"Is it safe to assume you would not be displeased if I were to ask Miss Lucas to marry me? Would you worry for your chances to make a good match if I married someone society would consider far below me?"

Georgiana was practically bouncing in her seat before Darcy had finished what he was saying. "Oh, Fitzwilliam, I can think of nothing I would like better than to have Rose for my sister!"

"Wait a moment, Georgie, there is one problem. On the two occasions when I have attempted to express my feelings for her, she has experienced a megrim."

"Of what are you speaking, brother?"

Darcy told her of the things he had said to Miss Lucas on the night of the harvest celebrations, as well as the previous day after tea. "How can I risk speaking to her when it may cause her to experience another of her painful headaches?" he asked despondently.

Georgiana was sure that was not the cause of her illness. After a moment, she said thoughtfully, "William, perhaps she has feelings for you but feels you could never return them because of her status. Perhaps it was the fear of unrequited love that brought on her headache." Georgiana sighed softly, thinking about the romance of the situation. She was determined to find a way to bring them together.

As Georgiana's thoughts were filled with romance, Darcy gave serious consideration to his sister's words. *Could Rose be uncertain of my feelings? Has she any experience in feelings of the heart? How can I show her I hold her in esteem in spite of her position? Perhaps she knows I esteem her, but thinks it is only in her capacity as a companion to Georgiana.* Suddenly Darcy was struck by an unpleasant thought. *Could she possibly think my attentions have a nefarious purpose?*

Darcy's thoughts were interrupted when Georgiana spoke. "Perhaps you need to invite her to do things alone with you without me always being present?"

"I would enjoy that, but how to do it without it being improper? If we are followed by a maid, she may feel I expect she will attempt to cause a compromise. Why could she not be more like the others who are always attempting to cause a compromise?" Darcy's frustration was obvious in his tone.

Georgiana laughed, saying, "If she were that type of young lady, you would not be interested in her in the first place!"

Darcy chuckled at the truth of her words.

"I will see what I can do about learning her thoughts on marriage and suitors. Though I doubt she will tell me of any feelings she may have for you," Georgiana continued. "I shall go up and see how she is feeling and see what I can learn."

Laughing again, he stood. "I am very grateful for your assistance," he said as he gave her an exaggerated bow.

"I will see if she feels up to having company. If so, perhaps we could all have dinner in our sitting room so she would not have to go far to join us."

"That is a wonderful idea, Georgie!"

As Georgiana left the study, she thought about what she could say to get Elizabeth to talk about her own feelings. Georgiana was pensive as she approached the door to Elizabeth's bedchamber. She knocked softly, and the door was opened by Lucy.

"How is Miss Lucas feeling? Do you think she would be up for some company?"

"She seems to be doing much better. I am sure she would enjoy company, as she seems to be getting a bit restless," the maid said with a smile.

Lucy opened the door wider and invited Georgiana inside. Georgie stepped close to the bed. "Are you feeling any better? I have missed your company today and wondered if you might be up for some company and conversation."

"Your timing is perfect, Georgiana. I am in much need of a distraction. I am feeling better and find it hard to stay in bed when I would much rather be taking a walk in the gardens." Elizabeth's rueful grin spoke of her boredom.

"Well, if it will help you to follow the doctor's orders, I will be happy to keep you company."

Lucy helped prop Elizabeth up on her pillows, the better to converse with her guest.

"You mentioned you have had headaches likes this before; what did your sisters do for you when you were feeling unwell?"

"My older sister, Jane, would tuck me up into bed and ensure I was comfortable. My next younger sister, Mary, would make me a special cup of tea with chamomile and lavender."

"Did you tell Lucy about it? I am sure Mrs. Mason would have been happy to prepare it for you."

"No, I did not wish to bother anyone, particularly if the ingredients were not at hand."

"Well, I insist you write down how it is to be made in case you should suffer from another headache. We will be sure to have the items on hand. Neither William nor I would wish you to suffer needlessly, and having the ingredients for this tea would not be a bother to anyone."

Georgiana's decisive tone brought a smile to Elizabeth's face and a quiet agreement with her request.

"What other activities did you share with your sisters?"

Lizzy smiled at Georgiana's question as she remembered the many special times she had shared with her sisters. "We often spent time re-trimming our bonnets to change the color or refresh the style. Jane and I particularly loved working with the flowers and herbs from the gardens. Jane could make wonderful perfumes and lotions. She created something special for each of the sisters. Jane's favorite was rose, while mine was jasmine. Mary, who was next youngest, liked violets. Then came Kitty, who liked Lily of the Valley, and the youngest, Lydia, liked lilac. I used to help Jane with this and knew how to make all the fragrances, but I have not done it in quite some time. I wonder if I could remember how," Elizabeth mused.

"Oh, that sounds fun! Do you think we could try it in the spring?"

Not knowing where she would be come spring, Elizabeth did not want to commit herself. However, at the look of excitement on Georgiana's face, she could not deny the girl the opportunity to learn something new. "We can attempt it. I will try to remember the steps and ingredients and write it down before then," said Elizabeth. "However, I cannot promise they will turn out as well as Jane's did."

"To which of your sisters were you the closest? From what you have said, I believe it was your sister Jane."

With a look of longing on her face, Elizabeth answered, "It was Jane. She was my best friend and the most wonderful sister anyone could have. I could tell Jane all my secrets and know they would be safe, and her serene spirit always made me feel better. I miss her terribly." Georgiana could see the tears glistening in Elizabeth's eyes.

"Do you mind if I ask you something?"

Elizabeth shook her head.

"What kinds of secrets did you share? Did you talk about your suitors or perhaps about the kind of man you wished to marry?"

"Of course. We shared all of our hopes and dreams, as well as our heartaches."

"What kind of man would you like to marry?"

Elizabeth stared at Georgiana before answering, wondering if there was a reason behind her question, but Georgiana's expression was innocent and expectant. "I always wanted to marry for love, particularly if the gentleman was intelligent and kind and could accept my intelligence. Many of the young men from my neighborhood did not wish to converse with me much. They loved it when my imagination could dream up wonderful stories and games when we played together as children, but even after spending time at university, many of them wanted only to talk about their horses or hunting. They did not seem to have much interest in books, or current events, or even running their estates."

"They must have been dolts," said Georgiana. "I know my brother enjoys your conversation very much. I have heard him say it is refreshing to talk with a young lady who can converse about more than the weather, the state of the roads, and ladies' fashions. The lack of intelligent conversation is one of the things he hates most about attending social events," said Georgiana with a laugh, bringing a smile to Elizabeth's face as well.

"Before you came, I could not even imagine how wonderful it would have been to have a sister. I do not know what I would have done if you had not been here to talk to me about Mr. Wickham. I wish I could have a sister just like you!" said Georgiana artlessly, closely watching her companion's reaction.

Elizabeth's face blushed a rosy pink at Georgie's words. "Anyone would be lucky to have you for a sister," Elizabeth answered earnestly. "I know when you no longer have need of me as a companion, I shall miss you dreadfully. You have helped fill the loss of my missing sisters. Is Mr. Darcy thinking about marrying? Is that why you are speaking of sisters?" Elizabeth hoped her questions seemed nonchalant, but Georgiana was not deceived. She could see the sadness Elizabeth was trying to hide at the thought of William's marriage.

"I think he has recently met someone to whom he is attracted, but he is shy and uncertain of her feelings. I think she would make him a wonderful wife," was Georgiana's enigmatic reply.

"I cannot imagine a young lady who would not admire Mr. Darcy. I hope he will be very happy," replied Elizabeth quietly, though without much spirit.

"Are you feeling up to company for dinner? We could dine in the sitting room and invite William to join us."

At the thought of seeing Mr. Darcy again, Elizabeth's face immediately brightened. It fell just as quickly as she remarked, "I would enjoy his conversation, but surely it would not be appropriate."

"He is often in the sitting room with us; I do not believe anyone would give the matter a second thought."

Georgiana could observe Elizabeth's obvious struggle to balance what she wished for while maintaining propriety. "Are you sure he would not feel like I am trying to compromise him?"

"I shall go and ask him, and then arrange things accordingly with Mrs. Reynolds. Will that satisfy your concerns?"

Elizabeth was not sure how to reply, so she gave a small nod. Georgiana stood and turned to the door. Elizabeth could not see the satisfied smile that graced her face.

Later that evening, Darcy, Georgiana, and Elizabeth shared a quiet supper in the ladies' sitting room. Darcy expressed his pleasure that Elizabeth was returned to good health. He was very attentive to her needs and comfort throughout the evening.

It had been six weeks since Caroline Bingley had begun her punishment. She had complained loudly for the first three weeks, nearly driving everyone mad, but then she had become very quiet. She went about the work she was forced to do in silence, but her angry expressions left no one in doubt as to her feelings about the situation. The servants tried to avoid her presence whenever possible, fearing a reprisal in spite of Mr. Bingley's promises. Mr. Hurst openly laughed at her, particularly if she struggled with a task she attempted. Louisa avoided her sister whenever possible. She had experienced her sister's wrath first hand and knew Caroline would be upset that she had not convinced Charles to rescind the punishment. In fact, Louisa was proud of Charles for standing firm with their recalcitrant sister. Charles, who knew his sister well, hoped she was learning from the experience, but he certainly did not completely trust her when she was this quiet and angry. He worried Caroline was most likely plotting her revenge.

The Hursts had spent a month in Lincolnshire, having returned only the day before. Because Caroline had gone about her punishment quietly for the past few weeks, Charles planned for her to rejoin the family beginning with dinner that evening. Charles had not yet found her a new lady's maid, so she was forced to prepare herself for the evening. She opened the door to her room to find her bodyguard still in attendance. With a glare at the man, she moved in the direction of the main staircase. She waltzed into the drawing room and seated herself on the sofa beside her brother. She noted her guard was standing just outside the drawing room door.

"Charles, is it necessary for the guard to continue to follow me?"

"You have been allowed to join the family for the evening, Caroline, but your behavior this evening will determine whether this will continue or whether you will be returning to your full punishment."

"Do not be ridiculous, Charles. This punishment has dragged on far too long; I have done all you expected of me. I have not mistreated any servants or even spoken to any of them," Caroline said with a sniff.

Charles quietly observed her with a slight shake of his head. "You may have finally settled down and handled the duties the servants usually perform for you, but what did you learn from the experience?"

"I am not a simpleton, Charles. I realize the work they do is hard, but that is what they are born to do, just as we were born to be ladies and gentlemen of the ton." The offhanded nature with which she delivered this sentiment showed she had not learned all he hoped she would.

"So the work is hard, that is all you learned?"

Knowing what he wished to hear, she said, "I shall not touch the servants to harm them. I will also refrain from throwing things when I am upset."

"Well, then, we shall see how this evening goes and whether or not you will rejoin the family during the day and for meals at home. However, I will not provide you with a lady's maid until I am certain she will be safe with you."

Caroline sniffed again and was about to argue when the butler announced that dinner was served. The family moved to the dining room to take their places at the table. The first course was served, but little conversation was heard as they ate their soup. After the soup had been removed, the second course was served. Louisa asked, "How was your dinner with the Gardiners last evening, Charles?"

"It was delightful. Any time I may spend in my angel's company is wonderful," he said with a moony-eyed look.

Louisa and Hurst exchanged looks and smiled at Charles' words, for they had heard much about Miss Bennet in Charles' letters while they were away, but Caroline's ears perked up in interest.

"Have you fallen in love again, Charles?" she asked with a slight tone of derision.

"Not again, Caroline. This time is different. Miss Bennet is the woman I will marry."

"And who is the 'angel'? I am not familiar with any families in the ton by the name of Bennet."

"Her name is Jane Bennet. She is the niece of Mr. Gardiner. He is a man of trade to whom Darcy referred me for a possible business deal and investments."

"A man of trade! Charles, what can you be thinking to fall in love with a tradesman's daughter? We have finally been accepted by several members of the ton. Are you trying to ruin every chance we have? A tradesman's daughter would never be accepted!"

"She is not the daughter of a tradesman. Her father was a gentleman with his own estate. She is above both of us, Caroline."

"A gentleman with an estate, that is different. What does his estate bring in? How big is her dowry?"

"His estate was entailed away upon his death; I do not know its value. Her dowry is five thousand pounds, but I do not need to marry for money. Father left us very well supplied."

"Not marry for money! Are you out of your senses?" Caroline turned to her sister and cried, "Why have you not put a stop to this? You know he is to marry Miss Darcy so that Mr. Darcy will wish to marry me!"

"Caroline, do not be ridiculous. Mr. Darcy has banned you from his homes. He will never marry you. As for Jane Bennet, she sounds like a sweet young lady and quite perfect for Charles. I look forward to meeting her and hope they will be very happy together."

While this conversation had been taking place, the footmen had cleared the table and were preparing to serve the next course.

Caroline was angry at what had gone on during the time she was absent from the family. "Have you both lost your minds?" she asked, looking from her brother to her sister and back again. Just as the footman prepared to place the next course before her, she raised her hands in exasperation. Her hand hit the bottom of the plate and tipped it into her lap. Abruptly shoving back her chair, Caroline cried out, "You clumsy fool! Look what you have done." She waved her hand at the mess on the front of her gown. The footman was trying to stammer out an apology when she shoved him out of the way, hard enough to knock the footman to the floor. She turned and stormed out of the room.

The other three stared in dismay and disgust at Caroline's behavior. The footman guarding her turned from the door and informed Charles he would follow Miss Bingley and ensure she remained in her room until he came to see her. Another of the footmen helped his comrade up from the floor. Bingley offered an apology and asked the young man if he was hurt. When peace again reigned in the dining room, the other three continued their meal.

"I will send an express to Aunt Agatha in the morning and we shall plan to depart for York by midday," said Charles hopelessly. "I will have to explain everything to Aunt so she knows what she is getting herself into, but she has always had Caroline's measure. Perhaps she can improve her behavior where we have failed."

"Charles, you are not to blame for Caroline's behavior. You have repeatedly tried to improve her behavior, and I believe you were very clever in your most recent attempt to reform your sister," Hurst said. "Her behavior was set even before your parents died. As her siblings, you and Louisa cannot expect to be successful when they were not."

"Do not forget to take the time to visit Miss Bennet in the morning and notify her about your trip," came Louisa's gentle reminder.

At the thought of Jane, Bingley realized he would be able to stop at Pemberley on his return to London. There he would talk to Darcy and possibly discover the truth about Miss Lucas.

When the meal was over, Charles made his way upstairs to his sister's suite. He knocked on the sitting room door, but received no reply. Slowly he opened the door to see Caroline pacing about the room.

Caroline had been deep in thought, trying to come up with the perfect apology for her brother. She did not wish to be returned to her room. Upon seeing him, she rushed forward, placing her hand on his arm. "Oh, Charles, please forgive me. I was so distracted by the conversation and then startled by what occurred that I spoke without thinking. Please, brother, I cannot stand to be trapped in this room another day. Please say you will forgive me."

"It is not me you should be begging for forgiveness, but the footman you abused," replied her brother. He did not miss the look of disgust that crossed her face at his suggestion. "You will be remaining in your room only one more night," began her brother.

"Oh thank you —" she said, but Charles raised his hand to interrupt her.

"The reason you will be here only one more night is because we shall leave for Aunt Agatha's by noon tomorrow. You should plan to take everything with you, as you will not be returning to this house. When we began this I told you what would happen if there was no improvement. In six weeks, you could not learn to control your temper and behavior. I can no longer allow you to remain here and risk the servants' well-being. In fact, should you choose to set up an establishment in London after you come of age, you may have difficulties finding servants willing to work for you. I am sure the treatment received by those you have abused has been shared with other servants. I imagine it would be quite humiliating if word got out that even servants did not wish to be in your company."

Charles knew his words were harsh, but nothing else had seemed to affect her. Perhaps the thought of humiliation by the ton would be sufficient motivation. He noticed the look of horror on Caroline's face at his words and hoped there might still be a chance for her.

"Louisa and several maids will be coming to pack for you. If you mistreat them in any way, Louisa and the maids will leave you to finish the work for yourself."

After leaving Caroline, Bingley made his way to his study to write to his aunt. An hour later, he put the message into the hands of the butler, asking that it be sent express at first light. When that was completed, he made his way to his room. After his valet had prepared him for the night, he poured himself a nightcap and settled into a chair before the fire.

He thought about what he would say to Jane on the morrow, and of the tediousness of the journey to come. He was sure he would be subjected to Caroline's pleadings and manipulations. He would take with him the two footmen who served as guards to ensure Caroline's compliance with his wishes.

20. THE TRUTH COMES OUT

IN THE DAYS SINCE THE DINNER in the ladies' sitting room, Darcy had made an effort to court Elizabeth, with Georgiana ensuring they had time alone to talk. Darcy was solicitous of Elizabeth's comfort, complimented her appearance, and asked her opinions on matters of both the household and business.

Believing Darcy was preparing to marry someone else had been hard for Elizabeth. However, during subsequent conversations with her charge, Georgiana spoke only of her brother's opinions about and feelings for Elizabeth. Eventually, Elizabeth began to believe the woman whom Georgiana's brother was interested in marrying was her. She could only hope such was the case, for Elizabeth knew she would never love another. Elizabeth thought Mr. Darcy was just what a gentleman ought to be, and he was exactly the man who, in disposition and talents, would most suit her. It was in this manner that the last weeks of November passed into the first week of December.

On a frigidly cold December night, the residents of Pemberley were enjoying their first course when voices were heard in the hallway. Soon, the butler appeared at the dining room door, announcing, "Mr. Bingley, sir."

"Bingley, though I am delighted to see you, what brings you here?" Darcy rose as he spoke and moved to shake his friend's hand.

"I am afraid I need to impose upon your hospitality for the night, Darcy. I was on my way to York to attend to some family matters when the carriage ran into difficulties. The blacksmith assures me he can have it ready by morning, but the inn in Lambton had no accommodations whatsoever. I also must request your indulgence and beg that you would allow Caroline to spend one night under your roof, as well." He saw Darcy's look darken, and anger appear on his face. "I am taking her to live with my Aunt Agatha in York and cutting ties. I do not believe she will ever change her ways." Bingley's words tumbled out in a rush, trying to forestall Darcy's anger and possible negative answer.

Darcy looked first at Georgiana and then at Elizabeth. Each gave an almost imperceptible nod. Trying to be a proper hostess, Georgiana addressed her brother. "Fitzwilliam, certainly we can make an exception for one night. After all, Mr. Bingley is your dearest friend."

"Very well, Bingley, she can stay, but I will not provide her with a lady's maid. And I am not above locking her in her room if the need arises," said Darcy sternly.

As Darcy turned to ask the footman to have someone set two more places at the table, Bingley rushed to the carriage where his sister waited rather impatiently. He whispered sternly to her and reminded her to control her tongue and her temper or she would find herself sleeping in the taproom of the inn. He helped her from the carriage and led her to the dining room, seating her at the place added beside Georgiana. Bingley then moved to take the chair beside Miss Lucas.

The footmen removed the plates from the first course, and the next course was brought in. After everyone had helped themselves, Darcy asked Bingley about the damage to the carriage. He was unsettled by the fact that Bingley's eyes frequently drifted towards Elizabeth. He stared at her quite a bit. Hoping to turn Bingley's attentions away from Elizabeth, Darcy asked, "Were you able to meet with the gentleman I recommended?"

"Indeed I was. We have come to an arrangement I believe will be mutually beneficial. He even invited me to dine with his family one evening, and I met the most beautiful angel. I have been calling on her for the past two months and proposed to her shortly before leaving London. She is in mourning, though, so we will wait until summer to marry." Bingley stared at Miss Lucas as he made this last comment.

Elizabeth had remained quiet through most of the conversation. She was very aware of Miss Bingley's glare, but it was Mr. Bingley's frequent staring that had her unsettled. However, it was Miss Bingley's startling words that caused her surprising distress.

"Mr. Darcy, please speak to Charles. He is going to ruin our family if he marries this tradesman's niece. How will we ever gain our rightful positions in society if he marries some obscure country miss with very little dowry?"

Darcy's cold, unrelenting scowl finally silenced her, but she continued to bat her eyelashes flirtatiously at him.

"That is enough, Caroline. I plan to marry Jane Bennet and there is nothing you can say to change that."

Darcy was still glaring at Caroline Bingley, but at the mention of Jane Bennet's name, he heard Elizabeth gasp. The next thing he knew her face had grown quite pale, her eyes had slipped closed, and she toppled sideways from her chair.

Darcy jumped up, knocking his chair over in the process, and caught her, lowering her gently to the floor. He braced her against his body as he began to chafe her hands. Georgiana rushed around the table to bring a glass of water and her napkin, which she waved over Elizabeth's face to stir the air.

"Miss Lucas," Darcy called, worry evident in his tone. "My sweet Rose, speak to me. Open your beautiful eyes, my dear." Darcy's soft, pleading words could be heard only by Georgiana and him. They did not have to wait long before Elizabeth's eyes began to flutter and then open. Georgiana held the glass to her lips and gave her several small sips of the water.

Eventually, she felt well enough to get to her feet, and Darcy helped her into her chair at the table. With a slightly shaky hand, she took a few sips from her wineglass. Caroline noticed the concern in Mr. Darcy's eyes as he continued to regard the servant.

"Miss Lucas, are you well?" asked Bingley. "I hope it was nothing my sister or I said that caused your distress."

"I am well, Mr. Bingley. It was nothing. I just have not eaten much today. It has never affected me so before." Elizabeth gave a shaky laugh, trying to lighten the mood.

"You must take better care of yourself, Miss Lucas. Georgiana and I would be devastated if you were to take ill."

"Really, Mr. Darcy. You should not say such things to a servant, particularly in front of your impressionable young sister."

Darcy turned his frigid gaze on Miss Bingley. "Miss Bingley, you have already been informed that

Miss Lucas is not a servant, but a distant cousin and dear friend to my sister, as well as a welcome member of my household. I advise you to take care how you speak about her," came his coldly formal reply.

"La, Mr. Darcy, the woman has been living in the family wing lo these many months. Everyone knows she is your mistress." Caroline's snide remark was made to no one in particular, and though she had lowered her voice slightly, she meant for the remark to be heard by all.

Elizabeth's face blanched, then blushed bright red. With what sounded like a sob, she bolted from her chair and ran from the room. Georgiana gasped in shock, tears filling her eyes at her friend's distress, while Bingley nearly shouted, "Caroline!"

Darcy was livid, and the anger was evident on his face. "Miss Bingley, on more occasions than I can count I have tolerated your poor behavior and fawning attentions because you are my best friend's sister. Tonight, against my better judgment and out of Christian charity, I permitted you shelter under my roof, but you have again betrayed my hospitality. I do not care if you have to sleep in the taproom of the inn or in the streets. I wish you gone from my home immediately!"

"Mr. Darcy, you cannot be serious," cried Caroline. "It is quite late in the day. You cannot mean to send me out at this hour! Where would I go?"

"I certainly do mean what I say, and where you go is none of my concern. Bingley, you are more than welcome to stay as planned, but your sister is not. I want her gone as soon as it can be managed." Darcy rose from his chair to exit the room, but stopped in the doorway. "Just to be sure there are no misunderstandings, listen well to what I say, Miss

Bingley. I would rather marry a servant if she behaved as Miss Lucas does than marry a selfish, conceited tradesman's daughter like you. If you were the last woman in the world, Miss Bingley, I could never be prevailed upon to marry you!" He turned and departed the room so quickly he did not see her faint and hit the floor with a satisfying thud.

Georgiana immediately excused herself and followed her brother.

Bingley angrily looked at his sister where she lay. How dare she be so rude after Darcy had made an exception and allowed her entry to his home in spite of his previous edict? Bingley would not worry about her. Instead, he must speak to Darcy. Seeing Jeffers, he said, "Please have my sister placed in her former room. There is no need for anyone to attend her." He then asked Jeffers to be sure the two footmen traveling with them were fed and to have their carriage prepared. "Lastly, can you tell me which direction Darcy took? I must speak to him on an important matter."

As Elizabeth blindly dashed from the dining room, she knew not where to turn. She was mortified by Miss Bingley's words, but even more so by the thought that perhaps others had thought the same of her, even if they had not done so out loud. Elizabeth rushed up the staircase, intending to hide in her room. However, upon reaching the landing, she noticed a pair of footmen coming down the hallway towards her. Not wishing to be seen, she ducked into the first door she saw.

She found herself in the library and quickly mounted the stairs to the loft. She tucked herself away behind the drapes in the window seat, where she pulled her feet up under her dress and dropped her head to her knees, sobbing softly.

Upon exiting the dining room, Darcy stopped and looked around. Miss Lucas was nowhere in sight. He noticed Jeffers standing at the foot of the stairs with an unusual look on his face.

"Jeffers, did you happen to see where Miss Lucas went?"

"I believe she went in the direction of the library, sir. She appeared to be in some distress. Is there anything I can do?"

"Yes, please have Mr. Bingley's carriage readied. Miss Bingley will be departing shortly, never to return," said Darcy grimly as he mounted the stairs two at a time. By this time, Georgiana, who had followed her brother from the room, saw him ascending the stairs and hurried after him.

Darcy calmed as he entered the room. He stopped and looked around, but did not see Rose anywhere. He closed his eyes to listen, then stopped and spun around at the sound of the door opening. Seeing his sister, he put his fingers to his lips to forestall her speaking. Darcy turned back around, closed his eyes, and listened. Finally, his eyes snapped open.

Darcy stepped closer to Georgiana and whispered in her ear. She moved to the sideboard while he quickly mounted the stairs to the loft.

Following the sound, Darcy found Rose hidden behind the curtains in the window seat. Kneeling beside her, he tried to take her hand, but she pulled it away as through burned by his touch. Trying not to take offense, he spoke soothingly, his voice gentle. "Miss Lucas, please allow me to offer my sincerest apologies for the abominable treatment you received from Miss Bingley. You did nothing to inspire her reprehensible words. She sees you as a threat. You are a beautiful young woman, residing in my home, and she recognizes my admiration of you." The tone of his voice changed with his last words, and a shocked Elizabeth looked up into his eyes. What she saw there was both comforting and frightening.

"You could not admire me, Mr. Darcy. I am your employee. If Miss Bingley suspects me of such reprehensible behavior, others must do so as well. Oh, no," she cried in distress. "The servants must have been thinking this since my arrival. I must find a new situation and leave immediately. I would never wish for my presence to cause harm to your reputation or that of Georgiana. I would only ask that you might provide me with a recommendation and perhaps inquire whether anyone of your acquaintance has need of my services. As soon as a new position can be found, I will leave."

"Please do not think of such things now. Just return to the library with me. Georgiana is waiting and very concerned for you. You are the dearest friend she has ever had."

This time when Darcy put out his hand, Elizabeth accepted it. He helped her to her feet and down the stairs to the library floor. Georgiana was seated on the sofa, a small glass of sherry on the table beside her. Darcy guided Elizabeth to the seat next to his sister. He handed Elizabeth the glass of sherry, encouraging her to take a sip or two to calm her. Darcy then pulled a chair close to the sofa and sat facing her.

"I understand your wishes, Miss Lucas, but you need not depart. Miss Bingley will be gone momentarily from my home and will never be welcomed at Pemberley, or any of my other homes, ever again, no matter how dire the circumstances. I have put up with her superior remarks, fawning behavior, and occasional attempts to create a compromise for far too long. I have never enjoyed her company and accepted her only for her brother's sake."

"Oh, yes, Rose!" Georgiana said. "Fitzwilliam is right; you cannot leave me, nor us. How would I ever make my debut without your strength and confidence to guide me? Please, please promise me you will not leave!" Georgiana was almost as distraught as Elizabeth as she thought of a future without the first true friend she had ever had.

"I sincerely appreciate your wish for me to remain. You have given me the family I was not sure I would ever again have. However, even if Miss Bingley leaves, what is to stop her from spreading her slander? If she does, I am not the one who will be ruined; I am a servant. Georgiana, you might never make your debut if it is rumored your brother's mistress was your companion. You, Mr. Darcy, might never find a woman who could love and respect you if she thought you had behaved in such a manner. I cannot let that be the future for either of you. I must leave."

The three talked a bit longer, and Darcy managed to convince Elizabeth to sleep on the matter. They would discuss it again on the morrow. If she still wished to leave, Darcy would assist her, but he was not above using guilt to make her change her mind.

As they stood from the couch, Elizabeth and Georgiana intending to retire for the evening, Mr. Bingley burst through the library door and slammed it behind him.

"Are you Miss Elizabeth Bennet of Hertfordshire?" he asked.

Darcy and Georgiana looked at Bingley as though he had lost his mind.

Darcy turned back to Miss Lucas in time to see her sway and begin to crumple in a faint. He reached out and caught her, lifting her gently in his arms. He then placed her carefully on the sofa and began to chaff her hands. Darcy immediately began calling out instructions. Georgiana rang for Mrs. Reynolds while Bingley poured a glass of brandy and handed it to Darcy. Having already learned Miss Bingley had caused some sort of disturbance that had upset Miss Lucas, Mrs. Reynolds bustled into the room, removing her smelling salts from her pocket as she came.

Bingley stood behind the couch on which Elizabeth lay, running his hands through his hair. Moving only slightly to allow Mrs. Reynolds to wave the smelling salts under Miss Lucas' nose. Darcy continued to warm her cold hands in his. Georgiana knelt by Elizabeth's head, gently stroking the hair from her forehead and whispering for her to open her eyes.

The sharp smell of the salts returned Elizabeth to consciousness, but the feeling of utter panic engulfed her, threatening to again overwhelm her. She tried to sit up, but was stopped as all those present reached out a hand to prevent her from doing so.

"I must go. He will find me if I stay. He will hurt them if I stay. I cannot let him hurt them. I thought I would be safe so far away."

Though she spoke her words in a murmur, all those present heard them and exchanged worried looks. Knowing she was not needed for the conversation to come, Mrs. Reynolds excused herself from the room, pulling the door closed behind her. Unfortunately, it did not latch tightly, but she did not realize that. She instructed all the servants who were close to the library to leave the area, knowing privacy was essential.

Elizabeth grew more alert and sat up. When she tried to rise from the sofa, Darcy stayed her. She would not meet his eye and kept repeating that she must leave as they were in danger if her presence were discovered.

In a commanding voice, Darcy stood and told Elizabeth she would not be going anywhere until he had a complete explanation of what was going on.

"It is not safe for you to know. I must go. I must get away from here to keep you safe."

"Enough, Miss Lucas or Miss Bennet, whatever your name is. I will protect you, but I cannot do so until you tell me what is wrong." Darcy's voice brooked no disagreement.

With shoulders slumped and a defeated air, Elizabeth began her tale.

"When you hired me, I did not tell you the complete truth. The information I withheld was done for both your safety and mine."

Darcy nodded for her to continue.

"My name is Elizabeth Rose Bennet, and my former home is the estate of Longbourn, outside the village of Meryton in Hertfordshire."

"Elizabeth Rose Bennet, ERB. Now I know and can stop wondering," Darcy whispered.

Elizabeth heard Darcy mutter something, but could not make out the softly spoken words. "When my life so drastically changed, bringing me to this point, my elder sister, Jane, was staying with my Aunt and Uncle Gardiner in London. My aunt was expecting a baby and having some difficulties. As she already had three young children, Jane had gone to assist them through my aunt's confinement. At the time, she was my dearest sister and friend. I have missed her every day and prayed for her health and happiness as well as that of the Gardiner family." Elizabeth proceeded to tell them the details of the accident that claimed her family.

Elizabeth paused to get her emotions under control. Georgiana, tears running down her cheeks, reached out and took Elizabeth's hand in hers. Darcy paced before the sofa. Bingley had slumped into the chair that Darcy had abandoned.

When she had her regained her composure, Elizabeth continued her tale. She told them of the arrival of the Collinses, the autocratic behavior of the heir, her isolation, his probable destruction of the letter she had written to the Gardiners, and all the rest. Then she spoke of the night she had attempted to retrieve her books and the many things she had overheard. "I knew I had to get away and I had to protect my remaining family, so I made my plans accordingly."

She continued to tell them of packing her family's belongings and gathering what monies she could find. "I tried to rescue items with special memories, packed them separately, and sent them to a friend for safekeeping." She proudly spoke of the help the servants had given her in escaping. Lastly, she gave them all the details right up to her encountering the Darcys at the Knight's Rest Inn in Stevenage. "I truly planned to travel about, looking for work. I never imagined I would be so blessed as to find the perfect situation on the very day I ran away from Mr. Collins.

"I gave you as much of the truth as I dared when you interviewed me, Mr. Darcy. The things I held back were to protect all of us. I am sorry to have deceived you. It was never my intention to use you. I have tried my best to do the job for which you hired me. I could not have imagined how dearly I would come to care for those I encountered in my new life. I simply needed to stay away until I reached my majority in April. I was trying to keep myself and my family safe. I did not mean to bring disgrace upon your family. As I said, it is best for everyone if I leave."

"That will not be necessary, but I do have a few questions," Darcy remarked. "If you had family remaining, why did you not go to them?"

"I was afraid of what Mr. Collins might do. From something I overheard him say that night in the library, there was a chance he had been involved in my family's death. I did not wish to place my only remaining family in danger. It is also why I did not wish to tell you the truth. I could never forgive myself if something were to happen to you or Georgie."

"You had no idea about an inheritance or what it might be?"

"No, nothing, but I think I have figured out why my father never said anything about it. You see, I was my mother's least favorite daughter. While carrying me, my mother was convinced I would be a boy, a son to break the entailment. Her disappointment that I was not the longed-for heir never went away. I am sure she would have spoken endlessly about how unfair it was that I was to inherit anything when I had not done my duty by being a boy and saving my family from the hedgerows."

"I do not quite understand," said Darcy, confused.

"My father's estate was not overly large and brought in only two thousand per annum. It could have done better, but he was more interested in books and the peace his library afforded him than in taking an active part in the management of the estate. He had taught me what was needed, and he knew I would take care of things in his stead. Mr. Collins' good opinion of himself made him look down on my mother, as she was the daughter of a country solicitor who had only five thousand pounds for a dowry. She knew the Collinses would remove us from our home immediately upon my father's death. There was not much saved for such a future. My sisters and I would have had only one thousand pounds each upon her death, so our chances of marrying would have been slight, with nothing more than our personal charms to interest a gentleman."

"When is your birthday, Miss Bennet?"

"I would prefer you continue to refer to me as Miss Lucas, sir. I will not reach my majority until the beginning of April. If you think it appropriate, I would like to stay with Miss Georgiana until then. I would be most grateful," Elizabeth said humbly.

The drama of the last hours had left Elizabeth drained. All she wished to do was retire and sleep for a very long time. She was about to request just that when a question occurred to her.

Turning to Mr. Bingley, she asked, "How did you find out my name?"

Bingley explained about meeting Jane and the Gardiners in the fall after being at Pemberley. He said he had spoken with Jane about the loss of her dearest sister. "She described you perfectly. I said nothing to Miss Bennet about my suspicions because I was not sure you were her sister. I am sorry for blurting it out. I had intended to find time to ask you quietly," he apologized.

"Do not be concerned, Mr. Bingley, but please tell me, how is my family? I miss them very much."

"They miss you too, Miss Elizabeth. Your loss has left a hole in the family, and they all feel it greatly," Bingley kindly responded. "Your sister is an angel, and when we are together, she seems to be happy, though she is quiet and reserved. Your aunt has given birth to a healthy baby girl, whom they named Allison Elizabeth."

Darcy was about to speak when they heard a noise at the door. Darcy and Bingley rushed towards the sound, finding the library door slightly ajar. They yanked it open and looked about, but saw no one. Darcy thought he caught a brief flash of orange down the hallway, but it disappeared so quickly, he was not sure.

Georgiana had followed them to the door, but remained behind her brother and Mr. Bingley. "What did you see?"

"There was no one there, but I thought I caught a glimpse of orange at the end of the corridor.

321

"Do you think it was Miss Bingley?" Georgiana asked quietly, with a glance at Elizabeth.

"Do you know anyone else who wears that color?" Darcy questioned sarcastically.

"What if she overheard what was said? She is very angry. Would she tell Mr. Collins where Rose, I mean, Miss Elizabeth is?" Georgiana's face clearly expressed her concern.

Not wishing to cause Elizabeth any more distress, Darcy asked Georgiana to take Elizabeth to their sitting room. "I will be along shortly to speak to you before retiring.

After the ladies had departed, Darcy applied his analytical mind to the problem of removing Miss Bingley from his home and containing any information she may have overheard. After a moment he spoke. "Could you use the rented carriage to transport your sister to York? I would be willing to provide outriders for her protection. It would get her there quickly and allow her little interaction with others if the footman you use to guard her could accompany her."

"You know the stable master in Lambton better than I. What do you think?"

"I am sure for the right price he will not mind, but that would necessitate waiting for the morning before the arrangements could be made," mused Darcy. Thinking further, he offered, "I will loan you my smallest carriage and the outriders so we may be rid of her immediately."

Darcy rang for a servant and Jeffers quickly appeared. Darcy explained what he needed, and the servant departed to make the necessary arrangements. Darcy and Bingley discussed a few additional details and Bingley began a letter to his aunt to be delivered by the footmen. In his letter, he informed Aunt Agatha that, in her anger, Caroline had threatened to spread gossip about the family. He instructed her to monitor all of Caroline's mail, incoming or outgoing. He included a list of names and topics that could not be contained in the correspondence and instructed her to burn any letters that did not comply. Explaining the information to Darcy, he said, "This should prevent her from spreading information she may have overheard, as well as her disgusting insinuations."

Within forty-five minutes, all was in readiness, and Bingley went to retrieve Caroline from her room. "Your usual room has been prepared for your use when you have seen to your sister," Darcy informed him.

The ladies entered their sitting room, and Elizabeth moved to stare out of the window. Elizabeth's heart felt like lead in her chest. She loved Georgiana like a sister, and, in spite of her best efforts to prevent it from happening, had also fallen in love with Darcy. It broke her heart to think that this night might be the last time she saw them, perhaps forever.

Hesitantly, Georgiana spoke. "Rose...excuse me, Miss Bennet...I am sorry for the difficulties you are experiencing on top of your loss. It is quite unfair you should have to bear so much."

With slow steps, Elizabeth moved to seat herself in one of the chairs. She felt drained and did not know how much more she could endure before breaking down completely. "I thank you for your kindness, Miss Darcy. I hope you know I have truly enjoyed my time here at Pemberley. You have become as dear to me as any of my other sisters."

Georgiana was pleased to hear of Elizabeth's affection, but she could not think of anything else to say to comfort her. Georgiana did not know what her brother would do. She had often heard him say, "Disguise of every sort is my abhorrence."

A knock was heard at the door. Georgiana rushed to open it, but Elizabeth did not look up from her lap. She was certain Mr. Darcy would ask her to leave, as he had remained silent throughout her story and asked only two questions afterward.

"I wish to inform you that Miss Bingley has departed, and she will never again set foot in Pemberley, no matter the circumstances. I wish you both a good-night. It has been an eventful day. We will speak more of this matter tomorrow."

"Good night, Brother."

"Good night, Mr. Darcy."

As Elizabeth's gaze remained fixed on her lap, she could not see the expression on Darcy's face. He was angry at Collins for the danger in which he had placed Elizabeth. He felt deeply for her loss, and he loved her more than ever for the courage and determination she had shown as she attempted to save herself and her remaining family from a difficult situation.

21. BETRAYED

CAROLINE WAS ROUSED FROM HER FAINT by the cold air in the chamber where the footmen had placed her. At first she did not realize where she was, but as Caroline came fully awake, she recognized the room as the one she had stayed in during previous visits to Pemberley. Caroline never believed Darcy would truly banish her from his homes for the sake of that conniving tart. To hear it a second time was disconcerting. She did not know how long she had been out, but she must try once more to speak to Mr. Darcy.

Exiting her room, Caroline tried to determine the most likely place to find him. Perhaps she could change Darcy's mind. If that did not succeed, she would have to arrange for a compromise. Deciding he would most likely be in the library, she headed in that direction.

Caroline ducked into an alcove when she saw Mrs. Reynolds exiting the library. Noticing the housekeeper left the door slightly ajar, she moved forward quietly. Caroline paused to listen for Darcy's voice before entering. What she heard was utterly shocking.

The voice she heard was not Darcy's but that of Miss Lucas, and the story she told was beyond belief. Caroline eased closer to listen. Miss Lucas—or Miss Bennet, whatever her real name might be—was nearing the end of the tale when Caroline shifted her weight and brushed against the library door, causing it to rattle. She turned quickly and ran down the hall towards the servants' stairs to return to her room.

Reaching safety, Caroline locked the room's door and crossed quickly to the writing desk. She pulled out a piece of paper and dipped the quill in ink. The pen scratched rapidly across the page, and in no time at all she was sanding and sealing the letter. As she addressed it, a sharp rap sounded at the door. Caroline shoved the letter into her pocket before stalking across the room to answer the knock.

"Caroline, the carriage is ready. You will be traveling directly to York. Aunt Agnes is already expecting you. The footmen will accompany you to ensure your good behavior. Darcy has loaned us outriders to serve as guards so you may travel through the night. You will stop only to refresh yourself. Meals will be taken in the carriage as you travel.

"As you have spent all your allowance for this quarter, you will have no funds except for what Aunt Agnes gives you. Upon your next birthday, I will arrange for the release of your funds to you. I was to be responsible for you only until your twenty-fifth birthday, which is just a few weeks away. You will find a home of your own and learn to live within your means. I will arrange for the lawyers to pay your bills directly and provide you with an allowance. You will need to learn to settle for less, as I will not cover overages. Your behavior has ensured you will no longer be welcome in my home, nor the Hursts' home."

Making sure her expression displayed her displeasure with Charles' plan for her, Caroline stuck her nose in the air and flounced out of the bedchamber. He caught up to her and took her elbow, guiding her down the stairs, out of the house, and into the waiting carriage. She refused her brother's offered hand and stepped into the carriage. The footmen were already seated on the rear-facing seat, their stoic expressions increasing Caroline's irritation.

Charles stood on the front steps as the carriage moved down the drive. When it had passed from view, Charles trudged into the house and went straight to his bed chamber. His valet prepared him for bed, and in a short time he was seated before the fire in his room, a brandy in his hand. For a brief moment, Charles felt guilty about sending his sister away, but he had made every effort to improve Caroline's behavior. He reminded himself that she had been aware of the consequences of failing to change. Darcy had even offered her a slight second chance, but with her desire to impress Darcy, she was not able to control her behavior through even a single meal. Realizing he had done his best and that Caroline chose not to change, Bingley set aside his guilt, downed his brandy, and went to bed.

It was quite late when Caroline departed Pemberley. She would never consider conversing with the footmen to pass the time, so she moved to one side of the carriage and leaned her head into the corner. She had been given a surprising gift and needed to find the opportunity to mail her note. Even if she would not have Darcy—though Caroline refused to believe she would not eventually get her way—she would get rid of the so-called "cousin" who was such a distraction to Darcy. If they were not to stop at an inn for any length of time, Caroline did not know how she would arrange for her letter to be sent. She closed her eyes to rest and hoped an idea would come to her as she slept.

Several hours passed and the carriage stopped for a change of horses. The footmen did not wake her at this first stop. When the carriage stopped the second time, Caroline was awakened and told to take a moment to refresh herself. One of the footmen went directly to the taproom and ordered breakfast to take with them. The other footman escorted Caroline to the necessary room. This footman remained close by to escort Caroline to the carriage when she was through. She chaffed at the supervision that was preventing her from carrying out the plan that had occurred to her during the late hours of the night.

Another woman approached the necessary room and stood near Caroline as they waited to use the currently occupied room. The newcomer looked askance at the footman hovering near the door. She cast him a frown and he moved a bit farther from the door. The door to the necessary room opened and a young woman exited. As Caroline moved to pass her, she knocked the young woman's reticule from her hand. She bent to help her retrieve it. As they stood, Caroline pressed the letter she had written into the young woman's hand along with her bag.

"Help me, please!" Caroline whispered urgently. "Please post this." Then Caroline brushed past and closed the door of the necessary room behind her.

The young woman hid the letter in her skirt and returned to the taproom to wait for the next coach. Soon she saw Caroline being escorted towards the exit of the inn. The uniformed man accompanying her looked grim. Caroline turned her head and spotted the young lady. She paused almost imperceptibly and mouthed, "Help me." The footman pulled her arm, forcing her to continue walking. The young lady observed the woman get into a carriage and two footmen follow her. As soon as the carriage was out of sight, the young woman walked to the counter where the innkeeper stood.

"Excuse me, sir, could you please ensure this is posted immediately? It is very important."

"Do you wish it sent by express?"

"Do you know what the cost would be?" the woman asked hesitantly.

After being given an amount, the young lady opened her reticule and removed the necessary coins, handing them to the innkeeper.

As she completed her business with the innkeeper, the next coach arrived, so the young woman hurried to gather her belongings and headed outside to get on the coach. As it moved away from the inn, she offered up a silent prayer for the distressed young lady who had asked for her help.

Caroline refused the food the footman offered. Reflecting her resentment of the treatment she was receiving, she would not lower herself to accept anything they gave her. Her anger revived as she remembered that Charles, her own brother, had assisted in her being thrown out of Pemberley. He should have done whatever it took to convince Darcy to marry her, as that was what she wanted. How dare he not assist her? Now, to make matters worse, he was having her escorted under guard to their dreadful Aunt Agnes. Agnes Bingley was a horrid old woman, her father's oldest sister. She had never married and was very strict and religious. Life with her would be miserable.

When he arrived in the breakfast room, Darcy was surprised to find only his sister. With a look of concern, he asked, "Where is Miss Lucas, Georgiana? Is she ill? Is she suffering from another megrim?"

"Relax, Brother. She was quite tired from all that occurred yesterday. I told her to rest, and I would have a tray sent to her. She promised to join me in the library by eleven. I will practice the pianoforte this morning, and we will have our lessons this afternoon." Georgiana returned to her breakfast while her brother filled his plate from the sideboard and took a seat at the table. When the servant had filled his cup and moved away, Georgiana took a deep breath and turned to her brother.

"William, what do you plan to say to Miss Lucas? Are you going to send her away?"

"Of course not, Georgie! Why on earth would you believe that?"

"I think Miss Lucas believes you will send her away for not being truthful. Please, William, she is my dearest friend. Please do not send her back to Mr. Collins!"

"Georgie, I would never do such a thing! I thought you understood my feelings for Miss Lucas."

"I thought I did, but I have often heard you speak of your dislike of lies and secrets. I was afraid her actions would cause you to dislike her."

"Right now I will not speak with you about what I plan to discuss with Miss Lucas, but you have my word, I have absolutely no intention of sending her away. I will also promise to do everything in my power to convince her not to leave, but to allow us to be of assistance to her."

"Thank you, Brother." With that, Georgiana finished her tea and excused herself.

Darcy finished his breakfast and went to his study to deal with any business that might be awaiting his attention. When he had completed all the work he found there, he looked at the clock and realized it was almost noon. Darcy pulled down his waistcoat and his outer jacket, then ran his fingers through his hair before moving in the direction of the library.

He opened the door quietly and observed the scene before him. Georgiana and Miss Lucas were seated on a sofa near the window, a low table before them. The sunlight shone on them, lighting their hair and giving a warm glow to their countenances.

"How are you feeling, Miss Bennet? You are not getting one of your headaches, are you?"

Without looking at Darcy, Elizabeth replied, "I am well, sir."

"Very good. Georgiana, would you mind moving across the room? I would like to speak with Miss Bennet, if she does not mind."

How I shall miss the sound of his voice, Elizabeth thought. She did not think she could bear the pain of him asking her to leave. "That will not be necessary, Mr. Darcy. I am sorry to have imposed myself upon your family. I will leave as soon as I can pack."

Darcy ignored her words and again spoke to his sister. "Georgiana, perhaps you could enjoy a book in the quiet of the loft while I speak with Miss Bennet."

"Yes, William." Georgiana gave Elizabeth's hand another squeeze and offered an encouraging smile before standing. As she moved towards the stairs to the loft, she gave William a stern look and was surprised to see him wink at her in return. Feeling more at ease, she picked up a random book from a table as she passed and moved to the window seat in the loft.

Darcy took a seat on the sofa beside Elizabeth. He stared at her, but she would not raise her eyes to look at him. "Miss Bennet, please look at me."

Steeling herself for the angry, disappointed expression she expected to see, Elizabeth slowly raised her eyes to meet Darcy's. Taking in his expression, her eyes widened in surprise.

"Miss Bennet, I have known since we met that you were pretending to be someone else." Elizabeth gasped as Darcy reached into his pocket and pulled out her handkerchief. "Elizabeth. I think it suits you very well."

"You have known all along that I was not being truthful?" she cried, astonished.

"I was drawn to you from the moment we met. I had been observing you in the dining room of the inn. There was something about you that made me feel protective. Then, when you confessed about the horse, I realized there was most likely more to your story. I also knew you were a good and kind person who was alone in the world. Georgiana and I know how that feels. Consequently, I could have done nothing but offer my assistance. I hoped one day you would feel comfortable enough to tell me the rest."

Darcy's softly spoken words brought tears to Elizabeth's eyes. He reached into a different pocket and pulled out his handkerchief to give her while he tucked hers safely back in his jacket.

"I was afraid to tell anyone the truth. Mr. Collins may have been responsible for my family's death. I could not put anyone else's safety at risk, especially yours and Georgiana's. I hoped, however, you might be willing to assist me after my birthday."

"I know of another way to ensure your safety."

Elizabeth looked at him in confusion.

"I have wished to do this for some time now, but it was not appropriate when I did not know your real name." Darcy slipped from the sofa onto one knee before her, smiling as her eyes widened yet again. "Miss Elizabeth Rose Bennet, I would like you to stay with me always. I love you most ardently. Would you do me the great honor of marrying me?"

Tears shimmered in Elizabeth's beautiful eyes. With a tremulous voice she asked, "You truly wish to marry me, even though I deceived you?"

"I do. I love you, my sweet rose. I cannot imagine my future life without you in it."

"But Mr. Darcy, I am the daughter of an unknown country gentleman and far below you in society. I have also been in your employ for several months now. Society could not possibly accept an engagement between us."

"Very few people are aware of that fact. Most think you my cousin, remember, and by the time you meet the ton, you will be Mrs. Darcy and a considerable heiress. They will see nothing wrong with me choosing you for my wife. We can even say the marriage was arranged before your parents' deaths, and you came to live with my sister and me for your protection from the Collinses."

Elizabeth was speechless. She wished to say yes, but that would certainly put him in immediate danger. Her eyes filled with tears as she gave him her answer.

"Mr. Darcy, my heart yearns to say yes, but being my intended would put you at even greater risk. If Mr. Collins were to learn of my location, you would be an impediment to his plans. If he did not hesitate to kill an entire family, I do not think one man would deter him. I could not live with myself if I were to cause you harm. Perhaps you could consider asking me again in three months?"

"I do not believe it is necessary for us to wait. Does wishing me to ask again mean you accept?"

"I am underage, sir, and cannot marry without permission."

"Then I shall obtain the necessary permission, or ask my godfather, the Bishop of Derby, to help us since your parents are both passed."

Tears slipped from her eyes and sparkled on her softly blushing cheeks. "Mr. Darcy, you leave me with only one choice."

Darcy held his breath.

"As I love you as well, I would be honored to be your wife."

Still holding her hand, Darcy stood and drew her up with him. He released one of her hands and brought up his to cup her cheek and gently brush his thumb across her petal soft lips. He looked from her eyes to her lips and back. She released his other hand and brought up both of hers to rest on his chest as his other hand slipped around to press against the small of her back. Slowly he lowered his head, his eyes never leaving hers until his lips barely brushed against her lips. He withdrew slightly and saw her eyes closed and her lips softly parted, and he again pressed his lips to hers gently at first, then more insistently. He nibbled her full bottom lip as he deepened the kiss. Her hands found their way to his hair as his insistent lips parted her mouth, and she allowed his tongue to touch hers. Not wishing to overwhelm her, he released her lips and held her close, tucking her head under his chin. She could hear the rapid beat of his heart and felt him place a gentle kiss on her hair.

He pulled her to the sofa and sat next to her, wrapping her in his arms. "I would prefer to marry sooner rather than later. What are your wishes?"

"I, too, would like to marry soon, but I am not sure it would be safe to do so. I am not of age and would need my uncle's permission. If Mr. Collins is watching them, he could discover where I am. If it were at all possible, I should like to have my remaining family with me when I marry."

"What is your uncle's name?"

"Edward Gardiner."

"Of Gardiner Imports and Exports?" asked Darcy, startled.

"Yes," Elizabeth answered hesitantly.

"Elizabeth, I have several investments with your uncle. We have been doing business for three years now. As we have corresponded on several occasions, I doubt a letter from me would give away anything."

"I would love to notify them and tell them I am well. Do you think they will forgive me for allowing them to believe I was dead?"

"I am sure they will understand once they know the circumstances. What would you think if we invited them to join us for the holidays? We could hold the wedding while they are here."

"You would do that for me? Oh, Mr. Darcy!"

He placed his fingers on her lips and said, "No more Mr. Darcy. I would be delighted if you would call me William, as Georgie does."

"Thank you, William. I would be most happy to marry you in just a few short weeks." A lifted brow and radiant smile accompanied her words.

"Shall we share our news with Georgie and Bingley?"

"Indeed, we should. Perhaps we should invite Mr. Bingley to remain for the holidays, as we are to invite my relations to Pemberley."

"That is an excellent idea, my Elizabeth Rose."

Harold Collins was seated behind the desk in the study when the new housekeeper shuffled in with the mail. She handed it to the angry man behind the desk and shuffled away. He glanced through the mail, tossing aside the bills. When he saw another envelope from his blackmailer, he cursed and threw it in the fire. He had received a similar note each of the last three weeks and was rapidly running out of ready cash and patience. He wondered what would happen if he did not make a payment. Did the blackmailer have proof, or was it just hearsay?

Returning to the stack of mail, he continued until he reached the last letter. The envelope was addressed in an unfamiliar and decidedly feminine hand. Curious, and hoping it was Elizabeth begging to return, Collins broke the seal and began to read.

December 3, 18___

Dear Mr. Collins,

I have recently met a young relation of yours, Miss Elizabeth Bennet. For the last several months, she has been staying with Mr. Fitzwilliam Darcy of Pemberley in Derbyshire. The young lady is using her arts and allurements to distract Mr. Darcy from his friends and responsibilities. If she is successful and marries him, you will have no chance of obtaining her inheritance.

I thought you might be interested in knowing where she is, but you must hurry or you may be too late!

A Concerned Friend

Collins' mouth puckered into an unpleasant smile when he read the first sentence, but as he continued to read, his face grew from red with anger to purple with rage. He slammed his hand on his desk and stood abruptly, beginning to pace. He knew he would need to make the trip to Derbyshire, but also knew he would need help to be successful at capturing Elizabeth. Walter was still at school and would be useless even if he could be convinced to take part. Then the perfect accomplice came to mind and an unpleasant yet satisfied smile appeared.

He returned to his desk and quickly jotted off a note to his new friend. He yelled for the housekeeper and told her to have the stable boy deliver it to the militia camp immediately. A short time later, there was a knock on the door to his study. At his call to enter, Wickham sauntered in.

"What was so important that you sent me such a rude summons?" he asked insolently.

"I need your help with something very important."

"Might I suggest you ask politely if it is assistance you need. I am not some lackey at your beck and call, Collins," Wickham grumbled.

"I will pay you five hundred pounds for your assistance."

At the mention of money, Wickham's interest increased. "Just what would I have to do for this money?"

"I have received word as to where my missing cousin is. She has been hiding in Derbyshire, though I have no idea how she could have made it so far on her own. She is at a place called Pemberley, and my informant says she is using her arts and allurements to entrap a man into marriage."

At the mention of Derbyshire, Wickham's ears had perked up, but when Pemberley was mentioned, his thoughts began to race with plans of his own. "And just what do you want me to do?"

"I want you to accompany me to Derbyshire, to this Pemberley, and help me get her back. The wench comes into a sizable inheritance in just a few months. I want that money and my revenge on the willful brat."

"I might be willing to aid you, and perhaps we can aid each other. I know Pemberley well. The owner is my old friend, Darcy, the one who denied me the living his father left me in his will. Darcy also separated me from the woman I loved, his sister, Georgiana. Perhaps, we can find a way to get both of the young ladies while dealing Darcy a crippling blow." Wickham chuckled evilly, and Collins was quick to join in.

Talking late into the night, Wickham and Collins laid their plans to leave for Derbyshire in two days' time.

Christmas was only a few weeks away, and Elizabeth and Georgiana had taken the carriage into Lambton to do some shopping. As agreed, after receiving the warning that had come in the colonel's last letter, they were accompanied by two armed footmen. Their first stop was the bookshop, where Elizabeth purchased a book for Mr. Darcy. Then they went to the tailor's shop, where Georgiana ordered a new waistcoat for her brother. She quietly told him she would have Mrs. Webb send over a dress fabric that the waistcoat should match. Next they went to the draper's. There they purchased supplies to make handkerchiefs for the staff members. Their last stop was the dressmaker. Because of their understanding, Darcy had convinced Elizabeth to accompany them to the Fitzwilliams' New Year's Eve Ball at Matlock. Both young ladies were to order ball gowns for the occasion. Elizabeth would have completed full mourning by then, and Georgiana would be permitted to stay until after supper and dance with family members only.

On their last visit to the store, Elizabeth had observed a beautiful deep green silk. She was delighted to discover the fabric was still available and immediately requested it for her ball gown. She chose a simple yet elegant design with a deep scooped-neck front and back trimmed with gold lace. The hem and short train were also trimmed in gold lace. The short puffed sleeves were made from interlocked and twisted gold ribbons and strips of the green silk. A gold sash under the bust tied in the back. There would be gold ribbons for Elizabeth's hair.

Georgiana chose a modest white silk gown embroidered with red roses around the neckline, sleeves, and hem. She also had a red sash under the bust; it tied in the back, with matching ribbons for her hair.

The ladies had finished making their choices and waited for Mrs. Webb to return with the cut ribbons they would use in their hair. The sound of scuffling footsteps in the back was followed by a thwack and then a thump.

Wickham and Collins had been in Derbyshire for nearly a week. They were staying in a small cottage just outside Lambton that had belonged to one of Wickham's long-dead relatives. Wickham had snuck onto Pemberley property and tried to learn what he could about the ladies' habits, but most often, Darcy accompanied them when they walked. Wickham and Collins also spent time in the pub gathering what information they could about how often the ladies traveled to Lambton and who accompanied them. They had learned very little of use and were growing frustrated.

Then, as they sat in the pub enjoying a game of cards, Wickham saw the Darcy carriage enter the village. Folding his hand, he stood and walked to the window. He watched as the carriage stopped in front of the bookshop and two ladies exited. A footman followed them into the shop and another remained outside the shop door until the ladies exited.

"Harold, we need to depart. I believe our package is ready to be picked up."

Recognizing the expression they had agreed to use when they spotted their quarry, Collins looked at the other gentlemen at the table. "Excuse me, gentlemen, I have business to which I must attend." He swept his meager winnings into his hand and stood to depart. He moved over to stand at the window with Wickham.

"What did you see?"

Nodding his head to the right, Wickham casually remarked, "See the carriage moving towards the stables at the end of town? It belongs to Darcy. I saw Miss Darcy and another young woman exit. She was petite with dark, curly hair. They entered the bookstore."

The two men sat at the table by the window and watched the shops across the street. After about thirty minutes, they saw the young ladies exit the shop. With the footmen following, they entered another shop two doors down, where again one footman entered with them, while the other took up his position outside the door. They had to wait only fifteen minutes before the ladies exited the second shop. They continued to observe as Georgiana and Elizabeth entered a third shop.

When the ladies walked into the dressmaker's shop, both footmen remained posted outside the door. Wickham muttered, "Finally! Come on; now is our chance."

Collins and Wickham quickly exited the pub and untethered their horses from the hitching post.

"Follow me," said Wickham. "I have never known ladies to finish at the dressmakers very quickly. Perhaps we can sneak in the back and abduct the ladies the same way." Pulling their horses behind them, he led Collins to the alleyway next to the bookstore. They entered undetected and made it to the small lane behind the shops that was used to make deliveries. When they reached the dressmaker's shop, they tied their horses to the post there.

"Do you have the gags and rope?" questioned Collins. Wickham responded by removing them from his saddlebags.

They quietly approached the back door of the seamstress' shop. Wickham squeezed the latch and eased open the door. He glanced about, seeing only an older woman at a table with her back to the door. Soundlessly, Wickham opened the door and stepped behind the lady, bringing down the butt of his pistol on the back of her head. The dressmaker slumped to the floor with a thump. They stepped over the woman, moving towards the curtain that separated them from the front of the shop and their prey.

"Mrs. Webb, is everything alright?" called Elizabeth as she moved towards the curtain leading to the shop's back room. No additional sounds were heard, but a man's hand appeared at the edge of the curtain. Elizabeth quickly stepped back, placing herself between Georgiana and the unseen trouble and edging them towards the shop door. Only a moment later the curtain was pushed aside, revealing two men. Elizabeth did not recognize the first man, but heard Georgiana's sudden intake of breath as she softly muttered, "Wickham." The man standing just beyond Wickham's shoulder was one she had hoped never to see again.

"Cousin Elizabeth," Harold Collins sneered. "I have been so worried about your safety. I was shocked to hear you have been trying to trap a gentleman into marriage. If you wanted to marry, you know Walter would have been happy to accommodate you."

"I had no wish to marry my cousin or to share my home with you," Elizabeth replied defiantly.

"I can easily remedy that for you, Cousin, but you will marry a Collins man before that occurs."

Elizabeth reached for Georgiana's hand as she took a step away from the men.

"Dearest Georgiana, why do you back away from your old friend? Now, step away from the door," Wickham commanded.

Neither of the women moved. With Elizabeth's hand holding tightly to hers, Georgiana found her courage. "What do you want, Mr. Wickham?"

"Why, I want what I wanted at Ramsgate—you." Wickham gave her his familiar, charming smile.

"You did not want me. You wanted my dowry, and you know you will not get that without William's approval."

"Then I will not marry you, just hold you for ransom. Though I may decide to enjoy the pleasures your brother denied me when he stopped our wedding," he said with a leer.

Elizabeth could feel Georgiana begin to tremble at Wickham's threat. She knew she needed to get Georgie safely away; then she would worry about her own safety. She looked back at Georgiana and whispered, "When I step towards the men, run for the carriage and help."

When Elizabeth faced the men, she noticed they had both drawn weapons. Still holding tightly to Georgiana's hand, she took a step forward. "What have you done to Mrs. Webb?" Elizabeth demanded angrily.

Startled at the surprising question, the men exchanged a glance. Elizabeth gave Georgie a backward shove when they did. By the time they looked back at the ladies, Georgiana had her hand on the door and was pulling it open. Elizabeth knew the guns were more for show than anything—they would gain nothing if the ladies were dead. Consequently, Elizabeth moved into Wickham's path as he stepped forward, arms extended to grab Georgiana and stop her exit. He angrily shoved Elizabeth aside, but it was too late; Georgiana was out the door, screaming at the footman to save Elizabeth.

Wickham turned the key in the lock to prevent the footmen from entering before delivering a backhanded blow to Elizabeth's face. He struck with such force that she fell to the floor, striking her head on a table as she did. "You just cost me thirty thousand pounds!" He raised his arm as if to strike her again, but his hand stopped in mid-motion when he felt the barrel of Collins' pistol in his back.

"You will lose more than that if you do not get away before the girl brings help. Now grab her other arm and let us get out of here." Collins and Wickham each grabbed Elizabeth by her upper arms in crushing grips and dragged her towards the back of the store.

They had just mounted when there was a crash as a footman barreled through the shop's entrance. He looked around and, not seeing anyone, continued towards the rear of the building. As he stuck his head out the back door, he saw only the swish of a tail as it turned the corner of the alley. The footman ran in that direction and caught a glimpse of two men on horses and a flash of black skirts stirred by the breeze as the horses galloped away. He noted the path they took and returned to the carriage where the coachman and remaining footman guarded Miss Darcy.

Colonel Richard Fitzwilliam had just entered the outskirts of Lambton after a long, hard ride. Thinking of the hot bath he would enjoy upon reaching Pemberley, he was startled to hear

Georgiana's voice crying for help. Seeing the Darcy coach parked in front of the confectioner's shop across the street, he spurred his horse quickly in that direction. He jumped from his mount and raced to Georgiana's side. Pulling her into a hug, he spoke softly and rubbed her back to calm her. Before she was able to explain what had occurred, the footman returned with the news that the men had gotten away, and it appeared they had taken Miss Lucas with them. He mentioned the direction he had seen them take.

"What men? Who took Miss Lucas?" barked the colonel.

"It was George Wickham and someone Rose called 'Collins.' They planned to take us both, but Rose helped me get away and must have prevented them from following. Oh, I should never have left her," Georgiana moaned as she again began to cry.

Richard turned to the footman who had investigated the store. "Run to the livery and tell them you need a horse immediately for Pemberley business. Return here as fast as you can." As the footman took off at a run, the colonel turned to the coachman and footman who had remained to protect Georgiana. "Get her to Pemberley as fast as you can. Tell Darcy what has happened. Have him bring the coach back and wait here for word. The footman and I will follow and see where the men have gone. We will send word back to the dressmaker's shop, as it is closer than Pemberley." The men nodded their understanding as the colonel helped Georgiana into the carriage. The coachman set off at a swift pace. The colonel had just settled back into the saddle when the footman appeared on his rented mount.

"Lead on and make haste," cried the colonel as the two men raced away.

22. THE COLONEL TO THE RESCUE

WICKHAM AND COLLINS DROVE THEIR HORSES to go faster and faster as they raced away from Lambton. They planned to return to the house they had been using and retrieve the carriage in which they had come from Hertfordshire. Then they would head for the border. Collins did not want to risk Elizabeth's escaping again before they were able to tie the knot.

They briefly laid a false trail in case they were being followed. Now, as they flew along the narrow track that would take them to the waiting carriage, Wickham fumed at the turn of events. Georgiana had, again, slipped through his fingers, and Collins had denied him the pleasure of taking out his anger on the other young woman. However, as they rode along, an idea struck Wickham. An evil smile crossed his face as he thought through his plan. He could always double-cross Collins and make off with the girl. Collins said she was to come into a large inheritance. Wickham did not know how large it would be, but even if it were less than Georgiana's dowry, the inheritance would certainly be better than walking away from this escapade with nothing.

On the other horse, Elizabeth began to regain consciousness. She was aware of a pair of arms encircling her, but rather than the pleasant smell of her intended, the stench was of alcohol and sweat, covered by a strong cologne. Between the smell and the rocking motion, she felt her stomach churn. Keeping her eyes closed, Elizabeth tried to recall what had occurred. When memory returned, she opened her eyes and cried, "Georgiana!"

Collins looked down at the troublesome girl held before him on his horse. "No, dear Cousin, it is I, your soon-to-be-husband." There was no love or pleasure in his look or his voice, and Elizabeth was truly frightened for the first time since the men had entered the dressmaker's shop.

Affecting bravado, she said, "I will not willingly marry you, and you cannot marry me. I am underage and you will need my uncle's permission, which he will never give."

"Perhaps were we to marry in England that would be true, but they do not worry about such formalities over the border." He glanced down at Elizabeth with an evil leer. "We will marry at Gretna Green and then immediately visit your uncle Philips so you may receive your inheritance. However, once it has been turned over, you will have very little opportunity to enjoy it."

He glanced at her again and laughed at the fear he saw in her face.

They rounded a bend in the road, and a dilapidated cottage came into view. As they stopped before the building, Collins dismounted from his horse and roughly yanked down Elizabeth. She was struck by a wave of dizziness and collapsed to her knees. Harold Collins grabbed her by the arm and pulled her to her feet. The next thing Collins knew, Elizabeth was emptying the contents of her stomach down the front of him.

With a curse, he pushed her away, and Elizabeth again found herself upon the ground. "Now I must change before we can depart," grumbled an irritated Collins as he stomped in the direction of the cottage.

Wickham moved to stand over Elizabeth, making sure to stay behind her, as she was still retching. When she had finished, he handed her a handkerchief with which to wipe her mouth. Then he gently took her arm and helped her to her feet before leading her into the cottage.

The colonel and the footman paused when they reached the corner of the alley. The colonel dismounted briefly to study the hoof prints the two men left behind, hoping to find an identifying mark that would help him track them. He noticed one of the horseshoes bore the mark of the military. It appeared Wickham had commandeered a horse from the militia for his most recent adventure. The other hoof prints were deeper, as Collins was a large man, and he was riding double with Elizabeth.

Remounting hastily, they continued on the path the footman had seen them take into the woods outside Lambton. They stopped occasionally to ensure they were still following the correct set of tracks. As the road veered to the left, a feeling of familiarity came over Richard, but he could not remember why the place seemed familiar.

The tracks continued to follow the road, so they continued in that direction. After traveling a few hundred yards, the tracks disappeared.

"Now what, Colonel?" asked the footman.

Richard dismounted and stared at the roadway ahead of them. He looked at the roadway and realized someone had brushed the center of the roadway to eliminate any tracks. They would have to backtrack, looking for a turnoff they may have missed. Richard returned to where the footman waited with the horses. It was then that he noticed another patch of brushed road.

The colonel hurried back to his horse and took off through the woods to his right, the footman following close behind him. When the woods thinned, Richard saw an overgrown track. From the way the undergrowth was matted down, it was obvious the path had recently seen steady traffic.

Again the feeling of familiarity returned, and suddenly the colonel realized why. There was a cottage nearby that had belonged to Wickham's maternal aunt. Turning to the footman, he said, "See that track? Ride in that direction. You should come out where we followed the bend in the road to the left. Return to Lambton as fast as you can to fetch Darcy. Tell him to meet me near the cottage that belonged to Mrs. Harris. I will watch for them to ensure they do not leave. Now, hurry!" The footman turned his horse and flew in the direction the colonel instructed.

The carriage raced up the drive to Pemberley at such a rapid pace as to cause Jeffers concern. He sent a footman to fetch Mr. Darcy from his study.

"What is it, Jeffers?" Darcy asked as he approached the butler, who was framed in the open front door.

"It appears to be your carriage, sir, and it is traveling rather fast."

Hearing the commotion, Bingley stepped from the library and moved to join his friend. By this time, Darcy had reached the open door and observed the carriage's approach with a feeling of dread. He rushed down the front steps, followed closely by Bingley, and ripped open the carriage door before it had fully stopped. Glancing inside to see if he could determine the problem, he saw only his sister, tears streaming down her face.

"Georgiana, where is Miss Lucas?"

Hearing her brother's voice, Georgiana launched herself from the carriage and into his arms. She sobbed so much she could not speak. Darcy attempted to calm her but was overcome with worry for Elizabeth. By this time, the footman had dismounted and was rapidly relaying the information and the colonel's message to his master.

Jeffers had called for Mrs. Reynolds, and the two of them stood under Pemberley's portico to see how they could be of assistance. After listening to the footman's account, Darcy began shouting for several horses and men to be ready to ride immediately. Hearing his orders, Mrs. Reynolds rushed forward to take over Georgiana's care and lead her into the house.

Darcy briefly told Jeffers what had occurred and said to send word to him at the dress shop should a message be received or in the event of an emergency. As he finished giving the butler his orders, Mr. Martin, his steward, and several mounted groomsmen appeared from the direction of the stables. Mr. Martin was leading Stargazer, and one of the grooms was leading a horse for the footman who had brought the colonel's message. Darcy was pleased to note that several of the men were armed.

After Darcy had settled in the saddle, Mr. Martin handed Darcy a loaded pistol. Darcy tucked the pistol into his waistband and kicked his horse into a gallop. He called over his shoulder, "Bingley, please watch over Georgiana while I am gone."

351

The men raced across the lawn and soared over fences, heading to Lambton overland, as it would save considerable time. Arriving at the dressmaker's, they were surprised to find a crowd around the door. Darcy pushed his way through the crowd and entered the shop. He immediately noticed the doctor kneeling near the opening to the back room. Dr. Powell was bent over Mrs. Webb, who was lying on the floor, unmoving.

"What is going on here?"

Mr. Watson, the constable, turned to order the newcomers out of the shop. At the sight of Mr. Darcy, he moved to speak to the gentleman.

"Begging your pardon, Mr. Darcy, but you need to step outside, sir."

"Do you know what is going on here, Mr. Watson?"

"It appears someone struck Mrs. Webb, but we do not know the reason, sir."

"I can tell you why."

Watson stared at Darcy in confusion. "What do you know, sir?"

Looking at the constable, Darcy said, "I need your promise that you will keep the information quiet to protect some of those involved. Do I have it?"

The constable nodded in assent.

"Then I will ask my men to move to the alley to wait for me while you disperse the crowd. I need to ensure we have privacy before I relate the story to you."

Nodding his consent, the constable moved with Darcy out the door. Darcy stepped up to Mr. Martin and whispered for all the Pemberley men to depart in different directions and meet again in the alley behind the shop.

Mr. Watson stood on the walkway in front of the shop. Raising his voice, he called to the crowd. "All right, everyone, it is time to go about your business. There is nothing to see here. Go on now, go home." The constable waved his arms at the crowd, trying to disperse them. When everyone had departed, Mr. Watson stationed his deputy at the door to prevent people from loitering or attempting to enter the shop.

Mr. Watson moved back into the shop. Darcy stood near Dr. Powell. In his most business-like voice, the constable spoke. "Now, Mr. Darcy, what information do you have regarding this matter?"

Taking a deep breath, Darcy began. "My sister and her companion, Miss Lucas, were in the shop at the time of the injury to Mrs. Webb. From what I was told when my sister returned to Pemberley, two men entered the shop with the intention of kidnapping my sister. One of the men was George Wickham and the other she did not recognize. Her companion managed to get Georgiana out of the store. Before my footman could return to investigate, the men had departed, and Miss Lucas was missing, as well.

"Good heavens, Darcy. Is Miss Darcy well?" cried Dr. Powell.

Darcy nodded and continued to relate the information he had. "From what I understand, my cousin, Colonel Fitzwilliam, had just ridden into town and heard my sister's cries for help. The footman who had gone to investigate told him there was no one in the store. He had my coachman and remaining footman return Miss Darcy to Pemberley while they took off after the men who took Miss Lucas. The message I received said to wait here for further information."

As the constable thought about the information he had been given, Darcy turned to the doctor. "How is Mrs. Webb; will she recover?"

"I hope so," responded Dr. Powell, concern evident in his voice. "She received a dreadful blow from a hard object. There is a depression in the back of her skull."

"Can you tell what caused the injury?" Mr. Watson inquired.

"From the shape, I would guess it was the butt of a pistol. From the depth of the injury, I would say the gentleman was considerably taller than his victim. He would have to have been to get enough leverage to cause this much damage." Dr. Powell shook his head. "She has not regained consciousness in the time I have been here. We can only hope she will. We need to move Mrs. Webb to my office so my housekeeper can keep watch over her. She will need to have someone sit with her at all times. My concern is that blood will build up, causing pressure on her brain. It can cause serious complications or death."

"I can have two of my men carry her," offered Darcy. "Will you need more than your nurse to assist in her care? I can arrange for one of the maids from Pemberley to assist."

"My housekeeper can handle things for now, and hopefully I can find some ladies from Lambton who will be able to take turns watching over Mrs. Webb. It would help if you would have your men move her."

Darcy stepped to the back door and found his men waiting there. "I need the assistance of several of you." Four immediately stepped forward. "Please carefully carry Mrs. Webb to Dr. Powell's office, then return here immediately. Dr. Powell will show you the way."

The grooms stepped inside and moved towards the prone figure on the storeroom floor. As the men bent to lift the woman, they heard the constable call out.

"Wait." He moved towards the men, carrying a blanket he had found folded over the back of a chair. "It might be easier and safer if we position her in this and then carry her. It will jostle her less."

Two of the men spread the blanket on the floor while the others gently rolled Mrs. Webb onto her side. They again rolled her to her back and smoothly moved her to the center of the blanket. Standing, they each grabbed a corner of the blanket and followed the doctor from the building.

After watching the dressmaker being carried from her shop, the constable turned to Darcy. "Do you plan to remain in the shop awaiting word from the colonel?" he inquired.

"Yes." Darcy was growing more concerned by the minute. The sun had almost set. Elizabeth had been missing for hours, and no word had yet come.

"I believe I will join you, sir. I would like to assist in the capture of these men. You can be sure I will see they are punished to the full extent of the law," came Watson's cold reply.

The words were barely out of his mouth when they became aware of a disturbance at the door. Looking through the window, Darcy recognized his livery. He flung open the door.

"Mr. Darcy, you must come with me. We are to meet the colonel at Mrs. Harris' cottage."

Darcy turned and ran through the shop and out the back door, where his men waited with his mount. Vaulting into the saddle, he called to his men, and they raced out of the alley. The constable, whose horse had been tied up in front of the shop, was hot on their heels. As they came to the overgrown track, Darcy pulled up.

He turned to the men following and said, "We will have to ride single file. Before we are too close to the house, I believe we should dismount and approach on foot. Just follow my lead." With that, Darcy moved his horse to the right and entered the woods.

When they had gone as far as he felt was safe, he dismounted and tied his horse to a nearby tree, leaving the reins long so the horse could graze. The others followed suit. When everyone had gathered, they moved forward as quietly as possible. When they were within sight of the cottage, Darcy saw his cousin a short distance ahead. Richard was crouched beside a stone wall that was crumbling in places. Picking up a small rock, Darcy tossed it at his cousin. It hit Richard in the back, causing him to turn. Placing his finger to his lips, he beckoned the men forward. As they approached, Darcy could hear raised voices, though they were indistinct, which made it difficult to determine what was being said. Reaching Richard's hiding place, the men spread out to hide behind the wall.

"What is the situation?" Darcy asked tersely.

"Wickham and Collins were just starting to argue when you got my attention. I have not been able to determine much of what is being said. I need to get closer so I can get a look inside and hear better. I believe we should have the men split up and surround the house. Listen for my command and we will enter."

As Richard was about to move off, Darcy said, "Wait, I am coming with you." Darcy looked at his steward and the constable, saying only, "You heard the colonel's orders."

Following Richard's movements, Darcy and the colonel crept closer to the cottage. They took up a position on either side of the front door. Closest to the window, the colonel pulled a small square object from his pocket. Positioning it carefully, he was able to get a look inside.

Elizabeth was seated facing the door. The two men facing each other were posturing in front of her. Now that they were closer, the words of their disagreement could be easily heard.

When he came through the door holding Elizabeth's arm, Wickham heard Collins cursing in the bedroom as he changed and cleaned his boots. Leaning close to Elizabeth, he whispered, "Keep your mouth closed and do as I say, and I might be able to get you away from him."

Elizabeth said nothing. She was sure she would be no better off with Wickham than she would with Mr. Collins.

"Tie her up," ordered Collins from the other room. "I do not want her running away again."

Displeased at being given orders, Wickham nevertheless did as requested. He pulled Elizabeth's hands behind her back and bound her wrists tightly. Once her hands were secured, he knelt in front of her to bind her feet. He reached out to take hold of her ankle. A smirk on his face, he allowed his hand to stroke her calf and drift towards her thigh. Elizabeth kicked out with her other leg, aiming for the most sensitive area of his anatomy. If she could cause enough injury, perhaps she could run. Unfortunately, the angle was wrong, and she merely succeeded in giving him a glancing blow.

Wickham backhanded Elizabeth again. This time, his ring cut into the tender flesh of her cheek. "Do you wish me to leave you to your fate with Collins?" he growled.

"I doubt my fate would be any better with you," she managed to reply.

Wickham leered at her. "That may be true, but I assure you, you would enjoy my attentions much more than Collins'." He laughed as Elizabeth shuddered.

Harold Collins entered the room to Wickham's laughter. "Has my dear cousin been entertaining you with her sharp wit? You know, Cousin Elizabeth, you must learn to hold your tongue. Intelligence in a woman is not an attractive quality." Turning to look at Wickham, he continued. "I am ready. We should depart. We need to get as far away as possible before we are discovered."

"I agree we should be leaving, but I do not think your company will be necessary."

"What are you getting at, Wickham?"

"You owe me, Collins. It was your cousin who cost me my fortune. I think it only appropriate I take her fortune from you."

Rage welled up in Collins as he grabbed Wickham by the throat. "The devil you will!"

With one hand, Wickham tried to pry Collins' hand from his neck, as the other hand struggled to remove the gun tucked into his back waistband. Finally, the gun came loose, and he shoved it into Collins' gut.

Collins let go of Wickham and stepped quickly to his right, placing Elizabeth between them. He yanked Elizabeth to her feet and attempted to use her as a shield as he reached into his coat pocket for his own weapon. However, as he tried to take a step away from Wickham, Elizabeth lost her balance and fell to the floor as two shots rang out.

Hearing the shots, Darcy and Richard burst through the front door. At the same time, Mr. Martin and the constable came in through the back. Darcy rushed to where Elizabeth lay on the floor and gathered her into his arms. The colonel moved first to Collins. He kicked the weapon away from his hand and leaned down to check for a pulse. He did not expect to find one because a large red stain was spreading across Collins' chest, but experience had taught him to always be sure.

He moved to where Wickham lay on the floor. There was a stain on his shoulder, and his eyes were closed. As the colonel leaned in to check for a pulse, Wickham grabbed the knife Richard kept in his boot, knocking Richard off his feet in the process. Richard screamed Darcy's name as Wickham raised the knife to plunge it into Darcy's back.

Recognizing from Richard's tone that he was in danger, Darcy gathered Elizabeth closer and rolled away from the body behind him, taking his beloved with him. Another shot rang out, and Wickham screamed in pain. Darcy turned his head to see smoke coming from the barrel of the constable's pistol and Wickham clutching his arm. There was a bloody stump where his hand should have been.

"Miss Lucas, are you well? Did I hurt you? Speak to me, please!"

"I am well, Mr. Darcy, just feeling a little battered."

Calling out for some of his men, Darcy stood and lifted Elizabeth in his arms. He directed one of the grooms to ride for Lambton and request Dr. Powell's presence at Pemberley. Turning to the others, he said, "I am taking the carriage that was outside and returning to Pemberley with Miss Lucas. Mr. Watson, Richard, I trust you can handle things from here."

"I will come to Pemberley tomorrow to speak with the young lady," said Mr. Watson. "I will need to take her statement."

Darcy nodded. Turning to another of the grooms, he said, "Please tie Stargazer and the horse you rode to the carriage. I will need you to drive for us. The rest of you can accompany us unless Mr. Watson has need of you."

"No, sir, you just take care of the young lady. I will be in touch soon."

Darcy strode from the house to the waiting carriage. With a groom holding the door, Darcy gently placed Elizabeth on a seat inside and climbed in after her. He quickly scooped her back into his arms and settled her onto his lap, holding her tightly.

Within a few minutes, the carriage was underway, and Darcy continued to hold Elizabeth, whispering words of love and reassurance as she sobbed. They were on the other side of Lambton by the time her tears had stopped.

"Oh, my perfect rose, when the carriage arrived at Pemberley without you, I thought my heart would stop."

"Oh, Georgiana! Is she safe? Did she make it home?"

"Do not worry, my love. She is safe, only concerned about you. I can see you have been abused by their hands. Are you truly well? If Collins were not dead, I would kill him for harming you."

Elizabeth could see the smoldering anger in Darcy's eyes. "It was not Mr. Collins who struck me; it was Mr. Wickham. The first time was when I stopped him from reaching Georgiana, giving her time to escape. Then, when he was following Mr. Collins' orders to bind my hands and feet, he attempted to take a liberty to which I objected. I tried to inflict some damage of my own, but, unfortunately, my aim was off. He took exception and my cheeks were again his target." Trying to distract Darcy's anger, she said, "With his last injury, he shall find his tendency to slap young women a bit more difficult to accomplish." Her smile, marred slightly by the swelling of her face, caused him to relax and smile slightly as well.

When the carriage pulled up in front of Pemberley, Georgiana, Mrs. Reynolds, and Dr. Powell hurried out. Darcy stepped from the carriage and reached in for Elizabeth. He carried her up the front stairs and directly to her bedchamber. He set her gently on the bed and Lucy stepped up to assist her mistress in shedding her outerwear. Mrs. Reynolds shooed Darcy out of the room, and she and Lucy continued to prepare Miss Lucas to be examined by Dr. Powell.

When his examination was completed, Dr. Powell again found Darcy pacing in the hallway. Placing an arm around the young man's shoulder, he led Darcy to the study. Once they each had a drink in hand, Dr. Powell said, "Rest assured, Darcy, Miss Lucas is quite well. Her cheeks will look worse before they look better. I treated the small cut, which did not require stitches. It should not be noticeable at all when it is healed. Other than a little bit of chaffing on her wrists and ankles caused by the rope and a lump on the back of her head, there are no injuries. I recommend she stay in bed for a day, but I imagine she will ignore that. She will likely be up and around tomorrow. I imagine she will most likely not wish to be seen until the bruising on her face is gone."

Darcy let out a relieved breath. "Thank you, Dr. Powell. How is Mrs. Webb? Has she regained consciousness?"

"Unfortunately, no. I will check in on her several times a day, but if you need anything, send someone to the office. They will know where I am. Is Miss Darcy well? Do you need me to check on her before I leave?"

"She says she is well, but I wonder if she will find sleep easily," was Darcy's reply.

"I could leave a draught for both ladies to ensure they get a good night's sleep if you would like."

"I believe that would be a perfect solution, Doctor. Again, thank you for all your assistance."

As Dr. Powell moved to the study door, Darcy's voice stopped him. "Were you able to find the necessary assistance for Mrs. Webb?"

"There are several ladies who are willing to sit with her during the day, but most of them must care for their families in the evening. I will sit with her tonight, and I may have to send for a nurse from Derby to stay with her in the nights to come."

"Please allow me to summon Mrs. Reynolds. She will be able to tell us which of the maids would be of the most use to you and Mrs. Webb."

Dr. Powell moved to sit before Darcy's desk again as they waited for Mrs. Reynolds to arrive. Once Darcy had explained the issue to Mrs. Reynolds, she thought for only a moment before she recommended one of the maids. Sending for the girl, Mrs. Reynolds explained the issue. The young girl hastily packed her belongings and left with Dr. Powell.

Darcy ascended the stairs and knocked on the door to Elizabeth's room. Lucy opened it to admit him. He saw Georgiana seated in a chair by Elizabeth's bed.

"How are my two favorite ladies this evening? I hope you are both recovered from your unfortunate adventure."

"We are well, William," said Elizabeth as she held out her hand to him.

"I came with some news I thought might be of particular interest to you, Elizabeth."

She looked at him questioningly when he pulled an envelope from his pocket.

"I received an express just after Dr. Powell's departure. The Gardiners will be arriving on December 20th. This note was included for you."

With a shaking hand, Elizabeth took the letter, recognizing her aunt's handwriting. Looking at the message for some time, Elizabeth finally broke the seal with trembling fingers.

Gracechurch Street
London

Dearest Lizzy,

It is a relief to know you are safe and well. To first hear you were killed and then to know this was not true but that you were missing nearly broke our hearts. What a blessing you landed somewhere safe and with such an exceptional and honorable gentleman as Mr. Darcy. However, do not dare worry us in such a way ever again!

Mr. Darcy's letter was succinct, yet there is much we wish to know—most especially why you would not come to us for assistance. Be prepared, my dear, to give a full accounting of everything that has occurred since the accident. Nothing less will satisfy us, you may be sure.

Mr. Darcy's messenger is awaiting this reply, so I must close, my dear Lizzy. Jane and your uncle send their best, and we will see you very soon.

With much love,

Helen Gardiner

As Elizabeth read her letter, Darcy watched her face closely to determine her emotions. As she closed her eyes and lowered the paper to her lap, he asked, "Are you well, dearest?"

"Indeed, Fitzwilliam, I am very well. Thank you for inviting them to visit. It appears I am forgiven, but must never frighten them again. My aunt also demands a full accounting of what occurred. I am delighted to have an opportunity to tell them, especially because it is occurring several months before expected."

"I have always enjoyed your uncle's company and look forward to meeting your remaining family. We shall be quite a merry party this Christmas, with family, a wedding, and a ball. I believe this is the first time I have ever looked forward to a ball," said Darcy with a laugh.

They moved to rejoin Georgiana and told her of the additional guests. "I look forward to meeting your sister Jane," said Georgie enthusiastically.

"There will be much for us to plan before the guests arrive, Georgie, but may we wait until tomorrow to begin? I find myself quite drained after the events of the day."

"Are you well, Elizabeth?" came Darcy's concerned question.

Patting the hand that reached out to hold one of hers, Elizabeth reassured him. "Yes, William, I am well, just very tired. Might we continue our planning in the morning?"

"Certainly, my dear, but any planning you do will be from this bed as per Dr. Powell's orders," came his firm reply. "I am sure Georgiana shall be happy to attend you here." Darcy stood and pulled Georgiana close for a hug as he placed a kiss on her head.

Waiting until his sister exited Elizabeth's room, Darcy picked up Elizabeth's hand. Reaching out with his other hand, he gently stroked her wounded cheeks. "Oh, my dearest love, I am so grateful you are safe and back at Pemberley where you belong forever more. I hope you will understand if I do not wish you out of my sight for some time to come."

She nodded shyly.

Darcy raised to his lips the hand he was holding, placing a lingering kiss on the soft skin. Glancing up with only his eyes, he noted the color that suffused her face. Never breaking eye contact, he turned her hand over, gently cradling it in his large, warm palm as he placed another lingering kiss on the tender flesh of her own palm. The color in her face increased, and her eyes looked fervently back at him. Giving her hand a gentle squeeze, he released it, placing it back on the bed. "Good night, my love," Darcy said as he moved to the door. He reached for the knob but was arrested by her voice.

"William, do you think I need to be concerned about the younger Mr. Collins? He was always pleasant to my family, unlike his father, but none of us had much use for the man. Do you think he will wish to gain my inheritance or seek revenge for his father's death? He never sounded as though he wished to marry me, but I am afraid today's events may anger him."

"We cannot know for certain, but from what Richard has told me of the investigation done on the young man, I do not believe so. However, until we can be certain, I shall make sure you are well protected whenever you are away from Pemberley. Now you must rest. We will talk in the morning."

She heard his footsteps as he descended the staircase. Finding Bingley and Richard engaged in a desultory game of billiards, he bade them goodnight before retiring. As he passed through the hallway to make his way up the staircase, Jeffers approached him. "Sir, Mr. Watson sent this note for you." Darcy moved to stand beneath a lighted wall sconce so he could read the note.

Mr. Darcy,

The enclosed letter was found in the dead man's pocket. I thought you would wish to have it, as it may help you identify the individual who started all the trouble.

Also, Wickham is suffering from a fever. Dr. Powell believes the wound in his hand has become infected. He will lose what remains of his hand and may lose the arm. However, be it from fever or hanging, he will definitely lose his life.

Watson

Darcy was surprised to note the paper appeared to be the same as was used at Pemberley. He opened the note and anger filled him. Though the note was unsigned, he had seen the handwriting often enough on invitations he had received. Darcy turned on his heel and returned to the billiard room.

"Bingley, I believe we have proof your sister overheard our discussion the last night she was here."

"Whatever do you mean?"

Darcy thrust the note into Bingley's hand as he paced back and forth. Bingley's face paled.

"Dear God! I wonder if she has any idea what her actions set in motion. She is responsible for Miss Elizabeth's kidnapping, the attempted kidnapping of Miss Darcy, and Mr. Collins' murder."

"You can add to that Wickham's death, as he will most likely hang unless the fever he has developed takes him, and quite possibly Mrs. Webb's if she does not survive her injuries," remarked Darcy. "You may wish to write to your aunt about this, Bingley. She should understand how dangerous Caroline can be. Perhaps you need to consider sending her to an asylum. If she heard our discussion, she knew the dangers to Elizabeth. I am uncertain as to whether she has the capacity to care for anyone besides herself. In any case, I am finally retiring. Again, good night."

23. CHRISTMAS AT PEMBERLEY

WITH LITTLE LESS THAN A FORTNIGHT between the events in Lambton and the arrival of the Christmas guests, those at Pemberley found their days filled. The first order of business was to satisfy Richard's demand to know the events that led up to the kidnapping and rescue. The residents of Pemberley gathered in the library after breakfast. Bingley spoke of his suspicions of Elizabeth's identity after meeting the Gardiners and Miss Bennet. Darcy related the events of the evening Bingley and his sister arrived and all that had occurred, and how Bingley's questioning of her identity forced Elizabeth to tell them the truth about her background. Elizabeth retold her story for Richard, who said it agreed with all he had discovered during his investigation. Then Elizabeth and Georgiana told of the events in Lambton, with Elizabeth giving them the details after Georgiana escaped from the shop. Darcy credited his cousin's timely arrival in Lambton with saving Elizabeth and Georgiana. Finally, Darcy and Elizabeth announced their plans to marry and told the others of the invitation to Elizabeth's family to join them at Pemberley for Christmas.

Next, Mrs. Reynolds and Jeffers were given the truth of Elizabeth's history. As both were very fond of the young lady, they were appalled at what she had endured and complimented her on her brave actions. They were further informed that she would become Mrs. Darcy at the earliest opportunity. Both expressed their happiness at the arrangements as they gave her their best wishes. The other members of the staff were to hear a slightly different version of the truth. They would be told it was Mr. Darcy's acquaintance with her uncle that brought Elizabeth under Darcy's protection and notice.

With these duties over, the gentlemen spent their days in leisurely pursuits. However, the young ladies had a great deal with which to contend. First they had to determine which rooms the guests would need so that those rooms could be prepared. Then they spent time planning the meals to be served while the guests were in residence, as well as activities and entertainments to be enjoyed.

Once those matters had been addressed, the ladies completed arrangements for the tenants' baskets and celebration. They determined they would have the celebration in the ballroom and provide cookies and wassail as the baskets and other gifts were distributed.

Fortunately for Georgiana and Elizabeth, Darcy realized Mrs. Webb's injuries would prevent the seamstress from completing their ball gowns. He contacted the seamstress in Matlock, and with a hefty gift, persuaded her to come to Pemberley for a day. With help from his staff, he was able to obtain from Mrs. Webb's shop the fabric and other items the ladies had selected for their ball gowns and had them brought to Pemberley. When the dressmaker arrived, she took their measurements and reviewed their wishes for their gowns before taking the information and the retrieved items to her shop. It was agreed the young ladies would arrive in Matlock two days before the ball and visit her shop for their final fittings.

One of the last things they did was decorate the house for the holidays. Elizabeth had learned from Georgiana and Mrs. Reynolds that the holidays had not been much celebrated in the years since the death of Lady Anne Darcy. Elizabeth was determined to change that practice. Christmas was her favorite time of year, and she felt they had much to celebrate this season. Mrs. Reynolds and the maids scoured the attics to find the family's heirloom decorations. Once they had been located and cleaned, the ladies planned what they wished to do.

On a gray morning just two days before their first guests were to arrive, they recruited the gentlemen to accompany them in pursuit of evergreens, holly, and mistletoe to use in their endeavors. The group dressed warmly for the cold weather, and Elizabeth and Georgiana each carried a large basket in which to collect nature's bounty. Darcy had requested the gardeners provide them with an ax, saws, and several pairs of clippers to aid in their activity. Seated in the back of a farm wagon driven by the colonel, they approached the forest and began their search. They called out to one another, talking and laughing as they gathered the needed items, which were placed in the wagon or the ladies' baskets.

Just before they finished collecting the needed greenery, snowflakes began to fall. It was a jolly group that returned with frozen fingers and toes, as well as rosy cheeks and noses. When they came in through the terrace doors, Mrs. Reynolds hurried them off to the warm baths she had waiting for them. She directed the maids to lay the items on the still room tables to dry. Then she ensured that warm drinks, scones, and other treats were prepared for their enjoyment.

371

An hour later they were all together in the drawing room.

"What plans do you ladies have for all we gathered?" asked Darcy.

"Oh, Brother, Rose...I mean, Elizabeth...had the most wonderful ideas. I cannot wait to see how it turns out!"

"May we assist you ladies in any way, or will you have the servants assist you?"

"It was our plan to have the servants assist us, but we would be delighted to have your company as well," said Elizabeth with a meaningful look at the three gentlemen.

"I am at your service, my dear."

"I believe it would be fun to participate," came Bingley's reply.

"You may count on my strong arm, ladies," said Richard, as he swept them a dashing bow.

The next day the house was filled with laughter as they used the red and gold ribbon Mrs. Reynolds had obtained and decorated every doorway and mantle in all the public rooms and the guest rooms that would be in use. They created a lovely pine garland that was becomingly draped on the stair rail and tied into place with the ribbons. The maids fashioned several kissing balls from the mistletoe, hanging them where they would receive the most use. A beautiful Nativity set was placed in a corner of the large drawing room.

As they stood in the hallway and observed the decorations around them, Mrs. Reynolds said, "I do not believe I have ever seen the house look more lovely and festive. Miss Bennet, you did a most wonderful job!"

"I quite agree, Elizabeth. The house is better dressed than I have ever seen it!" said Darcy as he took her hand and placed a lingering kiss on the back of it.

As the group admired the decorated hall and stairs, a knock was heard at the door. Answering it, Jeffers brought the message to Mr. Darcy. Darcy broke the seal and scanned the brief message with a sigh of relief.

"What is it, Darcy?" asked the colonel.

"It is from Watson. There will no longer be a need for a trial, as Mr. Wickham has succumbed to his injuries."

All those present stood silent for a moment—a silence broken by the colonel. "That is as it should be. All the harm he has done is at an end, and none of those who suffered at his hand shall be forced to face him and whatever lies he might tell in an attempt to save himself."

Still no one spoke or moved.

"The holidays and a new year approach," the colonel continued. It is time to put the troubles of this past year behind us and celebrate the joy that resulted from the evil intentions of others. I choose to believe everything is as it should be!"

"Hear, hear!" added Bingley.

Darcy, Elizabeth, and Georgiana each released a cleansing breath and smiled. "You are absolutely correct, Richard. We have a great many blessings to celebrate! Mrs. Reynolds, I believe we would all enjoy some refreshments." So saying, Darcy offered an arm to Elizabeth and one to Georgiana, then led them to the library as the remaining gentlemen followed.

Luncheon had passed, and the family and friends were gathered in the drawing room awaiting the arrival of the Gardiner family. Elizabeth's excitement did not permit her to remain still for long. She attempted to sew and read, but that resulted in her stabbing her fingers or reading the same paragraph over and over. Next she walked about the room, frequently stopping at the window in hopes of seeing a carriage.

When Jeffers announced a carriage was coming up the drive, Elizabeth rushed to the hall and threw open the front door. Darcy joined her, placing her cloak over her shoulders. He took her arm and placed it through his. She placed her other hand on his arm, and he covered her small, cold hands with his large, warm ones. When the carriage came into view, Elizabeth squeezed his arm tightly. The carriage finally came to a stop before the steps where Darcy and Elizabeth waited. Elizabeth released Darcy's arm and rushed forward, throwing herself against her uncle, who had just exited.

"Oh, my dear Lizzy, it is wonderful to see you again!"

"Oh, Uncle Edward, I am so happy you are here!"

He shifted Elizabeth to one arm and reached out to help his wife and other niece descend from the carriage. Elizabeth was quickly scooped up by her aunt and sister as the three hugged tightly to one another. Tears were on all their faces. A moment later the tugs of little hands at her skirts showed that Elizabeth's cousins had managed to escape the carriage as well. Elizabeth knelt to give each one a hug.

When Elizabeth returned to stand beside Darcy, he again tucked her hand under his arm. Looking at her family, she said, "Uncle Edward, Aunt Helen, Jane, Margaret, Benjamin, Luke, and little Allison, allow me to present your host, and my betrothed, Mr. Fitzwilliam Darcy. William, you already know my uncle, Edward Gardiner. Allow me to introduce you to my aunt, Helen Gardiner, my elder sister, Jane Bennet, and my cousins, Margaret, who is seven, Benjamin, who is five, and Luke, who is three. The littlest one, whom I am eager to hold, is Allison."

Darcy looked at his guests, "Welcome to Pemberley. I am very pleased to meet you, but might I suggest we return inside, where it is much warmer, before we become better acquainted?" With Elizabeth still on his arm, he turned and led the others into the house. Mr. Gardiner escorted his wife while Jane took the children's hands as they followed behind the Gardiners.

In the hall, Mrs. Reynolds waited with several servants to help the guests remove their outerwear.

"I am sure you would all like to rest and refresh before joining us for tea. Or, if you prefer, tea can be sent to your rooms."

"Thank you, Mr. Darcy, you are correct. We will take a moment to get the children settled and refresh ourselves. However, I believe the thing we most wish is to return to Elizabeth and have her explain all that has happened," said Mrs. Gardiner.

"If you do not mind, William, I shall go with Jane, but we will return soon, as I know Mr. Bingley is looking forward to greeting her." Elizabeth cast her sister a sly look and observed a deep blush appear on Jane's cheeks upon hearing that Mr. Bingley was in residence.

"Of course, Elizabeth." Darcy kissed her hand and returned to the drawing room, where they would await the arrival of the guests.

"Mrs. Reynolds, if you would not mind escorting my uncle and aunt to their room, I shall show my sister the way," said Elizabeth.

"Certainly, Miss Bennet." Within minutes, the hall was empty.

The sisters walked arm in arm to the guest room that had been prepared for Jane. It was a charming room done in shades of rose and overlooking the gardens.

"What a lovely room!" exclaimed Jane. Then, turning from her examination of the room, she hugged Elizabeth and said, "Oh, Lizzy, how I have missed you! I thought my heart would break when we received the letter saying you had all perished in an accident. I felt so lost and adrift."

"I missed you as well, Jane, but I was blessed to find dear Georgiana with whom to talk. We spoke much about my sisters and parents as I shared my memories of them with her. The Darcys were orphaned at a young age as well. They helped me deal with my loss."

"How did you ever end up in Derbyshire? Why did you not come to Uncle in London?"

"Oh, Jane, there is so much to the tale. If you do not mind, I would much rather tell it only once more when we are joined by Aunt Helen and Uncle Edward. Besides, I want to hear about you and Mr. Bingley."

Jane blushed and softly said, "We are to be married, though I have asked him to wait until my year of mourning is over."

"Oh, Jane. I am so happy for you! Who would have thought we would meet such men? And to think, they are best friends. We shall often be in one another's company, and I can think of nothing that would delight me more."

Hannah stepped into the bedroom and asked, "Is there a specific dress you wish to wear, miss?"

"Hannah, allow me to introduce my dearest sister, Miss Jane Bennet."

"A pleasure, Miss Bennet," replied the maid as she bobbed a curtsey.

"Hannah will be your lady's maid during your stay, Jane. Her sister, Lucy, is my maid." Turning to the maid, Elizabeth smiled and said, "You shall be much happier with Jane than the guest you previously served, Hannah, for my sister is the sweetest of people."

The girls chatted as Jane refreshed herself and changed her dress. When Hannah finished redoing her hair, the two sisters headed down to the drawing room to await the arrival of their aunt and uncle.

When everyone arrived, introductions were made to Georgiana and the colonel. Once all the guests were settled with a teacup in hand, Elizabeth began by telling her family of all that had happened since the fateful night of the accident. She related the story of Harold Collins and her daring escape. At times she heard the gasps from Jane and Aunt Helen and watched her uncle's face grow red with anger.

When she spoke of her time at Pemberley, Elizabeth's face glowed with happiness. When the glow dimmed, Darcy reached over and took her hand as Elizabeth related the incidents of a few weeks ago, ending with the deaths of the two men involved in her abduction.

To say her family was shocked would not begin to adequately express their sorrow, loss, anger, and outrage at the plans of Mr. Collins. When the telling was completed, Elizabeth breathed a sigh of relief. "Now that you are aware of all that has happened while we were parted, I should like every one of you to put it from your minds. Let us think only of the enjoyable time we shall have during your visit!"

The next few days passed pleasantly for the residents and guests of Pemberley. Darcy took the opportunity to speak with Mr. Gardiner and formally request Elizabeth's hand in marriage. A snowfall one night made for a delightful day as all but Mr. and Mrs. Gardiner and Allison spent the following morning playing in the snow. They built snowmen and had a snowball fight. After luncheon and naps for the children, Darcy had two sleighs prepared, and the entire party toured the grounds. Light snow began to fall as they returned to the house.

"I do hope the snow will not prevent your family from arriving, William."

"Not to worry, Elizabeth, they will come by sleigh if the snow gets too deep."

"Have you told Lord and Lady Matlock of our engagement?" Darcy noted the nervousness in her voice.

"Indeed I have, my love, and Richard has also praised you to them. They look forward to meeting you."

"I do hope they will like me." Again he noticed a trace of nervousness when she spoke.

"I am sure they will be quite pleased with my choice within a short time of making your acquaintance. You have nothing to fear. However, I should warn you, my Aunt Catherine will not be so welcoming."

A look of concern appeared on Elizabeth's face.

"Do not let it worry you, my love. I could be marrying Princess Charlotte and Aunt Catherine would not approve. For as long as I can remember, she has been trying to convince me to marry her daughter, Anne, saying she and my mother planned it from our infancy. I know that is not the case. My mother and her sister were not close, and my mother always spoke to me of finding someone to love when I chose to marry. I know my mother and father would have both loved you."

"I am pleased to know that. It grieves me to think our children will not have any grandparents."

"I also wish the situation were different, but I am certain Aunt Elaine and Uncle Anthony will happily fill that role. She has treated us as her children since my mother's death. They wish to introduce us as a married couple at the New Year's Eve ball. In fact, they have invited the Gardiners to attend as well. They could travel to Matlock with us and return to London from there after the ball."

"Have you spoken with my uncle about this?"

"I thought to do so after dinner tonight."

"Then I shall mention it to my aunt at the same time."

"Is everything ready for the tenant gathering tomorrow?"

Elizabeth pulled a paper from her pocket, saying, "I believe so. The ballroom has been decorated. The baskets are already there for distribution. The gifts for the children have been purchased and are sorted by age. Mrs. Mason has been baking for several days. I do not believe Georgiana or I have overlooked anything."

"I am sure it will be delightful, just as the Harvest Celebration was. Would you permit me to announce our engagement to the tenants?"

"How would your aunt and uncle feel if the news were to get out before the ball?"

"Word may get around, but I do not think they would mind. It is important for the tenants to see the estate will continue on as it has for another generation. I believe they deserve to hear the news before the ton, as they are far more important to Pemberley and to me."

"Your concern for those under your care is one of the things I most admire about you, Fitzwilliam."

The smile that showed his dimples appeared. Darcy was thrilled with her words, for he knew she was of the same opinion.

The day of the tenant Christmas party had arrived. It had been scheduled for the twenty-third, after luncheon. The Matlocks were to have arrived in time for luncheon, and the guests would be left to entertain themselves as Darcy, Georgiana, and Elizabeth attended to the tenants. However, the Fitzwilliams were delayed in arriving, and Darcy was forced to ask Mrs. Reynolds to greet them and see to their comfort while offering his apologies for his absence.

The courtyard filled with carts, wagons, and small carriages as the tenants arrived at Pemberley. A footman stationed at a doorway from the courtyard directed the tenants to the ballroom. Most were stunned when they arrived. Greenery and ribbons decorated the room's three fireplaces, each with a welcoming blaze in it. Greenery also decorated all the doors and windows. Red cloths covered the long tables in the room, and the food displayed thereon looked delicious. Small tables with chairs had been placed around the room. These were covered with white cloths and beautiful arrangements of flowers and holiday greenery.

When the majority of the guests had arrived, Darcy called for their attention. "We welcome all of you today and wish to share with you the joys of this special time of year. Before we distribute the gifts that have been prepared for you, I wish to share with you some wonderful news." He beckoned for Elizabeth to join him. "I am the fortunate man who has won the hand of Miss Elizabeth Bennet. We shall marry on December 27th."

Darcy heard the whispers of confusion as the tenants recognized her, but not the name.

"Many of you know her as Miss Rose Lucas. For Miss Bennet's safety, it was necessary for her to hide here at Pemberley. You are probably aware of the events that took place in Lambton a few weeks ago. Fortunately, those who wished Miss Bennet harm have been dealt with, and she is now safe. You have all been witness to her kindness. I am sure you will agree that you are quite fortunate to gain her as the Mistress of Pemberley!"

This time, Darcy's words were met with applause and cheers. Many of the tenants called out good wishes to the couple. Darcy moved to stand near the baskets for the tenant families while Georgiana and Elizabeth moved to the table where the children's gifts sat. Mrs. Reynolds and several maids stationed themselves near the food and beverages to ensure they did not run out of anything. The children lined up to receive their gifts. A great deal of laughter and excitement filled the room.

While the Darcys were busily engaged with their tenants, the Matlocks arrived. The butler, Jeffers, greeted them at the door, explaining what kept the Darcys from welcoming them. He informed them tea would be served in the green drawing room as soon as they had refreshed themselves.

As the Matlocks made their way down the stairs to the drawing room followed by their eldest son, Lady Matlock said, "Let us look in on the event in the ballroom, shall we?" Her husband nodded in agreement, and they turned in the direction of the ballroom.

They stood in the open door of the ballroom and looked over the party. They observed Darcy standing in the center of the room, an attractive young lady on his arm. Darcy and the young lady were speaking with some of the tenants, and the Matlocks were surprised to see the smile on Darcy's face. A moment later, they heard a lovely laugh ring out and observed Darcy turn to look at the young lady at his side before placing a kiss upon her hand. They were quite shocked at his easy behavior, but the look of love on his face was all the explanation they needed.

"I do not believe I have ever seen Darcy smile like that," said the viscount in surprise.

They moved away from the door quickly and headed for the drawing room where they would take tea. They heard the hum of conversation coming from the room. Entering, Lord Matlock was surprised to find a long-time business associate already there.

"Gardiner, I am surprised to see you here," said Lord Matlock.

Everyone stood upon the entrance of the newcomers. "Lord Matlock, a pleasure, sir. Darcy said you were expected today. They are finishing with the tenants' Christmas party, but are expected to join us at any time. Would you allow me to introduce you to my family?" At Lord Matlock's nod, Mr. Gardiner introduced his wife and niece. As he began to introduce Mr. Bingley, he was interrupted.

"Bingley, nice to see you again, young man. Are you joining us for the holidays?"

"Good afternoon, Lord Matlock, Lady Matlock, Viscount," Bingley acknowledged the newest guests. "Darcy was kind enough to invite me, as my betrothed, Miss Jane Bennet, is spending the holidays here."

"Congratulations, Bingley, Miss Bennet," offered the earl. "I believe I had best complete the introductions. Mr. and Mrs. Gardiner, Miss Bennet, allow me to introduce my wife, Lady Matlock, Elaine Fitzwilliam, and my son, Viscount Matson, Nicholas Fitzwilliam. I am Lord Matlock, Anthony Fitzwilliam." Everyone bowed or curtseyed at the introductions and settled into seats to await Darcy and Elizabeth.

Turning to Mr. Gardiner, Lord Matlock spoke. "I am surprised Darcy would drag you here on business at this time of year."

"Well, he did invite mc on business of a sort. He was seeking permission to marry my other niece, Elizabeth."

"And gratefully that permission was given," came Darcy's voice from the doorway.

Everyone turned to see Darcy standing there with Georgiana on one arm and Elizabeth on the other. Georgiana released his arm and moved to greet her aunt and uncle with a hug.

Darcy said, "Good afternoon, Uncle Anthony, Aunt Elaine, Nick. I see everyone has already been introduced. Allow me to make the most important introduction of all. I would like you to meet my betrothed, Miss Elizabeth Bennet."

Elizabeth curtseyed to the Matlocks as she was introduced to each.

Lord and Lady Matlock shared a look before returning their eyes to their nephew. "You wrote of an engagement, but I believe there is more to this story that you need to share with us." His uncle's tone was somewhat stern, and his aunt regarded him with a raised brow.

At that moment, Mrs. Reynolds and a maid arrived with the tray of tea things and another of refreshments, placing them on the table before Elizabeth. Darcy and Elizabeth exchanged a glance and she gave him a small nod. "Perhaps it would be best if we have some tea before I begin. It is a rather long tale," he said as Elizabeth began to serve the tea to everyone.

As everyone settled in their seats, Darcy recounted the tale of the loss of Elizabeth's family and her escape. Mr. Gardiner added a few details from the things they had been told and later learned upon the Philips' return to Meryton. It did not escape anyone's notice that Darcy and Elizabeth held hands throughout the recitation.

At the end of the tale, Lord and Lady Matlock again exchanged glances, while the viscount merely looked at his cousin with a bemused expression. Finally, the earl spoke. "Well, Miss Elizabeth, I am certainly glad you were fortunate enough to encounter my niece and nephew first. You could have found yourself in a great deal of trouble."

"My dear, how dreadful for you! I am sorry for your loss and all you were forced to endure. How can we thank you for protecting Georgiana from that dreadful Wickham? I can only be pleased he has received his just rewards for his lifetime of misdeeds."

"I was very fortunate. Mr. and Miss Darcy have become quite dear to me and been a blessing in my life.

"Do you know anything about your inheritance?"

"No, your ladyship. After the kidnapping, the most important thing to me was to contact my aunt, uncle, and Jane."

"Well, Darcy, we should look into this," offered his uncle. "Being an heiress will certainly help smooth Miss Elizabeth's entry into society."

"I will not come into my inheritance until the first week of April. I do not know if my Uncle Philips can release any information regarding the inheritance before then."

"Would you like me to write to Philips and ask, Lizzy?" asked Mr. Gardiner.

"If you believe it would be appropriate. I am not concerned about the inheritance. I have my family back and someone who loves me, as well as a wonderful new sister. I could not ask for more."

"Uncle, I do not feel the need to know. Elizabeth's settlement has already been completed, and I have received Mr. Gardiner's signature on it. After what she has been forced to endure, the inheritance should be Elizabeth's to do with as she pleases."

On the day before Christmas, the family and guests enjoyed a wonderful breakfast together. More snow had fallen overnight, and the grounds of Pemberley were covered in a pristine white. The family spent a pleasant day enjoying one another's company. Mrs. Mason served a sumptuous dinner, which included roast beef, roasted potatoes, Brussels sprouts, and Yorkshire pudding.

After the children had been put to bed, the adults loaded into the two sleighs and went to Pemberley chapel for the midnight service. The interior of the chapel was filled with evergreens, and the lights of hundreds of candles infused it with warmth. The Darcys and their guests sat in the first row of pews on both sides of the aisle. Many of the servants and estate families filled the remainder of the chapel.

It was a lovely service. The deep voice of the vicar, Mr. Hughes, resonated throughout the room as he read the Christmas story from Luke, beginning in Chapter 2. They departed to the sounds of the church bells ringing as they drove through the night. The light of the moon and the brilliance of the stars illuminated the snow-covered ground. When everyone arrived in their rooms, they found trays of hot cocoa awaiting them to chase away the chill of the nighttime ride.

On Christmas morning, the Darcys and their guests, arrayed in their Christmas finery, gathered for an enormous breakfast before, again, attending church services. It was a lovely morning, with the sun brightly shining and glistening off the snow. After services, they returned home to find that a stack of gifts had appeared in the drawing room.

Georgiana was delighted to have been given the task of distributing the gifts to everyone. Darcy had ensured there were gifts for all of the guests, as well as for Elizabeth and Georgiana. The others had also brought small gifts for their hosts and loved ones.

The children were delighted with their gifts. Margaret received a small tea set, Benjamin, a set of toy soldiers, and Luke, a set of blocks. Mr. Gardiner had brought bottles of French Brandy for the gentlemen. Darcy and Elizabeth had put together small baskets with bath salts, lotion, and perfume for the Countess of Matlock, Mrs. Gardiner, and Jane.

The last gifts Georgiana delivered were for Elizabeth. There were two wrapped rectangles, one considerably larger than the other. Elizabeth looked at Georgiana in surprise.

"Open the large one first!" cried the girl with an expression of suppressed excitement as she took the place beside Elizabeth on the sofa.

Taking the larger one onto her lap, Elizabeth untied the ribbon and put it beside her. She reached for the ends and loosened the paper, pulling it from the gift.

Immediately, one of Elizabeth's hands flew to her mouth and her eyes filled with tears. "Oh, Georgiana! This is the most wonderful gift I have ever received." Elizabeth could not take her eyes from the watercolor portrait of her lost family, surrounded by an elegant frame.

".Jane helped me select the correct colors for their hair and eyes, and William had it framed. Do you truly like it?"

"It is as if you have given me back my family. They look so like them!" Elizabeth turned the picture around for the Gardiners and Matlocks to see. "These are my family members who were killed in the carriage accident. I described them to Georgiana, and we worked for some time on getting them just right."

The Matlocks commented on the quality of the portrait, while the Gardiners and Jane, who were all somewhat teary, remarked on the outstanding likenesses.

"Oh, Miss Darcy," cried Jane. "I should dearly like to have a copy of this, if it is not too much trouble."

Darcy removed the large framed portrait from Elizabeth's hands as Georgiana placed the smaller one on her lap.

"Oh, how delightful!" Elizabeth exclaimed. "It is lovely. Jane, look." Elizabeth turned the second portrait to the others.

"I say, Miss Darcy, this is indeed a remarkable picture of Jane. I should love to have a smaller version I might keep on the desk in my study," cried an enthusiastic Bingley.

Jane blushed at the praise the picture was getting, but was quite pleased to hear Mr. Bingley request a portrait of her.

"Oh, there is one more," said Georgiana with a sly smile as she handed her brother a smaller rectangle, wrapped as Elizabeth's had been.

With a grin on his face, Darcy made short work of unwrapping the gift. "Just as I expected, and very much what I wanted, dear Georgie!" Darcy turned around the object in his hands. The others present gasped. "I see you finally made a portrait of your companion that satisfied you. I must say, Georgie, you have captured her perfectly—including the delightful sparkle in her eyes and the joy of her beautiful smile. I shall treasure this always." Though he spoke to his sister, his gaze was locked with

Elizabeth's, his eyes speaking of his overwhelming love for her.

After the gifts had been exchanged, everyone enjoyed refreshments, and then games were played that the children could enjoy. The day ended with a stupendous Christmas feast. There was a roast pig, goose, and fish, as well as several vegetables and breads. The meal ended with a flaming pudding. In the evening, the adults enjoyed several musical performances and the conversation that good friendships often produce.

On the morning of the 27th of December, Darcy and Elizabeth were wed in the Pemberley chapel. The evening before, Darcy had delivered a large box to Elizabeth, explaining it was a wedding gift. She had opened the box to find a beautiful wedding gown inside. Darcy had obtained a copy of the measurements the Matlock seamstress had taken during her visit to Pemberley. He had expressed them to Georgiana's modiste in town with specific instructions on a gown for Elizabeth, noting it was to be received at Pemberley by December 26th.

When Elizabeth appeared at the door of the chapel on her uncle's arm, William stood stunned by her beauty. The gown was of ivory satin, with a rounded neckline, empire waist, and long, fitted sleeves. A delicate blond lace trimmed the neckline and sleeves, as well as the hem and demi-train. Ivory and pink rosebuds crowned Elizabeth's dark curls, and she carried a bouquet of pink roses.

Darcy and Elizabeth had eyes only for each other, and they spoke their vows in voices filled with emotion. The family in attendance could be in no doubt of the love the two shared.

The Pemberley staff produced a spectacular and sumptuous wedding breakfast to celebrate the event, along with a delicious plum cake and champagne. The joy of the bride and groom filled the room.

The Matlock party departed after luncheon, including Richard. He had spent the majority of his leave at Pemberley, but would not dare miss his family's annual New Year's Eve ball. The Gardiners, Jane, Bingley, and Georgiana retired to the music room to while away the hours, and the bride and groom disappeared to their suite, not to be seen until breakfast the next morning.

24. TROUBLE FROM ROSINGS

THE PARTY FROM PEMBERLEY ARRIVED AT Matlock on the afternoon of December 28th. The next morning, Georgiana and Elizabeth went into town to visit the seamstress to have a fitting for their ball gowns. The woman had done an excellent job with the gowns, and both Elizabeth and Georgiana were pleased.

They had received word before their departure that Mrs. Webb would recover. However, it appeared the injury to her head had caused some difficulties, and she was unable to do the fine stitchwork required of a seamstress. Darcy sent her a note informing her he would send word to Georgiana's London modiste asking if she knew of someone qualified to assist Mrs. Webb in her shop. By the time Mrs. Webb was recovered enough to return to her shop, two seamstresses, sisters Eloise and Chloe, had arrived to assist her. Darcy had a second floor added to her shop as living quarters for the sisters.

Elizabeth and Georgiana returned to Lockwood Hall, the Matlock estate, where they learned Darcy was out riding with the colonel and the viscount. Lady Matlock was waiting for them in the drawing room and eager to hear about the gowns they would be wearing to the ball.

The ladies were enjoying tea together when the gentlemen returned from their ride. Knowing the countess would not permit them in her drawing room in their current state of dishabille, they quickly retired to their rooms to change and later rejoin the ladies.

As Darcy and his cousins descended the stairs, he heard Elizabeth's sweet laugh ring out, and he could not help but smile. Richard nudged his brother in the ribs, nodding his head in Darcy's direction.

"I say, Darcy," came the viscount's teasing voice, "marriage seems to agree with you. You seem to wear a silly grin quite frequently on that usually somber face of yours."

"It suits me very well indeed," came Darcy's challenging reply. "Were you married to such a remarkable woman, I imagine you would look even more ridiculous. I feel for you, Nick, to have only the simpering, silly women of the ton from whom to pick. Perhaps you should give thought to scouring the countryside for someone more unique." Darcy patted his cousin on the shoulder and quickened his pace, eager to rejoin his beautiful bride of one day.

Richard and Nick stood rooted to the stairs where he had left them. After their surprise had passed, they grinned at each other before loud guffaws overtook them.

"Have you ever seen Darcy smile like that? Perhaps there is something to be said for our cousin's thinking," said the viscount as he sobered and looked at his brother thoughtfully.

"Let us hope he did not find the only remaining 'original' left in England!" replied the colonel as he slapped his brother on the shoulder, then moved to join those in the drawing room.

The family passed the remainder of the day pleasantly and retired early, looking forward to another enjoyable day together. Had they known what the morrow would bring, none of them would have rested well.

In spite of the cold weather, Elizabeth and Georgiana were enjoying a quiet stroll through the sunny gardens of Lockwood when they heard the rumble of a carriage. Because this was not their home, neither young lady gave it another thought as they continued their walk.

A short time later they heard the crunch of gravel behind them and turned to see two people bearing down on them. Both young ladies paled and wished for the presence of Fitzwilliam.

"Is this person your runaway relation, Mr. Collins?" came the harsh, nasal voice of a tall, imperious-looking woman with iron gray hair and a hat topped with plumes that made her seem even taller.

"Yes, your Ladyship, this is —"

"Georgiana what are you doing with this harlot?" screeched the unknown woman.

Unwilling to allow her overbearing aunt to insult her new sister, Georgiana courageously replied, "How dare you speak so of my friend and —"

Before she could add sister, Georgiana received a slap to the face from the older woman. "Talking back! Obviously your brother's recent dreadful behavior is rubbing off on you, but I shall correct that. You shall come to Rosings with me, and I will ensure you know how to behave as a proper young lady of society."

"I shall not go anywhere with you. My home is with Fitzwilliam and Eliz —" Georgiana took a step back as the woman raised her hand to strike the young girl again.

As her hand came forward, it was stopped short of its intended target by a tight grip on her wrist. "I do not know who you are, madam," Elizabeth said, "but it is obvious from your behavior you know nothing about the proper manners of society." She heard a gasp from Mr. Collins at her statement.

"Get your hands off me, you doxy. I shall have you arrested for laying hands on a member of the aristocracy."

"I care not who you may be. You shall not treat Georgiana in such a way," Elizabeth replied bravely, still holding onto the woman's arm.

Mr. Collins began to pull at Elizabeth's arm. "This is my illustrious patroness and Miss Darcy's aunt. You must release her, Cousin," came his distressed voice.

Elizabeth was forced to release Lady Catherine's arm to free her own arm from her cousin's grip. She took a step away from the two intruders, grabbing hold of Georgiana's hand as she did so. She pushed Georgiana behind her and continued to back away.

"Georgiana, do you know who this creature is? You should not be in the presence of such a conniver. Now come here to me," Lady Catherine demanded, her voice growing louder.

"It is you, Aunt, who knows nothing. This my dearest friend and now —"

Again Lady Catherine interrupted. "I know perfectly well who she is. She is a liar and seductress. She is your brother's mistress, and he had the poor judgment to install her in his home near his impressionable sister. If word that you are living with your brother's mistress were to get out, you would never be able to make a good match." By now Lady Catherine was practically shouting.

Darcy had been informed that Lady Catherine's carriage had been seen on the drive, but when she did not appear in the house, he grew concerned. Knowing Elizabeth and Georgiana were in the gardens, he went to join them to protect them from his aunt. As he stepped onto the terrace, he could hear his aunt's raised voice speaking vile words and moved quickly in the direction of it. Stepping around his aunt and the unknown gentleman, Darcy placed himself in front of his ladies as he worked to control his outrage at the words his aunt had spoken.

"You are being utterly absurd, Aunt Catherine. Who in the world would be surprised Georgiana is living with her brother and his wife?" He reached his hand behind him, searching for Elizabeth's. She moved to stand beside Darcy with her arm firmly around Georgiana's waist.

"Have you completely lost your mind, Darcy? First you bring your paramour into your home, and now you speak of a wife. There has been no wedding, though Anne and I have been waiting for quite some time for you to do your duty by her."

"Aunt, you have been told time and again that I will not marry Anne. And now it is impossible for me to do so, as I am already married to Elizabeth. We were wed but two days ago."

"This is not to be born! You are engaged to my daughter! I will have this annulled immediately! I shall go straight to the Archbishop if necessary! I must see my brother, for he shall certainly assist me."

"As Uncle Anthony and Aunt Elaine were at the wedding, as well as Richard and Nicholas, you shall get no support from them."

"I shall not be forestalled by any impediment. You are engaged to my daughter, and you will marry Anne—and soon!

Meanwhile, the carriage, which had stopped to let out Lady Catherine and Mr. Collins upon their noticing the two women walking in the garden, made its way to the front entrance of Lockwood Hall. The two footmen jumped down. One rushed to the front doors to announce the arrival of Miss Anne de Bourgh while the other assisted the young lady from the carriage and escorted her to the entry. Extremely weary from the arduous trip, she collapsed into a chair in the entry before anyone could assist her with her outerwear.

"Anne, dear, what are you doing here? Did your mother relent and allow you to attend the ball?" the countess said as she reached the bottom of the staircase.

She had not yet reached her niece when her husband's voice was heard behind her. "Where is my dear sister? Do not tell me she allowed you to make the trip without her?"

Taking in her niece's appearance, Lady Matlock spoke in concerned tones. "My dear girl, has something happened. You look quite ill. Here, let me assist you to a bedchamber."

Lady Matlock assisted Anne in standing and began to move in the direction of the stairs, where her ever-efficient housekeeper stood waiting. Before she began the climb, Anne looked at her uncle and said, "I believe you will find Mother in the garden. She heard some tale of Darcy having his mistress at Pemberley with Georgiana in residence and that he even intended to marry the woman." Anne attempted to laugh, but it turned into a cough. When she finally recovered, she scornfully remarked, "As if my proud, unbending cousin would ever stoop so low."

Lord and Lady Matlock looked at each other in surprise at her harsh words before Lady Matlock continued up the stairs with her niece.

Worried at the upset his sister might be causing, Lord Matlock moved to join the group in the garden. As he drew closer, he heard his sister say, "You must be out of your senses, Darcy, to have allowed some money-grubbing tart to have tricked you into marriage. I will see you in an asylum, and then I will take Georgiana to Rosings and raise her properly."

"That is enough, Catherine!" came Lord Matlock's authoritative voice. "You will desist with this nonsense immediately!"

Catherine turned at the sound of her brother's voice. By now Lady Catherine's rage had pushed her beyond reason. "You cannot speak to me in such a fashion. Perhaps you, too, have lost your senses, as you allowed this ridiculous marriage to take place. I demand you summon our cousin. We must begin the process of having the marriage annulled for Anne's sake."

"As if you have any concern for your daughter. She appeared beyond exhausted and unwell when she entered the house. If you were so concerned about her, you would not have dragged her halfway across the country in the dead of winter."

"Not care about Anne? I am doing this for her! It is you who failed to protect her interests when you allowed Darcy to marry this nobody, this tart!"

"Lady Catherine, do not speak of my wife in such disgusting terms again! She is a gentleman's daughter and heiress, and I will not allow her to remain in your presence another moment. Come, Elizabeth, Georgiana, we are returning to the house."

"Indeed, get this person out of my sight, but I am not finished with you yet. I demand you remain here until I have been satisfied. Now let go of that female and attend me." She grabbed Darcy's arm while attempting to push Elizabeth away from him. Caught unawares, Elizabeth stumbled and would have fallen but for the fact that Mr. Collins reached out to steady her. Unfortunately, he caught only her arm and tore the dress from her shoulder.

Darcy was immediately at Elizabeth's side. He quickly repositioned her cloak to cover the torn dress and preserve her modesty. Keeping an arm firmly around her, he faced Elizabeth's assailant. "How dare you lay hands on my wife, sir? I should call you out for such behavior!"

Walter Collins stammered, "I meant no harm, sir, truly. I merely wished to prevent my cousin from falling."

"Cousin?" came Darcy's startled question. "Just who are you, sir?"

"My name is Walter Collins. I am the fortunate man who was given responsibility for the parish at Hunsford by your esteem — by Lady Catherine."

"What are you doing here? How did you know Elizabeth was here?"

"I did not know she was here. Some time ago, I received a letter from my father, who said my cousin had been located at a place named Pemberley in Derbyshire. I waited to hear further from him, but no word came. As I had heard Lady Catherine mention she had a nephew who lived in Derbyshire, I asked her about the area. When I mentioned Pemberley, she demanded to know why I inquired. After explaining, she insisted we depart immediately for Derbyshire."

"I warn you to stay away from my wife. Her inheritance is forever out of your reach."

"Sir, I have never had any desire for my cousin's inheritance, and I did try to discourage my father's efforts to obtain it, for all the good it did me. In fact, I have not heard from my father in more than a month. However, Mr. Darcy, be warned he is not a man to be crossed."

Darcy looked at Elizabeth, who nodded imperceptibly at her husband. "A moment of your time, Mr. Collins. Elizabeth, you and Georgiana go into the house; I will join you shortly." Darcy kissed her hand before releasing it, and she and Georgiana hurried for the warmth and comfort of Lockwood.

"Come with me, please, Mr. Collins," said Darcy as he indicated a path away from where his aunt stood.

"Come back here, Darcy," cried Lady Catherine. "I said I was not through with you."

Ignoring his aunt, Darcy continued to lead Mr. Collins away. When they were some distance apart, Darcy indicated a bench. "You may wish to sit down, Mr. Collins." When the man was seated, Darcy began to pace. "I am sorry to be the one to tell you this, but your father is dead."

"I beg your pardon, Mr. Darcy?" the man said in confusion.

"About three weeks ago, your father and another man, Mr. George Wickham, were here in Derbyshire, actually in the village of Lambton just five miles from my estate. They severely injured the dressmaker in their attempt to kidnap my sister and were successful in kidnapping my wife, injuring her in the process. I was very fortunate in that my cousin, Colonel Richard Fitzwilliam, arrived in Lambton within moments of the event and was able to follow. When he found their hiding place, word was sent and I met up with him so my wife could be rescued.

"As we approached, we heard the men arguing about which of them should take possession of Elizabeth. We heard two shots ring out just before we burst in. Your father had been shot in the chest. I am sorry. He did not survive his injury."

Mr. Collins' face was shocked. "My father attempted to kidnap Cousin Elizabeth? How could he have been so foolish?" Mr. Collins shook his head. "I am very sorry, sir. Please extend my apologies to my cousin. I assure you, Mr. Darcy, I am nothing like my father. Elizabeth is safe from me. If the Lord and a relative chose to bless her with an inheritance, I am happy for her. If you would excuse me, sir, I wish to be alone with my thoughts."

"Of course, Mr. Collins," said Darcy. He bowed and walked away.

Lady Catherine and the earl continued to argue throughout Darcy's conversation with Walter Collins. The grand lady harangued her brother about his need to assist her in dissolving Darcy's marriage.

"That is enough, Catherine. I do not want to hear another word! Darcy is married and that is the end of it. He and Elizabeth are happy and in love."

"In love! Humph! As if that were of any value! He has been engaged to my daughter since her birth. Their marriage has been spoken of frequently. Are you willing to have your niece humiliated for the sake of some country nobody who behaves no better than a courtesan?"

"If you and Anne are embarrassed, you have only yourself to blame. It was you who spoke about it in public as though it were a certainty, even though Darcy had never committed himself to her."

"How dare he ignore his mother's wishes and fail to do his duty to his cousin!"

"Darcy is his own man and the head of his family. He does not answer to us, Catherine, but you cannot accept it when people do not bow to your wishes. This is one time you will have to accept it. There is nothing you can do to change things. Darcy is married, and I am quite sure the marriage has been consummated. There are no grounds for an annulment."

Lady Catherine's mouth opened and closed several times, but before she could utter a word, the earl raised his hand to silence her. "That is enough! I will not hear another word about this."

Lady Catherine glared at her brother, still prepared to argue, but he continued to speak.

"I will arrange a room for you tonight, and you will depart for Rosings in the morning. If Anne is not sufficiently recovered, she can remain longer, but you will not. Darcy and Elizabeth are our guests, and I will not allow you to disturb their visit. Please follow me and we will get you settled. I will have tea and dinner sent to your room."

"Anthony, how dare you treat me in this reprehensible manner? I am your sister, and my wishes should supersede those of our nephew. I demand you help me!"

"Need I remind you, Catherine, I am the head of the Fitzwilliam family, and it is you who must obey my directives? As the head of this family, I insist you leave Darcy and Elizabeth alone, nor will you speak one word against Elizabeth. If gossip starts and I learn of your involvement in it, I will make sure you regret it. Am I understood?"

Without responding, Lady Catherine flounced away in the direction of the house. Unfortunate was the first footman she encountered, for he was the recipient of her ill temper and abuse when she demanded to be shown to the countess. However, her brother had followed quickly after her, and, dismissing the young man, he took her by the elbow to lead her upstairs to the room adjoining Anne's. He opened the door for her and stood aside.

Lady Catherine walked into the room and turned to face her brother. Giving him a look of loathing, she slammed the door in his face. The earl heaved a sigh of frustration and went in search of his dear wife.

Upon leaving Mr. Collins, Darcy rushed to the house to find Elizabeth and Georgiana. He located them in a small sitting room at the back of the house, where they continued to watch those remaining in the gardens. Georgiana held a cloth to her cheek, her head resting on Elizabeth's shoulder, and Elizabeth's arm around her. Darcy rushed to kneel before the two women he loved more than his own life.

"Georgiana, what has happened?" cried Darcy with concern.

"It is nothing, William."

"If it were nothing, you would not have a cold cloth on your face."

"Your aunt struck Georgiana for trying to defend me." Elizabeth's soft voice was filled with guilt. "She tried to do it again, but I prevented her. She said she would have me arrested for laying hands on a member of the aristocracy."

Darcy lifted the cloth from Georgiana's cheek to see what injury had been done. He saw a bit of swelling and a visible handprint. He stood and rang for a servant. When the maid appeared, Darcy said, "Would you please escort my sister to her room and bring some ice for her cheek? Also, ask the countess to go to my sister's chamber."

"Certainly, sir."

Once the maid and Georgiana had departed, Darcy swept Elizabeth into his arms. "Oh, my Elizabeth. How can you ever forgive me for allowing my aunt to attack you in such a way? What can I do to make it up to you?"

"It is I who owes you an apology. I failed to protect Georgiana as I promised. It never occurred to me a peeress would do something so despicable, especially to her own niece.

Darcy was extremely angry at his aunt's actions and became concerned that Elizabeth had been injured, too. "She did not lay her hands on you, did she, Elizabeth?"

"No, William. After releasing her arm, I wisely put some distance between us with Georgiana safely behind me."

"Will you tell me what she said?"

"It is not necessary to speak of it, William. You warned me she would not be pleased when she learned of our arrangement. Suffice it to say she speaks extremely loudly and has a wide and varied vocabulary," said Elizabeth with a slight laugh.

"I am so sorry, my dearest rose. You should not have been forced to endure such treatment. I will cut ties with her until a proper apology is given to both you and Georgiana."

"William, I do not wish to be the cause of a breach in your family. Please simply allow your aunt time to adjust to her loss."

"No, Elizabeth. She has tried to force her desires on me too often. I shall not allow her to get away with such egregious behavior."

"I will check on Georgiana. Do you wish to join me?"

"I should be delighted." Darcy rose and offered his arm to Elizabeth. Upon arriving at Georgiana's door, her maid, Amy, admitted them. They were pleased to see the handprint was less obvious and the redness somewhat reduced. Realizing it was almost time for tea, Georgiana decided to join her family as they made their way to the drawing room.

Lady Matlock had learned of her niece's injury, but was shocked when she discovered how it had been attained. When Lord Matlock found his wife, she had just exited Georgiana's room. Her husband was surprised at the militant look in her eyes.

"Is anything wrong, my dear?" he asked as he took her hand in his.

"There certainly is! Would you please join me in our sitting room for a moment?" As soon as they entered their sitting room and the door was closed behind them, Elaine Fitzwilliam whirled to face her husband. "Anthony, Catherine struck Georgiana hard enough to leave a handprint on her face."

"What?" cried her husband. "Catherine would not dare do such a thing."

"She did dare. In fact, she attempted to do it a second time, but Elizabeth stopped her."

"Does Darcy know?"

"He does."

"Catherine has done it now. Darcy will cut all ties with her for such an offense."

"He should," said the countess angrily. "You do plan to make it perfectly clear to your sister that such behavior is not acceptable at Matlock?" Though the countess phrased her statement as a question, her husband knew it was her polite way of saying she wished Catherine gone from the house.

"As things currently stand, I have put my foot down and told her she may not leave her room until she departs in the morning. I wonder, my dear, do you think Anne shares her mother's feelings on this matter? I was rather surprised by her less-than-complimentary comments about Darcy."

"Though I have always believed she had no interest in Darcy, I, too, was shocked. We have been allowed to spend so little time with Anne over the years, I have no idea of her feelings about anything," the countess said. Then, realizing the time, she added, "It is nearing teatime, dear. Will you accompany me to the drawing room so we might await our guests?"

"It would be my pleasure, my dear," said the earl as he opened the door for his wife to pass through. In the hallway, he offered her his arm and they moved towards the green drawing room.

Anne had been resting on her bed when she heard her mother's raised voice. Walking to the sitting room door, she opened it to complain to her mother for disturbing her rest. "Is it not enough, Mother, that you drag me all about the countryside? Now you will not even be quiet enough for me to rest."

Lady Catherine neither noticed her daughter nor heard her words as she paced to and fro, muttering to herself.

"Mother!" said Anne louder. "Whatever is the matter with you? Was it not enough to drag me halfway across England? Are you now going to disturb my rest as well?" The peevish whine in Anne's voice was abundantly obvious.

"He is married, Anne! We are too late."

"Who is married?"

"Fitzwilliam. He has already married that, that —"

"Darcy is already married?" Anne said, confused.

"Yes, and your uncle has given the union his blessing. He has forbidden me from interfering."

"Darcy is already married?" Anne said again. "How dare he treat me like this? He did not even have the courtesy to ask me!" Anne began pacing the room as her mother had been doing. "This is unacceptable. I will not allow him to treat me in such a fashion. How dare he ignore me for some insignificant nonentity."

"Perhaps you should calm down, my dear," said Lady Catherine. She had never seen her daughter so angry.

"No, mother, I shall not calm down. Fitzwilliam Darcy shall not ignore me now. I shall enjoy telling him exactly what I think of him." Anne yanked open the door and marched down the hallway. Of the first servant she encountered, she demanded to know where Mr. Darcy could be found.

The Countess of Matlock was seated in the drawing room, happily observing her guests as they enjoyed afternoon tea. Mr. Gardiner and the viscount were recounting to the gentlemen tales of their catches from the morning, which they had spent fishing. Mrs. Gardiner was entertaining the ladies with stories of the children from her morning spent in the nursery. The room hummed with pleasant conversation and occasional laughter. Consequently, when the drawing room doors burst open, the occupants were quite startled. Seeing a young lady standing in the doorway, the gentlemen rose. Anne de Bourgh, her eyes blazing, stormed across the room and glared at Fitzwilliam Darcy.

"Good afternoon, Anne," he said stiffly.

"How dare you?" she nearly shouted at him.

"I beg your pardon?"

"How dare you marry when you are engaged to me?"

Attempting to control his temper, Darcy coldly replied, "We were never engaged, Anne. That was a dream of your mother's. My mother told me I should marry only for the deepest of loves, the kind she had for my father."

"Love? Love has absolutely nothing to do with marriage. Marriage is about money and connections. You owed me the courtesy of a proposal! How dare you pass me over for some country nobody!" Anne glanced around the room and discovered three unknown women. The most beautiful of the three was deep in conversation with a man who seemed vaguely familiar. Looking at the other two, she quickly determined that the younger one must be Darcy's new wife. Anne looked Elizabeth over with blatant disdain, though she could not help but notice that the older woman and Georgiana both held tightly to the young lady's hands.

She turned back to Darcy, a sneer evident on her face.

"Have a care with your words, Anne," warned Darcy.

Taking in the look on his face, Anne took a quick breath before saying, "You owed me the courtesy of a proposal, Darcy. I had been waiting my whole life to turn you down and tell you what a bore you were. I would never settle for someone so stern and somber. Life with you would have been utterly dull."

Anne turned on her heel to depart, but from the corner of her eye she saw Darcy's wife rise and move towards him. Spinning again, she moved to stand in front of Elizabeth. Before anyone could stop her, she slapped Elizabeth across the face. Darcy was immediately at her side and pulled Elizabeth into his arm, while Richard stepped up and grabbed Anne's arms to prevent her from striking again.

Animosity blazing in her eyes, Anne screeched, "You are beneath me. You are both beneath me! You have ruined yourself with this marriage, Darcy, and I shall be happy to tell everyone so!"

Lord Matlock stepped between Anne and Elizabeth. "That is enough, Anne." Giving Anne a hard stare, he said, "You would do well to look to your own future. Go home and take up your inheritance. Send your mother to the dower house. It is unfortunately quite evident you have been spending far too much time in her company. If you continue in this behavior, you shall spend your life alone, just as she has been all these years."

In spite of her brother's edict, Lady Catherine had left her room and followed her daughter to the drawing room. She remained hidden outside the door in case Anne needed her assistance. She had been shocked when Anne spoke of refusing a proposal from Darcy. Catherine's gasp when her brother spoke of Anne's inheritance was heard by the occupants of the room.

Anne turned to look at the door. "Mother!" she called. "What is this inheritance of which Uncle Anthony speaks?"

Struck by an idea, Lord Matlock turned to stare at his sister. "Catherine, have you never told Anne of her inheritance? Is this why you were so adamant about Anne marrying Darcy?"

"Of course. If she married Darcy, they would live at Pemberley and I could remain in charge of Rosings."

"You underestimate our nephew if you believe you would have continued to do as you wished with no accountability. Rosings would have belonged to Darcy upon the marriage, and he would have cared for it as diligently as he does all his other holdings."

"Stop it!" cried Anne with a stomp of her foot. "What is my inheritance? What have you kept from me, Mother?"

Lady Catherine clamped her mouth shut and refused to speak, so Lord Matlock answered his niece's questions. "When you reached the age of five and twenty, Rosings became your estate. You are the mistress and can do as you wish, including sending your mother to the dower house."

Looking at her mother, Anne shrieked. "How dare you, Mother? How could you deny me this opportunity? I had no need of Darcy all this time. With an inheritance such as Rosings, I could find a much better man for my husband. You shall pay for this, Mother. I will not forget what you have cost me!"

As the two women began to argue with each other, Lady Matlock reached the limit of her patience. She moved to the door and called for her housekeeper. She ordered that someone immediately pack for the de Bourghs and that their carriage be made ready immediately. "I wish them gone within the half hour!"

Moving to her younger son's side, Lady Matlock whispered in his ear. She stepped away and put her fingers in her ears as Richard gave a shrill whistle that ended all the confusion in the room.

When the room quieted, she spoke in her usual elegant tones. "Catherine, Anne, your carriage will be at the door momentarily, and your bags are being packed. I am afraid you will have to stay at the inn in Matlock, for you are not welcome in my home. You arrived uninvited two days before my annual ball, bringing with you nothing but turmoil. Then you caused a scene, insulted my guests, and physically assaulted two young women. I shall not tolerate your presence for a moment longer, so take your ill manners and arguments from my home now."

Two large footmen appeared and, taking each of the ladies by an arm, escorted them from the room.

Their resumed argument could be heard growing fainter as they moved down the hall.

Turning to her guests, Lady Matlock said, "Mr. and Mrs. Gardiner, Miss Bennet, Mr. Bingley, Elizabeth, please accept my sincere apologies for the disgraceful behavior you were forced to witness. I can only hope you shall not judge the rest of the family based on Catherine and Anne." She walked over to Elizabeth and took her hands. "My dear girl, are you quite well? Is there anything I can get for you?"

"I am well, Lady Matlock. Fortunately for me, Anne has not the strength of her mother."

"You must call me Aunt Elaine now, dear. I should have said something after the wedding or even last evening, but I have been distracted with all the arrangements for the ball."

"I should be happy to do so, Aunt Elaine. I should also be most willing to help you in any way you might need."

"Thank you, dear," said the countess as she embraced Elizabeth the best she could, as Darcy had not released her from his protective hold.

"Aunt, if you will excuse us, I believe the three of us shall retire to rest until dinner." Darcy said. "My ladies have had a rather challenging day, and I need to see to their comfort."

"Shall I send you a tea tray?"

"No thank you, Aunt. We shall see you at dinner." So saying, Darcy, his arm still about Elizabeth's waist, offered his other arm to Georgiana and escorted them from the room.

The Gardiners and Miss Bennet gave their excuses and retired after the Darcys, and Richard, Nick, and Bingley took themselves off to the billiards room. When the door closed behind their sons, Lord

Matlock opened his arms and his wife settled herself in his comforting embrace. After a few moments, he offered her his arm and said, "Shall we retire as well, my dear? I believe you, too, could use a little comfort." He wrapped her hand around his arm, and they mounted the stairs together.

The day before the ball passed quietly for the residents of Lockwood. No one spoke of the events of the previous day, as they could not be too soon forgotten. Elizabeth and Georgiana assisted Lady Matlock as she checked on the remaining items to be addressed for the ball. The four young gentlemen accompanied the Gardiner children to the stables to see a new foal before taking the children in front of them on their horses for a quick ride about the stable ring. It was a relaxing and pleasant day.

The next morning the staff bustled about, attending to the last-minute details for the ball. After an early dinner, everyone retired to dress for the evening.

Lucy was putting the last pins in Elizabeth's coiffure when Darcy entered his wife's dressing room. Meeting his eyes in the mirror, Elizabeth could see the look of appreciation on his face. Darcy stepped closer and leaned in to nibble on Elizabeth's neck.

"You look beautiful, my love. However, I thought perhaps you would enjoy wearing these for the evening." Darcy handed Elizabeth a flat box covered in a forest green fabric. Opening the box, Elizabeth gave a gasp of surprise. Nestled on a bed of dove gray satin was a choker of alternating round diamonds and emeralds that grew larger as they reached the center. The center stone was a diamond of good size, and from this stone was suspended a very large tear-shaped emerald surrounded by small diamonds. There were also matching earrings. "William, this is exquisite!"

"It is part of the Darcy jewels, my love, and as Mrs. Darcy, they are all intended for your use." Reaching to remove the necklace from the box, Darcy said, "Allow me to assist you, my dear." He clasped the necklace around her neck before again leaning in to nuzzle its side.

When he moved away, Elizabeth quickly put on the earrings. With a last glance in the mirror, she rose and turned to face her husband.

"Shall I embarrass you, do you think?" Elizabeth asked with a small smile playing around her lips.

In spite of her smile, Darcy knew Elizabeth was nervous. After Lady Catherine's reaction, she was not particularly desirous of meeting other members of the ton.

"Let me see," said Darcy thoughtfully as he surveyed her appearance. Elizabeth's gown was made of emerald green satin that clung to her curvaceous figure. The neckline was a deep sweetheart cut and was overlaid in velvet of the same color. The overlay was similar in style to the top portion of an open robe. The upper portion created delicate cap sleeves, with a tight band under the bust, which emphasized Elizabeth's figure. The gown was what some would consider plain, but it flattered her immensely and allowed the jewels to appear at their best. When Darcy again met her eyes, Elizabeth noticed their darkened color and the unmistakable look of passion in them.

"No, you shall not embarrass me, my wife, but I shall have to keep you close to my side, for every

413

man in the room shall be tempted by your beauty. Indeed, Elizabeth, you look magnificent." Darcy offered her his arm and escorted her to where the Matlocks stood in the entry to greet their guests.

Hearing the footsteps on the stairs, all the Matlocks turned to greet the new arrivals. Darcy could easily see the reaction of his cousins and tucked Elizabeth's arm more firmly to his side. The looks on the faces of his aunt and uncle made Darcy swell with pride.

Lady Matlock moved across the floor towards Elizabeth, who stepped away from Darcy. Lady Matlock took Elizabeth's hands and stretched them to the side. "My dear Elizabeth, you are resplendent. You shall have all the gentlemen clamoring for an invitation and all the women wondering who designed your magnificent gown."

"Thank you, Aunt Elaine. I shall do my best to dazzle your guests."

"You need only be yourself, my love, and they shall not be able to resist you," said her husband with an indulgent smile.

They were shortly joined by the other members of their party. As the clock struck nine, the Gardiners moved in the direction of the ballroom with Jane and Bingley. The countess insisted that Darcy and Elizabeth join them in the receiving line. Lord and Lady Matlock were first, followed by Darcy, Elizabeth, Richard, and Nicholas.

Having feared the receiving line would be tedious, Elizabeth instead found herself very entertained. After greeting her guests, Lady Matlock often indicated Darcy to her right, saying something like, "You know my nephew, Fitzwilliam Darcy, do you not?" The ladies' faces would immediately change. The mothers appeared calculating, and the daughters began to simper. Then Darcy would quickly introduce his "wife, Elizabeth" and the smiles would instantly vanish. Elizabeth's amusement kept her from being nervous, and she was able to greet and converse easily with everyone she met.

Mr. and Mrs. Darcy danced the opening set together, taking their place next to Lord and Lady Matlock in the set. It was the first time they had danced together as husband and wife, and they were quickly lost in each other's eyes. Elizabeth danced with her husband for the supper set. The supper was timed to conclude as midnight approached. The servants delivered glasses of champagne to all the guests for a toast to the new year. When the last bong of the clock sounded the stroke of midnight, there were cheers of "Happy New Year!" Darcy managed to steal a kiss from his wife.

Elizabeth and Darcy made a circuit of the room with Lady Matlock after supper, and Elizabeth met many of Pemberley's neighbors. The final dance of the evening again found Darcy and Elizabeth paired. Lady Matlock had arranged for the final dance to be a waltz, and Darcy was thrilled to hold Elizabeth in his arms. When they fell into bed after the ball, both Darcy and Elizabeth had a feeling of satisfaction. It had been a delightful evening, and Elizabeth had been well received by the majority of those she met.

The Darcys remained at Lockwood one additional day before returning to Pemberley. Bingley traveled with them. He would spend one night at Pemberley before journeying north to see Aunt Agatha and his sister, Caroline. He must determine what was best for his sister before he could look forward to his future with Jane.

The Gardiners and Jane departed Lockwood the same day as the Darcys. They were returning to London, with Mr. Bingley's promise to call as soon as he returned to town. He expected it to take two or three weeks before his business was completed.

25. INHERITANCES

THE DARCYS HAD REMAINED AT PEMBERLEY throughout the winter, departing for London the second week in March. On their way to town, they stopped in Cambridge so Elizabeth could visit with the Hills and introduce them to her husband. She had already written them about all that had occurred, and they were anxious to see for themselves that she was safe. Darcy offered his thanks for their assistance to Elizabeth and promised them their custom whenever they were in the area.

The days leading up to Elizabeth's birthday were spent obtaining a new wardrobe for the season and preparing for her presentation to the Queen. Her curtsey to the Queen had taken place just two days earlier.

Finally, Elizabeth's birthday arrived. She was quite nervous to learn about her inheritance. It had caused her upheaval and great loss, but it had also been the means of uniting her with her beloved husband.

She and Fitzwilliam left London early in the morning, arriving in Meryton just before noon. Stopping at the inn, they enjoyed a luncheon, then presented themselves at Mr. Philips' office promptly at one o'clock. When they were shown into his office, Mr. Philips jumped from his chair and came forward, enfolding his dear niece in a tight hug.

"Oh, dear girl, how delighted I am to see you again. When we first heard the news of your death, we were heartbroken. Upon returning to Meryton, we were informed you had not died in the accident, but that you had not been seen since the day of the viewing. I tried to speak with Mr. Collins, but he refused to see me. Consequently, I went to see Sir William Lucas. He called for Sam, and I was given all the information regarding the events surrounding your parents' deaths and your disappearance. Though I was immensely relieved to learn you had escaped from Collins' plans, I was greatly concerned for your safety. I notified the Gardiners of what I learned, but there was little either of us could do. If we were to search for you, Collins might get to you before we could. We knew your intelligence and wit would help you and we prayed for your safety and wellbeing. Your aunt and I were greatly relieved to learn you were safe and to be married to an excellent man."

"Speaking of that excellent man, let me introduce you to my husband, Mr. Fitzwilliam Darcy."

"A pleasure, Mr. Darcy. Thank you so much for taking care of our dear girl."

"That was my very great pleasure, Mr. Philips," said Darcy with a loving look at his wife.

"Shall we get down to business?" said Mr. Philips, as he indicated two chairs before his desk.

Darcy helped Elizabeth into a seat before taking his own. He reached across and took Elizabeth's hand comfortingly in his.

Turning to a gentleman they had not noticed, who was seated at the side of the room, Mr. Philips said, "Allow me to introduce Mr. Townsend of Townsend and Hall of London. Mr. Townsend's firm handled your aunt's will and remains the executor of her estate."

Darcy stood to shake the solicitor's hand as Elizabeth nodded to him.

"Mr. Townsend will read to you of your inheritance. It was left to you by your great-aunt Rose; she was your grandmother Bennet's younger sister. She was your father's favorite aunt, and that is why you were given her name. Rose was considered quite the beauty and married very well. As she passed many years ago, the majority of the bequeaths in her will have already been handled. It is only your inheritance that remains."

Mr. Townsend looked at the papers, searching for the part he wished to read. "Ah, here it is," he mumbled. Clearing his voice, he began to read. "To my niece, Elizabeth Rose Bennet, I leave the following: First, I leave her the estate of Windhaven as well as my house in town. I also leave her the sum of fifty thousand pounds and a special piece of jewelry."

Elizabeth was astounded. She had never dreamed the inheritance would be so large. She looked from her uncle to her husband in astonishment before returning her gaze to the solicitor.

"Now, about Windhaven," continued Mr. Townsend. "The estate is located in northern Warwickshire and is of a good size, with a large manor house as part of the property. The estate brings in about four thousand pounds per annum, all of which has been placed in an account for you, with the exception of the funds needed to maintain the estate. Here is the ledger containing a record of all the funds for your perusal. The house in town is located in Mayfair and has been rented out so the rent could cover its maintenance and upkeep. Here is the ledger showing the accounts for that property. Lastly, the money has continued to earn interest since your aunt's death and has grown considerably. Mr. Darcy, if you will provide me with the name of your solicitors, I will have the monies from the estate and those held for the former Miss Elizabeth transferred to your account upon returning to town."

Darcy looked at Elizabeth, who merely raised her eyebrow at him.

"Mr. Townsend, I would prefer to have my solicitor contact you after we return to town. My wife and I would like to discuss this situation before making any decisions."

"Certainly, sir. Lastly, here is the jewelry that was left for you, as well as a letter from your great-aunt." The lawyer handed Elizabeth a small wrapped package, which she tucked into her reticule.

Mr. Townsend stood and produced a card from his waistcoat pocket. "I will look forward to hearing from you soon, Mr. Darcy." So saying, he handed the card to Darcy, expressed his farewell to everyone, and left Mr. Philips' office.

"Lizzy, dear, there is one more thing I need to discuss with you before you depart." Mr. Philips shuffled papers on his desk before finding the one for which he was looking. He placed the paper in the center of his desk and put on his glasses before picking up the paper to begin. "I had a very unusual letter recently which concerns you. I have complied with the requests in the letter and need to make you aware of the contents."

"Certainly, Uncle." Elizabeth looked at her husband, not sure how many more surprises she could handle.

"As I said, I handled the work as requested, and there is a letter for you. Do you wish to read it or should I?" asked Mr. Philips.

"Please, you read it, Uncle."

Hunsford Parsonage
Hunsford, Kent

Dear Cousin Elizabeth,

    I am extremely sorry for the suffering you received at my father's hands. I tried to discourage him from his course, but as you probably know, he has never paid much heed to me or my opinions.

    Because I feel strongly that my work in the church is a calling from God, I do not wish to become a landowner. Consequently, I have asked Mr. Philips to have the entail ended and to arrange for the estate to be deeded to you.

    I know this in no way makes up for the harm my father has caused you, but I hope you will find peace in having your family home returned to you.

    May God bless you always.

Sincerely,

Walter Collins

Elizabeth stared at her uncle in amazement. "Can he so easily have the entail broken? Why could Father not have done so?"

"It is because he is the last male in the line that he can break it. So, here are the deed and keys to Longbourn. I hired someone to clean it after all the paperwork was handled, so you should find it in good order should you wish to stay the night. I hope you will dine with your aunt and me tonight, and I am sure I can find someone to attend you if you decide to reside there briefly," offered Mr. Philips.

Elizabeth turned to look at her husband, who could easily read the desire in her eyes to see her home again.

Turning to Mr. Philips, Darcy said, "Thank you for your offer of help and dinner; we would be happy to accept both. I shall drive Elizabeth to Longbourn immediately. What time should we return?"

"We dine at seven," replied Mr. Philips.

"We shall see you at seven, then." Darcy stood and shook Mr. Philips' hand before helping Elizabeth to her feet.

Elizabeth stepped up to her uncle and kissed his cheek. "Thank you for everything, Uncle Stephen. We shall see you later."

"Certainly, my dear. I was very happy to help with this particular matter. I believe old Mrs. Allen is looking for work now that her husband has passed. I will call upon her and send her over if she is agreeable."

"Thank you, Uncle." Elizabeth kissed his cheek once more before taking her husband's arm. Within minutes, they were underway and headed for Longbourn.

As the carriage turned into the drive, Elizabeth was disappointed to see the grounds had not been tended to for some time. Tears filled her eyes, but her husband squeezed her hand and said, "Do not worry, my love. We will have everything returned to its former glory before you know it."

She gave him a brilliant smile before turning back to the window. The carriage pulled to a stop in front of the house. Elizabeth was shocked to see Sam walking towards the carriage from the direction of the stables.

Opening the door before the footman had a chance, Sam said, "Welcome home, Miss Lizzy—I mean, Mrs. Darcy." A huge grin covered his face.

"I cannot tell you how happy I am to be back," said Elizabeth with a matching smile. "Seeing you coming from the stables makes it even better!" She turned to Darcy. "Fitzwilliam, allow me to introduce you to Sam Bailey. He and his family have been tenants of Longbourn for several generations, and Sam worked in the stables. It was he who assisted me in escaping the morning I ran away from Longbourn."

"My thanks, Sam," replied Darcy, offering his hand to the young man.

"It was a pleasure to be of assistance, sir. Mrs. Darcy is a fine woman. Always had a kind word for everyone, she did. Will you be staying long, miss?"

"We are not sure yet," said Darcy, "but we will need the carriage at half past six, as we are dining with the Philips this evening."

"I will be sure to have it ready, sir. This way," Sam called to the coachman.

Darcy and Elizabeth stepped up to the door and Elizabeth pulled the key from her pocket. With trembling fingers, she inserted the key into the lock and turned it. Darcy turned the knob and opened the door for his wife.

Elizabeth entered the house, pleased to see that everything looked much the same. Darcy helped her remove her pelisse before she moved towards the sitting room and drew the curtains, letting sunlight into the room. After discarding his outerwear, Darcy joined his wife in the sitting room. He clasped her hand and whispered, "Are you happy, my love?"

"Oh, William, I never thought I would set foot in Longbourn again. I am so very happy."

She tugged on his hand as she moved from room to room, opening the curtains. When she opened the door to her father's library, she paused in the doorway, overcome by the wonderful smell of leather and parchment, as well as by the memories that assaulted her. Tears filled her eyes as she released Darcy's hand and moved farther into the room. She ran her hands along the books on the shelves and across the top of her father's chair. Finally, she turned to look at her husband.

"I spent much of my youth in this room with my father. I can almost feel him here with me," came her soft words.

Darcy crossed to where she stood and enfolded her in his arms. "I am sure he is, my sweet Elizabeth. I am quite sure he is smiling down on you, knowing the house is again in good hands."

She led him to the kitchen and pushed him down into a chair at the table. "Would you like some tea if there is any?"

"You do not need to trouble yourself."

"It is no trouble," came her reply as she looked for the canister that had always held the tea. "I believe there is just enough for a pot of tea. If we are going to stay for a day or two, perhaps we should go back into the village for a few supplies."

"Is there a tea shop in Meryton?"

"Yes, and they serve wonderful pastries there, too."

"Allow me to call for the carriage, my love, and then we shall go."

"Would you mind if we were to walk? It is only a mile, and I used to walk to Meryton often with my sisters."

"I would be pleased to accompany you." He held out his hand to her, and they moved to the front door. Soon they were walking down the drive.

The bright sun was warm, but the air was still on the cool side, making for a pleasant walk. They first visited the mercantile and purchased a few necessities, requesting the items be delivered to the Philips' home before seven that evening. Next they visited the tea shop. They found a quiet table in the corner and enjoyed tea and pastries. When they finished there, they crossed to the bookshop.

At the jangle of the bell, the owner called out from the back room. "I will be right with you."

Smiling at her husband, Elizabeth put her finger to her lips to stop him from acknowledging the words. Then she called out, "Do you have anything new for me to look at today?"

They heard the thud of a book being dropped. The curtain to the back opened. "Bless my soul," said the older gentleman who approached her. "If it is not my little Miss Lizzy. Oh, my dear girl, I am delighted to see you again. You gave us quite a scare, running off like that. Why did you not seek me out if you needed assistance?"

"Hello, Mr. Stevens. I am very happy to see you again. My adventures are a very long tale, and I do not wish to think about the past, only about the future. Allow me to introduce you to my husband, Mr. Fitzwilliam Darcy of Pemberley in Derbyshire."

"Pleased to make your acquaintance, Mr. Darcy. Did this young lady make you show her your

425

library before she accepted your proposal?" the shop owner teased.

"Indeed, she did. I am glad it was to her requirements so that she willingly agreed to marry me."

Elizabeth smiled at her husband and turned to Mr. Stevens. "It is a library even you would appreciate, sir. I believe it is quite ten times the size of your shop and filled from ceiling to floor with shelves and shelves of books. Mr. Darcy even has a most ingenious system he uses to find specific books."

"Well, Mr. Darcy, I would imagine that makes you a man worth knowing. Anyone who loves books as much as Miss Lizzy does must be the best of gentlemen. Believe it or not, my dear girl, I did set aside a few books for you. I was not sure if you would have the chance to purchase books wherever you had gone. I did not wish for you to miss out on anything you might enjoy." He moved to the counter at the front of the shop. There on a shelf behind him was a bundle of books tied with a green ribbon. He lifted the books and set them on the counter. Elizabeth untied the ribbon and looked at the titles.

"Oh, William, here is the latest volume by Byron! We had planned to purchase it but had not yet had an opportunity."

"Mr. Stevens, can you show me any first editions you may have while my wife looks through the books you set aside for her?"

"Certainly, sir." Mr. Stevens led Darcy to a set of shelves near the door. "These three shelves contain first editions, and these three contain new releases."

By the time Darcy returned to the counter with several books under his arm, Elizabeth had finished looking at her books. She decided to purchase all but one, as she had already obtained a copy of it. Darcy set his books next to hers and paid for them.

"Mr. Stevens, would it be a problem for you to deliver these to the Philips' home by seven this evening? We walked into the village, but we will be returning to dine with them this evening."

"I will drop them off on my way home, Mr. Darcy."

"Now, my dear wife, I believe we must head home before it becomes dark. I should like to make one more stop before we do."

"Goodbye, Mr. Stevens." Lizzy gave him a wave from the door.

"It was good to see you, Miss Lizzy, and a pleasure to meet you, Mr. Darcy."

They exited the shop and moved towards the inn. Elizabeth paused to look in the milliner's window as Darcy stepped inside briefly.

As they moved off towards Longbourn, Elizabeth asked, "What was your last errand, dear husband?"

"I sent a note to Palmer requesting that he and Lucy pack enough for us for a fortnight and come along with it early tomorrow morning. They should arrive by about ten. We will stay until we are certain things at Longbourn are settled and running smoothly."

"Thank you, William. I would like that very much."

As they turned down the drive towards the house, Elizabeth was surprised to see many of the tenants working to tame the overgrown yard and flowerbeds. They all stopped to welcome Elizabeth home, and she tearfully thanked them for the welcome and for the wonderful work they were doing.

"It is a pleasure to have a Bennet back at Longbourn," said Mr. Bailey, Sam's father. "The way Mr. Collins was going, Longbourn would have been ruined before too much more time had passed. I am glad we were here to see your return."

Elizabeth introduced her husband to the group and told them they would stay for a time to be sure that things at Longbourn were in good order again.

As they reached the front door, they found Mrs. Allen seated on the porch, waiting for them. After entering the house, they explained the situation to Mrs. Allen. They informed her their personal servants would arrive in the morning and instructed her to hire what additional help she would need for the weeks they were to be in residence.

As a surprise for her niece, Mrs. Philips arranged for the Lucas family to join them after her husband had mentioned Elizabeth and her new husband would be joining them for dinner. When they stepped into the Philips' parlor, Elizabeth heard her name called.

"Eliza!"

"Charlotte!" Elizabeth rushed to greet her friend and the two hugged in the center of the room. Elizabeth was immediately surrounded by her friends and family, but quickly extricated herself and brought over Fitzwilliam to make introductions.

The time before dinner was spent with Elizabeth recounting her adventures and explaining she had just been given the deed of Longbourn by her cousin Walter.

The meal was very pleasant, and Fitzwilliam went out of his way to be sociable. He listened patiently to Sir William's recounting of his knighthood at St. James. He also heard stories of Elizabeth's youth from the two oldest Lucas siblings.

After dinner, when the gentlemen rejoined the ladies, Sir William moved to sit near Elizabeth. "Miss Eliza, I am afraid I have some news that might be upsetting to you."

Darcy stood speaking to Robert Lucas, but seeing the look on Elizabeth's face, he moved to sit beside her. Robert followed, as he realized what information his father was sharing with his childhood friend.

"When Sam first came to us, he told us of your suspicions regarding Mr. Collins and your parents' accident. At the time we were recovering your family from the accident scene, he pointed out to Robert the carriage shaft. It appeared to have been sawed partway through."

Tears welled up in her eyes, and Fitzwilliam reached over to take one of her hands in his.

"We could not confront Mr. Collins without proof, so our hands were tied. However, when he took off in early December, we seized the opportunity to search the house one day. Sam, Robert, and I entered with the housekeeper's permission, obtained by the offer of a few coins. We found a letter addressed to Mr. Collins, signed only with "J," confirming he wished assistance in making the deaths of the Bennet family look like an accident. It contained a description of you and said that if you were with the party, nothing was to occur. With the proof we needed, Mr. Collins would have been arrested on his return to Hertfordshire and most likely hanged for his crimes."

By this time, Elizabeth's tears had spilled onto her cheeks. Darcy offered her a handkerchief. When she had dried her tears, she said, "I am relieved to know the truth, but I do not understand how anyone can value money and things over a life. I am glad to know he can never harm anyone again."

Not wishing the evening to end on such sad news, Mrs. Philips called for music. Later, they enjoyed cards, ending the evening on a pleasant note. The footman who had accompanied the Darcys loaded their purchases into the coach. The Lucases had even brought the trunk Elizabeth had sent to them for safe keeping.

When they arrived home from the Philips', they went into the library and Darcy poured them each a glass of wine. As he settled on the couch beside her, Darcy asked, "My love, have you opened the package from your great-aunt?"

"I almost forgot about it." Elizabeth reached into her reticule and retrieved the box and letter. Opening the letter, she began to read it aloud.

Philadelphia, Pennsylvania
United States of America

My dear niece,

Though I have not had the chance to see you, I have heard much about you from your father. Thomas was always very dear to me and kept up a regular correspondence with me throughout my lifetime. From his many stories, I believe we are much alike. I was always filled with a thirst for learning and rather outspoken.

I was fortunate enough to have been afforded a season in London when I was eight and ten. It was there that I met my beloved husband, Daniel Smythe-Hill, Lord Havenwood. He was several years older than I, but it was love at first sight for both of us. Daniel was in the government and served as an ambassador for many years. It was an exciting life, moving around the world to the different countries where he was posted. Our final posting was to the former Colonies. It was an exciting young country full of growth and new ideas, and we very much enjoyed our time here. Before we could return to England, my dear husband came down with a fever and died. I could not think of leaving him behind, so I decided to remain in the United States until I could join him in Heaven.

Daniel was the last of his line, and though we lived a full and wonderful life, we were never blessed with children. The title died with him, but all of the properties were left to me.

I understand the difficulties of being an intelligent young lady in a world that refuses to recognize your value. I did not wish you to suffer those same trials. With this inheritance, I wished to ensure you would always have the opportunity to continue to learn and grow and to see the world if you so desired.

The one piece of jewelry I have left you is a piece that is special to me. It is a cameo my husband had commissioned for me on my twenty-first birthday. He had the figure on the cameo made from a sketch of me that had been done for my birthday that year. I hope when you wear it you will be reminded of me and reach for whatever dreams you desire.

With love to my namesake,

Rose Smythe-Hill, Lady Woodhaven

When Elizabeth unwrapped the box and removed the lid, she gasped in surprise.

"What is it, my love? Are you well?"

Wordlessly, Elizabeth removed the rose-colored cameo from the box and handed it to her husband.

Darcy looked down at the brooch in his hand and gasped as well. "It appears you and your great-aunt shared more than a name and a personality. You look exactly like her."

Later that evening, Elizabeth lay curled against her husband in the bed she had slept in at Longbourn. "William, you once said I could do with my inheritance anything I wished. Did you mean it?"

"Of course, my love. Did you have something particular in mind?"

She looked up into his eyes and said, "As a matter of fact, I do have a few ideas." She told him her thoughts, concluding by saying, "The money should be set aside to increase our daughters' dowries or to purchase an estate for one of our sons should it be necessary."

"I agree with your suggestions, my dear. Shall we issue the invitations to everyone tomorrow? If you write them out, I will arrange for their delivery by express."

The next morning, Darcy and Elizabeth walked to Oakham Mount to watch the sun rise. They were enjoying a late breakfast when their carriage arrived with their clothes and personal servants. After bathing and changing for the day, Elizabeth went to the desk in the parlor and began to write out the invitations to their guests. When they were completed, she looked for Darcy, finding him in the study with the steward, going over the books for the estate.

"I have finished the invitations, William."

Darcy rang for a servant, and one of the footmen appeared. "Please take these to the village and arrange for them to be sent express." Darcy tossed a bag of coins to the footman. "This should cover the expense."

"Certainly, Mr. Darcy."

"William, I shall be in the gardens when you are through," Elizabeth said. "I wish to see what work needs to be done there."

"I will find you shortly, my dear."

Elizabeth wandered around the gardens, pulling a stray weed here and there as she looked at the beds. The spring bulbs were blooming, but she could see that the rose bushes had not been pruned as they should have been. She made a mental note to find a gardener to attend to them so they would bloom in their season. William joined her a short time later, and they continued to stroll through the gardens.

433

When they returned to the house, Elizabeth led the way to the conservatory. Upon entering, her heart plummeted. Several of the windows had broken, and most of the tender plants had frozen over the winter. Again, tears welled up in her eyes. "How could Mr. Collins have allowed this to happen?"

"Do not worry, my love, I will arrange for the glass to be replaced and we shall obtain new plants. We can arrange for some cuttings to be sent from Pemberley."

"That would be wonderful! Thank you, William."

Two days later, the house was prepared for the visitors, the meals were planned, and Elizabeth was anxiously awaiting the arrival of their guests. Darcy was amused by her inability to sit still, but he refrained from teasing her. He was extremely proud of the decisions she had made regarding her inheritance and was anxious to see the reactions of their guests.

Those traveling from London arrived shortly before luncheon. They were shown to their rooms so they could refresh themselves before the meal was served. The only local people invited to attend were Charlotte Lucas and her Uncle Philips.

After luncheon, everyone settled in the parlor and the doors were closed.

"William and I would like to thank all of you for joining us on such short notice. I am delighted to share my family home with you. As you are all aware, I recently attained my majority and received my inheritance. The gift from my great-aunt Rose was astounding, but even more overwhelming was the gift

I received from Mr. Collins. Mr. Collins informed me he felt his work with the church to be a true calling. Consequently, he deeded Longbourn to me to compensate for the foul deeds of his father."

Gasps went up from those present.

"As I am married to a man who owns several estates, I would like to give Longbourn to the Gardiners. It would allow them the opportunity to raise their children in a wonderful country setting, but it is close enough for Uncle Edward to make trips to town to oversee his business there. You shall also receive the equivalent of five years of Longbourn's income to help restore the estate from the damage done through Mr. Collins' neglect. If you will agree to accept this gift, Uncle Philips will draw up the necessary papers for the transfer.

"Lizzy, oh, my dear girl! Are you sure you wish to do this?" asked Mr. Gardiner.

"I am sure, Uncle. You and Aunt Helen have always been as close to me as my own parents. I can think of no one to whom I would rather give this than you. It can never begin to repay you for all you have done for me throughout my life."

Edward Gardiner looked at his wife, who had tears streaming down her face. She nodded imperceptibly as they rose to their feet.

"'Thank you' seems so inadequate, but we do thank you from the bottom of our hearts, Lizzy." They both enveloped her in a hug before returning to their seats.

"Though it is hard for me to believe, the inheritance from my great-aunt Rose was even more grand. Mr. Bingley, while we were in Derbyshire for the holidays, you purchased an estate for you and Jane that would be near Pemberley. Consequently, I would like to give you and Jane the townhouse I inherited in London. It is in Mayfair and is currently being rented, but we will notify the tenants that the lease will not be renewed. I do not know the exact date on which the lease ends, but as you have not yet married, you will have no need of it in the immediate future. When we are all in town, Darcy and I will look over the property and ensure it is in good repair. We will fix anything we find wanting. You will also receive the last two years of rent from the property to allow you to make any purchases necessary for making it feel like your home.

"The last portion of the gift is for you, Richard. If you had not arrived in Lambton when you did, I might not have lived long enough to inherit. As I know how deeply Darcy and Georgiana worry for you and fear your being sent abroad, I would like to gift you the estate of Windhaven in Warwickshire. It brings in about four thousand pounds per year. There is also a manor house on the estate that, I am told, has been well maintained. In addition, you will receive the last three years of income from the estate."

Richard sat stunned, for once at a loss for words. Lord and Lady Matlock sat next to their son. Her ladyship had tears streaming down her face, and the earl's eyes were suspiciously moist. He reached over and clapped his son on the shoulder, finding words before the colonel could. "Elizabeth, Darcy —"

Darcy interrupted. "I had nothing to do with these decisions, Uncle. I gave Elizabeth total control of her inheritance. It is her generous heart that came up with these gifts."

Lady Matlock rose from her seat and moved to embrace Elizabeth. "How can I ever thank you for giving my son this opportunity? Now I shall never again have to fear that he will be sent to the continent to face the French."

"There is no need to thank me," said Elizabeth softly. "Richard saved my life. I am simply returning the favor."

"Truly, Elizabeth, there are not enough words to express our gratitude," added the earl. "You have ensured we will be able to enjoy Richard's presence for a long time to come."

Finally, Richard rose. "You have given me the gift of a lifetime. Not only can I support myself if I leave the army, you have also allowed me to have the family I never dreamed I could have on my army salary. If only there were another lady like you!"

"Richard, my Elizabeth is one of a kind. However, because you now have an estate and are the son of an earl, I am sure the ladies of the ton will be throwing themselves at you this season. You shall be able to enjoy the torture I once endured," said Darcy with a laugh.

"Things are looking up already, but I doubt I will find anyone like Elizabeth among the ladies of the ton."

Everyone laughed as Elizabeth added, "I will keep my eyes open for you, Richard. I am sure there is at least one original young lady out there somewhere."

Elizabeth's remarks made everyone laugh harder as Richard's face turned bright red.

"I have one last gift to give." Elizabeth turned to Charlotte. "You have been my dearest friend throughout my life, and you were kind enough to keep all my family's treasures while I was away. I would like to give you five thousand pounds to add to your dowry. William and I would also like to have you join us for the season."

Charlotte was speechless. "Eliza, I could not possibly accept such a gift."

"Yes, you can, Charlotte. I insist you accept it and I shall not take no for an answer. Now, would you care to join us in town?"

"I should like that very much. Thank you, Eliza."

"Lizzy, did you keep any portion of the inheritance for yourself?" asked Jane.

"I did, Jane; there was also a substantial sum of cash, which will continue to earn interest. It will either be used to increase our daughters' dowries or to purchase an estate for a younger son should William not already have enough," said Elizabeth with a laugh. "There was also a beautiful rose-colored cameo that was left to me. I believe you might find it rather interesting. Aunt Rose said her husband had it specially made from an artist's rendering of her at the age of one and twenty." Elizabeth pulled the piece from her pocket and handed it to Jane.

"Lizzy, this looks exactly like you!" cried Jane in surprise.

"It is rather ironic I chose to use her name when I was hiding from Mr. Collins."

"Indeed it is, and you shall always be my perfect rose," said William as he pulled Elizabeth into his embrace.

Colonel Fitzwilliam and the Matlocks returned to town the following day so Richard could resign his commission. Jane, Bingley, and the Gardiners stayed on for another week. While Jane acquainted Mr. Bingley with Longbourn and Meryton, Darcy and Mr. Gardiner met with the steward and went over the books for the estate. They made arrangements for repairs to all the tenant homes and outbuildings on the property.

At the end of the week, the Gardiners, along with Jane and Bingley, returned to London and began to make arrangements for their move. They took possession of Longbourn at the end of June.

On the day before they departed, everyone, including Mr. Bingley, went to the churchyard in Meryton to visit the graves. Unbeknownst to Elizabeth, Darcy had arranged, through Mr. Philips, to have headstones carved and placed for the departed members of the Bennet family. Upon seeing the beautiful markers, Elizabeth knew her wonderful husband had done this for her. She gave William a blinding smile, the tears that pooled in her eyes making them sparkle more than usual.

Darcy and Elizabeth remained at Longbourn long enough to observe the beginnings of the repairs. When everything was well underway, they made the journey back to London. This time as Elizabeth departed, she knew she would see her home again, and it filled her heart with joy.

EPILOGUE

ELIZABETH'S FIRST SEASON AMONG THE TON was a success. Some of the details of her inheritance were purposely leaked by Lady Matlock. The size of her fortune, as well as her marriage to Darcy, ensured she was well received. However, it did not take long before her acceptance was for herself alone. Her intelligence and wit helped her deal with the less pleasant members of the ton. Elizabeth's humor, vivacity, and ability to put others at ease drew people to her. It would not be many years before she was considered one of the leaders of society.

At the end of that first season, Darcy and Elizabeth journeyed to Longbourn with the Gardiners and Jane. Just before departing, Elizabeth shared with her husband and family that she and Darcy would be parents before the end of the year.

Upon returning to Pemberley after Elizabeth's first season, the Darcys learned that because of her injuries, Mrs. Webb had retired and was living with her daughter on a farm outside Lambton. The two young women who had come to assist her were paying her a small monthly amount to purchase the shop.

They enjoyed the many beauties of Pemberley as they awaited the birth of their first child. On a cold November morning, after a long labor, Thomas William Darcy and Sophia Helen Darcy were born. The Darcys went on to have four additional children:

Andrew Richard, Bennet Charles, Anne Elizabeth, and Eleanor Jane. The children grew up surrounded by love, and in each was instilled a thirst for learning.

Jane and Mr. Bingley decided to marry from Longbourn. Though Jane had not lived there for a year, Reverend Carter happily called the banns for the three weeks before the wedding. Her uncle gave Jane away. Just as she had always dreamed, she married in the Meryton church and from her family home. She and Mr. Bingley journeyed to Weymouth for their honeymoon, spending a month at the seaside before settling at their new estate in Derbyshire. Jane and Bingley would go on to have five children. The firstborn was their son, Charles— Charlie to the family. He was followed by Mary, Katherine, Lydia, and Mark.

Charlotte Lucas and Richard Fitzwilliam were often in company during that first season in London. With her new wardrobe and a chance to be herself without the eyes of Meryton observing all she said and did, Charlotte began to shine. She was an intelligent young woman, pretty in an understated way, sensible, and kind. Richard found her conversation enjoyable and did not mind when she teased him about all the ladies who fluttered their eyelashes at him.

Just before the season ended, Richard proposed to Charlotte and was accepted. When he returned to Meryton for Bingley's wedding, he received Sir William's blessing on the marriage. After the wedding of Charles and Jane, Charlotte and her parents traveled with Richard to Windhaven to see his new estate. A wedding date was set for the middle of October, as Richard would be required to remain at Windhaven for the harvest. After their wedding, Richard and Charlotte returned to their estate, where they remained until joining the rest of the Fitzwilliams at Pemberley for Christmas. Charlotte and Richard would have four children of their own. The first three were boys, but the last one was the little girl Charlotte had dreamed of having.

When Nicholas Fitzwilliam, Viscount Matson, saw that his brother had also found a gem in the countryside, he accepted every house party invitation he received that summer. During the second one, at the home of a university friend, he met the young sister of another friend. This young lady, Miss Maria Chapman, had not yet made her debut and possessed a freshness of face and independence of spirit that utterly charmed the viscount. Miss Chapman's parents wished her to make her debut before committing herself to marriage, but she was quite adamant in her determination to not wait so long. As a result, she and the viscount wed at the end of November after she had briefly participated in the Little Season.

Walter Collins did not remain in his position at Hunsford. Lady Catherine had been extremely displeased with him for returning Longbourn to his cousin. Though she would not give him a reference, through the auspices of Lord Matlock and Mr. Darcy, he found another parish in Somerset where he served faithfully for the remainder of his days. He met a pleasant young woman of the congregation, and they eventually married. Unfortunately, they were never blessed with children. Mr. Collins was much beloved by his parishioners, who turned out in large numbers to pay their respects upon his death.

As for Lady Catherine, all of her worst fears were realized. Learning she had been the mistress of Rosings for two years, Anne determined to take her place and had her mother removed to the dower house. Anne then began to socialize with her neighbors, something her mother had never allowed. At a dinner one evening, she met Jacob Simpson, a cousin to one of their neighbors. Jacob was visiting in the area; he was a handsome young man with charming manners and a pleasing address. After a whirlwind courtship, they were married and settled at Rosings.

Unfortunately for Anne, Jacob's interest did not last long. Shortly after their marriage and the receipt of the property Anne brought to it, Jacob disappeared one morning along with all of Rosings' liquid assets. As a result, Anne had to practice economies and learn to live on considerably less as her Uncle Anthony tried to save Rosings from bankruptcy.

What happened to Miss Bingley, you might ask? When confronted by her brother regarding her part in the abduction of Mrs. Darcy and the attempted kidnapping of Miss Darcy, her only comment was of disappointment that the men had failed to remove the obstacles to her marriage to Mr. Darcy. Shaking his head in disgust, Bingley and his aunt decided Miss Bingley was unbalanced and the only solution would be to put her in a sanitarium, where she spent the remainder of her days.

After two years of observing the marriage between her brother and Elizabeth, Georgiana made her debut. By that time, she had become the strong, confident young woman her brother hoped she would be. It was in her second season (accompanied by Lord and Lady Matlock, as Elizabeth was increasing) that she met the Viscount Winsford, eldest son of the Earl of Evesham, whose seat was in Worcestershire, less than a day's travel to Pemberley. After a courtship of six months and a two-month engagement, they were married in Pemberley's chapel. The young couple was very happy together and had a small family, with two sons and a daughter. They had been married for more than fifteen years before her husband inherited his father's title. Georgiana made a lovely countess.

Darcy and Elizabeth shared a long and happy marriage. They spent most of their time at Pemberley, though they forced themselves to spend at least part of each season in town. Along with the obligatory social events, they often walked in the park, visited the museums, and took in the theater and opera.

Darcy and Elizabeth lived to see all of their children marry for love and begin families of their own. They doted on their grandchildren and were fortunate enough to become great-grandparents before their deaths.

Drenched in a sudden downpour while walking on a late October day, Elizabeth caught a severe cold. Her body ravished by fever, Elizabeth died in her sleep one night, surrounded by her family. It broke Darcy's heart to lay his dear wife of fifty-six years to rest. He ordered that pink rose bushes be placed on either side of her headstone.

When the roses bloomed the next summer, Darcy's son, Thomas, found his father seated on the ground at his wife's grave. Darcy was leaning back against the bench that rested in the shade of a large oak tree. Coming quietly to his father's side, Thomas placed his hand on his Darcy's shoulder and was surprised by the coolness he felt in spite of the warm day. Realizing his dear father had passed from the world, Thomas noted the pink rose that lay in his open palm. The children had all heard the story about how their parents met and had often heard their father call Elizabeth "his perfect rose." A few days later, Darcy was buried beside his beloved wife.

END NOTES

(1) This is a variation of a quote by William Shakespeare from *Hamlet*.

(2) Written by Ludwig van Beethoven. Full Title: Opus 81a: Piano Sonata No. 26 in E-Flat Major (Les adieux/Das Lebewohl) (1810).

(3) An English folk song and nursery rhyme dating from the 17th century. Author: Unknown.

(4) *Pride and Prejudice* by Jane Austen.

NEW FROM THIS AUTHOR

A Matter of Timing

They say that timing is everything . . .

Their chance meeting at Pemberley helped Elizabeth Bennet to realize her true feelings for Mr. Darcy. That same meeting gave him the opportunity to show Elizabeth that he had taken her criticism to heart and made improvements to his behavior. Would this new start finally lead to their happily ever after?

How might the relationship between Elizabeth and Darcy have been different if they had become betrothed before Elizabeth learned of Lydia's elopement? Would they have traveled to London together? Would Elizabeth have assisted in her sister's recovery? Would Lydia and Wickham still have married or would there be another way to save Elizabeth's youngest sister?

A Matter of Timing answers all those questions and more.

OTHER BOOKS BY LINDA C. THOMPSON

Her Unforgettable Laugh
Book 1

Dark curls and an unforgettably sweet laugh was all he knew of his sister's rescuer. Later, a second glimpse showed her to be lovely, and he heard her melodious laugh again. Darcy wondered what it would be like to meet this remarkable, and remarkably lovely, young woman. Would the spirit that caused her to go to the aid of a stranger be able to bring some joy to his lonely life? Would they ever meet, or would he always be left wondering?

Little did Fitzwilliam Darcy know that his trip to Hertfordshire to help his friend would bring him face to face with the lovely young woman whose unforgettable laugh had haunted his dreams for the last several years. Would she be anything like the woman he had built up in his dreams? Would he be able to avoid Miss Bingley long enough to discover more about this mysterious young woman?

Laughter Through Trials
Book 2

Dark curls and an unforgettably sweet laugh . . .

In Book I of the series, Her Unforgettable Laugh, a trip to Hertfordshire brought Fitzwilliam Darcy face-to-face with the woman who had haunted his dreams for five years. Their chance meeting led to a courtship, in spite of those who wished to separate them. Now Elizabeth Bennet is traveling to London where she will be introduced to Darcy's family and the ton. How will Elizabeth be received? Will their love flourish and grow or will new trials overwhelm them?

The Laughter of Love
Book 3

Dark curls and an unforgettably sweet laugh . . .

In Book 2 of the series, Laughter Through Trials, Darcy and Elizabeth celebrated their courtship as Elizabeth was introduced to the Fitzwilliam family and London society. Their sojourn in town held a few difficulties, but the strength of their love allowed them to face the challenges and outwit their enemies.

Now Darcy and Elizabeth are returning to Hertfordshire for their wedding and Elizabeth worries there is still one trial to be faced—Mrs. Bennet. Her mother refuses to prepare the simple, elegant affair the couple wishes for their wedding day. Will it be the day of their dreams or a disaster?

However, the wedding turns out, Darcy and Elizabeth are excited to begin their life together. The bright future before them fills their hearts with joy. Both know they will face periods of contentment and heartache, but united they will confront whatever comes their way. Will those they have previously encountered allow them to enjoy their happiness or will there be more misfortune for them to overcome?

FOR YOUR ENJOYMENT

I am delighted to share an excerpt from *The Netherfield Affair*. It is the first book in a four-book series, each containing a standalone mystery that helps bring Darcy and Elizabeth closer together. The mysteries involved are solved in each book, but the resolution of Darcy and Elizabeth's relationship does not occur until the final book in the series.

These intriguing books, by JAFF author Penelope Swan, are well-written, mysterious, and entertaining.

Happy reading!

The Netherfield Affair

A Pride and Prejudice Variation

By

PENELOPE SWAN

EXCERPT

Elizabeth awoke to the muted sounds of wind and rain. It seemed that the storm had abated—at least temporarily. Pulling her shawl around her, she hurried to the window again to look out. Now that she had the benefit of daylight, she could see that it was just as her father had described: one of the tall beech trees on the front lawn had been wrenched from its position and was now lying prone across the drive, barring the way for anyone attempting to bring a carriage or even ride a horse up to the front entrance of Longbourn.

When she went down to breakfast, however, Elizabeth learned that she had been mistaken in her supposition that a horse rider could not cross the barrier, for a message had just arrived from Netherfield Park—a letter from Jane, addressed to her.

"Well, open it, Lizzy—make haste!" said Mrs Bennet, looking up eagerly from her plate of kippers. "Perhaps it is Jane writing that Mr Bingley has proposed already!"

This elicited giggles from the younger girls and a moue of disapproval from Mary. The latter pushed her spectacles up her nose as she clasped her hands primly on the table in front of her and said:

"It behooves us to remember what is said in the Book of Proverbs 20:25: 'Marriage is based on sacred vows. Entering those vows rashly and hastily generally leads to a snare. But after you are married, it is too late to reconsider your vows'. Thus we are told that if we marry in haste, we shall repent at leisure."

"Oh Mary!" said Lydia, rolling her eyes.

Elizabeth ignored all this as she concentrated on the letter before her. It was certainly from Jane although the hand was shakier than her sister's usually beautiful penmanship. As she read the contents, Elizabeth soon understood the reason for such frail script. It appeared that Jane had taken ill and was even now awaiting a visit from Mr Jones, the apothecary, at Netherfield Park. Although Jane wrote of a simple cold, Elizabeth suspected that her gentle sister—forever concerned about giving pain to others—had made light of her illness so as not to worry her family.

"We must go and see her," declared Elizabeth with some unease.

"I would be more than happy to visit Jane, but will the carriage be able to pass the fallen tree?" asked Mrs Bennet.

Mr Bennet shook his head. "I am afraid we will not know the answer to that, my dear, until I can bring men from the farm to attempt to shift it. At present, it seems unlikely that a carriage will be able to pass. You may have to delay your visit to Jane until later today."

"I feel that I must go to Jane immediately," said Elizabeth, standing up from the table. "I shall walk to Netherfield Park."

"Walk?" gasped her mother, her eyes widening in horror. "Why, in the wind and rain… you will not be fit to be seen!"

"I shall be fit to see Jane, which is all I care about," said Elizabeth. "My mind is quite made up."

"Would you like me to ask the groom to fetch one of the horses so that you may attempt the journey on horseback?" asked Mr Bennet.

"No indeed, Papa," said Elizabeth. "It is barely three miles to Netherfield and I would welcome some fresh air after being confined indoors for so long." She glanced out of the dining room windows. "I believe that the rain has ceased for the time being and the skies look like they might be clearing. I think a refreshing walk would be the very thing."

"Have care when you arrive at Netherfield, Lizzy, for we have heard that it is haunted!" said Lydia suddenly.

Elizabeth paused and looked at her younger sister quizzically. Lydia and Kitty had been huddled together whispering for the past few minutes while Elizabeth had been discussing her plans for travelling to Netherfield, but now they hastened to inform everyone at the table of their news.

Lydia leaned forwards excitedly. "They say that there is a ghost—the spirit of a poor serving girl who was deflowered by the old master of the house many years ago—"

"Lydia!" gasped Mary.

Lydia ignored the remonstration as the rest of the table looked at her agog. She was enjoying the sensation of holding everyone's attention rapt and she was determined to make the most of her temporary advantage. "Yes, and her ghost wanders the house at night—and can even be seen sometimes looking out of the windows. On dark and stormy nights, it is possible to hear her wailing for her lost virtue and if you do not take care, she may claim your soul to keep hers company!"

"From where did you hear such an extraordinary tale?" asked Mr Bennet.

"Sarah told me," said Lydia. "And she had it directly from the Netherfield parlourmaid, who heard it from the kitchenmaid who—"

"You should know better than to listen to servants' gossip," said Elizabeth severely. "And it is well known that ghost stories are merely created to titillate and entertain. I certainly have no fear of ghoulish spirits for I do not believe that they exist."

"Aye, Lizzy," said her father with a smile. "That is a good attitude to have."

"It is not mere titillation!" insisted Lydia as Kitty nodded vehemently next to her. "Sarah told me that the servants at Netherfield have themselves observed such occurrences as to make the blood run cold—strange noises in the night, mysterious disappearances of household items, and once even a dark figure creeping up the stairs—"

"Oh! Do not talk of such things!" cried Mrs Bennet, fanning herself with her lace handkerchief. "To think of my dear Jane in such a household!"

"Perhaps now you may feel that the pursuit of Mr Bingley is not worth such gruesome risks?" enquired Mr Bennet of his wife with a teasing smile.

Mrs Bennet sniffed and looked away.

"Well, I believe that any threats that Jane may be exposed to are of an infectious rather than a supernatural variety," said Elizabeth firmly. "I thank you for the warning, Lydia, but I believe I may be safe from any ghostly attack during my visit at Netherfield."

Catching her father's twinkling eye, Elizabeth smiled, turned, and quitted the room.

Ten minutes later, Elizabeth set off on foot for Netherfield Park. She had been right in her estimation of a break in the rain, but her appraisal of the sky had been too optimistic. It did not look like it was brightening—in fact, the edges of the horizon were lined with an ominous black, which spread across the sky like an inky stain. Thick clouds loomed above, heavy with the promise of more rain, and Elizabeth hastened her steps as she cast a worried look at the heavens. It would not do to be caught in another downpour and become ill like Jane!

Elizabeth was well used to walking in the country—indeed, she enjoyed the activity immensely and indulged in it often—but today, the going was decidedly difficult. Heavy rain had turned most of the roads into a veritable quagmire and she sank up to her ankles in mud as she negotiated the stiles between the fields and attempted to avoid the puddles. She was delighted when the house at Netherfield Park finally came into view, and hastened her steps even more.

As she approached the house, Elizabeth raised her eyes to trace the outline of its elegant architecture. She had seen it several times in her rambles about the countryside and had always admired the beauty of this country manor. Today, however, it looked very different. Outlined as it was by a nimbus of black cloud in the sky behind it, the house had an almost menacing air as it sat brooding in the middle of its rain-sodden grounds.

Elizabeth laughed and chided herself for her fanciful imaginings. She was letting Lydia's wild tales and the mood of the inclement weather prevail upon her good senses, and incline her towards melodrama!

She bent her head to negotiate the last section of muddy field, then jumped as an eerie scream filled the air. Elizabeth gasped and looked around, searching for the source of the sound. Then her steps faltered as she raised her gaze once more and her eyes caught sight of something at the top of the house.

Elizabeth blinked and looked again, but she was not mistaken. There, in a small attic window, showed a ghostly white face, with black eyes that bored into her very soul.

So great was the shock upon seeing the apparition at the window that Elizabeth tripped and stumbled in the mud. Indeed, she would have fallen, but for the hand that shot out and caught her arm in a strong grip. A tall, dark figure loomed over her and Elizabeth drew breath to scream before she realised that she recognised the handsome countenance.

"Mr Darcy!" she cried, struggling to regain her composure.

He sketched a slight bow. "Miss Bennet."

Elizabeth was very conscious of his hand, still solicitously underneath her elbow. "I… I must thank you, sir. It would seem that were it not for your quick reflexes, I would be prostrate in the mud."

"It is I perhaps who should offer my apologies," said Darcy. "It appears that my sudden appearance may have startled you into missing your step."

"Oh no, that was not the reason. I stumbled because I believed I saw—"

Here, Elizabeth faltered, suddenly aware of who she was speaking to. She had no wish to confess her fanciful imaginings to such a stern gentleman. She coloured at the thought of repeating Lydia's wild assertions regarding the house in which her sister was a guest. A quick glance from the side of her eyes reassured her that there was no longer any face at the top window.

Perhaps there had never been.

"Yes, Miss Bennet?" asked Darcy with a raised eyebrow.

"'Tis of no consequence," said Elizabeth quickly. "Um… I have come to see my sister Jane. We were all very concerned to hear of her illness."

"I believe it is merely a cold," said Darcy. "Bingley has already sent for the apothecary and every effort is being made to see to her comfort."

"Oh, I am sure Jane could not want for better care," said Elizabeth hastily. "But I hope you will understand a sister's concern. Will you take me to her?"

Darcy inclined his head. "Certainly. This way, Miss Bennet."

Turning, he led the way back to the house. Elizabeth followed silently, marvelling at the turn of circumstances that had led her to now be walking next to this formidable man. It seemed that Mr Darcy was a great walker for Elizabeth could not help noticing his powerful strides and the ease with which he moved. It brought to mind an illustration she had once seen of a great jungle cat from the Orient—a savage, beautiful beast with inky black pelt and glittering green eyes, and such a fluid, commanding grace in movement.

Elizabeth blinked as she realised where her thoughts had led her and was glad that Mr Darcy was not looking her way, so as not to observe the high colour in her cheeks. Lydia's histrionic tales must have affected her more than she realised! It was not like her to be prone to such wild, fanciful imaginings—and about this man, no less! She was relieved when they reached the house and Mr Darcy—with another elegant bow—handed her over to the care of a manservant. As Elizabeth followed the servant across the hall, she put Mr Darcy from her mind and resolved to think no more of him.

She was shown into the breakfast parlour where a footman announced her arrival. Mr Bingley received her with great enthusiasm, but Elizabeth noticed the shocked expressions on his sisters' faces. They made little effort to hide their disgust as they eyed her appearance and responded to her greeting with cold civility. Mr Hurst merely grunted as he mumbled a greeting, obviously keen to return to his seat at the table and his overflowing plate. Mr Darcy said nothing at all. He simply walked over to the side buffet and upon pouring himself a cup of coffee, stood silently drinking this while his dark eyes rested on the visitor. Elizabeth cared not about the cold welcome from all but Mr Bingley—all she wanted to do now was to see Jane, and she made her excuses gladly as soon as a maid arrived to take her to her sister's room.

Jane was surprised to see her, but it was evident from the expression of delight on her face that while she had not wanted to worry them, she had longed for Elizabeth's company.

"Have they been treating you well, Jane?" asked Elizabeth anxiously after she had settled in the room. "I know your Mr Bingley is all amiability and kindness, but I confess I cannot imagine that his sisters would provide much in the way of solicitude."

"He is not *my* Mr Bingley," said Jane with a shy smile. "And indeed, you are wrong about his sisters, Lizzy! They have been all goodness and kindness to me, from the moment that they perceived I was not feeling well. They have visited me once this morning already, while Mr Jones the apothecary was here, and left with promises to return again soon."

Elizabeth made no answer, but continued to sponge Jane's forehead with the cool water from the basin while she looked at her sister with concern.

Jane felt hot and feverish, and her eyes were unnaturally bright. Though she seemed much happier now that Elizabeth was here, it was not difficult to see that she still suffered badly from the symptoms of the cold. Elizabeth administered the draughts that Mr Jones had left behind and hoped that they would prove effective soon.

She was about to begin brushing Jane's hair—which had become tangled from the tossing and turning in the night—when a soft knock sounded at the door. It was opened by a servant girl bearing another basin of fresh water. She curtsied when she saw Elizabeth and offered a smile. She was uncommonly pretty, with hair of a fiery shade of copper, caught up with a blue satin ribbon. Elizabeth was surprised as she had not seen such finery on a maid before, though the rest of the girl's costume was as plain as any other maid's outfit.

"If you please, miss," the girl said. "I have brought Miss Bennet some fresh water for spongin' an' a bed warmer for her feet."

"Oh yes, come in, come in," said Elizabeth, making way for the girl to enter.

"Lizzy, this is Tilly—she is one of the kitchen maids at Netherfield, but Caroline Bingley has very kindly offered her services to me as my lady's maid during my stay here, so that I may be more comfortable," said Jane from the bed.

Tilly curtsied again and looked at Elizabeth worriedly. "Is somethin' the matter, miss?"

The latter realised that she had been staring. "Oh, no… 'tis naught. I was struck by the sight of your hair ornament," said Elizabeth, her eyes going once more to the length of blue satin in the servant girl's hair. "It is uncommonly fine. Did you purchase it from a shop in Meryton?"

Tilly flushed slightly and curtsied awkwardly. "'Twas a gift, miss." She seemed disinclined to say anything else and Elizabeth decided to abandon the questioning. She took the bowl of fresh water from Tilly and went back to sit at the edge of the bed to minister to Jane, whilst the servant girl positioned the bed warmer under the blankets, then moved quietly about the room, straightening clothing and clearing away soiled items.

"Tilly is skilled in the use of herbs and flowers to prepare healthful cordials and other recipes," Jane said with a smile. "I do believe that the syrup of violets she gave me is superior to Mr Jones' draughts in bringing about relief for my symptoms." She pointed to a small glass bottle filled with a beautiful, clear lavender liquid, sitting on her bedside table.

Tilly beamed with pleasure. "You're too kind, miss. I do like spendin' most of me time in the still room."

Elizabeth reached over and picked up the bottle. She uncorked it and held it up to her nose, inhaling the delicate violet aroma. "Ah, I have rarely smelled anything as sweet! I have no doubt that this is far superior to Mr Jones' concoctions."

"Oh, the power of violets be greatly overlooked, miss," said Tilly earnestly. "I make violet tea an' infusions, syrups an' ointments, an' they work great to cure everythin'— 'ague, epilepsy, inflammation of the eyes, sleeplessness, pleurisy, jaundice, an' quinsy'. The syrup does wonders for those with colds. It eases the coughs an' the roughness of the throat. Even the flowers chewed can dispel a headache."

"Such a catalogue of benefits from so humble a flower," said Elizabeth with a smile. "We must beg a recipe from you, Tilly, for our own use before we return to Longbourn."

"With pleasure, miss." Tilly shyly returned the smile. Then she pointed to Elizabeth's gown. "If you like, miss, I can clean the hem of your gown for you."

Elizabeth followed the direction of the maid's gaze and realised that the bottom of her gown was caked in mud. It was no wonder that the Bingley sisters had looked so shocked upon her arrival! Indeed, she must have been trailing mud all over the house as she moved about.

"I should have tied my gown up before my walk," said Elizabeth with chagrin. "Then at least the mud would have only gone onto my petticoats, which could be covered from view when I let down my gown. Now I fear that it will be no easy task to remove these stains."

"'Tis no trouble, miss," said Tilly. "I can have the gown clean an' back to you within an hour an' no one'll ever know."

"Why, that is very kind of you," said Elizabeth gratefully. She thought of the disdainful Bingley sisters again and realised that it would be in her favour to maintain a respectable image, no matter how much she disliked their company. As a member of the same family, her own conduct and appearance played a role in Jane's position of respectability and she did not want to do anything which may hamper her sister's chances of finding matrimonial happiness with Mr Bingley.

"Thank you, Tilly, I will accept your offer," said Elizabeth, standing up from the bed.

She undressed down to her petticoat and handed the gown to the servant girl, who hurried away, promising to be back within the hour. She was as good as her word and Elizabeth was delighted to perceive the clean gown, with the hem barely showing any sign of soiling. And not a moment too soon, for Tilly had barely finished helping her dress again when there came another knock at the door, and this time it was opened to admit the Bingley sisters.

The two fine ladies entered the room and exclaimed over their dear friend. Elizabeth retreated to the far corner and watched with a cynical eye as Caroline Bingley and Mrs Hurst showered the invalid with effusive expressions of concern. They talked of their own dislike for colds, the miseries they had suffered in the past when afflicted with a cold, and their fears for the possible fatal consequences of such an illness—none of which was designed to cheer the patient.

To Elizabeth's indignant ears, it seemed that the two ladies were more intent on talking about themselves than enquiring after Jane's health. She was convinced that they were only visiting because of the lack of other suitable activities to occupy their time in the inclement weather. When at length they had run out of their melodramatic platitudes and finally quit the room, Elizabeth shut the door behind them with some violence and turned impatiently to Jane.

"I cannot understand how such creatures could be related to your excellent Mr Bingley," she expostulated, approaching the bed. "Where he is warm and sincere, they are indifferent and false; where he is generous and good, they are contemptuous and full of their own self-importance!"

"Lizzy…" chided Jane gently. "Caroline Bingley and her sister have been all that is polite and pleasing. You cannot expect them to care for me as if I were their own sister and I do think it is very good of them to wait on me, when they could be doing much pleasanter things downstairs."

"I am sure Mr Bingley would prefer waiting upon you to any other activity, should propriety allow it," teased Elizabeth, regaining her good humour as she watched Jane blush. "You should try and get some rest now," she added. "You look tired. I am sure some sleep would do you good."

"I believe you may be right, Lizzy," said Jane, stifling a yawn. "I confess, I did not sleep well last night. Aside from the headache and sore throat, I was disturbed by strange noises."

"Strange noises?" said Elizabeth. "You mean from the storm?"

Jane shook her head. "No, these were noises that came from within the house."

"Perhaps it was only the servants going about their duties," said Elizabeth.

"Perhaps," said Jane doubtfully. "But it seems a strange time for them to be active. It was a few hours before dawn, I believe—a time in the very middle of the night when all should have been asleep." She shivered. "One could almost imagine that there was a sinister presence about."

Elizabeth wondered if Jane had heard the stories of Netherfield being haunted and this was why her sister's thoughts had moved immediately towards a sepulchral explanation for the nocturnal disturbance. But if Jane did not know of the rumours yet, Elizabeth did not want to add to her sister's cares now by repeating Lydia's wild speculations. Instead, she bent over Jane and smoothed her sister's hair back from her hot forehead.

"Sleep now, Jane. I shall be sitting there by the window if you should need me."

Printed in Great Britain
by Amazon